DARK IMPERIUM

GODBLIGHT

More Warhammer 40,000 from Black Library

• DARK IMPERIUM •
Guy Haley
BOOK 1: Dark Imperium
BOOK 2: Plague War
BOOK 3: Godblight

• DAWN OF FIRE •
BOOK 1: Avenging Son
Guy Haley
BOOK 2: The Gate of Bones
Andy Clark
BOOK 3: The Wolftime
Gav Thorpe

INDOMITUS
Gav Thorpe

BELISARIUS CAWL: THE GREAT WORK
Guy Haley

• WATCHERS OF THE THRONE •
Chris Wraight
BOOK 1: The Emperor's Legion
BOOK 2: The Regent's Shadow

RITES OF PASSAGE
Mike Brooks

KNIGHTS OF MACRAGGE
Nick Kyme

CADIA STANDS
Justin D Hill

CADIAN HONOUR
Justin D Hill

• VAULTS OF TERRA •
Chris Wraight
BOOK 1: The Carrion Throne
BOOK 2: The Hollow Mountain

MARK OF FAITH
Rachel Harrison

EPHRAEL STERN: THE HERETIC SAINT
David Annandale

DARK IMPERIUM
GODBLIGHT

AN ERA INDOMITUS NOVEL

GUY HALEY

BLACK LIBRARY

A BLACK LIBRARY PUBLICATION

First published in 2021.
This edition published in Great Britain in 2022 by
Black Library, Games Workshop Ltd., Willow Road,
Nottingham, NG7 2WS, UK.

Represented by: Games Workshop Limited – Irish branch,
Unit 3, Lower Liffey Street, Dublin 1,
D01 K199, Ireland.

10 9 8 7 6 5 4

Produced by Games Workshop in Nottingham.
Cover illustration by Vladimir Krisetskiy.

A CIP record for this book is available from the British Library.

ISBN 13: 978-1-80026-203-4

This is a work of fiction. All the characters and events portrayed
in this book are fictional, and any resemblance to real people or
incidents is purely coincidental.

See Black Library on the internet at

blacklibrary.com

Find out more about Games Workshop
and the world of Warhammer 40,000 at

games-workshop.com

Printed and bound by CPI Group (UK) Ltd, Croydon, CR0 4YY

It is the 41st millennium.

Ten thousand years have passed since the Primarch Horus turned to
Chaos and betrayed his father, the Emperor of Mankind, plunging the
galaxy into ruinous civil war.

For one hundred centuries the Imperium has endured xenos invasion,
internal dissent, and the perfidious attentions of the dark gods of the
warp. The Emperor sits immobile upon the Golden Throne of Terra,
a psychic bastion against infernal powers. It is His will alone that
lights the Astronomican, binding together the Imperium, yet not one
word has He uttered in all that time. Without His guidance, mankind
has strayed far from the path of enlightenment.

The bright ideals of the Age of Wonder have withered and died.
To be alive in this time is a terrible fate, where an existence of
grinding servitude is the best that can be hoped for, and a quick death
is seen as the kindest mercy.

As the Imperium continues its inevitable decline, Abaddon, last
true son of the Primarch Horus, and now Warmaster in his stead,
has reached the climax of a plan millennia in the making, tearing
reality open across the width of the galaxy and unleashing forces
unheard of. At last it seems, after centuries of valiant struggle,
mankind's doom is at hand.

Into this darkness a pale shaft of light penetrates. The Primarch
Roboute Guilliman has been wakened from deathly slumber by alien
sorcery and arcane science. Returning to Terra, he has resolved to
set right this dire imbalance, to defeat Chaos once and for all, and to
restart the Emperor's grand plan for humanity.

But first, the Imperium must be saved. The galaxy is split in twain.
On one side, Imperium Sanctus, beleaguered but defiant. On the
other, Imperium Nihilus, thought lost to the night. A mighty crusade
has been called to take back the Imperium and restore its glory. All
mankind stands ready for the greatest conflict of the age. Failure
means extinction, and the path to victory leads only to war.

This is the era Indomitus.

CHAPTER ONE

A HOMECOMING

With a blast of equalising pressure, the Overlord's assault ramps clanged down onto the deck of the Palatine Hangar. The ramps were locked on to combat settings – hard drop, no dampers – not the done thing when attending the last loyal primarch, but Tetrarch Decimus Androdinus Felix was not in a mood for niceties.

Felix strode out of the gunship first, the Chosen of Vespator at his heels. They were his bodyguard, ten Space Marines in varied livery, one chosen from each of the Shield Chapters of Ultramar. They made a colourful crowd, clashing to some sensibilities, only united by the golden device of the tetrarch emblazoned on their left pauldrons. Their boots rang loudly as they spread out, guns ready. Even aboard the primarch's flagship, they scanned their surroundings for threat. Each one was a lord of battle, and they could not easily put war aside.

A small delegation of unmodified humans awaited Felix. A chamberlain hurried forward from amid the banners and the floating servo-skulls. Small and feeble though the man was, he stepped boldly into the path of the giants of Ultramar, bringing them to a halt.

'My lord Felix, welcome back to the *Macragge's Honour.'* The chamberlain sketched a quick yet perfect bow. 'If I might direct you to the quarters the primarch has prepared for you, you may refresh yourself.' The official's critical gaze roamed over the damage marking the battleplate of each and every Space Marine. 'And perhaps make yourselves presentable?'

A fussy statement from a fussy little man. Felix didn't intend to growl, but the noise of irritation he made came out as one from the voxmitter of his helm.

'There will be no need. My errand is urgent. I will see the primarch now.'

'He bids you wait awhile – he is aware of your efforts at Alveiro and is most pleased that you have come to see him, but requests you await his call for a proper audience.'

'Now,' said Felix firmly. 'I am the commander of the Eastern Tetra of Ultramar. The task I am upon cannot wait.'

'My lord–' the human began, but Felix cut him off.

'You said he requests.'

'Yes, my lord,' said the chamberlain.

'Then tell me, does the Imperial Regent command me to my quarters?' Felix asked. 'Are these orders you give me, or suggestions?'

The official hesitated. 'Your comfort and your wellbeing are ever at the forefront of the Imperial Regent's mind–'

'Not orders,' said Sergeant Cominus, head of Felix's guard, whose armour was the red and white of the Sons of Orar. 'Is that not right, chamberlain?'

The man's calm did not waver. 'Not orders,' he admitted.

'Then take me to him. Now.' Felix leaned forward, a weight of armour and gene-engineered flesh with cold glass for eyes. The joints of his Gravis plate purred menacingly. He still smelled of war, of blood, and oil, and fire. Few men would stand firm in front of something like that.

The chamberlain had a heart of iron, and so submitted gracefully. He gave another bow, even slower this time, and stepped aside.

'I shall escort you, my lord. I–'

'Do not trouble yourself, chamberlain, I know the way.'

'Then I shall send heralds ahead of you to announce your arrival.'

'If you insist,' said Felix. 'If they can keep up.' By then he was already moving.

The heralds ran to match the Space Marines' pace, doggedly calling out the name and ranks of the tetrarch in every hall and corridor as they made their way up from the Palatine Hangar into the Palace Spire, the personal domain of Roboute Guilliman.

Several months had passed since the Relief of Parmenio and the battle at Hecatone. Fleet Primus had made great strides in evicting Mortarion's forces from Ultramar, but one crucial campaign remained. The garden world of Iax, the epicentre of corruption, was still in enemy hands. Felix had not been recalled to take part in the invasion, yet although that might have explained his rage, it was not the cause. Felix was angry for an altogether darker reason.

'Make way for Decimus Felix! Make way for the Tetrarch of Vespator, lord of the Eastern Marches!' the heralds called breathlessly. Their announcements caused some consternation, for the corridors were heavily trafficked, and the Chosen proceeded as lightly as bull grox, their marching steps booming around the *Macragge's Honour* like artillery. By habit Guilliman kept his palace empty when he could; even a being as singular as the primarch needed space to withdraw, like any man. On the occasion

of Felix's visit the palace was full of rushing scribes and poten-
tates. The men and women the Chosen encountered seemed
unused to Space Marines, and scattered out of their way, despite
their high ranks. They were all lords and ladies of one adepta or
another, for by then Felix and his party were deep into the spire,
where only the exalted and their servants went.

'Is it just me,' voxed Cominus to Felix, 'or is this place infested
with bureaucrats?'

'Infested is not the word I would use for such valued Imperial servants,' said Felix drily. 'But in essence, your observation
is correct. This is not the primarch's only war. Beyond the Five
Hundred Worlds the Indomitus Crusade continues. He will be
done soon in Ultramar. He is preparing to move on, once the
final blow is struck at Iax.'

They made straight for the primarch's personal scriptorium,
Felix knowing from his long association with Guilliman that
this was his preferred place. The heralds evidently expected the
Imperial Regent to be within also, and raised no objection, but
enquiries with the historitors there revealed the primarch to
be elsewhere, and they were redirected further upward to the
Chamber Imperius.

They took lifters to the pinnacle of Guilliman's Palace Spire.
It was a dome of armaglass, a meeting place for matters of the
most important sort. Felix knew it well.

He led his men down a vaulted approach corridor as ornate
and high as a cathedral nave. As they neared the great doors
to the Chamber Imperius, twenty of Guilliman's Victrix Guard
trooped out from rooms to either side and stepped in front
of the gates, forming a perfect semicircle, and halting Felix's
progress. They stamped once, slammed their shields down,
then clashed them together, presenting a blue wall of ceramite
decked with skulls and wings to the tetrarch. In the centre they

left a gap wide enough for a single Space Marine to pass, and through this stepped Sicarius, once captain of the Ultramarines Second Company, now commander of Guilliman's personal guard. He came forward unhelmed and stopped before Felix.

'Greetings, Tetrarch Felix,' said Sicarius, with a slight bow of his head. He gripped his sword hilt. His hand was never far from the weapon, either resting on its pommel or toying with its decoration. Sicarius had always resented keeping it sheathed, and that appeared to be ever the case since his return from the warp. 'To what do we owe the honour of your presence?'

'I think you know why.'

Sicarius stared at Felix. 'Do I, tetrarch? Enlighten me.'

Felix looked down on him. Sicarius was unusual for so high ranking a Space Marine in not yet having crossed the Rubicon Primaris. He was older than Felix, at least in terms of active service, though if one counted birthdates, Felix had greater years than nearly every human alive.

'The primarch. He has my prisoner. Let me through.'

'He does,' said Sicarius, but he gave no ground. The Chosen of Vespator and the Victrix Guard stared at each other. A tension stretched the air. Wherever the Adeptus Astartes went, violence was not far behind. There was no hatred between them, but there was an aggressive curiosity. Both groups wished to test themselves against the other.

Felix looked past the shorter warrior to the chamber gates. 'Was the regent expecting me?'

Sicarius inclined his head. 'What do you think, brother? He is a primarch.'

'Then whatever I do, he anticipates.'

'It is not a failing of yours, I assure you,' said Sicarius.

'Does he ever make you feel like a fool, captain?' said Felix.

Sicarius let out a snort. 'Compared to him, tetrarch, we are all fools. I wonder how he stands us, sometimes. We must seem so limited to him.'

Felix reached up and undid the seal clasps of his helm, eased it off his head and out from under his Gravis armour's cowl. His face was rough with dried sweat. He had been in his armour for days. He'd intended to bathe before they arrived, for by the standard measures Alveiro was six days' journey from Iax, but the warp was unpredictable away from the calming presence the primarch had on its storms, and the journey had been accomplished in minutes.

Destiny, perhaps. Felix had expected to arrive once it was all over, to vent his fury after the fact. He was not prepared for this. He suspected the hand of smirking gods in the run of events, pushing him and his master towards confrontation.

'Never second-guess him,' said Sicarius. 'I would have thought you were his equerry long enough to know that.'

'I was. But it goes against me too, for I forget sometimes that he is not a man.'

Sicarius' hard face did not change. 'Neither are we.'

'He is going to interrogate my prisoner. That is his intention, is it not?'

'That is for him to say, brother,' said Sicarius. He looked around at the Chosen, whose weapons were not raised, but not held at rest either. 'Have your men stand down. They can wait in the portside antechamber. There's enough room for them. It looks like you have some skilled warriors here. We should test ourselves and our men against one another. You have won a high reputation.' Sicarius appeared altogether grim as he made his offer. It was not an extension of brotherhood, but came from a need to prove himself against all comers.

Felix ignored the invitation. 'So you are going to let me in to see him?' Another unexpected eventuality. He thought he would have to exert his authority, for he outranked Sicarius. Fight, even. He was ready to.

Sicarius was far more phlegmatic, and shrugged. His armour whined as his pauldrons displaced themselves. 'I am not going to let you do anything, tetrarch. You are being admitted according to the primarch's express command.' Sicarius' battle-worn face became less dour; there was even a hint of a smile about the corners of his eyes. 'You were right. He was expecting you.'

The doors of the Chamber Imperius swung wide onto darkness. The lumens were out, though the shutters were open, admitting a pale wash of starlight from the high windows that made up the walls. Like the dome overhead, the walls were almost entirely of armaglass, and numerous enough that they gave a near-complete view of the ship, from its gargantuan ploughshare ram to the outer edges of its city-sized engine stack. Felix stopped, momentarily taken aback. There was no better way to see the *Macragge's Honour*, one of the last Gloriana-class battleships left in the galaxy, than to view it from the Chamber, and he was arrested by its majesty. It was immense, of a scale that defied description. It was surrounded by many more massive craft, the core of Battle Group Alphus, chief spearhead of Indomitus Crusade Fleet Primus. But these others, though huge themselves, were but slivers of metal against the *Macragge's Honour*. There were no women or men who could build its like any more. The science was lost. The will was lacking. The *Macragge's Honour* was a relic of a better age, a monstrous weapon from higher times, and in that it was exactly like its master.

Roboute Guilliman was on the far side of the room, near the raised stalls where the Council Exterra sat when in session. Just then, there were no others present, and the chamber was completely empty but for the primarch, making it seem larger than usual despite all the chairs and thrones that took up its floor.

Guilliman cut a lonely figure against the field of stars and ships. The primarch was not looking at the view, but had a hololithic light weave, depicting a world, open in front of him, and it was to this he gave his full attention. The hololith shone a wan glow up into his face, lending him an ashen cast. Even from the far side of the room, Felix recognised Iax. The signs of a planet sickened by Nurgle's maladies were clear, and seemed to infect the primarch by reflection.

Not for the first time, Felix thought Roboute Guilliman looked tired.

Guilliman looked up from the image. Shadow trapped his eyes.

'Decimus,' Guilliman said. Felix's given name echoed around the Chamber Imperius, as if looking for somewhere to settle. It found no home, but died quietly, lost in the high peak of the dome. 'It is good to see you.' He sounded sincere.

Felix approached his lord. In Felix's body were numerous additional organs, and coiled supplemental strands of gene-code, all taken from the primarch. Guilliman was not truly his father, but Guilliman was as close to kin as Felix had. Their blood was mixed.

Felix knelt with difficulty, his heavy armour hampering his movements, and bowed his head. He waited for Guilliman to speak. When he did not, Felix spoke instead.

'You are not angry that I came?' he said quietly, expecting rebuke.

'Should I be?' said Guilliman mildly.

'I have come to recommend you do not do what I think you are about to do.'

Guilliman's smile was audible in his voice. 'You disapprove so much you will not specify my actions? How do I know you and I refer to the same matter?'

'Such things as you intend should not be named,' said Felix.

'Perhaps,' said Guilliman. 'But you do not have to agree with everything I do, my son. You do your duty as you see best. You are not an unthinking man, you are not afraid to defy me. I gave you the role of tetrarch because of that. If anything, I am pleased you came.'

'And if I had remained at Alveiro instead?'

'Then I would also have been pleased,' said Guilliman. 'But you are here. Your instincts are good. What we are about to attempt is a risk. You see that. You come to warn me. Good intentions should not be punished.'

Felix looked up. He was mystified. No matter how much he thought he understood the primarch, he realised he never would. If one of Felix's own men were to behave as he had, then Felix would not hesitate to censure them. Often, Felix felt himself to have left humanity behind, but Guilliman had never been human, not truly.

'You plan to question it. That is why you called it back rather than allowing me to destroy it when it was found. I am right?'

Guilliman did not answer, but looked down at him, giving him his full attention for the first time. Felix felt his gaze as a weight on his soul.

'There is no need to kneel, Decimus. Please stand.'

Felix got to his feet. The smallest noises were made large by the chamber. Its acoustics were perfect, designed to amplify the reediest voice of the most ancient sage, and it lent the sounds of his panoply, even the swish of his cloak upon the mosaic floor, great portentousness.

'There, that is better,' said Guilliman. He clenched his fist in the heart of the hololith, banishing it. The primarch looked Felix up and down, and approved of what he saw.

'You seem well. Strong. The office suits you, my son,' he said. 'How do you like your new domain?'

Felix was still angry, and could not keep it completely from his response, so his words came out tersely. 'I was on Vespator for precisely twenty-three hours before I moved on to continue my inspection of the province, my lord. I couldn't tell from so short a visit, but it seems defensible enough.'

Guilliman smiled again. He had a sad smile, full of the pain of understanding. His melancholy smothered the fire burning in Felix's heart. 'I meant the people, Felix, I meant the world.'

'Both seem pleasant enough,' said Felix, less angry now. 'But neither of those things are worth much if they cannot be protected. Your entire realm is under threat. Mortarion's hordes are not the only danger.'

Guilliman nodded. He was distracted. The running lights of voidships close by the *Macragge's Honour* filled his eyes with stars. 'What about the rest of the Eastern Tetra? Will you be able to bring it under our control?'

'May I speak honestly?'

'When have I ever asked that you do otherwise?'

'It is a shambles,' Felix said, and in remembering his tour of the worlds he was responsible for ruling, he tasted the primarch's burden. 'Nearly every planet is in disarray. Mortarion's armies have not done much direct harm to the east, but the Sotharan League was hit hard by the tyranids, and there has been raiding by orks, and recently by the necrons. Human pirates are also a problem. But the hive fleets are the worst. There were a dozen inhabited worlds stripped to bedrock at least. I do not know how many unknown planets suffered the same fate. If the xenos were not rapacious enough, years of corruption have hollowed the old League out. I have not been to a single planet where the defences, or any other asset for that matter, military or otherwise, match the records. Tithes have been falsified. A significant proportion of sector finances have been embezzled. Much has been stolen, sometimes openly. They have no fear of Imperial authority there, but they will. I have begun an inquisition. Agents of the Ordo Hereticus and the Adeptus Arbites assist me. There will be executions. A great many.'

Guilliman's face was unreadable, prompting Felix to apologise.

'I am sorry, my lord, I do not have time to be gentle. Examples have to be made.'

The primarch shook his head. 'No, no, you do right, the League was the worst of all political systems,' said Guilliman. 'Enough centralised power to embolden the elite, not enough to keep them in check. Untrammelled flow of coin amplifies greed. It allows acquisitiveness while enabling the shirking of responsibility, and so the weak suffer. It must be corrected with maximum prejudice. Again my errors confront me. I say once more that Ultramar should never have been divided.'

'Things will change,' said Felix. 'The Sotharan League is no more. The populace will find direct rule by Ultramar a more just solution.' He paused. 'I have wondered what the Scythes of the Emperor were thinking, letting it get so bad.'

'They had their own wars to fight,' said Guilliman, 'and they paid dearly to fulfil their duties. It was not their place to interfere with civilian governance. That too will change.'

Felix could not disagree. The tyranids had stripped Sotha, the capital of the League and the home world of the Scythes of the Emperor, and nearly annihilated the Scythes in the process. He'd exchanged a few messages with the reduced Chapter, continuing negotiations to supply them with Primaris reinforcements to bring them back to full strength, but they were a ruined brotherhood, and shame dripped from every message they sent him.

'One good thing to be said, is that the people were pleased to see us,' Felix said. 'We will not find much resistance there to reimposing direct rule, not if the ruling classes know what is good for them.'

'In your experience, do people often know what is good for them?' asked Guilliman.

Felix said nothing for a moment. 'In truth, I do not know. I was a boy when I was taken by Cawl's agents. I have been active only a dozen years since my reawakening from suspended animation, during which time I have known nothing but war. You told me I retained much of my humanity when many firstborn Primaris brothers did not, but I have had to take that on trust. I do not know people, my lord. So how can I tell?'

'You are wrong, Decimus, you do know people. You have a facility for empathy. What does your instinct say?'

'My gut says that people do not know what is good for them.' He hesitated.

'And?'

'As individuals, people are intelligent creatures, but as a group, they are animals, and animals need a firm hand.'

'I see,' said Guilliman, and there was the space for an ocean of disappointment between those two words.

'The philosophy is unimportant,' Felix said hurriedly. 'Action is. I have not had much trouble with the Imperial governors, and if any oppose us the people are ready to rise up. They have had enough of human greed and xenos terror.'

'Then I trust you to put it right for me, my son,' said Guilliman. He looked out of the window. 'This war will never end. We can only fight for brief moments of peace. Once Mortarion is driven off, there will be other foes. The tyranids, the necrons, the t'au. I must leave you and the others to deal with them here. I have a galaxy to save.'

The primarch was unusually troubled. He stared off into space, then seemed to come back into himself.

'Ultramar is nearly ours,' Guilliman said briskly. 'Not before time. This war has been a dangerous distraction from the Indomitus Crusade, and although I have tried to spare most of its assets from my duties here, relying instead upon forces gathered from the surrounding sectors, several battle groups of Fleet Primus are still occupied in Ultramar, where they could be liberating other worlds.'

'It is all the same fight,' said Felix. 'Chaos must be defeated wherever it is found. This is an important war zone.'

'It is,' agreed Guilliman. 'Ultramar is important for all sorts of reasons. But we must take politics into account, and politics do not speak the same language as logic. There are those who use my desire to save Ultramar as a weapon against me, naming it a sign of favouritism for my own people. Terra seethes with discontent still. The agents of the enemy are everywhere. The greed of humanity is not restricted to the dead league of Sotha, but is found wherever mankind goes. Avarice clouds men's vision, it makes them blind to anything but the short term and their own gain.

'The Council Exterra does what it can to refute these claims, but its members are not the High Lords, and even its existence is another fact used to prove my desire to become Emperor. The politicians in the Imperial Palace call them lapdogs. There has been rebellion on Terra while we fight for survival,' he said, referring to a plot of several deposed and new High Lords to usurp him. Guilliman glanced at his gene-son. 'I have limited time to save the Imperium from the external threats of Chaos and xenos before the whole rotten structure implodes. I must be triumphant here. The heart must be torn from Mortarion's efforts. The crossing of the Attilan Gap to Imperium Nihilus cannot be delayed any longer. Abaddon pushes hard at the Nachmund Gauntlet and around the remains of the Cadian Gate. Marneus

Calgar must return to Vigilus soon. I have been here too long. No doubt this is part of the Warmaster's plan. He strikes at what I hold dear to distract me, and I am ashamed to say it has worked.'

'Do you believe Mortarion is working with the Warmaster?'

Guilliman let out a bark of mirthless laughter. 'He does no bidding but his own. This is not the Heresy. There is no central command, only the whim of madness. No, Mortarion only wishes to humble me. He will care nothing for Abaddon, but his actions play into other plans. He is unaware that by following his supposedly indomitable will he is merely the puppet of others, like all the followers of Chaos. He has been manipulated into this. I need a quick solution. I need to know what is happening on Iax before we attack, and I need to know now. I am in some peril. I cannot go in blindly.'

'Is that why you are going to speak with the inquisitor's slave?'

Guilliman's mouth set. 'We come to the crux of our disagreement. You disapprove. That is why I knew you would come.'

'Why did you not tell me?'

'Because in all honesty, my son, I anticipated this, and realised it would be easier to handle your anger in this situation, rather than having you arrive with the slave. I calculated that you might attempt to destroy it, there and then, at terrible risk to yourself, in order to save me from making a mistake.'

'You are making a mistake.'

'That is not impossible. If it calms you, the slave's destruction is only deferred. It will die.'

'But not before you use it. It is a thing of the enemy, my lord. Inquisitor Tjejren went too far. He is a dangerous radical who has betrayed his office.'

'His actions enrage you, and yet he eluded you,' said Guilliman. Felix felt the sting of criticism.

'I regret to say he is still at large,' he admitted, ashamed.

'No matter,' said Guilliman. 'Tjejren was a servant of the Emperor once. He still believes he is. He may yet serve.'

'I fear he is beyond hope. Everything touched by the warp is corrupted.'

Guilliman looked down at him. 'Then we are all corrupt, for in the existence of our souls, a fragment of the warp is lodged in us all.' He shifted. The Armour of Fate growled.

'Have you seen the slave?' said Felix harshly. 'Have you seen what Tjejren did to this interrogator yet?'

'No, I admit I have not,' said the primarch. 'I have many matters to occupy me.'

'Then you may speak differently once you have, my lord. Remo and his parasite will bring you nothing but evil,' said Felix.

'You underestimate the strength of will of the Emperor's servants. I have been told Interrogator Remo clings on. He is in thrall to the thing occupying him, but he desires to perform one last service, and I trust that will see the creature remain truthful while it is interrogated. It is an opportunity, Felix. Understand that I do not undertake this course of action lightly. Only a thing of the warp can tell us what occurs on Iax. It teeters on the brink. One push may see it turned to a daemon world, or sucked into the empyrean entirely, and it may take many other worlds with it, no matter how much damage we have done to Mortarion's plans. This is an opportunity that I cannot pass up. It will save lives by the million. It may save my life. I cannot win this war if I am dead.'

Felix was silent a moment.

'You swear you will kill him afterwards?' said Felix. 'My lord, forgive my presumption, but if you witnessed what it did to the kill-team sent to apprehend Tjejren…' Felix let his sentence trail off. He had no heart to put his memories into words.

'It will be a mercy to the interrogator, if nothing else.' Guilliman moved away from the window. 'Do you wish to attend the questioning, now that you are here? Perhaps if you see the interrogation and execution it will put your mind at ease. I would have no differences come between us.'

'You will kill him afterwards?' Felix asked again.

'I swear,' said Guilliman. 'Do not be afraid, it can do no harm. The Concilia Psykana hold it, under Brother-Captain Ionan Grud's guidance.'

'The Grey Knight?' Felix asked. 'He who bested Typhus aboard Galatan before Parmenio?'

'The same. He is strong, and incorruptible. I say who better than the Knights of Titan to chain a daemon?'

CHAPTER TWO

DAEMONHOST

The Space Marine Librarius occupied the tower behind the palace, and it was to here that Guilliman and Felix went next, going by swift lifters and private ways until they were hidden in halls of adamantium far from the ship's hull. Heavily armoured, only the vulnerable reactor was more protected than the Librarius' inner wards, and they needed to be.

Most capital ships belonging to the Adeptus Astartes carried replications in miniature of the various subdomains found in their fortress monasteries: forge, reclusiam, apothecarion and the rest, each one necessary for Space Marine forces to act independently for protracted periods. One section of such ships was always set aside for psykers, and the needs of the esoteric battles they fought. The Imperium faced many differing forms of supernatural foe. Warded cells and ritual sites were as necessary as guns and tanks to its most elite armies.

Where the Librarius of the *Macragge's Honour* differed from those on other Space Marine ships was only partly due to scale – though it was undoubtedly larger than most. The chief difference was in its purpose. Rather than the mystics of one Chapter, the Librarius of the *Macragge's Honour* played host to Librarians of many brotherhoods, and others who were not of the Adeptus Astartes, for there were unaugmented human psykers present there, and a few who were not human at all. Whatever their origin, the occupants were mighty in the warp, and the chiefs of this group made up Guilliman's Concilia Psykana: his council of seers. Once, a long time ago, Guilliman would have thought the idea of his council ridiculous – something from children's tales, a cabal of wizards to guide a king. Now, he found them indispensable.

The membership of the Concilia Psykana was fluid, as members came and went on to other missions or fell in battle. There were never more than a hundred, and never fewer than a dozen. Though the Concilia changed with time, of their number there were a handful Guilliman had come to rely on especially, and they were a valuable constant to him in his war against the gods.

Guilliman and Felix arrived at a cell made entirely of iron rusted to the colour of old blood. It was small, hardly fifty feet across, beehive shaped, taller than it was wide, with warding runes cut into the metal in such number that there was not a smooth surface in the room. The single caged lumen at the apex of the ceiling was barely sufficient to illuminate the place. Rings of tarnished silver lay on the floor, the staples holding them in place sunk deep into the deck. Narrow observation slits ran all around the room at a Space Marine's head height. Black glass glinted deep in them, and their frames and transoms were made of sanctified lead, also cast with many sigils. It was a place of extreme spiritual danger, best looked on from outside, but Guilliman and Felix went within.

'We must see what we are to see first-hand,' said Guilliman, before they passed the threshold.

The thick door squealed aside. Guilliman put on his helm, told Felix to do the same, then bent to go through. He did not pause once inside, but crossed the floor and took up a place by the far wall. Felix, on the other hand, hesitated. He smelled blood. He sensed suffering. There was a wide iris hatch in the floor, and from it emanated a foreboding of dread so intense it made the hair on his neck prickle.

'This is a wicked place,' said Felix.

'There are degrees of wickedness,' Guilliman replied. His machine-projected voice seemed robbed of power, dulled by malice, a bell with its clapper muffled. 'In a perfect universe, I would not have anything to do with this, but the universe we have been given is not perfect, and so some wickednesses must serve, dangerous though they be. Enter, Felix, no harm will come to you, I promise.'

Reluctantly, Felix joined the primarch, and turned to face the door. A Space Marine Epistolary and two Codiciers came in. One, Felix knew as Donas Maxim of the Aurora Chapter, the others he did not. They were helmed, their eye-lenses already glowing with gathering psychic power. They arranged themselves equi-distantly, their silence adding a sense of dolefulness to the evil permeating the metal.

The next person to come in would have surprised some in the fleet, for he was not a Space Marine, nor was he even human, but an aeldari, garbed in the black robes and mystic gear of a farseer of Ulthwé. His tall, curved helm nearly touched the doorway top as he entered.

He was Illiyanne Natasé, emissary of Eldrad Ulthran, Guilli-man's ally.

Felix was born of a more tolerant age, and the xenos incited curiosity in him rather than hatred. Natasé was a valued advisor to Guilliman, but his presence in the Concilia was not widely known, and for some time he had been away from the flagship treating with his own people, who had come to aid the fight in Ultramar's west. Despite Felix's closeness to Guilliman, even his own dealings with Natasé had been minimal. Natasé was a secret, much like what was about to happen. Both were secrets of the most damaging kind.

Natasé performed an elaborate greeting to the primarch, closer to a dance than a bow. If a human had performed the same actions, he would have seemed absurd, but the aeldari was graceful, the movements beautiful, and the fine charms he wore all about his person only accentuated his elegance as they swung with his movements.

'My lord Roboute Guilliman.'

'You are ready?' asked the primarch.

'I am,' said Natasé. 'I have consulted the skein, difficult as it is, surrounded by so many crude minds. You will be able to interrogate the daemon. It will answer you.' The xenos was hard to read, his body language rich but alien. Guilliman understood it better than Felix.

'You are like Decimus here. You do not think we should perform this questioning,' said Guilliman.

'I do not,' said Natasé firmly. 'The daemon bound to this man is a fragment of the Great Changer. Nothing you will hear from its mouth will be the truth, even when it is speaking the truth. You are intelligent for something derived from human stock, Lord Guilliman, but I fear you will do yourself nothing but harm should you proceed.'

Guilliman stared at the xenos. Natasé was so slight, Felix thought, like a bundle of rushes dressed and set to look like a man, so feeble the weight of Guilliman's regard alone should have crushed him, but he stood firm.

'Your prognostications told you this?' Guilliman asked.

'Eldrad Ulthran commanded me to be as straightforward with you as I can, for yours is not a subtle species, and there is much you will never understand,' he said. 'In truth, I cannot see what will befall you. The pathways created by the Changer of the Ways are convoluted, and lead never to where one thinks they might, before they reach their inevitable destination.'

'Corruption. Madness. Damnation,' said Guilliman.

'Terse, unpoetic, but apt,' said the aeldari. There was a hint of mockery in the way he mimicked Guilliman's speech pattern. 'My advice to you is dictated partly by this uncertainty, but partly because I know these daemons of old. Every word they utter is a trap.'

'Then do you refuse to help me find it?'

'No, I will not refuse,' said Natasé, and his arrogance was tempered by regret. 'I am bound by oath to aid you in whatever way I can. Eldrad Ulthran said that I was to listen to you. He said that you are...' The xenos considered his words carefully. 'Superior even to us, in some ways.' It was evident he found the idea distasteful.

'I thank you for your counsel, seer. We will go on. Let us be about it. I will not have Remo suffer for any longer than is necessary. Bring in the prisoner,' Guilliman commanded.

As soon as the words were spoken, the temperature in the room dropped. The iris hatch lensed open. Lifter wheels squealed, a silvery unlight shone up from the shaft, and frost spidered over the rusted walls. The runes burst into life with audible cracks as psychic power shocked the metal. A hexagrammatic circle around the hatch, invisible before, glimmered, then flared so brightly that Felix's helm reacted, and darkened his eye-lenses.

The possessed man and his guard rose up on a platform.

Despite the timeless prison of the stasis field the daemon-host had been held in, Chaos had pushed itself deeply into the clay of Remo's body. His skin had become a sickening, mottled pink, and was covered with sores. He was emaciated, the twisted bones showing, obviously in the process of turning into something new. Knobs and spurs protruded from his joints. A group of horns sprouted from one side of his face, covering over his features completely on the left, all but the mouth, whose down-turned tusks pulled into a permanent, drooling sneer. Black teeth sharp as flints crowded bleeding gums. Though it should have made the daemonhost look like a witless fool, somehow the expression managed to convey a dangerous cunning, and amusement.

As for the man Interrogator Remo had been, little was left of him but his suffering. His arms were looped over the crossbar of a T-shaped crucifix of shining metal, his hands manacled behind him in rune-stamped chains of the same blue steel. Loops of razor wire about his elbows and his waist tied him in place. Fiercely glowing warding charms hung from it in bunches. His feet were pinned to the metal upright by a single silver nail, whose head was struck with a complex sigil. This, and all the other arcane symbols around him, glowed with an unnatural heat. Black flames licked around his bonds, burning his flesh wherever they touched. It was an agonising position to be bound in for any length of time, yet Remo held himself utterly still, single yellow eye staring ahead. It locked with Felix's gaze. It was deep, he thought, that gaze. Two pupils swam around the iris, shifting with ever-changing patterns like the Great Rift that split the galaxy. Behind them were infinities.

Before Felix could look away, memory rose unbidden.

Felix remembered the day he had uncovered Tjejren's plot. A so-called scrying ritual to find the network of Mortarion's corruption. He had no warning the inquisitor was going to bind a daemon to his servant until the last moment. He had intervened,

Tjejren had fled. Remo remained, already damned. Felix had lost six good men before Remo had been subdued. Stasis and psychic lock had contained him, just.

Felix's misgivings redoubled. A coldness touched both his hearts. He had sent Remo back to Vespator to be safely dealt with by his psykers, fearing that merely killing him might unleash the daemon trapped in his flesh, for what did he know of these matters, even now? Yet he had returned from Alveiro to discover the daemonhost not dead, but already on board a Null Ship of the Anathema Psykana, and heading out of the system. He was appalled to find the order had come directly from the primarch himself. Doubt assailed him. He loved Guilliman as a father, but this, surely, was a step most assuredly in the wrong direction. Remo was possessed by Chaos, and should not be treated with in any way. His memory of fighting this thing collapsed into fire, and he saw a bloody future, where a dark mockery of Guilliman presided over an Imperium of despair and suffering. This is how damnation began, as a single bad action made in good faith. History turned on the point of spear.

If only it could be stopped, he thought. A single sword thrust. A moment's work. He would die, but the future would be…

Felix tore his gaze away from the daemon. He was sweating under his armour. His hand was around his sword hilt, ready to draw.

Guilliman glanced at him.

'Be wary, Decimus,' said Guilliman. 'Do not heed its temptations.'

Felix nodded, and recovered himself. 'Yes, my lord.' He avoided its gaze from then on.

Around Remo's neck was a collar, also alight with warding sigils. A chain led from the collar. The end of it was held in the hand of his guard, a warrior in unusual Terminator battleplate, and he too was terrible to behold in his way.

Where Remo raged with heat, Ionan Grud radiated a chill deeper than the void, and Felix realised it was from his influence that the frost came and the air froze. Felix was used to psychic matters. His own advisors included among their number many potent psykers, and he had fought against all manner of warp abominations and sorcerers since he had been awoken, but the sense of power coming off Grud was of an entirely different order of magnitude. He imagined this was what it must feel like to be close to the Emperor Himself. Felix's soul trembled in its presence. The tetrarch was a mighty warrior, but he knew without a doubt that if the Grey Knights captain turned on him, he would die in moments, and that along with his body his soul would be annihilated.

Guilliman was unaffected by either daemon or warrior-mystic.

'Captain Grud,' he said, 'are you prepared?'

'I stand ready,' said the captain. His voice was condemnatory, a tone accentuated by the harshness of his voxmitter.

'Natasé,' said Guilliman, 'begin.'

The aeldari was shaking, profoundly affected by Grud's sledge-hammer presence. Farseers were immensely powerful psykers, but their talents were less aggressive than those of the Grey Knights, and the sensibilities of his race were altogether finer than those of humans. He came forward carefully, as if approaching a raging fire, reaching into a pouch by his side as he did so. Speaking quickly in his own tongue, he drew out a number of small objects; angular runes, they appeared to be. With great care he set them spinning one by one in the palm of his hand, then threw them up into the air, where they took up orbits around the daemon and his gaoler, trailing silvery light, until Grud and Remo were surrounded by a complex, intersecting pattern. Felix heard the names of various aeldari deities in the liquid speech coming from the farseer's helm, but caught nothing else.

When the cage was woven, the farseer stepped back. His runes continued their orbit.

'He is bound,' said Natasé hoarsely.

The daemonhost continued to stare ahead, only at Felix. The tetrarch felt the thing was attempting to share a private joke with him.

'Interrogator Remo,' Guilliman said. 'Speak to me.'

Instantly, the thing's head snapped back and forth so quickly it became a blur, and the possessed man gave out a deep, feline growl.

'Remo. Fight,' commanded the primarch. 'There is will left in you yet.'

The daemonhost's head ceased jerking about, and came to a dead stop. It laughed.

Thy servant is no more, consumed by me, he is part of me. Part of the Lord of Change, as all things were and all things are and all things will be,' the daemonhost said. *'No hope for him, or for thee, my petty mortal lord.'*

Guilliman glanced at Grud. The Grey Knight yanked hard upon the chain, tugging the daemonhost forward. Blue fire sped up the links, and seared the thing's flesh. It let out an outraged snarl.

'Let forward the spirit of Remo, so he may speak with us,' said Guilliman.

'No,' said the daemonhost. *'This body is mine. His soul is mine. I will not let him speak.'*

'Already you reveal your weakness and your lies. How can he be gone and yet still able to speak? Release him,' Guilliman said. Again he looked to Grud.

Runes flared all over the Grey Knight's armour as he declaimed a litany of ancient Gothic, finishing with a series of sounds that tortured the hearing of all in the room and echoed in unseen spaces. The bound daemon screamed at the speaking of its name, thrashing in its bonds. Natasé staggered back. The Space Marine Librarians braced themselves, eye-lenses glowing as they exerted their formidable wills to contain the daemon. The Grey Knight ceased speaking, and the words died away, only slowly, leaving sibilances that seemed sharp enough to draw blood hanging long in the room.

Remo hung slackly from his pole and crossbar. He seemed more human now, afflicted instead of dangerous. The wires mortified his flesh, and blood, the bright red of mortal kind, ran down his body.

'I have your true name, daemon,' Guilliman said. 'Do you think I would petition you like some footling sorcerer, ready to sell my soul for scraps of knowledge? I am the last son of the Emperor of Terra. You will heed me and you will obey!'

'Speak, then, with your puling serf,' said the daemon's voice.

Remo's head rose, and now the surviving eye was human, light brown and full of pain.

'My lord, it knows you will destroy it. I...' He winced, and gritted his black teeth. 'It will not tell you what you wish to know. I cannot force it to be...' He shook violently. Blood poured from his mouth, and his chest convulsed. He groaned, and rallied himself. 'My lord, help me, I wish to serve, but I cannot bear this much longer. Kill me, I beg you.'

'It will tell me,' said Guilliman coldly. 'We have its name. It has no choice, is that not correct?'

Remo's head jerked, and his eye rolled back, performing a complete rotation, until the yellow iris with its double pupil appeared again.

'Curse thee, son of the Anathema!' it said. *'Curse thee and all thy feeble kind! Great Tzeentch is rising, thou art his pawn. Canst thou not see it? I will tell thee nothing!'*

'You will speak.' Guilliman rested his hand upon the pommel

of the Sword of the Emperor. 'You will speak now, and then with this blade I will burn your essence from existence. There is nothing you can do about this. I abhor you. I abjure you. But before your wickedness is seared from reality for all eternity, you will speak and damn your very master!'

The daemon writhed. *'Never!'* it said, though its words were pained.

'Tell me, what is my brother Mortarion's plan?'

'I will not speak.'

'Speak!' Guilliman shouted, and Felix was buffeted by his force of will. The scene in the room was horrifying enough, but beneath the skin of reality, rival currents moved, great tides of psychic energy that tore at the tetrarch. All of them, the farseer, the Grey Knight, the Space Marine Librarians, were affected by it, but not Roboute Guilliman. 'You are a weaver of schemes, your master is my brother's sworn enemy. Tell me of his plans, and you shall at least die in service to your twisted liege, who might enjoy a little victory when I destroy my sibling.'

'No!'

The daemon writhed. The razor wire cut into its stolen flesh, carving bloody strips from Remo's body. The black fires around its hands and feet burned up, consuming the host. Acrid smoke filled the room. Felix heard Remo's all too human screams beneath the daemon's howls. Again, the Grey Knight intoned the daemon's name, causing it to shriek. One of the Space Marine Librarians collapsed, his armour tolling loudly on the floor. Natasé's runes rotated faster and faster about the daemonhost.

'Speak,' commanded Guilliman.

The daemonhost suddenly slumped forward. The raw wash of conflicted spiritual energy subsided. A hot silence fell.

Natasé said something in his alien tongue. 'Now comes the most dangerous time, beware!' he added in Gothic.

The daemonhost raised its head. In twinned voices it spoke, the Neverborn's subordinate now to Remo's. Black tears ran down its face.

'Ask thy questions, oh son of the Anathema. Nine shalt thou have, as is Tzeentch's boon.'

Guilliman was ready.

'Where is Mortarion?'

The daemonhost shuddered. *'He awaits thee upon Iax, as he told thee himself. Eight questions remain.'*

'What is his intention?'

'To kill thee. Seven questions hast thou left.'

'How?' said Guilliman.

'By disease, in honour of his god, Nurgle, lord of blights, the master of seven and three. Six more you may ask.'

Guilliman stopped to think. The bound daemon was true to the ways of its kind, giving the most limited answers. All would be misleading. The primarch had to be careful.

'I am a primarch, created by the Emperor. I am immune to all disease. If Mortarion is to slay me by sickness, it must be of an uncanny sort. By what means is this possible?'

The daemon hissed. Remo sobbed, choking up the words. *'Upon Iax, Ku'Gath Plaguefather works, thrice-cursed Unclean One, first in favour of Nurgle. He stirs the pot of Nurgle himself. It is by the pestilence brewed within the cauldron that he would kill thee, foolish mortal. He has thy blood. Five more.'*

'That was a full answer, my lord, and liable to be full of treachery,' warned Natasé.

'I will not discount it,' said Guilliman. 'Tell me, daemon. I have read of this cauldron. It is known to my loremasters. Does it have a role to play in the net of corruption Mortarion has cast over my realm?'

The daemon howled. *'Yes! Yes! Yes!'* It thrashed and cried, cursing its own words as they poured from its mouth. *'It is the source, the cesspit, the giver of corruption, the heart that pumps filth throughout thy realm. Four answers I will give thee now, no more!'*

'And if it is destroyed, his hold on Ultramar will be broken?'

'A grievous blow will be dealt to him, who is son of plague and son of Anathema both! Three left.'

'Where is it?' said Guilliman.

The daemon became sly. *'In the warp. In Nurgle's Garden. Two.'*

Guilliman shifted, annoyed. he had formulated his question poorly.

'Where is it upon Iax?'

'Everywhere. Nowhere. On Iax,' said the creature. *'One.'*

'Do not toy with me!' Guilliman said, and took a step forward. He pulled the Emperor's Sword a finger's width out of its scabbard. Bright fire burned along the exposed blade. 'You know this sword. In moments, I will use it to end you.'

Gurgling laughter sounded. Though its source was the daemon, it seemed to come from all corners of the room, and it ate at Felix's soul like acid.

'Thou threatens me with annihilation, then why should I tell thee anything at all?'

'Because you are bound! Tell me, where upon Iax will I find the cauldron so that it might be destroyed?'

'It is nowhere, it is everywhere. Iax is become Pestiliax. It is no longer yours, or of this realm.'

'Speak! Tell me more!'

The daemonhost writhed. Remo's voice became stronger, more urgent. *'He will drag your kingdom entire into the warp, you are the key. It will become the stinking playground of the Plague God. You rush to this end, and your recklessness will see his plans come to pass.'*

'That is no answer to my question, where is the cauldron? I command it!'

The daemon shook, resisting the compulsion laid upon it, the conflict within lifting it up from its cross. Dark light blazed a halo about its twisted head, and a smell of burnt spices choked the chamber's occupants. *'A place of life made one of sickness, where neither earth nor water hold sway, but both are lords. Death's garden, where the plague lords play. Iron bound, the king of poxes wreaks his deadly design upon thy mundanity.'*

With a great heave, the daemon coughed up squirming coils of corposant that let short-lived monsters into being. They roared, and fought, and spat venom in a mist over all present, before dissolving into pleading screams.

'No more questions shall I answer, but be free, and complete the task given me,' the voice boomed from every quarter, battering Felix to his knees. The lumen failed. *'Nurgle shall not have thy head, but many-pathed Tzeentch!'*

Blood streaming from his eyes, Felix hardly saw what happened next, but experienced it as a series of vignettes stamped into his memory by strobing psychic light. Natasé's runes exploded in showers of wraithbone and the farseer was flung back against the wall. The cage of light collapsed inward, cutting scores into Captain Grud's armour. The razor wire burst, and the daemon shucked its bonds. The chain about its neck glowed red and melted into smoke. Remo's ruined body convulsed and changed, taking on a shimmering iridescence. Feathers sprouted from his arms and his back. His neck lengthened, becoming wattled, the head long and avian. Talons burst bloodily from his toes. The silver nail shot from his flesh, burying itself in the wall, and the daemon stepped down.

Grud moved to counter it, his armour still smoking from the cuts of Natasé's cage, but the beast, now twenty feet tall and growing still, swatted him aside, sending him into one of the Librarians. Felix tried to rise, but the thing's head swung around on its neck. One look from its beady eyes was enough to pin him in place. His body seemed ablaze with fire, and he roared with the pain.

Then there was light, a soothing flame that washed him as a balm, and he turned his head in time to see Guilliman, last loyal son, the sword of his father raised high over his head. The daemon shrank from it a moment, then attacked, striking faster than the eye could follow. There was an explosion, and a screaming that seemed to last forever. The fires of the sword burst outward, whirling around. The daemon shrieked. White smoke boiled from it, its screams turning to pathetic squeals, and it shrank, reduced again to human size. Felix saw the burning Remo transfixed upon the point of the Emperor's Sword, then fall down to the floor.

The screams died. The fires died. The room went black.

For an age Felix lay stunned. He had not even managed to lay his hand upon his sword.

Silence passed. Felix moved. He was tender all over, but he could stand. He saw the glowing eye-lenses of Grud, the Librarians and, finally, to his relief, those of Roboute Guilliman's Armour of Fate, unmistakable by their size and height above him.

'Lumen,' commanded Guilliman.

The single lamp on the chamber's roof spat sparks, then slowly returned to life.

The Space Marine Librarians were on guard, weapons out. Nimbuses of psychic energy returned to play around the heads of all the psykers. Natasé was at the back of the room, his elaborate helm discarded. His face was paler than alabaster, his black eyes slits. He shivered quietly, battered more by the power of the Immortal Emperor's Sword than the daemon's manifest-ation, Felix thought.

Of Remo only a charred corpse remained, his limbs clutched in by fire-tightened sinew, his teeth white in a screaming mouth. Grud walked over to the dead man and looked down, his eye-lenses flashing an angry blue. It was he that spoke first, and he addressed Guilliman.

'You are the lord of the Imperium, the Imperial Regent, the Lord Commander, the last loyal son of the Emperor Himself, my master and my general,' Grud said. 'But I shall never do the likes of this for you again. Mark my words well, primarch, you stray into dangerous waters with what has passed here.'

Later, Felix learnt that the entirety of Grud's brotherhood departed from Fleet Primus that day, no matter where its battle groups were, and they would not serve at Guilliman's side for some time.

Guilliman watched Grud go. The Sword of the Emperor was sheathed at his side, as if it had not left its scabbard.

'A dangerous course indeed, and a heavy price. This man lost his life and his soul to bring us this information,' Guilliman said. 'But I now know what must be done to remove Mortar-ion from Ultramar.'

CHAPTER THREE

A GREAT CHANGE

'There were cities here, once,' said Cherala. She coughed, and spat out a gob of phlegm. Her hip was hurting again, and her foot dragged. Another dubious gift from the jolly Grandfather.

'Shut up, Cherala. There never were.' Odifus had a honking voice, a legacy of the ear-worms that had got into his head when he was a babe. He could barely hear still over their trilling, and shouted all the while.

Cherala cringed. Odifus' shout stirred up clouds of bile flies from the mounds. Giant fungi quivered and turned squelching on their stalks to watch them pass.

'There were! Grandpa said,' said Cherala. She pushed greasy hair out of her good eye. The other was half closed by throbbing growths. The witch kin in the village said the tumours might go, they might not; it depended how hard she prayed, to her other grandfather, the fat one, merry lord, Nurgle-in-the-mist. 'There was a city right here, in the Stink Forest.'

'Rubbish!' boomed Odifus. 'No cities on Noxia. None at all.' The pair of them had only the faintest conception of what a city was, but they knew there were lots of people in them. 'Stupid, cramming together like that. Fastest way for pox to spread.'

Pox: they used it as shorthand for everything, whatever sickness, disease or malady, though when it came to proper description, when it mattered, they had myriad words, one for each of Grandfather's gifts.

'It's true,' Cherala said. Odifus' dismissal of her tale annoyed her, and she fought back for once. She pointed up to the towering toad-trees, a thousand mottled slime caps growing on every one. 'These was buildings, big as the sky, and this...' She pointed at the squelching mosses they walked upon. 'This was roads, all hard.'

'First things, this is moss. Second things, roads is mud and muck,' said Odifus. 'This is a forest, always been a forest. Trees and slime and flies. No buildings, nothing *hard.*'

'Yeah, that so?' Cherala grumbled quietly, but Odifus heard her fine for once.

'That's so,' said Odifus.

They came to the edge of the scrounging grounds. Beneath the profusion of creepers and trees, square, regular oblongs could be made out, stacked in places five high. Their rusted doors hung half open, showing foetid darknesses within. From a distance, they looked like blocky boulders, and a little kidling might take them for such, but Cherala was twelve years old, halfway through her life, and wise as they come. The blocks were metal, rotted through for the most part, and in places sunk half into the swamp, but when her grandpa – her human grandpa, that is – told the tale of the city that was, she believed, because she had seen the boxes.

'Then what are these then?' she said.

'God boxes,' shouted Odifus. 'Gifts from Grandfather's pantries in his Black Manse. Way, way up in the garden.'

Odifus turned back to look at her. His face was swollen with a goitre, so that it was stretched, and his jowls hung upon his chest. Sweat stained his mouldering clothes. He looked as old as fifty, though he was only Cherala's age.

'That's what the god talkers say. They say,' he bellowed, 'that if you keeps on walking here, on and on in the Stink Forest, then you'll come out the other side, and there you'll find yourself in the most glorious of places, Nurgle's Garden! Lovely it is, where the rot takes you, but you don't feel it.' His stomach growled, and he let out a pungent fart.

They went between the god boxes. This close to the village they had been picked clean a generation ago. Cherala's grandfather had said a hundred years had passed since the forest came, and he was right. He was also wrong, for only a dozen years had gone by outside the three systems of the Scourge Stars. There, in Mortarion's mortal empire, time sickened as much as flesh.

'Nah,' she said. 'Nah! These are...' She searched for the unfamiliar words. Grandpa's soft palate had been lost to the mouth rot, and he didn't speak so well. 'Rargo tainers,' she said. 'This was a... a... *port*. He said these boxes came from other places, full of all the good things we take from them now, in the big Perium, before we met jolly Grandfather, and worshipped another god.'

She spoke loudly herself now, annoyed. Her blasphemy slipped out as easy as a belch, and proved just as acid. The shrieking of the insect things in the trees dipped. The mangy birds stopped their crowing. They watched her, and judged.

Odifus didn't seem to notice, but slapped his hand against his neck, mashing a bloodskeeter. He flicked the goo off his hands. 'Your grandpa said that?' He guffawed. 'Your grandpa can't speak worth dung. He's the oldest man in the village, and his head is as soft as his mouth.'

The animal sounds of the forest burst back, living their frantic cycles of life and death again. Cherala held her sore tongue still. She didn't want to offend jolly Grandfather with her grandpa's tales, bad things happened to those that did, but she knew that they were true. He said his great-great-grandfather had worked here, and he didn't mean grubbing about under decayed trunks for food.

Tree roots were thick in that part of the forest, shoots growing a foot a day, before collapsing into black ruin, and then again, so a treacherous web of snags replaced the moss. They went into the stacks of rargo tainers, or god boxes, if you were of Odifus' opinion. They made green canyons topped with trees and hanging beards of lichen. Animals ran ahead of them sometimes, all of them blessed, not one – and Cherala shuddered at the thought – *healthy*. Such were jolly Grandfather's gifts.

They banged on a few of the tainers, which boomed hollow as empty skulls, when the sides didn't crumble in. All of them were empty, their contents filched long since, or rotted into mush. Many were the lairs of Noxia's teeming life forms. When they opened doors, hissing rats bounded from their nests, or swarms of vile beetles clattered past on shimmering wings, giving Cherala a fright and making Odifus laugh loud as one of the temple bells.

The forest thinned out. The port must have been as big as the whole world, Cherala thought. The toad-trees and their crowds of slimy caps retreated. The god boxes stretched away, thousands and thousands of them. Millions, maybe. Away to the north they slumped into one another where the swamps began in earnest, but there, still near the edge, hints of regimentation persisted under the mats of green and black.

As many boxes as there were, Cherala and Odifus found

nothing. Every knock boomed back. Every door opened onto emptiness. They ate a couple of rats each, raw and dripping, so they'd not kill off any gifts jolly Grandfather might have hidden inside for them to suffer.

The forest canopy opened out. The stands of trees on the god boxes thinned out. Soon they could see the boxes themselves, properly now, bright with rusts, but definitely *made*. Cherala traced the hints of faded lettering with her fingers, and found on one skulls cast in metal.

'See!' said Odifus. 'That's the mark of jolly Grandfather, Nurgle's skull. He gave us these, not some Perium,' he scoffed.

'Get well soon,' she cursed him, and scrambled up the side of one of the god boxes, using the vines to get on top. She stood and looked out to lumpy horizons, over the landscape's discord of organisation and chaos.

The skies of Noxia pulsed with colour, livid as a fading bruise, a melange of greens and yellows, purples and browns. It was beautiful, and she watched the clouds swirl awhile, her pain forgotten. A veil of rain drew her eye down, and then a shaft of light penetrated, and lit upon something that made her yelp in triumph.

'What about that then?' she said, pointing.

Odifus looked up from the ground, where he was poking about with a stick.

'What?' He couldn't see. A little way down the box lines, one had fallen off the stacks and blocked his view.

'Over here.' She broke into the quickest hobble her stiff hip would allow, along the long, square ridge made by the god boxes. Odifus followed her along the road between the boxes, and she could now see that it *was* a road, for there were patches of wet, flat stone visible, with little metal studs set into it, and gratings full of leaves.

On this road was what she'd seen. Odifus clambered over the fallen god box blocking it from view, and she wheezed a triumphant laugh.

'Look under there! That's got to be something!'

'That's nothing,' said Odifus, approaching the weed-shrouded shape she pointed out.

'Liar! You can see it! It's a machine! A machine! That's no forest thing! City. Here. Ha!' She clambered down off the ridge, and pulled off moss and decaying cloth, revealing a heavy, brutal-looking thing, square edged in all the curves and swell of the jungle, with a cage atop it for a man to sit in, and a long arm with a pronged hand for lifting heavy stuff. *Like the tainers,* she thought.

Odifus lifted up tangles of dead vegetation and sniffed dismissively. The metal was rusted paper thin. Flakes of paint dropped off like scabs.

'Something from Grandfather's men. The Death Guard. They have tanks and such.'

'You ever seen one?' shrieked Cherala. 'They'd never fit in there! That's for a normal man, like my grandpa.'

'Health on your grandpa,' said Odifus moodily, stomping away from the machine. 'This way, chatterling, these god boxes look untouched.'

'Rargo tainers,' insisted Cherala, and stuck out her tongue.

Sure enough, Odifus was right. The boxes there were stuffed. Some had contents that had festered away to uselessness, solid blocks of flaking wood pulp that might have been crates, the things inside mysterious lumps. But in others, brittle plastek and sturdy metals protected the contents, and when Odifus opened up a god box with a couple of bangs on the lock, and an avalanche of metal spilled out, he wheezed with joy.

'Good steel!' he said, lifting up a heavy bolt. 'Good iron!'

They were machine parts of one kind or another, once protected by filmy bags full of oil. The bags had perished, the oils dried to sticky tars, but the metal itself was barely spotted. Odifus picked one piece up, then another, dropping them when he spied something better. He waded inside, pulled at the contents, and more fell from within.

'Riches!' he said. 'Such riches! Hey, Cherala, hey! How many swords can we make from this? How many muck-ploughs?'

Cherala was not listening. There was a strange noise that had caught her attention, almost lost beneath Odifus' wading through the spilled metal: a high chiming, pure, the cleanest sound she had ever heard. It entranced her, and she moved off towards it.

'Cherala!' shouted Odifus, but she didn't listen to him, and he went muttering back to his treasure.

She limped ahead, and before she knew it was half a mile away from her friend. The noise didn't get louder so much as more distinct, a ringing melody of chimes that wasn't exactly music – it was too random for that – but which *almost* was.

Then she saw the lights.

The run of god boxes or tainers or whatever they really were came to an end. There was a wide space ahead, marked out by circles raised off the ground on pillars of metal. A vibrant pink-and-blue glow shimmered atop one of them, twisting about, so that she fancied she saw dancers moving in the sky. Vine-choked stairs ran up to the circle, and without thinking she ascended them, entranced by the light and the music.

When she got to the top she found the circle covered over in twisted vines, all knotted and heaving with fungus. They seemed lethargic in their growth, fat and sluggish. They had half engulfed another machine waiting there, a big thing, like a fat avian with broken windows at the front. The source of the light, and the noise, came from behind.

'Voidskup,' she said, recognising it from another of her grand-pa's stories, about the craft that brought the god boxes down from the sky. She crept around it, and gasped.

In the centre of the circle everything had turned to clear crystal: roots, plants, metal and all. From this the light shone. The crystal was creeping outward, very slowly, but each inch it gained turned more of its surroundings to the same, clear, glassy substance. The air was dry there, and a cool wind blew outward, bringing with it scents that Cherala could only describe as clean. As she watched, she noticed that the chimes sounded when a root or toadstool was transformed, the crystal moving or contracting in some way to play the tones. The light grew brighter, moving from golds to greens and back to pinks. She gave a little cry of delight. She had never seen such beauty. A thought struck her, coming from outside her head. It spoke to her and said that, until then, she hadn't really known what beauty was, thinking that deformity and sickness were the prettiest of things, when this, this was true beauty, clean and lovely and ever-changing.

The lights brightened, became thick and slow, coalescing into shining birds that broke out of the light and flew about. They had such plumage, and were free of all sickness. Their voices gave the finest of all musics that joined the chimes of the crystals. Glowing orbs burst from the shine, and danced about, shedding drops of gold. Where these hit the ground, more crystal appeared, and spread, while the music played all the louder, and the light shone all the brighter, reaching up for the sickly clouds and filling them with new glories.

For a moment she was happy. Only a moment.

The light swayed. A shape moved within. It had arms and legs like a man, but for a head it had a leering moon, such a vibrant yellow she could not look upon it. It came out of the light, and began to prance, waving around itself a staff of crystal, with more crystals swinging from it. Gibbering in some unknowable tongue, it let off bolts of fizzling magic that struck the ground all about, the voidskup too, turning its metal hide and the blighted plants that choked it into one giant, shining sculpture. She did not like this newcomer or his staff, but found herself unable to leave, frozen to the spot by its capering.

The light became harsh. The creature noticed her, and its leer spread. It said no word, but lowered its staff. It flashed.

She hardly felt the magic touch her. She tried to move then, but could not, and when she looked down she saw her feet had gone to crystal that was spreading up her legs with a feeling of unbearable tightness. Her new glass skin vibrated with the energies of change.

Screaming things with slow beating wings flew from the light in flocks, and they were not so pretty. The bobbing spheres touched down upon the platforms and the ground beyond, burst with soft sighs, and from them sprang gangling things of violent pink that bounded cackling into the trees. They whooped and called, blasting fires of many colours from their palms, and setting the wet trees ablaze.

The last she saw was a hideous giant: scab-skinned, dusty smelling, with a bird's head as long as a man's body. It hauled itself from the light, and spread wings covered in madly swivelling eyes.

The crystal closed over her face, then the top of her head, and yet still she could see.

Her soul screamed for release from its prison. As her mind collapsed into fractal insanities, swift daemon beasts galloped from the growing rift. By then Odifus had seen what was happening away on the old landing pads, and tried to run, scattering his prizes in his terror. He did not get far before he was torn to pieces, and his thin blood was drunk by the jungle. The crystal growths spread faster, and faster, and more of the daemons of Tzeentch poured onto Noxia.

The gods were fighting.

The War in the Rift had begun.

CHAPTER FOUR

FIRST IN NURGLE'S FAVOUR

In the horarium of Mortarion, all the clocks were still. The daemon primarch of the Death Guard was enwrapped in black filaments that penetrated his skin and his eyes. By the dark miracle of the Mycota Profundis, he communed with his estranged gene-son, Typhus, and the primarch did not like what he was hearing.

'I cannot come to Iax, Mortarion, I have orders from a higher power,' Typhus was saying. 'The First, Third and Fourth plague companies are with me. We are returning to the Scourge Stars.'

Typhus' sepulchral voice emanated from a perfect recreation of his shoulders and head, a living bust, presented in cross section like a vivisected anatomical specimen. Tubes and organs moved beneath layered bone, fat and armour. The wound given Typhus by the Emperor's witch-brothers troubled him still, months after the battle for Galatan. There were blackened areas within his body that were new, that even the regenerative powers of Nurgle struggled to make good. The blade of Captain Grud had cut deep. The constant buzz of the Destroyer Hive his body played host to was subdued.

'You are injured. Fear has you,' said Mortarion. The pleasure the primarch felt at his son's setback was transmitted between them along with his words, and Typhus bridled.

'Fear has nothing to do with it, my gene-father,' said Typhus. 'I am the Mortal Herald of Nurgle. I am bidden to return by our god. I must go, and so must you. Your material holdings are under attack at this very moment. The Great War between the gods has begun.'

'No!' said Mortarion. *'I will not abandon my campaign. We are close. Guilliman will die by my hand, and his realm will be ours. Not three worlds dedicated to corruption, but hundreds! Billions of souls are ripe for the harvest. My brother comes now. The trap is set. I will snare him.'*

'Listen to me, Mortarion,' said Typhus patiently, infuriating the primarch further. 'You must heed these tidings. I come to you not as your son, or your First Captain, but as the Herald of Grandfather Nurgle. You must return. This is not a request. He cares nothing for your feud with your brother. Change disrupts the cycle of death and rebirth. This is the real war. Put aside your petty rivalry, you are commanded to do so by your god.'

'How dare you,' said Mortarion. *'How dare you treat me in this way, as if I were a child to be scolded.'*

'I perform my role, as our god ordains,' said Typhus. 'You would be wise to perform yours as his champion.'

'And where are these commands, Typhus?' Mortarion's expression twisted so much the black filigree of the mycelia broke and re-formed on his face. *'Has Nurgle himself come down from his dark house to tell you? I have heard nothing, from manse-warden, the uncleanly or any other of his princes, therefore he does not command me. I refuse to be manipulated by you again.'*

'He makes his will known to me in his way, father,' said Typhus. 'There are portents, there are impulses. I have been sent visions, I have been given signs.'

'Not even a visitation?' scoffed Mortarion. *'In that case I must immediately abandon my victory,'* he said sarcastically.

'No herald would be necessary, my lord – if you were but to listen to the warp, you would hear it too,' said Typhus calmly. 'I rise in his favour. The command is sure, and imperative. Leave now.'

'I am well enough occupied here,' snapped Mortarion. *'Begone. I am the son of his mightiest enemy, and among his foremost servants. If he wishes to command me, then he may do so himself.'*

'Father, you said it yourself, you are a servant. Do not forget it. You are a primarch but you serve a god. I warn you now. There is a hierarchy. Grandfather does not make himself seen. He is everything. He is everywhere. He will know you defy him. This is as clear a command as you will get. View it as warning.'

'I take no orders from you, First Captain.' Mortarion's wings beat once, wafting the noisome vapours of his horarium about. *'You owe everything to me.'*

'You have it the wrong way round, my lord. It is I who led you to your current status. Once again, I fulfil my duties of messenger for your advantage.'

'You are a serpent, Typhus. You always have been. You always will be.'

'So be it,' said Typhus. 'You overestimate your worth. Your arrogance blinds you. You defied Nurgle's will to make this war, and you defy it again to remain. Nurgle is an indulgent grandfather. He delights in the activities of his children, wayward though they may be, but he has limits. You rapidly approach them. If you transgress them, there will only be one consequence, Mortarion. Grandfather will be displeased. The mightiest rages come from the best-humoured. Do not make him–'

Mortarion let out a hiss of rage. Green and purple smokes boiled from the respirator fixed to his face. He swung Silence, his great scythe, cutting through the stalk of the fungus that bore Typhus' image. Typhus growled as phantom pain reached over the warp for him, and the image tumbled, already dissolving. It hit the ground in a splash of black matter, and was gone.

The mycelial spread that sustained the Mycota Profundis shrivelled. Mortarion wrenched himself free of its embrace before it had fully decayed, causing the warp-fed fungus to keen with a human voice.

'I am Mortarion, lord of the Death Guard! Bringer of plague, the mighty, the indomitable,' he said. In the glass prison upon the great central clock, the soul of his alien foster father raced around and around in terror. *'No one commands me!'*

Mortarion's anger manifested as a blast of psychic energy that washed out from him and through his thousands of clocks. As it touched them, they set into motion and began to chime. Broken time clattered around the horarium.

'No one,' he repeated. *'Do you hear me? No one!'*

Mortarion's rebellion did not go unnoticed.

In a house as big as forever, in a garden of repugnant fecundity, something monstrous stirred. An eye that could encompass a universe rolled stickily in its socket, and its gaze fell upon Ultramar.

Ku'Gath was stirring the cauldron when the storm began. He looked to the sky where purple-and-green clouds crowded out the sun. Lightning of sickly colour played within them, and when they cracked they made a noise like rotten tree boughs breaking.

'It's going to rain,' he said miserably. He didn't like rain. It

reminded him of his rival, Rotigus. He turned to say this to Septicus, but his lieutenant was gone, slain at the hand of Roboute Guilliman. No mere banishing, but the true death, his existence burned from reality. Daemons were timeless, and the day would come when they would meet again. However, those moments had already passed, and though they would be fresh to Ku'Gath, there would be no more made. Septicus was dead.

Everyone was sad. The nurglings feeding the flames with damp wood went about their duties sullenly. They did not sing or shriek. Their silence would have suited Ku'Gath perfectly, if it did not remind him of his loss. The plaguebearers chanted out their counts much subdued. After aeons of singular misery, Ku'Gath finally had others who felt the same way, and he did not like it one bit.

'*I even miss his pipes,*' moaned the lord of plagues. A slow, fat, greasy tear rolled down his cheek. His loose eye followed, and vanished with a plop in his cauldron.

'*Damn and blast,*' he muttered. Thunder boomed overhead. He looked up again. '*And now the rain will come and dilute my potions! Oh for botheration, botheration!*'

He pushed his hand into the liquid, searching for his eye.

Nurgle's cauldron was full to brimming, the potion within the brightest green. Its glow lit up the rotting face of Ku'Gath. Lightning teased the shine, driving it back mischievously, and making Ku'Gath seem a statue of a moment, cast in blacks and whites.

Ku'Gath fished about, pushing his arm deeper, and deeper. The mixture was potent, dangerous even, and stripped his unearthly flesh from his arm as he swirled it round and round. But he exerted himself, drawing a little more energy from the warp, remaking his flesh as quickly as it was melted. He enjoyed the pain. It burned and tickled in a most effervescent way.

'*Where is it? Where is it?*' he muttered. '*I need my eye for I must… what?*'

His hand grasped something hard, something spined. He tugged upon it. It would not move.

'*What is this?*' he growled; then he roared. '*What is* **this?**'

He tugged, he heaved; his belly knocked against the cauldron, sending it rocking on its stumpy legs. Tides of thick slime slopped over the edge, sending nurglings screaming. Their tiny stampede was beneath his notice, but hundreds died beneath the clawed feet of their brethren. The fire steamed. The smell it put out was truly abominable, but Ku'Gath was far too outraged to enjoy it.

'*Something in my stew! Something in my pot!*' he roared. '*Out, out, out, foreign ingredient!*'

He yanked. Whatever it was did not move. He yanked harder, and then there was movement. Too much movement. Ku'Gath fell. He let go of the object, spraying the elixir everywhere as he toppled back, demolishing a fair part of the hospital's ruins, and further, so that he landed on his spongy behind in a rising cloud of dust, and moist rubble was his seat.

The object rose. It broke the surface, and showed itself to be an antler. A filthy hood followed, then wicked eyes, and a nose, and a mouth, bent upward in a superior smile. A warty hand slapped upon the cauldron's side, and pushed down, so that from the brew shoulders came.

Out from the poisons Ku'Gath had so carefully concocted rose another Great Unclean One, and this fellow Ku'Gath knew only too well.

'*Rotigus Rainfather, second in Nurgle's favour,*' he gasped.

Rotigus rose from the deeps, slopping the precious fluid over the side in gloopy waves.

'*No! No! Stop!*' shouted Ku'Gath. He pushed himself back to his feet, tripping on his own rolls of flab as he raced back to his mixture. His talons tore at his guts and ripped his skin, but he was far too angry to notice. *'Grandfather lent me this cauldron! It is mine to use, not yours!'*

Rotigus coughed, and a wash of Ku'Gath's precious elixir spilled from his mouth. He tried to speak, but gurgled, then hawked and spat a gob of maggots and slime, clearing his throat.

The rain fell heavier, and heavier.

He coughed again and again, spewing into the mix. Finally, the rancid contents of his mouth were in the stew, and he smiled wider, and then spoke.

'Well met, my festering kin.' He held out a hand. In it a glistening orb swivelled. *'You dropped your eye.'*

Ku'Gath snatched his eye and screwed it back into place. *'There is nothing well about this meeting. Now get out of my cauldron.'*

'Ah, ah, ah!' Rotigus admonished. *'Not your cauldron, rot sibling, Grandfather's cauldron.'*

'He gave it to me to use!' snapped Ku'Gath.

'Well, he allowed me to manifest in it. What do you think about that?' Rotigus grinned, dipped a finger in the mix, and sucked it clean. *'Most filthy, most contagious. What is this?'*

'None of your business, precipitator of precipitation,' growled Ku'Gath.

'This is the blight, isn't it? This is what you and the half-son intend to slay Guilliman with.' He took another taste. *'Tangy,'* he said.

Ku'Gath's ire boiled his brains, to the extent that steam puffed from his ears and mouth.

'Get out of there! You're spoiling it!'

'Making it better, you mean,' said Rotigus. He reclined in the cauldron and made a satisfied sigh. *'I'll give you this, it is rather invigorating.'*

'Is it now?' said Ku'Gath. He took up his paddle and gripped it hard, like it was a halberd or a spear, and not a utensil of

medicine. *'Sit in it, and die. Drink it, and die. This is the most potent ailment ever conceived of!'*

'Really?' Rotigus slurped up a mouthful of the stuff and spat it high in a small, green fountain. The maggots that fell perpetually from his mouth surfed high upon the spout.

'This disease is the Godblight. It will kill the primarch. It would kill any of the Anathema's little toy men. There was one, a foe of all, who dreamed of similar, long ago. I shall finish what he did not have the wit to unleash. Mine is better. Refined. And best of all, I shall free it.'

'Lovely,' said Rotigus. *'Would it kill Mortarion?'*

'Yes it would kill Mortarion. It would kill him dead!' shouted Ku'Gath indignantly. *'This disease rots body and soul, in and out! Nothing is immune to it. You will die! Not just the short death of banishment, but the true death! Your being will be corroded, your essence will be the feast of soul-bacillae. You will feed the next generation of spirit pox, and thereby become bountiful. But Rotigus, the Rainfather, he will cease to be.'* Ku'Gath gloated. *'Dead!'* he added for emphasis.

'Ah, dead. But will I? Really?' said Rotigus. He flopped his flabby arms out over the sides of the cauldron as if he were in a refreshing bath. His skin hissed on the hot iron, but that did not seem to discomfort him overly much, and the tentacles that fringed his left hand moved with lazy pleasure, and the mouth above them in his wrist lapped at the potion. *'Thing is, Ku'Gath old fellow…'* He grinned now, wide and yellow and horrible. *'I'm very much alive, aren't I? In fact, I am positively refreshed!'*

Ku'Gath deflated a little, and wrung his hands anxiously around the paddle.

'It is not yet finished,' he said. *'But it will–'*

'Yes, yes, yes,' said Rotigus. *'I am sure it will do all those things. It will kill the primarch, it would kill me, but right now, well.'*

He splashed his hand in and out. *'Right now it will not, will it? Right now, I am sitting in it, and I am still alive, no?'*

'But–'

'That's why I am here.' He leered. *'You are running out of time. The Changer is making his move on Grandfather's grounds. There will be fighting in the flowerbeds. War in the glasshouses of the damned. It is starting now, in the Scourge Stars.'*

Ku'Gath was taken aback. *'But the treaties! Why would…'*

Rotigus lay his head back on the cauldron's iron rim. *'Ku'Gath, let me be frank with you. I understand why Grandfather Nurgle loves you over all we others. You are very charming in your grumbling. He likes you. I like you! You might not know it, because you are an old misery guts, and probably think everyone hates you, because you are so terribly self-centred.* **Everyone's thinking about me, everyone hates me.'** Rotigus mimicked Ku'Gath's voice, and rolled his eyes dramatically. *'But nobody* **cares.** *They don't think about you, and when they do, you are liked.'* He slapped a wet hand, large as a man, against his chest. *'You are, however, a little naive. The godswar never ends. The treaties struck between the brothers will not hold, they never do. There will be another accord, I am sure, but for now we have new war. You know this, I know this.'* He smirked. *'We all know this! They move. Ilhorio and Tzeentch's legions have allied. They are jealous of Grandfather's gains, and work to take the Scourge Stars from us. Personally, I blame Mortarion. It is not right to allow mortals to play the great game, even ones like him.'*

'What?'

'You heard,' said Rotigus. *'If I were you, I would have a little rearrangement of my priorities. The Grandfather will not look kindly upon those who aren't ready for the muster. You know, the kind of daemons who are off doing their own thing, so to speak. Things like this.'* He looked meaningfully into his bath. He went

a little cross-eyed. Flatulence bubbled from him, popping in large brown bubbles at the surface. *'Ah, that's better.'*

'You mean... you mean I should leave?' asked Ku'Gath.

Rotigus scooped up a handful of liquid, poured it over his tentacles, and shrugged.

'But, but this is a catastrophe!' said Ku'Gath. *'My plague is nearly finished! I... I... I have crafted something special, something delightful that will kill the Anathema's son, spirit and body. This is as good as the plague that made me. It is better!'*

'Ach, nobody cares,' said Rotigus, and dabbled his fingers in his bath. *'The Anathema's son,'* he said mockingly. *'Oh do shut up. What is he? One man? One counterfeit demigod? This is the game of real gods! This reality is doomed, Ku'Gath. The mortals here are finished. They always lose, in the end, and this bunch have already lost, they just can't see it yet. The gods fight over the spoils, before the next corruption begins. Fresh realms await.'* He gave Ku'Gath a sly look. *'Surely that makes even you happy, miserable one?'*

Ku'Gath drew up his saggy chest. *'I am working towards the aims of Grandfather. Why, our entire scheme here is to bring these disgustingly clean worlds into the garden, and cultivate them as new beds of rot and glory. I–'*

Once again, Rotigus interrupted him.

'Don't lie to yourself, you follow Mortarion's plan because you want the Grandfather to forgive you for being born. When, really, all that's happened is that you've let yourself get sucked into mortal obsessions.'

'He's a daemon!'

'Pfft,' said Rotigus dismissively. *'Only half. You have lost sight of the bigger picture. You want to be careful. All plagues wax and wane, Ku'Gath Plaguefather. Could it be that your time is coming to an end, and mine is beginning? I am feeling most excellently contagious.'*

Ku'Gath scowled. *'If you are so mighty, why do you not lend your strength to us here?'*

Rotigus examined his fingernails, scowled at them, pulled one free, popped it into his mouth and crunched on it.

'I might, I might. But I am busy on other worlds, on other planes, in other places. Severally, in matter of fact. I have none of my being to spare for this conflict. Besides, why would I wish to steal your thunder?'

'Then why are you here, if you are so occupied, dear Rotigus?' said Ku'Gath with a vast and insincere smile. *'Best be away, not to trouble yourself with our little war.'*

'Oh it's no trouble at all!' said Rotigus. *'I am always happy to make time for the first in Nurgle's favour. Though you better work harder if you wish to maintain the position.'* He wagged his finger admonishingly. *'All things grow and die, Ku'Gath. Reputation too, and Grandfather's love. I am second in his favour. For how much longer shall you remain first? You never know, I could be getting a promotion.'*

The sky rumbled like a dyspeptic gut. Fat drops of rain plopped into the cauldron.

'Rain, eh?' said Rotigus with a grin. *'I thought that my signature. They do say imitation is the sincerest form of flattery.'* Rotigus looked out over the stinking marshland. *'I suppose I should feel very flattered indeed.'* He winked. *'Until later, oh Ku'Gath, currently first in his favour.'*

So saying, Rotigus sank beneath the surface. Fat bubbles welled up and popped in the cauldron. Ku'Gath thrust his hand into the mix, and searched about for his rival, but Rotigus had gone.

'Flattery,' said Ku'Gath. *'Indeed!'* His mood worsened further when he gave his hand an experimental lick and found that Rotigus had been right: the pox was better.

Grumbling about the iniquities of life, Ku'Gath Plaguefather took up his paddle and began stirring again. His efforts were at first fast, driven by annoyance, but as he stirred, he thought, and as he thought, he slowed.

'Hmmm,' he said to himself. *'I wonder if Mortarion knows? Surely, he must.'*

He didn't really wish to speak with the primarch, but they were allied, and he could not make the assumption he did know, he realised.

'Oh botheration,' he said, and reluctantly tickled the fungal infestation on his thigh that would call up the Mycota Profundis.

A short while later, he conferred with the ex-mortal, the half-son, dratted Mortarion, and discovered that he knew all about the invasion, and that he was quite piqued by it all. But the news he had made things even worse.

Typhus, Mortarion's truculent lieutenant, had abandoned their war, and was leaving Ultramar.

CHAPTER FIVE

UPON THE NATURE
OF GODS

'It was not wise, what we did,' said Donas Maxim.

Guilliman gave him a hard stare.

'No,' said Guilliman. 'But it was necessary.'

'To interrogate daemons is to invite them in. It does not matter that you destroyed the beast afterward. And the blade you carry, do not think it will protect you from the slow poisons of the warp, my lord. We are taught this by rote and rod in our Librarius, according to texts you set down. Why did you ask us to perform this act of daemonology? We are not sorcerers. Will you make them of us?'

They spoke in Guilliman's library, his most sacred sanctum. Guilliman had removed the Armour of Fate, though it physically pained him to do so. Like Maxim, he wore a tunic and trousers. The primarch's clothes were ultramarine blue to Maxim's forest green, and unlike Maxim's heavily embroidered garb, Guilliman wore no decoration besides the buckle stamped with the ultima that fastened his belt. As usual, he sat at his desk, working while he talked.

Maxim watched the primarch closely. He could feel the pain in him. Not only from the wound across his neck, which ached still, nor the nick it had cut in his spirit, but also a deeper hurt, buried beneath pragmatism and duty; a sense of loss, a sense of loneliness, broadcast so potently from that engineered soul it pressed on Maxim's consciousness as hard as a gauntleted finger grinding against a wall. Speaking with the primarch was as taxing as any metaphysical battle.

'I will not make you sorcerers,' said Guilliman. 'I seized the moment. We are running out of time. Tjejren's daemonhost was there, available.'

'Expediency has damned many noble spirits, my lord.'

'Has it damned you, Donas? Your knowledge of the esoteric brought you into my service. You were close to censure yourself.'

'We are all damned, my lord,' said Maxim. 'But if I am lost to the warp, it would be a lesser blow to the Imperium than if you were. I urge you, be careful.'

'As always, I value your forthrightness, Codicier Maxim,' said Guilliman. 'It is why I retain you on the Concilia, but the matter is done. I have what I need. I will not pursue the same course of action again, if it sets your mind to rest.'

'A little,' admitted Maxim. 'I have known others who have taken similar chances. None have escaped harm entirely.'

'You are right to be concerned. I lost more than one brother who thought they could master such beings. They could not, and I know I cannot. Now, I must speak with you of other things.'

'Gladly.'

Guilliman paused. 'I must also ask for your utmost discretion. What I am about to tell you will be shocking.'

'I am intrigued, for I am not easily shocked.'

'Trust me, you will be,' said the primarch. 'There is another whose counsel I seek on this matter. Please, take a seat.'

He gestured to a chair made for transhuman stature by a table that was low enough for a mortal man to use. Maxim took it. Guilliman called down a cyber-construct and sent it away to bring in refreshments, and then activated a vox-unit set into the wall near his desk.

'Send in our guest.'

Illiyanne Natasé entered, dressed in soft black robes with a high neck, long gloves and his ever-present charms, though he too bore no physical armour. Guilliman bade him sit also. Maxim had killed several aeldari psykers in his time. Although farseers were mighty with the warp, they lacked the brute martial power of a Space Marine Librarian.

Natasé glanced at him haughtily as he took his seat, letting Maxim understand that he knew what Maxim was thinking.

'My lord primarch, Librarian,' he said. 'What manner of inadvisable peril am I to be embroiled in today?'

'You are insolent, xenos, for a lone seer surrounded by the might of humanity,' said Maxim.

'Do you expect me to be your friend, murderer of my kin, or scared of you?' said Natasé, not deigning to look at Maxim. 'I am neither.'

'You are our ally,' said Guilliman. 'Please, Donas, show him respect.'

'No disrespect was intended,' said Maxim. 'I merely wished to know why our ambassador here thinks it suitable to openly display his hostility. It is an unwise action from such a wise being.'

'We have a surfeit of such actions at the moment,' said Guilliman meaningfully.

Natasé hunched forward, and laced his fingers together, a

most un-aeldari-like posture. He fixed the floor with his black eyes, as if addressing a confession to it.

'I will tell you why. If you were to ask my people, they would say I was sour, like a young wine.'

'Is that a compliment, or an insult?' asked Maxim.

'Neither. Both. Your language is unbelievably crude.' Natasé gave a cruel smile. 'Take that word, "unbelievably", for example, that I employed just now, a word that does not mean what it means when I use it, and as no fine metaphor, but as crude hyperbole to reinforce an obvious statement, and grant it a little impact. Your speech is insipid. To convey what is meant by me being a "young wine" in your tongue would take dozens of your words. For us, two suffices, and both are rich with meaning that you cannot comprehend.'

Maxim pulled a face of mock offence. 'Did you summon the alien to give us a lecture on linguistics, my lord?'

'You jest, but your wit is as blunt as your mind,' said Natasé. He sighed. He seemed a little shrunken. 'I shall be blunt. Spending time with your people is hard for one of my sensibilities. The smell, for a start, and the food! A few months with Prince Yriel the Reborn was a blessed relief.' He raised his gaze from the floor. 'It is your minds that press hardest on me. Lumpen, open to corruption. You are not a stupid people, but you are unsophisticated, as like to we aeldari as the orks are unto you. So I apologise if my manners seem abrupt, but your company is almost unbearable.'

'Eldrad Ulthran chose the most diplomatic of his comrades to advise us,' said Maxim.

'You see?' said Natasé, appealing to Guilliman.

'I understand,' said Guilliman calmingly. 'If it would soothe you, I can release you from your mission and send you back to your home. You have aided me on many occasions, and shall depart with all due honour.'

'Do not tempt me,' said Natasé. 'A decade of your years I have been with you, and they have seemed an eternity. Each moment brings another lick of tedium.' He scowled. 'It is a wonder I have remained sane. But I must stay with you. That was Eldrad Ulthran's command to me, and I swore to obey. Although I may be a young wine, I keep my word.'

'If it's that bad, I can see why he did not come himself,' said Maxim.

Natasé grinned, a savage expression. 'Now you begin to understand. In any case, Ulthwé lies across the Rift. Maybe when we cross it, I will leave you and return.'

'You could open up your webway to us, master seer,' said Maxim. 'The return would be quicker.'

'Quite impossible,' said Natasé. 'War afflicts the web. Since their awakening, the necrontyr have penetrated it, and Chaos rules supreme in many branches. Even were it not so, taking a force of this size through the way is impossible in this diminished era. In the days of my ancestors, perhaps, but not now.'

'Transit across the Rift is not what we are here to discuss,' said Guilliman. 'That lies in our future.'

Some of the primarch's servants arrived, summoned by the cyber-construct, bringing with them meat and drink. They placed them on the table.

'Go, I will attend to my guests personally,' Guilliman told them when they began to serve the wine. 'I am not to be disturbed.'

The servants withdrew.

'Engage full privacy field,' Guilliman said. Somewhere beneath the library, a fresh hum joined the endless thrumming of machines, and faded away, taking with it all the mumblings of the vessel. The library fell silent. Even the vibrations of the engines seemed to have stilled, so that Maxim felt like they floated, alone, in a vault of knowledge cast adrift between the stars. For a moment, he thought of the Librarius on Firestorm, and wondered how the Chapter planet fared.

There was a box on Guilliman's desk. He picked this up and joined his guests at the lower table, where he put it down and opened the lid, revealing the pale blue gleam of a stasis field. He pushed the box towards them. There was a book inside, and upon its cover was the title, *Lectitio Divinitatus*.

Guilliman poured wine while they looked at it.

'The central text of the Imperial Cult?' said Maxim.

'Yes,' said Guilliman. 'That is what it is.'

'This is old,' said Natasé. 'Other than that I fail to see the significance of this book. As the Librarian says, this is the text of your people's religion, the one you do not follow yourself, but hold in contempt.'

'Correct,' said Guilliman. 'But only partially.'

He passed out goblets to Maxim and Natasé. Maxim drank his in a single draught. Natasé sniffed his disdainfully.

'A young wine?' asked Maxim.

'A bad one,' said Natasé. He drank it anyway.

'May I?' said Maxim, gesturing at the book. 'It seems more than old, it seems ancient.'

'I sense it is several thousand years old – that is old, not ancient, to me. Age is a matter of perspective,' said Natasé haughtily.

Maxim turned off the stasis field and picked up the book. The cover was a flaking, light brown leather. The bottom right corner was stained darker by skin oils. Maxim opened it, and examined the first lines.

'Very ancient. I can barely read this. It is Gothic, but archaic in the extreme.'

'You have read the central texts of the Adeptus Ministorum?' asked Guilliman. He took a drink of the wine. The goblet he used was heroically sized, a mythic horn of plenty.

'Of course,' said Maxim. 'It is mostly nonsense, so our Chapter cult says.'

'There is some truth in it,' said Guilliman. 'Fragments of history in an age where history has been suppressed. The current scriptures are the work of thousands of hands. Nothing in this carcass of an empire has survived the years intact, certainly not the truth, and the *Lectitio Divinitatus* is no exception. It has been meddled with, redacted, added to, and retold so many times that what is real and what is not is impossible to tease apart. But this particular volume is different. This is a copy of the very first scripture.' He looked at Maxim gravely. The information he was about to impart was doubtless known to Natasé, but would be news to any human. 'It was written by my brother Lorgar.'

'What?' said Maxim. 'The traitor primarch?'

Guilliman nodded. 'The originator of the Imperial Cult was one of my brothers. Indeed, it was the Emperor's spurning of Lorgar's worship that sent him looking for other, more amenable gods. Terrible, yes?' he said. He poured himself more wine.

'You do not react. You knew this,' Maxim said to Natasé.

The aeldari gave a subtle nod that managed to express every variation of self-satisfaction. 'The identity of the author is known to my people.'

'For want of a better word, this is the *Lectitio Divinitatus* in its purest form, or as near as is possible,' said Guilliman. 'I have had the material dated and psy-read. This particular book is around eight thousand years old, and so was printed less than a millennium after the Heresy.'

Guilliman paused. He drank more wine. Maxim thought he seemed disturbed.

'I have recently read it. I never did so in my prior life, in fact I made a point of not reading it to show my scorn, and I tried my best to have every copy burned. I was too naive to see that it was too late. The cult was growing. Faith had taken root, and in such barren soil, I thought.'

He refilled Maxim's goblet. Natasé placed a graceful hand over the cup when offered more.

'The Emperor smashed every idol He came across. He threw down churches and temples, even the meanest shaman's hut was burned to the ground. We were commanded to destroy every sign of religion we found. Iterators stood in the ashes of belief and spread the Imperial Truth. The Emperor would brook no cult but that of reason.' Guilliman laughed. 'To think I believed it all.'

'My lord?' asked Maxim, cautious now of Guilliman's rancour.

'Do not worry yourself, Donas,' said Guilliman. 'I merely mean that reason is a faith of its own, with its own traps and heresies. I have not fallen into worship. Lorgar's arguments are persuasive, but are built on several fallacies for all that. The Emperor said Himself that He was no god, over and over again. You should have seen Him when He commanded me to punish Lorgar. His anger was no sham. I cannot see any situation in which He would be happy with the way the Imperium has turned out.'

'Then why show me?' asked Maxim. 'Why have you burdened me with this secret. Why not Lord Tigurius, or another, higher mind?'

'You are here. I wish to discuss it now. You are most appropriate,' said Guilliman. 'Do you need another reason for my confidence?'

Maxim bowed his head in wonder, and put the book down. 'This information is explosive. If you could get anyone to believe it.'

'Your species is fractious. Someone would believe,' said Natasé. 'You are correct, it is damaging.'

'Then my question is even more pressing,' said Maxim. 'Why?'

'There have been many events that have occurred since I returned that make me question my assumptions. I wish to speak with you both on the nature of godhood,' said Guilliman.

'Should you not ask a priest?' said Maxim, half joking to cover his discomfort.

'I have had more than my fill of priests,' said Guilliman. 'I have no psychic ability. This world around us...' He gestured around the hall. 'It is the only one I can perceive. I am aware of the warp, I respect its power, and understand it better than I ever did, but it is not in my nature to comprehend it completely. You have many abilities, Maxim. Natasé, your people is far older than ours, and you know much, should you choose to share.'

'Ask, and we shall see what I will tell,' said Natasé.

Guilliman paused. 'What is a god?' he asked. 'What is the definition of divinity?'

'Everything I have ever met that called itself a god has been my enemy,' said Maxim. 'That is good enough for me.'

'Does that make your master your enemy also?' said Natasé.

'The Emperor denied always that He is a god,' said Maxim.

'Denied, but does He still? I believe that is the heart of the matter under discussion here,' said Natasé. 'Is that not so, lord regent?'

Guilliman ignored his insinuation. 'Clarify further, Codicier,' the primarch said.

'Power defines gods, but they are all false,' said Maxim. 'Falsehood is the essence of godhood. They are lies. They may seem to be divine to primitive minds in their ability to grant favour, but they are inimical to all mortal life. The gods of Chaos bring only horror. They see us as playthings, and would destroy us all in the end. They are evil, every one. Man needs no gods. The Emperor was right.'

'Natasé?' asked Guilliman.

'Not all gods are evil,' said Natasé. 'You are wrong, Donas Maxim. And you speak only of the gods born out of the immaterium. You neglect the C'tan, the Yngir, we called them. They too were gods.'

He sighed, collected himself, as if he were a schoolmaster about to deliver a much simplified lesson to children that would still not understand.

'You are right when you say that power defines a god,' he said. 'Temporal, spiritual, physical – it matters not.' He fell silent a moment. 'My people define godhood in several ways, but there are two broad categories. The gods of the othersea, who are reflections of what you call the materium, and the gods of the materium itself, who you know as the C'tan, though there are other, more ancient and even more terrible things than they. The gods of the materium are an essential part of its fabric – they are able to influence its structure, such is their intimate connection to it, but they are bound nevertheless by the laws of this reality. The gods of the warp are more ephemeral, and more diverse in type. Many are mere concentrations of feeling, some were once mortals themselves, before the belief of others changed them. The gods of my ancestors were of both sorts, I believe, though this is not the only philosophy propounded by my kind, and I have heard many heated debates on the subject. It is impossible to say now, for our gods were slain when we fell, and even if they could be asked, they would not know the truth of it, for the truth would change anyway, as it must, according to the beliefs of those who had faith in them.

'Yet another kind are agglomerations of souls of those who were once living, or so say the Ynnari, whose supposed deity Ynnead was unleashed by the breaking of Biel-Tan. But who, in truth, can say? One, two, all or more of these things can be true at one moment, and may change at another. There are gods that eat gods, gods that are eternal, gods that were but now never were, and gods that come into being only to have existed for all time. The origins of gods are therefore impossible to catalogue. They have no histories but the histories people impose upon them. I would agree with your sorcerer here, to an extent. Puissance is the defining aspect of them.' A grave expression crossed his face. 'Faith is another, though this does not apply to all. Some beings do not require faith. But falsehood is not intrinsic to them all.'

'Explain,' said Guilliman.

'The C'tan, as far as our legends attest, were essential components of creation – hungry, evil to mortal eyes, but part of it. They require no belief to live, in the same way the suns they devoured require no observer to be. Nor do the great four gods of Chaos, who have become so all-powerful they are in essence self-sustaining, though the faith of their followers makes them stronger. Nor does the Great Devourer, the mind of the tyranids, a being that is generated by the unthinking actions of its physical component parts, and that is perhaps greater than all the rest. Is that a god? Some of our philosophers argue so. Others vehemently disagree. But for other gods, lesser gods, faith is vital. Without faith, they collapse into formlessness, becoming non-sentient vortices of emotion. Unstable, they die.'

'But if the people of the Imperium ceased to believe in the Emperor, He would not vanish,' said Guilliman. 'He has a physical presence, even now. He sits upon the Throne. By that measure, He is not a god.'

'How can you be so sure, simply because He existed before He took to His Throne? You base your supposition on the idea that He was actually a man to begin with, and that He did not lie. You also suppose that what sits upon the Golden Throne still has a mortal life, and would persist should His worship cease,' said Natasé. 'Did I not say there are gods who were once mortals? These beings become focal points for belief, and belief begets faith, as the pure gods of the warp do, those that are consciousnesses which emerge from the othersea. The difference is, for gods who were something before they were gods...'

Guilliman raised an eyebrow.

'Hypothetically speaking,' said Natasé smoothly, 'not assuming that is what happened to your father – in cases like that there is an existing being to mould. Faith hangs from them, changes them, elevates them, if that is a correct word.' Natasé smiled his thin, cruel smile. 'We come to an unpalatable truth. To many of your people, primarch, son of the Emperor, you are a god. Because they believe in their billions, does that not make it true?'

'A status I deny,' said Guilliman icily. 'I am no god.'

'Deny it all you will,' Natasé insisted. 'Where you go, victory follows. Your presence inspires your people. In this age of storms, the very warp calms at your approach. How long is it until the first miracle is proclaimed in your name, and when that occurs how will you be able to say that you were not responsible for it? The incident on Parmenio with the girl, the way her power freed you from the grip of the enemy, drove back daemons, actions already being ascribed to your maker.' Natasé paused. 'But if divine, was it truly Him?'

'Are you saying that was *me*?'

'I am asking you to consider it.'

'I have no psychic gift,' said Guilliman.

'It does not matter,' said Natasé. 'We are talking here not of sorcery, or what you refer to as psychic power, but of faith. Faith is the most powerful force in this galaxy. It requires no proof to convince. It grants conviction to those who believe. It brings hope to the hopeless, and where it flourishes, reality changes. A single mind connected strongly to the warp can bend the laws of our universe, but a billion minds, a trillion minds, all believing the same thing? It matters little if they are psykers or not. The influence of so many souls has a profound effect. My kind birthed a god. Perhaps now it is your turn.

'Faith is your race's greatest power. It is also the greatest peril to us all. It is the faith of every human being that moulds reality. Psychic power washes through our existence, heightening everything. It is their despair that threatens us. You have said to me before, Roboute Guilliman, that you will save my people, yet it is your people who are damning us all. They damn you, too. For all your will, how can your single soul stand against the collected belief of your species? You brought us here to ask if the Emperor is a god, for that is where this conversation is going, but the questions you should be asking yourself are, "Am I a god?" and "If I am a god, am I free?"'

'That is not what I wish to know,' said Guilliman. 'For my status is in no doubt, in my eyes.'

'You should consider it, nevertheless,' said Natasé.

'You cannot entertain this idea, my lord,' said Maxim.

Guilliman frowned. 'It is your belief that the Emperor is a god, then?'

'My belief is unimportant in the balance of belief,' said Natasé. 'It is reflected proportionally in what you call the empyrean. This is what I am trying to convey to you.'

'How do you perceive the Emperor, when you look into the warp?'

'I see no god or man. I see the great light of your beacon. From it comes pain, and suffering,' said Natasé, uneasy for once. 'Who can tell if what I see in the light is true? Our lore tells us your master ever was chameleonic. Maybe He is truly dead. Perhaps if you turned off your machines, then the light would die. It is impossible to say. Every thread of the skein that leads to Him is burned to nothing. His path cannot be predicted. He cannot be looked upon directly. Some of my kind maintain that He is the great brake on your species, yet its only shield, that He is the poison to the galaxy that might save us all, that He is not one, but broken, fractured, and properly healed and with His power marshalled again could outmatch the great gods themselves. Others say He is nothing, that the light that burns so painfully over Terra is but an echo of a luminous being long gone. We must judge His worth to our species by inference alone.'

'Maxim?'

'He is a light, my lord, that is too bright to look at, as Natasé avers. He is a roaring beacon. He is a pillar of souls. His presence burns the spirit. He is singular, and obvious, yet too intense to perceive. On the few occasions I have dared turned my witch-sight near Him, I too have felt His pain. It scarred me. But I believe He is there. I have felt His regard on me.'

'This is not a common action among Space Marine Librarians,' said Guilliman.

'As I understand it, no. All of us are trained to find the beacon, for we must occasionally serve as Navigators when the Chapter mutants fail, but His light is too much for us to gaze upon for long. Few dare to look closely. I have.'

'I have heard Natasé's opinion on this matter, but I ask you, Donas Maxim, to set aside your Chapter beliefs and tell me, is the Emperor a god?'

Donas shook his head and shrugged. He looked perplexed, as if he could not understand the question. 'He is the Emperor, my lord.'

Guilliman looked to the book. 'Lorgar was wrong about our creator. He was no god when I knew Him, but now...' His voice faltered. 'If He were truly a god, whatever we take that word to mean, what does it mean for our strategy? I cannot allow my own convictions to get in the way of truth, for only in knowing the truth can victory be secured. If I ignore the reality of the situation simply because it does not fit my own theoreticals, then I will fail. But contrarily, if I adopt this mode of thought as actual, and base all future practicals upon it, then what manner of victory will that deliver us? What kind of Imperium do I wish to see? I would rather it was one free of religion, and gods, and all their perfidy.'

'Is it not enough to accept the Emperor's power, my lord, and to countenance that He may be at work again in the Imperium?' said Maxim. 'Upon Parmenio we have seen evidence of that.'

'We have seen evidence of something,' said Guilliman. 'Perhaps I have seen enough to discount the machinations of other powers. Maybe it is the Emperor.'

'Caution is due,' said Natasé. 'Discerning the source of these phenomena is beyond me, and therefore the rest of your Concilia Psykana.'

'Indeed,' said Guilliman. 'On the one hand, I have the fervent belief of the militant-apostolic that my father fights at my right hand. On the other, we must be alert to possible manipulation.' He looked at Natasé.

'I understand your implication, but my people are not responsible, nor any others of my race,' said Natasé. 'So far as I am aware.'

Guilliman was thoughtful a moment, then moved decisively. He bent over so he could reach the box and reactivate the stasis field, then flipped the lid shut.

'Thank you both, you have given me much to think on. In the meantime, we have other problems to deal with.'

'As my oath demands, I shall fulfil it, my lord primarch,' said Natasé.

'You may go, farseer. Codicier, please remain.'

'My thanks, primarch. Donas Maxim,' Natasé said to the Space Marine.

Maxim gave the aeldari a nod of acknowledgement. The doors opened. Maxim caught a glimpse of the aeldari's bodyguard waiting outside: four of them, black armour, bone-coloured inset masks and the tall plumes of the Dire Avengers warrior aspect. Allowing armed xenos to roam about the fleet was a source of consternation in all quarters. Maxim shared it.

'My lord, is there something else I may help you with?' said Maxim when the doors had closed.

'There is nothing,' said Guilliman. He stood, and so did Maxim. 'A courtesy only, from me. I have heard that you are to cross the Rubicon Primaris soon, and I wanted to give you my good wishes for a safe transition, and a speedy recovery.'

'I thank you for your concern, my lord. I hear the procedure is much safer now than it was.'

'It is not entirely free of risk, I am afraid,' said Guilliman. 'Would that it were so. I commend your bravery in stepping forward.'

'I do it so I may serve you better, my lord.'

Guilliman nodded. He was turning to other affairs. Maxim felt a surge of thought patterns from his strange, engineered mind, and quickly disengaged from them. Guilliman went to his desk and began to reorder the papers and data devices there. Maxim recognised it as preparatory to undertaking a considerable amount of work. He used the same focusing technique himself.

He wondered then how much of his character he owed to this ancient giant. Despite their conversation, he could half believe Guilliman were indeed a demigod.

'When do you undergo the procedure?'

'Tomorrow,' said Maxim.

'Should you survive, then, I make the same offer to you as I did to Natasé, Donas. You too may return home, though you may find it easier to do so once the campaign here is over.'

'It is a welcome thought. I have been in Ultramar since the Rift opened and cut my strike force off. I have brothers at home, and duties too long neglected. But I think not.'

'Then I ask that you and your warriors accompany me further after we have crossed the Rift, and to whatever we may find there.'

'Gladly, and with all my heart,' said Maxim. 'I will serve at your side for as long as I may, my lord, for what true son of yours has ever dreamed of anything other?'

'Your devotion touches me. It weighs on me that it may mean your death.'

Maxim bowed. 'Death in service is what we aspire to.'

'Sadly, I can offer that to all,' said Guilliman. 'Thank you, Codicier, that will be all.'

The doors swung open to let him out. Maxim looked back before he passed out of the library, and saw the primarch staring thoughtfully at the box that contained Lorgar's book.

CHAPTER SIX

THE TATTLESLUG

'Drat and botheration. Misery and woe,' muttered Ku'Gath. He left his stirring to his minions and waddled through the court-yard, glumly mumbling, ignoring the cheery halloos of his nurglings and the droning reports of his plaguebearers. A few broken walls were all that was left of the hospital's outer pre-cincts, slumped like corpses under strangling vegetation that perished as quickly as it grew. The paving was lost beneath layers of toxic algae. Clicks of stinking waste dribbled through the mortar.

'Where are you going, master, where are you bound?' gibbered choruses of nurglings.

'For a walk, curse you, not that it is any of your business!' Ku'Gath blustered, and lumbered at them. The tiny imps screeched and made to run, but they could not escape, and burst like grapes under his dragging belly. Did he feel at all uplifted by this small, malicious act? No, he did not, not one jot.

The lone Great Unclean One in the court wisely kept his

peace. Ku'Gath Plaguefather excepted, the greater daemons of Nurgle were jolly beings, but the defeat at Parmenio had knocked their mirth squarely out. Ku'Gath had new lieutenants, sent by Nurgle's manse-wards themselves to guard him, to replace his comrades languishing in the Great Garden, where they awaited rebirth. He did not trust these newcomers.

Ku'Gath was being watched.

'And I don't need the likes of Rotigus to tell me that,' he grumbled. He pushed his way through part of the remaining perimeter wall, toppling it into a mush of foamcrete and putrid vegetable matter. Chunks plopped into the mud.

Out he went from the plague mill, down through the filthy camp of his daemon legion. The Hythian wetlands had overflowed, and turbid waters lapped at the bottom of the hills the mill commanded. Still grumbling, Ku'Gath slipped in, and began to wade.

The noise of the daemon camp diminished quickly. He left behind the sombre count of the plaguebearers and the grating singing of nurglings, and a morose silence fell. The ground he traversed had been pasture for bovids, crossed by roads and dotted with human habitations. Now it was a sea of ooze, the farmland and the marsh wholly indistinguishable. The sole signs that mortals had dwelled there were the rusty stumps of wind turbines a mile or so away, and they were so choked with slimy vines it was difficult to tell what they had been.

Ku'Gath's choler was dampened by the swamp. Cool muck washed in through his open belly, bathing his intestines with filth. It was rather pleasant, and he almost began to feel upbeat; the thought of the new infections he might contract came close to bringing a smile to his lips. That just wouldn't do, so he reminded himself of what was at stake until he was sufficiently miserable again.

He paddled on, his huge bulk thrusting up a bow wave of muck, until he deemed the distance sufficient that he could perform his summoning unobserved. He stopped. He turned around. The roofless plague mill was lit red by the fire warming the cauldron, from which toxic vapours drifted. Gelid biolumi-nescence bathed the exterior and campfires burned for a mile or more beyond it, but away from the mill all was dark and drear, and would be until dawn came; then all would be dim and drear instead, which was only right.

'These cursed mortals have no appreciation for the gifts we bring them,' complained Ku'Gath, surveying the glories of the ooze sea. How could they could not see its beauty? He wondered at it, truly perplexed.

Unnatural things disappeared under the water with gloopy plops when they felt the touch of his gaze. He let out a little of his soul, letting it brush all things around him. The mud boiled with eager life as his essence leaked into the marsh, but he felt nothing that could think, or that would care what he was about to do, or, most importantly, tell anyone about it.

Anyone like Rotigus, for example.

He looked around one last time, and softly cleared his throat.

'Tattleslug, Tattleslug, come, come, come,' he sang, very qui-ctly. *'I have a secret I must tell. Wriggle out, wriggle out, ears aflap, under revelation's spell.'*

He looked around again. No sign of the thing he would enlist to his cause, no sign that he had been heard. A cold wind, red-olent of flatus, blew over him.

'Hmph,' he grumbled. The Tattleslug was a lesser thing than he, but he could not simply command it: its allegiance must be bought. He sighed. He was going to have to appear more enthusiastic.

'Tattleslug, Tattleslug, come, come, come,' he sang again, more

loudly now. *'I have a secret I must tell. Wriggle out, wriggle out, ears aflap, under revelation's spell.'*

The wind blew stronger. Tree branches rattled. Damned souls moaned further out in the wastes. He listened hard, and heard a faint and ghostly tittering.

Encouraged, he sang again, and louder still. *'Tattleslug, Tattleslug, come, come, come. I have a secret I must tell. Wriggle out, wriggle out, ears aflap, under revelati... Oooof,'* he said, and gripped his stomach. A most pleasing reflux burned his gullet. Gas bubbled, forced its way out, ballooning his exposed guts, where it escaped from an ulcer with a hissing, wheezing stink.

Ku'Gath gritted carious teeth. *'Tattleslug, Tattleslug, come, come, come. I have a secret I must tell. Wriggle out, wriggle out, ears aflap, under revelation's spell!'*

The pain moved outward, as if something with sharp claws was swimming through his innards, up, up to the surface of his body. The something pushed against the inside of his leathery hide, and bit.

Ku'Gath gasped. Again he sang his little song, and the pain became a blister upon his skin. A sixth repetition of the spell saw the blister grow, until he sang for the seventh and final time.

'Tattleslug, Tattleslug, come, come, come. I have a secret I must tell. Wriggle out, wriggle out, ears aflap, under revelation's spell.'

The blister burst. A slippery, slug-like thing encased in a membrane slipped free in a wash of fluid. Ku'Gath lunged for it, grasped it, but it popped through his fingers like a well-greased stool, and he found himself grabbing at it three times before he had it cradled in the palm of one vast hand. It squirmed within its birthing sac, and Ku'Gath licked at it gently with his sticky tongue until the sac was free, and the creature exposed.

It uncurled, and shook, flinging off mucus, and lifted a broad, eyeless head. It had a body like a tadpole crossed with a maggot, round at the front, tapering to a muscular tail. The face was simply a broad mouth set with flat teeth, and lurid purple lips. It had no legs as such, but four stumpy arms tipped with sharp-clawed, three-fingered hands.

'*Tattleslug,*' said Ku'Gath. '*You came.*'

'*Great and mighty Ku'Gath Plaguefather,*' said the Tattleslug. It thrust itself up on its tail, spread its tiny arms wide and bowed. It had a soft, incipient voice, full of cunning and treachery. '*What service might I provide you, oh first in Nurgle's favour?*'

'*First indeed, but for how much longer?*' grumbled Ku'Gath. '*I have been told of many things by a rival of mine.*'

'*You speak, of course, of Rotigus,*' said the Tattleslug.

Ku'Gath's cold blood boiled that this insignificant thing should know of his woes, but that was its nature.

'*Yes. Rotigus. I must complete the plague I brew in yonder plague mill, or else I shall suffer a subtraction of regard, and find myself lower in the estimations of our Grandfather. I will not kowtow to that arrogant bringer of weather. Never!*'

'*You would know his designs then, his plans, his schemes, so you might foil them?*' said the Tattleslug.

'*No!*' snapped Ku'Gath. '*Foolish mite. That is too unsubtle. I do not want to move against him, and risk the Grandfather's ire. I say I must have success, is all, right here on Pestilius.*'

'*How so then, mighty one?*' asked the Tattleslug.

'*I have to prove myself right, and him wrong. My plague must work. I have to kill the thrice-cursed, seven-times-damned Anathema's son. Only then will Nurgle esteem me higher than the rain-dripper.*'

'*You want to kill Mortarion?*' said the Tattleslug slyly.

'*No! Not Mortarion, though I can think of sadder worlds than ones where he does not exist. But no! I mean Roboute Guilliman.*' His jaw clicked and spasmed as he forced out the name. '*He is coming here, soon. I would know his plans.*'

'*I cannot pierce the veils of light that surround him. He is protected by...*' the Tattleslug shuddered. '*Him.*'

Ku'Gath chewed his lip. '*I thought as much, though dared hope otherwise, so I had simpler methods in mind. I need a cunning mind to fare in mortal lands. Gather intelligence, and suchlike.*'

'*A spy then?*' The Tattleslug cocked its head and stuck out its lip. '*Such work I have done, and I was made to do, for Grandfather enjoys to eavesdrop. Spy it is. Who?*'

'*Someone who can see and hear him, but not too close. None of his sons, or the golden beasts of the Emperor, nor any of his priests or his warrior women, or those checked by and close to the same.*'

'*Then a normal man? A mortal who can come and go, not too important, but invested with sufficient authority to move freely. One of this world perhaps, not of his crusading host. The son of the Anathema is wary, but he is alone. His attention cannot be everywhere at once.*'

'*Yes! Yes!*' said Ku'Gath enthusiastically. '*That sounds good, that sounds right! Important, but not too important.*'

The Tattleslug nodded. '*That way, then, it shall be done.*' It clasped its hands before its pallid gut. '*You know the price. If it is secrets that you seek, then it is secrets you must trade, like for like, that is my custom. Whisper a thing unknown for me to have as my consideration.*'

'*How do I judge what is worthy to tell?*' bubbled Ku'Gath.

'*You are far above me, mighty one, first in Nurgle's favour. I am lowly in the hierarchy, nine thousand nine hundred and seventeenth, but in this case my will supersedes yours. I shall judge the weight of your secret. It will dictate the length and nature of my service. The greater the secret, the greater the risks I am permitted to take.*'

'*Hmmmm,*' said Ku'Gath. '*A secret.*' He thought long and hard. The Tattleslug waited patiently in the Great Unclean One's hand.

'*I have it!*' said Ku'Gath. He bent his pocked face forward. The Tattleslug cocked its head, and cupped a hand around the place where its ear would have been, if it had had ears.

'*Speak!*' said the Tattleslug.

'*I…*' wheezed Ku'Gath, his voice very quiet. '*I never really liked Septicus Seven.*'

The Tattleslug stood back on its tail and folded its little arms. '*Is that it? Is that the best you can do? For that morsel I would not risk stealing a baby's name by listening to its mother. This is most pathetic, my lord.*'

'*I… Oh, um. Well.*' Ku'Gath leaned a bit closer. '*I really don't like Mortarion either, or Typhus, and I* hate *Rotigus.*'

'*Oh great one,*' said the Tattleslug, not entirely unsympathetically. '*I appreciate that you try your best, and that these confessions cause you a little embarrassment, but they are of no use, because the very nature of a secret, my lord, is that it is unknown to others, and if the great and good of Nurgle's Garden know one thing about you, it is that you hate everybody. So I suggest you try again. Go on, I know you can.*'

'*Very well.*' Ku'Gath dropped his voice even further, until it was nothing but a tickle on his halitosis. '*I have a drop of the primarch's blood.*'

'*It's, yes,*' said the Tattleslug eagerly, clapping its hands. '*Give me more. This is known, but I sense a secret coming.*'

'*I got it on the battlefield of Hecatone. It will enable us to kill him.*'

'*Go on. Tell me something I do not know.*'

'*I still have it.*' Ku'Gath rooted about with ragged fingernails in one of his many unhealed wounds. He pulled out a tiny phial, and hung it from a chain before the Tattleslug. The glass was clean, the chain free of corrosion; a single ruby drop slid around the inside, resolutely unpolluted. '*I keep this about me* at all times, even though it burns me so! This is not a pleasant suffering, being the awful touch of the Anathema Himself.'

'Most impressive,' said the Tattleslug. 'But not enough. It is known you require it for your concoction. No secret, no service.'

Ku'Gath dropped his voice. 'I do not need it all for the Godblight. I was careful. It is precious. I could do all manner of wondrous things with this, things that even Mortarion would be powerless against. They are siblings, you know. They share some of the same strengths, and some of the same weaknesses, because they share the same blood.'

The Tattleslug clapped its hands and spun around on its belly. 'Excellent! Excellent! Plots and schemes are the best of secrets. I would say yours are safe with me, but then I am the Tattleslug, and that would be a lie. This information suffices for my employment. Our compact is sealed. I shall perform the duty you require.'

Crimson slits appeared on the Tattleslug's back, and a double set of ragged wings unfolded. They beat swiftly with the sawing sound of fly swarms, and the Tattleslug rose up.

'What I shall learn, you shall know, oh great one,' said the small daemon, executing an aerial bow. Obeisance given, it buzzed away into the night.

Ku'Gath watched the Tattleslug until it was lost to sight. 'This had better be worth it,' he sighed, and waded back to the plague mill and his work.

Captain Diamider Tefelius slept uneasily beside his wife. It was a hot night, as all nights were now on Iax, with damp winds coming off the infected lands. Counterseptic-soaked sheets hung in his windows, filling his quarters with a chemical fug that made his head buzz and his mind sluggish in the mornings. His dreams were vividly unpleasant, but whether that was down to the diseases the enemy had unleashed upon the garden world, corrupting fully four-fifths of it, or the measures the humans living in the last free lands were forced to take against them, he could not say. He was no medicae expert, and had to trust what he was told.

But by the Emperor, he hated the smell of the counterseptic. He was dreaming about it: how when he put his sanctified, bio-pure uniform on, the smell clung to him; how it was worse when the helmet respirator was sealed in place. He could taste it on his food, on his wife's kisses, and he could taste it in his sleep.

In his dream, he was an infantryman again, and Sergeant Sovaset was bellowing at him to put on his helmet, even though it was full of counterseptic. He'd hated Sovaset, thinking him a bully. Although in his later years he understood why the sergeant had behaved that way, in his dreams Tefelius was still terrified of him.

'But I'll drown, sir,' he said.

Sovaset's reply was an incoherent stream of rage, nonsense sounds and spittle that made Tefelius cringe. Tefelius was suddenly even younger, a child, the sergeant still shouting at him though Tefelius was half the sergeant's size. The uniform pooled around his feet and hung off his body, and the helmet had grown to four times life-size. Now Sovaset wanted him to get into the bath of stinking fluid the helmet contained.

The dreaming Tefelius cried, then cried more when Sovaset began to beat him. He had never wept at punishment in real life, but throughout his training Tefelius had feared he would, and dreamed about it often.

He felt a feather touch upon his mind, and a curious soul peer in.

'Would you like to see something else?' a soft, friendly voice asked.

Tefelius, now curled upon the floor as Sovaset's hard stick whacked into his ribs, whimpered.

'Yes.'

Then he was someone else, or something else, perhaps – a little fellow who flew so freely through the air. The dream was calming, and a relief after Sovaset's rage. He was flying over the plague-racked world of Pestiliax – he knew that name was wrong, but could not remember what its proper name was – towards the city-port of First Landing, where the mortal lords lived, and where the primarch would undoubtedly land in a few days' time. Tefelius was confused; he had no information about the primarch's whereabouts, and never in his life had he had a glimmer of foresight, but he seemed to be in possession of a store of secret knowledge, and he knew, he just knew, that Roboute Guilliman would be coming to his city soon.

As he neared the bladed karst mountains where First Landing lay, the land grew less and less sickly. For some reason this upset him.

He saw the passing world as if he were there himself, but he did not direct the flight, and the wings that he could feel as his own were not his to move. The view tilted. The stepped gardens of First Landing raced up to meet him. He saw the first, second and third-tier walls, ranked up the mountain like an Ascension Day cake, and the broad Spiral Way that wound about the blade. The buildings, the castella, the dying hanging gardens. Soon he was over the district of his domicile, then his home tower, tall and conical like that of a termite colony, then his window, the counterseptic sheets wafting in the breeze.

There was a soft thump, a skid as of a sack of fat slung along the ground, and his flight was done. A pallid hand, also not his own, but nevertheless somehow his, lifted aside the drapes with a hiss of discomfort. The smell seemed worse than ever.

Awake, a voice in him said with some urgency.

The room was dark, but in the city glow he saw sleeping forms ahead in a bed of carved wood. His bed. It seemed huge, tall as a cliff. A curl of brown hair he knew to be his wife Almeya's poked out from the covers to hang over the edge, and over the top there was a lump that could only be his own back. The sleepers slumbered, unawares, as malice crept towards them.

Awake now, or be damned, the voice said.

Grunting softly, dream Tefelius hauled himself up the bed sheets hand over hand, wriggling onto the brocade bedspread. The cleanliness of the stiff cloth was painful on dream Tefelius' body, and he squirmed quickly to the head of the bed to avoid touching it too long. A small hand reached down, and pulled back the sheets.

Before him, mouth slightly open, was his own unconscious face.

Awake! Awake!

In his dream sight, Tefelius twitched and moaned, but could not shake off the dream.

'*Hello, human,*' dream Tefelius said to his own sleeping self. '*By dream we have touched, and by dream become one.*' The small, clawed hand reached out, and pressed into his cheek, moist and horrible.

Awake!

With a gasp, Tefelius awoke. For a moment, he experienced a strange sense of bilocation, looking down at his own shocked features, and up at the disgusting, slug-like creature squatting on his chest.

'*Such a sweet, sweet little soul you have. But I don't need that.*'

Wings folded moistly back beneath the thing's skin. Tefelius opened his mouth.

'*I only need your eyes,*' said the Tattleslug.

Before Tefelius could scream, the Tattleslug's soft head thrust itself into his mouth, jamming his jaw wide. Pushing hard, it forced itself down his throat, wriggling, stretching, choking him on its noisome body, until with a slippery give, it slithered inside his chest.

Tefelius sat bolt upright, drenched in sweat; he gasped hard, choking for breath.

'My love, are you unwell?'

Almeya's concerned face came into sharp focus. It was no longer night. Weak daylight poured through the curtains. On the stand, where his uniform hung, his vox-bead was honking.

He put his hand to his chest. He was soaked. A hard lump seemed to sit behind his breastbone, and he had the most disgusting feeling it was laughing, quivering his viscera with its mirth. He blinked sweat from his eyes, and turned to look at his wife.

'I...'

'Diamider?' she asked, thoroughly unnerved.

He grasped the front of his nightshirt, but the awful feeling in his chest faded away. He gulped. His throat was raw.

'A nightmare,' he said. 'I had the most terrible nightmare!' He laughed with relief.

'Of what sort?' she asked. The priests had asked that nocturnal terrors be reported. Tefelius was having none of that.

'Not that kind, not the kind that needs to be tallied with the others, I'm sure,' he said, although he wasn't sure. He was so very far from sure, although he would not report it. A compulsion grew in him not to tell, and became stronger the more he thought on it.

'Your vox-bead is clamouring,' she said sleepily. She flopped down onto her side of the bed. Her hand flung out and touched his side. 'You've soaked the sheets,' she mumbled. She was falling back asleep.

'Then have the servants deal with it while I am on duty.' He got out of bed on legs that still trembled, went to his uniform stand, and fumbled at his collar. He had to try twice before he managed to press the vox-bead response rune.

'Captain Tefelius,' he said.

'*Captain, your presence is needed immediately at the command centre, by order of Planetary Governor Costalis.*'

'Are the enemy coming?' he asked. They had been expecting an attack for months. It would be a relief to get it over with.

'*No, sir,*' the officer on the other end of the line said, and Tefelius noted his excitement. '*It's the primarch. He's coming here. The crusade fleet made warp egress an hour ago. They will be in orbit of Iax within a few days.*'

Tefelius didn't listen to the rest of what the lieutenant had to say. All he could think of was his dream, and his certainty that the primarch would be here soon. He stood, struck dumb.

'*Sir? Sir?*' The lieutenant's voice cut through his numbness.

'Sorry, lieutenant, you were saying? The primarch?' His throat was still sore. How much more of his nightmare had been real?

'*I said, should I inform Lord Costalis that you are on your way?*' asked the lieutenant.

'Yes. I will be there soon.'

He washed quickly at his nightstand, and pulled his uniform on. When he reached it, the command suite was already heaving with activity. As soon as he arrived he was taken up by his duties, and he forgot his nightmare.

It, however, did not forget him.

CHAPTER SEVEN

IAX RELIEVED

'We near the enemy blockade, my lord, boarding range will be reached in five minutes. Prepare for your assault on termination of approach countdown.'

Fleetmaster Isaiah Khestrin's voice was thinned to a nasal whine by the voxmitters of the transit bay, though it was clear enough, and the high pitch helped it cut through the hum of power-armour reactors.

'Very good, fleetmaster,' responded Roboute Guilliman. 'I may be uncontactable for part of this operation. Please proceed according to your own decisions.'

'I shall, my lord. The Emperor go with you.'

Khestrin's voice cut out, taking with it the background hiss of the vox. A bank of red lights illuminated at the forefront of the transit bay, bathing the occupants of the compartment in a sanguine glow. Gold-and-blue armour appeared dark and blood-soaked. Glowing eye-lenses and ready lights on battle-plate reactors and weapons gave the occupants a daemonic air.

There were over fifty of them, transhuman giants all, clustered around the greatest of their number, the primarch Roboute Guilliman. Arrayed behind him were twenty of his Victrix Guard, all clad in Ultramarines blue. All were heroes, tall and proud, the angels of the Emperor. Yet they were not the most glorious of the beings within, for archangels flew with them.

Most impressive of all was Stratarchis Tribune Actuarius Maldovar Colquan and his Custodians, their great height made yet more imposing by their tall, conical helms. They included three Allarus Terminators, five Wardens and two squads of five Custodians of lesser rank. Lesser was a subjective term, for every one of them was the match of a hundred mortal men, or a dozen Space Marines. They were second only to Guilliman himself in might. They could, together, perhaps beat him. It was rare so many fought in a single host, even in Fleet Primus, where their numbers were the greatest.

And all because the primarch had decided to wet his blade.

'Are you sure this is wise, my lord?' asked Maldovar Colquan.

Guilliman, who had yet to don his helmet, gave Colquan a narrowed glance.

'Wise?'

'You are the living hand of the Emperor, yet you put yourself in danger,' said Colquan.

'And do you think, tribune, that asking me this question several times will avail you of a different answer?'

'No, primarch,' said Colquan. 'I only–'

'Then I ask you to desist,' said Guilliman. 'I am sure the collections of writings on myself and my brothers that exist in your citadels make it very clear that we are unlikely to change our minds once a decision has been reached.'

'That is indeed so.'

'I am also sure they relate that our minds were constructed

very much like yours, and that we are unlikely to forget anything, and that we are skilled at reading the hearts and minds of all men.'

When Colquan did not respond, Guilliman rotated at the waist so he could look down at him, for he was significantly taller than even the tribune. The primarch raised his eyebrows at Colquan to prompt an answer.

'Yes, my lord,' said Colquan.

The *Aquila Resplendum* juddered. A soft alarm sounded somewhere deeper back in its interior. A stray shot from the foe, extreme range. There would be many more of those coming.

'Then let it be noted and recognised by both of us,' said Guilliman, having his fun with the tribune, 'that you are displeased with my decision to undertake this action personally, that you desire that I am aware of said displeasure, and that you are eager for me to reconsider. I understand all these things perfectly, but I will not change my mind.'

The voxmitters of the ship gave out a metallic blare, and one of the red lights in the bank at the front of the transit bay turned green.

'You have fought beside me many times, Maldovar, though I know you still do not trust me. Although you have, on occasion, made similar protests, there have been more than an equal number where you have not.'

'It is a matter of risk and reward, my lord. Boarding actions are dangerous. You could be destroyed at distance with relative ease. The blockade could be easily overwhelmed by Fleet Primus. There is no need for you to be here.'

'In deference to your insistence, and also to display my own irritation at your constant prompting that I abandon this task, I will again take you through my reasoning. Are you ready?'

'Yes, my lord,' said Colquan. The ship bounced. Trembles

ran through its frame. The transhumans, all mag-locked to the deck, swayed.

'Do not sound so peevish, Maldovar. I am in high spirits. I am going to fight. It is about time.'

'Yes, my lord.'

'If you are annoyed by this, then be glad my brother Russ did not return in my stead. For humour's sake he would punch you to the ground and then scold you for not laughing with him. He did it to me once. I shall tell you the tale some time. And yet, I am not being entirely bull-headed. There is strategy here.'

'I am aware of the str–'

'You should have held your tongue and then you would not have to hear it again, would you?' interrupted Guilliman. 'The enemy are numerous. The sons of Mortarion regard themselves superior to all others, for they have embraced despair and pain, and believe that they have emerged on the far side of it. To them, or to many of them, life is a cosmic joke. Thus, they fear no pain, no privation, no death. But they are not without fear. They are arrogant, but even they know that to face me is the doom of them. I will go among them, and I will slay them. I will scuttle their vessels from the inside, not because it grants any immediate advantage, but because it gives us an opportunity to erode their morale, to make them doubt the dubious gifts of their patron god. Let them come at me, by all means. Let them die. Let the few that survive spread the rumour of my coming so that all may doubt and fear. Let them attempt to blast this vessel from the sky as it flies at them, golden and pure, a symbol of all they have turned their backs on, and let them fail. They will remember the might of the Emperor and His unsullied primarchs before this day is out.'

'It is possible that Mortarion may have some ruse in wait for us, my lord. What then, if the fleet finds itself surrounded or otherwise disadvantaged? You will not be there. You may be captured.'

'You do not believe Fleetmaster Khestrin to be equal to the task of deflecting Mortarion's designs?'

The ship took a direct hit. They felt the pulse of the void shields as they swallowed kinetic energy and pushed it out into the warp. A hit like that would have caused some damage to another vessel, but the *Aquila Resplendum* was crafted to the very highest specifications, and a slight deviation from its flight path was the sole result.

'Khestrin is not a primarch, my lord.'

Another of the lights went green. There were four more to go.

'Nor is Mortarion, not any more,' said Guilliman. 'He is more a thing of the Plague Lord than the Emperor. Power cannot be taken from the likes of the so-called gods freely. They give no gifts. His cost him his will. He lacks freedom, though he will not see it. He is a slave. The Emperor allows a little more self-determination.'

More incoming fire rattled the aquila-shaped craft. The attacks were coming frequently. Guilliman and Colquan were obliged to raise their voices to continue their conversation.

'I will also show him that I have no fear. No doubt you would be happier if I turned away from Iax completely, but I cannot. I must face my brother. I must goad him into action that we may then oppose.'

'What if it does not work?' Colquan said testily.

Another green light. The ship closed in on its target.

'Do not tell me that you, a tribune of the Emperor's own guardians, only ever have one plan.'

'No, my lord,' said Colquan.

'And so I never rely on one outcome either. I will kill Mortarion. Or I will not. But in either eventuality, Mortarion will be leaving Ultramar, you may be certain of that.'

Again, the harsh warning blurt, again the click as a lumen switched from red to green.

'Then why risk yourself, if your victory is assured?' Colquan looked up at this dangerous weapon, created by his Emperor in the distant past. He could not trust Guilliman, not ever, he thought, but he had held stronger views once, and now the being brought as much hope as he did misgiving to his heart. 'I ask you, please, my lord, in recognition of the understanding that is growing between us, that you answer me without dissembling, and with as much honesty for me as you would bestow upon yourself.'

Guilliman smiled.

'I think you know the answer, tribune, I think you know the answer very well.'

'It would not hurt me to hear it,' he said.

Another light turned green.

'Because, tribune, sometimes one has to work off a little anger. After what Mortarion has done to Ultramar, I am very angry indeed.'

Guilliman placed his helm over his head, and it hissed shut, closing out all the dangers of the void and the toxic environment they would encounter in the plague ship.

Thereafter the final light went green, and mayhem followed.

Guilliman's vessel had been a gift from the Adeptus Custodes when he had arrived on Terra. In the years since, it had proven a valuable asset. It was not his only ship, but it was among the most magnificent, and the one he favoured when an impression needed to be made, whether that be in peace, or in war.

The *Aquila Resplendum* lived up to its name, being fashioned in the shape of the two-headed eagle that served as the Imperium's chief emblem. Each of its heads housed flight decks. Its landing claws were the eagle's talons. Its furled wings wrapped over powerful engines. Unfurled, they were bedecked with weaponry.

They unfurled now, a golden span stretching wide to embrace the void as surely as the Emperor's own hands. Sculpted feathers folded back to reveal gun ports. Long barrels and gleaming warheads emerged from concealment. The eagle's twin heads swung inward, jutting forward, flattening out its belly where its vulnerable transit bay was located, so that it resembled a true eagle hunting.

There were few ships of its kind. No others matched its grace. It was far from the blocky, utilitarian designs favoured by the Imperium.

Many of the weapons it displayed were melta cannons. Too short-ranged to play a role at distance, but they would soon find employment.

The *Aquila Resplendum* flew into the maelstrom of fire crossing the space between Guilliman's fleet and the Death Guard blockade. As the lead elements of Battle Group Alphus closed, the Chaos ships turned broadside, and opened up with corroded cannons. Guilliman's assault ships replied with prow-mounted weaponry, but although greater in number, the strategy of the day placed speed of approach over fire arcs, and they could not bring their main gun decks to bear. In the first minutes of the battle, the damage inflicted by both sides was equal.

Ships powered through the flare of discharging void shields. Las-light flicked a deadly ribbon display. Plasma and particle trails cut burning paths across the blackness of space. All the while gargantuan shells detonated, filling the vacuum with clouds of hyper-velocity shrapnel.

Into this the *Aquila Resplendum* sped, trailed by flight after flight of Thunderhawks, Overlords, assault cruisers and boarding rams. Thousands of Space Marines raced across the deadly gulf, Guilliman's strategy being to overwhelm the blockade by boarding action, quickening his landing on Iax and sparing the battered world the trauma of munitions overspill from high-orbital battle. Mortarion's ships walled-in the garden world. Every shell or stray missile that passed them by would slam into the planet below.

The *Aquila Resplendum* was an obvious craft, drawing much enemy fire. Guilliman did not care. It was more important to him to announce his presence. He wished to provoke his brother into hasty action. Void shields flaring, the eagle-ship roared through storms of fire, weathering multiple hits while lesser ships travelling behind it were consumed. Enemy fighters locked on to the *Aquila Resplendum* and began a rash pursuit, only to find the eagle had many claws. Missiles raced rearward from the wing housings, lascannon fire flickered from ball turrets mounted along its sides. Potent data weapons made in the ephemeral digital forges of Mars were unleashed to slay the machine-spirits of enemy craft, and where these had been replaced by unclean Neverborn, disrupt their ability to control their mechanical shells. Whole squadrons vying to bring down the primarch were reduced to tumbling wreckage, their corruption cleansed by fire and the timeless purity of the void.

The corroded hulk of Guilliman's target grew rapidly. A massive grand cruiser of ancient design, its Imperial origins all but obscured by corrosion, mutation and accumulations of filth. Patches of pale paint suggested an original livery in cream, but these were tiny, hidden fragments of a forgotten past, and its hull was otherwise black from long exposure to the void.

The pilots dived and banked around incoming fire, outpacing the ability of the ship's anti-fighter turrets to turn. A trio of rusted missiles, drive units shining an unclean red, raced at the

Aquila Resplendum. In response it drove downward, then climbed steeply, and the missiles raced away past it, target lock lost.

The side of the enemy vessel rose up, giant cliffs of metal studded with weapons large and small. The *Aquila Resplendum* aimed for a specific spot between two rusting macrocannons, and fired.

The melta-arrays activated in carefully arranged sequence, each targeting a spot close by its fellows. Gimbal mounts allowed them to move like searchlights, playing over and across each other, and cut into the hull in an expertly conceived pattern. The wall seemed solid still as the eagle's talons extended and it came rushing in to land like a raptor stooping on its prey. The fusion beams continued to fire, until, the instant before the golden ship was obliterated on the hide of its target, the hull gave out, exploding in a rush of superheated metal gases, which roared over the *Aquila Resplendum*'s void shield and dragged a teardrop of iridescent light behind it. Debris wheeled by, but the eagle-ship flew right through it, reared up and entered the vessel.

It flew into what had been a large repair and manufactory space for the grand cruiser's strike fighters, but the shops had been abandoned millennia ago, left to fungal growths and the strange play of half-daemonic beasts. Its thick, noxious atmosphere was vented in one filthy exhalation. Pallid fungi were ripped out into the void. There was a large amount of infrastructure tenuously clinging to the ceiling – catwalks, lifters, cranes and remote-assembly rigs – though all had lost their original form beneath centuries of accreted dross. A large part of this crashed down, wrenched from its mountings by the decompression gale, and the *Aquila Resplendum* clutched clawfuls of the wreckage as it set down. Its wings remained spread, weapons ready, the articulated neck mounts of its twinned flight decks allowing the crew to look across the empty hold.

Ancient protective protocols were enacted. Shuddering on dry bearings, blast doors shut across the ingress ways to the deeper vessel, and the howl of gas escaping into space diminished, then ceased. In the silence of the vacuum, cunningly wrought feathers on the ship's belly unlocked from one another, and the ramp of the golden eagle opened, spilling flawless light upon the vessel's tainted decks.

Out of this glow came Roboute Guilliman and his men, angels venturing into ancient hells.

'Secure this area,' said Guilliman. 'Get these doors open. We will tear out the innards of this ship with our bare hands.'

CHAPTER EIGHT

THEORETICAL, PRACTICAL

Roboute Guilliman strode halls where no loyal man had trodden for millennia, and wondered if he had walked this way before.

The ship was ancient, the design dating back to before the Great Crusade. Although naturally that did not mean the ship was that old, time flowed differently in the warp, so it was possible that the craft had served under the Emperor's banner, long, long ago. Had it, perhaps, been in the flotilla that had arrived at Barbarus with the Emperor, bearing the first of the Legion, then known as the Dusk Raiders, to meet their father? Had it taken the message of the Imperial Truth to forgotten worlds? Had it been joyously received by the scattered scions of humanity, or had it forced compliance on those who had rejected the Emperor's dream of brotherhood?

Guilliman knew those times were brutal, and believed the methods used extreme. He had privately disapproved of some of what his so-called father had done, though in truth even the worst atrocity was but what Guilliman himself had performed in Ultramar, writ large. The intent of an act of violence, he thought, was the same, whether a single murder or the destruction of a city resulted. During the Great Crusade, he had wholeheartedly accepted the Emperor's cruelties as a means to an end.

And yet...

The worlds burned. The civilisations wiped from existence, the alien species driven to extinction. So much death to achieve peace.

And then came the Heresy, and the truth of what the Emperor had withheld was thrown in his face.

Even during the Crusade, Guilliman had wrestled with his conscience. He had argued with his brothers as to the morality of their actions. He had disagreed with some of their methods. Some of them, like the monster Curze, he had openly despised. But when he walked these corridors, dripping with ooze and unnatural decay, these spaces that held an atmosphere against the laws of all physics; when he saw what had been done to the domain of the Emperor, what had been done to his own kingdom of Ultramar, then he thought all those methods just.

Wherever this ship went now, it would never be greeted with joy. It would never be seen as a liberator or a bringer of safety. Whether its shadow fell across the worlds of mankind or xenos, it had nothing to offer but cargoes of pain, corruption, disease and decay. It was catastrophe trapped in a bottle, wilfully unleashed.

Perhaps nothing should be ruled out, in the end. Perhaps no deed was too dark to hold back the horror that Chaos brought. There were no ethics, no morals, nothing, that could not be sacrificed to preserve the species, to ensure that mankind survived against the odds.

Maybe that was what Guilliman had not understood before.

He was beginning to think he understood it now, though it burned his soul to accept it.

Theoretical: the Emperor had been right, after all, about everything.

The aeldari, the necrons, the rest of the galaxy's thinking beings, they were worse than men by far. The aeldari insisted they were more moral, more sophisticated, while half of them manipulated every being they possibly could to ensure the smallest advantage, while the other half cravenly offered the suffering of innocents to save themselves. All of them were equally arrogant.

The necrons took another route, worse in its way – that of a soulless existence. Now they were openly pitted against humanity, a second and terrible enemy. An unexpected war raged around the Pariah Nexus, tying up untold numbers of Guilliman's ships as the Imperium sought to contain the threat, and yet the technology they employed might save them all, according to Belisarius Cawl.

He thought on. The boarding group went along huge processionals now so covered in organic matter they resembled the insides of diseased beasts.

He thought to the times he had raised his concerns, and had them soothed away. The Emperor had made impassioned cases for the unity of humanity, for the rediscovery of lost might and lost technology. He had never mentioned Chaos. Not once.

Guilliman thought he understood that too, for a brutal galaxy demanded a brutal regime to keep it safe. Chaos would always offer an escape from oppression, tempting the vast and teeming herds of humanity to run from the one thing that kept the nightmares away, straight into their arms.

Theoretical: the Emperor had intended this phase to be temporary. Instead, it had persisted since His internment on the Golden Throne. Practical, it was up to him to set that right.

A normal man can accomplish a dozen things at once, a great man can accomplish a thousand, he thought, recalling words his foster father, Konor, had said to him. *But no man, no matter his ability or his will, can accomplish more than one grand scheme at a time.*

His thoughts strayed to the Codex Imperialis, sitting unfinished in his scriptorium.

'One thing at a time, Roboute,' he said, rebuking himself for his impatience.

'My lord?' Colquan asked.

'Nothing,' said Guilliman.

Yet, he thought on, he could not afford to tarry. Colquan was one of a thousand spurs digging into Guilliman's side. Their relationship had improved in recent years, but the tribune still did not trust the primarch. He was poised, constantly, to act should Guilliman even look like he was thinking of moving on the Throne. That was why Valoris had given Colquan the rank, and sent him on the crusade.

Then there was Mathieu, whose growing movement would see Guilliman second only to the Emperor in the Church. Or the radical lords and politicians who wanted him on the Throne. There were the conservatives who resented him for trammelling their power. He liked to say to those close to him – a precious few, with whom he would not share the thoughts he was currently entertaining – that he had a score of enemies outside the Imperium, but a billion within.

High-level strategic chatter filtered through his vox-beads throughout these ruminations. Screeds of information played down his helmplate, layered so deeply some of it was presented as almost solid blocks of colour. He flicked through it, analysed it. His conclusion was that Khestrin was handling the attack well.

He wondered what Mortarion thought of all this, if he still had the freedom of independent thought. He and Guilliman had never got on. Guilliman found him pessimistic. Mortarion always saw the worst in everything, and expecting no joy, he found none. He had been obsessed with overcoming hardship to the point that he would deliberately seek it out, and he was not reserved in imposing the same suffering on his gene-sons. His obsessions were manifold, and once he became fixated on something, it was impossible to redirect his attention until it had been resolved to meet his always miserable expectations. Were it his sullen resentment at the Emperor's rescue of him, or the vexed question of the use of psychic power within the Legions, he pursued it until the bitter end. Could he not see he had been manipulated? Did he not realise that he had become a slave, that a far darker master than the Emperor laughed at him, and rejoiced in making him a parody of everything he had despised? Or did he still see himself as the wronged victim, and rejoice in his so-called triumphs? He was like Perturabo in that regard. Selfish, self-obsessed, cynical.

And yet, Guilliman felt sorrow that he had turned, that any of them had turned: broken Angron; the magnificent Fulgrim; even Curze, whose greatest crime was madness, and that was no crime at all. Guilliman had not loved each one of them the same, but these promethean beings had been his brothers in every way, and he could not help but mourn them.

He could tell no one this. He had told no one this. When his thoughts went down these roads, he was the loneliest traveller of all.

That was why he led this boarding party. That was why he rejoiced when a blast door a hundred feet wide and fifty feet tall grated back, and a wall of Mortarion's daemon machines rolled out. That was why he drew the Emperor's Sword, and without informing any one of his retinue of his intention, charged immediately into the fray.

'For the Emperor! For Ultramar!' he bellowed, his godlike voice amplified by his helm to shocking levels, and it was a bitter war cry indeed.

CHAPTER NINE

A PRIMARCH UNLEASHED

Colquan's sensorium registered the power surge that presaged the opening of the door, and painted up in illuminated outline what waited behind it. Guilliman's actions, though unanticipated, were to be expected. The Imperial Regent had been in fiery mood of late.

But though Colquan had expected Guilliman to attack, the speed of his charge took him by surprise, and he cursed himself for underestimating the physical prowess of the primarch again.

'Custodians, form up, protect the regent!' he commanded after the fact, when Guilliman was already halfway to the enemy. 'Reading thirteen daemon engines in the medius threat range. Twenty-plus Traitor Astartes in the rearguard.'

The foe opened fire before the door was fully open. Bolts and compact missiles streaked out on smoky trails at the Imperial boarders. A meltagun roared. One of Guilliman's bodyguard took the hit directly on his storm shield as he tried to keep pace with his lord. The power field gave out with an almighty bang, and the Space Marine hurled the smoking wreck towards the foe, where it skidded on the ground and crashed into their legs. They were unmoved by his response.

Guilliman was into the thick of the foe in a moment, projectiles turned aside by the Armour of Fate. Though powerful, neither the Custodians nor the Victrix Guard could keep pace with Roboute Guilliman. A mortal man his size would have moved slowly, clumsily, but Guilliman was no genetic outlier; he was a perfectly designed being, and he ran swift as the wind, the fires flowing from the Emperor's Sword stretched out into a banner behind him. With a crash of armour, he hurled himself at the lead engine shoulder first, rocking it on its motive tracks so hard it pivoted pathetically on the rearmost, and toppled over. Guilliman finished it with a downward thrust that blew out its engine, not even noticing the crash and explosion of bolt-shells going off all over his armour's energy field. The primarch was moving before Colquan could formulate his next exhortation that he be protected.

The daemon engines were myphitic blight haulers, a light, anti-armour construct the Death Guard deployed in large numbers. Their loadouts of multimeltas and missile launchers were equally useful in slaying power-armoured troops as tanks, and all of them were wheeling about to bring their weapons to bear on Guilliman. Yet he moved too fast to be accurately targeted, and Colquan lost sight of him among the vapours the haulers' engines belched.

'By the Emperor, to the primarch!' he roared. Men were running forward. They were strung out. The primarch's heedlessness had put them all in danger.

Doors opened along the side of the corridor. More Traitor Marines were behind.

'Ambush! Ambush!' a Space Marine shouted over the vox-link.

The shouter's icon blinked out as soon as it lit, and Colquan could not tell who had spoken. In dismay he saw more of the diseased progeny of Mortarion taking up firing positions along the railings of the upper level. He levelled his bolt caster and let fly, blasting out the chest of a hulking Plague Marine with its double shot. The warriors coming out into the corridor on the lower level were equipped with short-range plague belchers and rusted melee weapons, and moved in to engage the party hand to hand.

'In the Emperor's name, get up there! Move in! Protect the primarch!' Colquan's fear that Guilliman would be slain was the only thing that outweighed his misgivings about his survival.

But the Space Marines and the Custodians found themselves embroiled in their own battles. Those who had moved forward to guard the primarch were attacked on three fronts, and slowed, the Space Marines struggling to reform their battle line, while Guilliman was a lone flash of blue and gold surrounded by rust and greening metal.

Colquan swore and pushed on, finding himself in an unseemly jostle of armoured bodies. Plague Marines who chuckled constantly vied with those grumbling about their ailments to get to him. Colquan cut a tentacle from an armoured warrior so fat it was a surprise he could move at all. He whirled his guardian spear about and drove the tip into his swollen belly. Black guts, already well into the last stages of decay, gushed liquidly all over the Plague Marine's armour, their acids eating into the plates and making them smoke as he dropped dead to the ground.

'The primarch! The primarch! Protect him!' Colquan shouted.

He crossed the golden haft of his spear with a rust-blunted plaguesword, throwing back the wielder. A lamprey face pushed out through a wrecked breathing grille, and Colquan headbutted hard, mashing the thrashing thing to pulp. A spear blow followed through the mess of the crushed mutation, and gleaming auramite caved in brittle ceramite. But his foe was strong, and gifted incredible resilience by his patron. It pushed out wildly, and Colquan found himself shoved back into Varsillian the Many-Gloried, one of his fellow Custodians.

'We have to get to Guilliman!' Colquan growled, as he fended off the blows of rusted blades. 'If he falls now...'

Colquan put his opponent down, ending a thousand years of treachery with a cut up through the helm. The space opened in front of him and for a few seconds he could see Guilliman fight.

The Hand of Dominion vomited a stream of bolts into the blank frontplate of a blight crawler, cratering the rusty metal and bringing out a seepage of watery oil. The damage was minimal, but the flash of so many explosions all over the forward arc of the daemon machine blinded it, and Guilliman stepped in with his sword to deal the killing blow.

Always, it was the sword that did the damage. It roared with fire as Guilliman swung it, seeming to flare brighter as it sensed the presence of the daemon caged inside the machine. Too late, the Neverborn understood the danger it was in, and tried to flee.

Guilliman spun the sword around, pivoting over crossed feet, executing a full turn, and struck. The Emperor's Sword hit the bulbous front of the machine in a brutal uppercut, tearing through the metal easily, and setting it ablaze with unearthly fire. Thick liquid burst from the innards as the sword ripped up through materials technological, organic and diabolical, Guilliman's great strength and the sword's supernaturally keen edge slicing them all as easily. The sword exploded out of the top as Guilliman finished his turn, almost cutting right the way through the daemon engine. Half the armoured frontplate fell off, exposing the mess of guts and wires that served as the machine's workings.

The daemon made a horrible, keening noise that ran sharp

claws down the surface of one's being. The shadow of the escaping daemon rushed up from the top of the engine, seeking escape to the warp, but the Emperor's Sword permitted no mercy for its kind. The fires from the shell seemed to leap after it, and embrace it, dragging the shadow back. Colquan had an impression of a horned face screaming in the fire, suddenly going to tatters.

As surely as if a promethium jet had been turned off, the fires died, their soul-fuel consumed. Guilliman was already onto his next target.

'We're supposed to be guarding him?' said Varsillian. He had recently completed his fifth century of service, and taken the honour robes of the Wardens. 'He needs no guarding, tribune. We are, I fear, entirely ancillary to purposes here. Guilliman cuts through the machines of the Death Guard as if they were paper stage props.'

'Yet we must watch him,' growled the tribune. 'He is not invulnerable. And you must watch your tone also, Varsillian. Primarch he may be, but in him dwells the hopes of us all, for the moment. I will not have him die under my protection because we allowed ourselves to stumble into this ambush.'

Privately, he conceded that Varsillian had a point. There was nothing to greet them in that chamber that could even slow the primarch down.

For all his suspicions of Guilliman's intentions, Colquan could not fault him as a warrior. The Adeptus Custodes' records maintained that the primarchs had been created primarily as weapons. Having seen Guilliman fight many times now, he judged the fact proven. Guilliman exhibited many other qualities in governance, administration and law especially, but he was, ultimately, an unsheathed blade. All his other skills were adornments on the hilt.

Guilliman vanished again. Around Colquan, the press of

combat slackened, enough that the two Custodians could part. Colquan reversed his grip, slashed down with the blade of his halberd, taking off the leg of a warrior at the knee. The Plague Marine toppled over, and Colquan slew him with a thrust through the neck. He twisted his blade when it had passed through, separating what was left of the Space Marine's head from his body. The disruption field blasted most of it apart, and what went skidding through the feet of the warring parties was little more than a smoking skullcap.

Varsillian wielded a great castellan axe, which he swung around now at chest height, forcing back the three Plague Marines who sought to trap him. One moved in to engage him from his right, but Varsillian switched his swipe to a stab, thrust far out, using his back leg to put as much power as he could into his blow. The top of the axe blade punched through the Plague Marine's breast-plate, the power field flared, and Varsillian drove the axe top right through the man's chest, bolt caster and all. It rammed into the reactor pack powering the traitor's armour, and it exploded with a dull crump and an effusion of brown fume, scattering cor-roded pieces of armour and flesh everywhere. Varsillian stepped through the cloud, unharmed, his axe rising again.

Colquan thought back to the days before the Edict of Restraint was overturned. Then, the Adeptus Custodes ventured out from Terra rarely, clandestinely, and in small numbers. The missions they undertook were for the most part diplomatic, for conceal-ing their presence after battle was nigh impossible. Fighting made them conspicuous. Politically, they could not afford to attract attention to themselves. The most combat the majority saw was in the Blood Games held on Terra itself.

The Games were no substitute for battle. To see twenty of the Emperor's own guardians fight side by side as he did now was an honour his kind had waited millennia to witness.

Maldovar Colquan slaughtered the enemy, and it felt good to do so. He could see the primarch's point.

By now the Allarus Terminators had forced their way through the press. Colquan caught a glimpse of them forming up around the regent, who was very much alive. He had time for a breath of relief, then a new foe presented himself.

A champion came at him, whirling a two-handed flail around and around his head. Weighted skulls on rusty chains vomited a stream of green gas that threatened to burn through Colquan's softseals. Colquan resisted the urge to attack immediately, holding back to judge his foe. The Plague Marine was powerfully built, his height and strength increased by the gifts of his patron god. Through gaps in his corroded armour the tribune saw the movement of flabby muscle. This champion was stronger than his fellows, and he would be as inured to pain as all of them. That made him dangerous.

The champion's followers gave their leader room, opening up a duelling ground in the swirl of the melee. Colquan paced around his opponent, noting everything about him. The Death Guard were among the last of the Traitor Legions to retain their organisation, and had kept up their numbers by aggressive recruitment, but the greening brass honour badges and tokens of devotion this champion wore marked him out as ancient, perhaps one of the original traitors who had followed Mortarion down his dark road. His armour was streaked with rust and congealed oil. His power plant shook and coughed smoke from its exhaust ports. Viscous saliva ran from his arched breathing grille. A cyclopean eye-lens glowed green above this, and above that a single horn, slightly off-centre, thrust outward.

The censer skulls thrummed around and around. Balefires glowed in their eyes. Colquan made a feint to draw an attack, to see what response his opponent would offer, but the plague lord did not fall for the trick, and repositioned himself, kept up the whirl of the skulls, and spoke.

'I was born upon Barbarus,' he said. His voice was surprisingly pure. 'I have fought the Long War since the days of Horus himself, where I walked the ground of Terra, and saw the Imperial Palace burn.'

More fluid welled from his mouth as he spoke.

'But I have never slain one of your kind, corpse-watcher.'

Then he struck.

The skulls hissed through the air at Colquan. It was a blow that would shatter tank armour, delivered fast. Colquan was faster still, and sidestepped, and the skulls passed by to smash a hole in the deck. Pipes beneath the plating ruptured, gushing steam into the hall. Colquan went to attack while his opponent was off balance, only to meet the spiked butt of the flail thrust at him. His guardian spear's jab hastily turned to a parry, and he turned it aside. The adamantium blade met iron shaft in an explosion of lightning, but the champion's weapon was undamaged, durable despite its rusted appearance.

The champion followed up his counter-attack skilfully, dipping the head of the flail and circling it up, round and over in a figure of eight to send the chains whirling again. He kicked out and down towards Colquan's foot, scraping sparks from his auramite greave and slowing the tribune's backward step enough that the champion was successful in bringing the flail around and into the tribune's helm.

Colquan's head snapped to the side, staggering him. Encouraged, the champion attacked again, but Colquan got his spear up, and the chains wrapped about the powered head. Yanking hard, the blade cut through two of the three flail chains, and the skulls bounced along the floor. The third remained wrapped about the haft of his halberd, and there followed a contest of strength where Colquan attempted to wrest the flail from the grip of his opponent and the champion tried to stop him.

Gene-forged strength vied with Chaos power, and the two were drawn into a warrior's embrace, chest to chest.

'You are weak, corpse-guard. Feel my strength, my vitality. This is the gift of my god. Where are the gifts of yours?'

Colquan threw himself back, dragging the plague champion with him. He planted his back foot solidly, and the Plague Marine stumbled into him. Colquan released the haft of his guardian spear with his right hand, and drew his misericordia. The champion wrenched hard on the tangled weapons, only to find Colquan's power knife punched through his breastplate, and buried in his primary heart.

Black blood gushed over Colquan's hand. He let go of his spear, grabbed the warrior about the head, and pulled him close. He leaned in to the fallen Space Marine's helmet.

'We have no need of gods,' he said, and ripped the misericordia sideways. He was almost thrown back by the force of sundered atoms, but took the explosion on his auramite, the plague champion still clasped close, and obliterated his second heart.

He worked his arm around further, thrust his fingers into the traitor's respirator grille, twisted hard, and broke his neck, kicking the body back before it hit the ground so he could retrieve his spear.

The Plague Marines were retreating. On the left Guilliman's Victrix Guard had gained the gallery, and were fighting ferociously to clear the upper level. On the right, the Custodians had blocked and then turned back the tide of reinforcements coming through onto the main deck. The Death Guard fell back in good order, still firing, retreating through the doors they had arrived by, leaving their dead behind.

Guilliman fought the last of the daemon engines while the Allarus Terminators fired bolts after the foe. Whatever havoc the Death Guard had thought to wreak upon the boarders had gone unrealised. Several blue-armoured bodies were mingled with the fallen, but none of the golden warriors had died, and the sons of Mortarion lay all about in heaps, and their daemon engines were blazing shells emptied of their possessing spirits.

With a blow of the Hand of Dominion, Guilliman punched in the front of the last blight hauler. A few more bolt-rounds crackled off. Custodians and Victrix Guard went among the fallen, finishing off wounded enemies with misericordia and power gladius.

There was no need to call for a halt. The veteran Space Marines and Custodians did not pursue their foe into the labyrinth of the ship, but re-formed, and waited.

Colquan quickly appraised the standing of his troops. Two of the Custodians were injured, but their battleplate was uncompromised, and the plagues of the enemy had no hold on their Emperor-designed physiology.

An Apothecary's reductor whined as it cut out the gene-seed of fallen Space Marines. A moment's tense silence passed.

'Onward, to the command deck,' Guilliman said.

Guilliman's group encountered little more resistance. A few packs of lesser daemon engines attempted to delay them, but these were quickly dealt with, and the Imperial advance proceeded rapidly down corridors silent but for the reports of the ship's main armaments. It appeared the main strength of Plague Marines had come against them in the hall, and having failed at that ambush, those remaining either hid themselves away or fled for the planet, as fleet auguries suggested they were doing now from several other boarded vessels.

Few mortal crew presented themselves. Those that did were summarily executed. Daemon-infested devices were smashed. Pitiful agglomerations of flesh blended with the vessel were scoured with fire.

There were a few moments for rest as automated defences covering the approaches to the command deck were dealt with, and it was by the light of a burning skin wall infested with eyes that Colquan and Guilliman spoke.

'This is disappointingly easy,' said Guilliman.

Roasting eyes popped and hissed in the fire. Rancid fat dripped flaming to the ground.

'The enemy has few of his real warriors aboard this ship,' said Colquan. 'He preserves his strength. Nothing can stand against three crusade battle groups. I am surprised he even bothers with this pitiful blockade.'

'It is the same story across the fleet,' said Guilliman. 'It is as we expected. This is no serious attempt to prevent our landing, but a delaying tactic. The majority of Mortarion's forces will be on the surface, if his goading me to come here was not simply a diversion, and he intends to strike elsewhere.'

'I do not believe so,' said Colquan.

'Nor do I, but all possibilities must be accounted for, examined and evaluated,' said Guilliman. 'Nothing is impossible until the moment for it to occur has passed. Mortarion's freedom to move through the warp makes pinning him down irksomely hard, yet if he means to kill me, he will be on hand to gloat. This is obviously a trap, and yet it is one we must willingly go into. Mortarion uses himself as bait. This a dangerous strategy for him, because if his trap fails, I shall have his head. He will know this.'

There was a bright flash and a shower of sparks up ahead, followed by a short burst of bolter fire. Shouts came back down the corridor that the next bulkhead door had been cleared. Guilliman's guard gave a thunderous advance and presented their shields in a wall across the now open way.

A turret cannon encased in jelly-like growths opened up. The Space Marines raised their shields, deflecting the heavy-calibre rounds with their power fields, and ran forward. They kept up their formation until they were past the maximum depression of the gun and into its blind-zone. One of their number stepped forward, and lopped the barrel off. Ammunition exploded inside, and the gun sagged, bleeding, in its mount.

'Clear!' the warrior shouted.

They reached the final portal to the command deck. A hundred deranged baseline humans, mutated beyond reason, mounted a brief but futile defence, and were cut down in short order. Melta bombs blew wide the bridge doors, and Roboute Guilliman strode into the nerve centre of the vessel.

It was filthy, and stank. Stringy growths hung from machinery, linking them to one another. Shuffling humans worked failing machines. Tallow sticks gave off a greasy light. The crew did not look up from their tasks as the regent of the Imperium of Man strode among them.

'Kill these wretches,' Guilliman said. 'All of them.'

With murderous efficiency, the Adeptus Custodes and Adeptus Astartes despatched the bridge crew. They were simple, idiot beings, their will decayed, and put up no resistance beyond a pathetic mewling.

'The Death Guard and their officers have withdrawn,' said Guilliman. He looked around him at the flesh-clotted control galleries and servitor choirs, the occupants of which were reduced to grinning, green skulls engulfed by rampant organic growths. 'Colquan, secure a teleport lock and have us removed from this vessel. *Aquila Resplendum*, launch. All other assault parties withdraw.'

'This ship has been primed to self-destruct?' asked Colquan. There were no signs that this was the case, no alarms or fail-safe announcements, and no change in the ship's reactor hum, but what the primarch was saying made perfect sense.

'A very probable practical,' said Roboute Guilliman. 'It is what I would do. Mortarion put this target here for me to select. He staged enough resistance to keep us occupied.' He went to the cracked oculus and looked out over Iax.

'The opening moves of his game,' said Colquan.

'Our match of regicide continues. Doubtless it will for all time,' said Guilliman. 'It would be too much to ask the universe to allow me simply to kill him.'

Guilliman watched the void battle, if such a feeble resistance was worthy of that name. Mortarion's fleet was falling to pieces. From the command deck, it was even more obviously a delaying tactic rather than a concerted effort to win. The largest, more valuable ships were sailing away, and the lead vessels were already passing over the horizon of Iax. What was left were medium-sized craft, and the grand cruiser they currently stood upon.

'He intends to slay as many Space Marines as possible,' said Guilliman. 'Most of these ships will be rigged for detonation. A costly gambit, but Mortarion always plays the card of attrition.' Guilliman contacted fleet command, and gave orders that all boarding parties on every ship were to retreat immediately, and that engaged warships were to pull back to safe distances. 'I wonder where that putrid cur he calls a son is to be found? Typhus commands the largest plague fleet. His presence would have presented some difficulties.'

'A shame he is not here, my lord,' said Colquan. 'I can think of few other traitors who I would more gladly slay.'

The last of the human crew were executed, and the Custodians began to arrange themselves for emergency teleport extraction, while the Victrix Guard prepared to be retrieved by ship. Doctrine would dictate that Guilliman withdraw to the centre of Colquan's group, but he remained by the oculus, looking over Iax. He remembered a blue-green jewel of the void, a perfect marble, an example even to wider Ultramar as to how mankind could live in harmony with his environment. Mortarion had struck deliberately at this place to wound him. Guilliman felt his jaw clench. All he could see now were clouds the colour of jaundiced skin. From galactic beauty to a weeping sore on reality. His anger grew, but that was what his brother intended.

'Teleport lock secured,' announced one of the Victrix Guard.

'Then withdraw us, immediately. Sicarius, do not delay to get your men off the vessel.'

'Yes, my lord.'

Guilliman kept his eye upon his ravaged garden as arcs of power crackled over his armour. The metallic smell of warp energy crowded his senses. There was a flash, that infinite instant of suspension, where he felt his soul called to join the wide seas of the warp, then a strobing, and he was suddenly aboard the *Macragge's Honour*, wisps of corposant curling from his limbs and his eye-lenses spidered with warp-frost.

Decontamination teams moved forward, slow in their high-hazard suits. Wide nozzles sprayed counterseptic all over him and the other returnees. Conclaves of human psykers played their powers about the room, for the maladies of the Plague God were not all beholden to physical law.

As Guilliman underwent the first phases of cleansing, he voxed the command deck.

'Khestrin,' he said. 'How goes it?'

'We are withdrawing to safe range according to your orders, my lord,' the fleetmaster responded.

'Do we have any lock upon surface targets?' asked Guilliman, already knowing the answer.

'Negative, my lord, we have no indication of surface features beyond the provinces around First Landing. Our augurs are blind over eighty per cent of the planet. I commanded attempts at clairvoyant scries, but our astropaths too report a lack of success. What they can see is not where it should be, and it moves.'

'Then it is as I predicted,' said Guilliman. 'Iax is so drenched in the warp it renders geography meaningless. We must go down to the surface.' He lifted up his arms to allow the counterseptic jets access to his armpit joints. His battleplate ran with chemicals. Full decontamination would take over an hour.

'The first of the enemy ships has auto-destructed, my lord.'

'Helm feed,' demanded Guilliman.

A thumbnail view of the void appeared in his vision. The fading glow of plasma marked the demise of the first ship. As he watched, another craft detonated, his primarch's sight unflinchingly taking in its blinding death. His attention strayed to a list of casualty figures scrolling down another part of his helmplate. He found his irritation with Mortarion redoubled. By stationing these ships where he had, the daemon primarch had forced him to choose between the lives of his Space Marines and his subjects on the planet below.

'As soon as they are done with this pathetic display of pyrotechnics, take up geostationary high anchor over First Landing. Prepare for limited combat drop around the capital, and get me some charts of the place. Assault on Iax's primary space port will begin at my command.'

Another signal cut into Guilliman's communication with Khestrin. A fleet control officer, by the sigil appended to his request to communicate.

'Speak,' said Guilliman.

'*My lords, I am sorry to intrude, but we have an unsanctioned force already making their approach to the target planet.*'

'Who, and under what authority do they claim rights to land?' demanded Guilliman.

'*It is the militant-apostolic, my lord,*' said the officer. '*He has his crusade and takes the Cadian Four Thousand and Twenty-First with him. He invokes the right of Bellus Primus of the Adeptus Ministorum, claiming the authority of the God-Emperor Himself as his justification for assault.*'

Guilliman had to restrain himself from giving any indication of his anger.

'Thank you for informing me.' Guilliman severed the connection. 'Can you call the Cadians back, at least, Isaiah?'

'*They are unaffiliated to any particular command,*' said Khestrin. '*When they joined the crusade they pledged themselves to the office of the militant-apostolic almost immediately, and he accepted. We could order them back, but they will be under no obligation to obey.*' Khestrin paused. '*We could cripple their ships instead, my lord.*'

Guilliman felt an uncommon fury. 'What, and risk providing the Church with a martyr, and my detractors with proof of my contempt for their beliefs?' said the primarch. 'What is his target?'

As a reply, Khestrin played Guilliman a short audex extract. Mathieu's voice had become more strident since the happenings on Parmenio. His zealotry was now openly expressed. Guilliman was not surprised by this, for he could not explain satisfactorily what had happened at the Battle of Hecatone himself.

'*For the glory of the Emperor we land first!*' Mathieu was shouting. '*For the glory of the primarch, we shall take the port!*'

'The void port, then,' said Guilliman. 'Let him be. He may save us the effort of fighting for it ourselves. I shall deal with him myself, if he survives the landing.' He thought a moment.

'Send strike craft to cover his descent. Let him come to no harm. Prepare my diplomatic barque to take me down, not the *Aquila Resplendum*. We go with the branches of peace extended. I will land myself as soon as I am cleansed.'

Having spoken, the primarch broke the channel.

'*My lord,*' said Colquan over a vox-link. '*What has occurred?*'

'Not what, but who. Frater Mathieu has slipped his leash.' Guilliman gritted his teeth. 'He is a most turbulent priest.'

CHAPTER TEN

FAITH'S LIGHT

The transit hold was full of singing by the time the ship came in to land. It competed with the roar of engines, it shook the hull more than the violence of atmospheric entry. The lander was old. It grumbled its way through the upset skies of Iax, and upon hitting the ground, sank into its landing gear like a dowager settling into her skirts.

But it got them down safe, praise be to the Emperor.

Trumpets blasted with such volume they stirred the hair of the occupants, and sent their banners waving. Mathieu exulted at the holiness contained within that ship, his army of true believers, come to purge the garden world with flamer, sword and song. The noise his battle congregation made was a tonic to the soul. Any daemon that heard that sound would surely quail, for the Crusade of the Witnesses was going to war.

Giant pistons slammed back. Atmospheric seals uncoupled. A hiss of equalising pressure joined the crusaders' song. Cogs twenty feet high ratcheted backward, then locked; the drums they restrained were released, unspooling lengths of chains with man-sized links. As they clanked through their guides, the grand stair-ramp descended ponderously, allowing in a slot of leprous light. Decorations unfolded themselves from their stowed positions, unfurling like paper sculptures, making pulpits and statues. Anticipating release, the cyber-constructs that accompanied the Crusade of the Witnesses rose up from their roosts, flocks of wooden angels and sanctified skulls. Mathieu's own companion was up there among them, and Mathieu rejoiced that the spirit of his teacher would see yet another world, and experience another morsel of vengeance for her murder.

There would be plenty of opportunity for revenge, he thought, for Iax was poisoned to the point of death, and much of it was in the hands of the enemy. The ship quivered to the impact of guns on its void shield. The atmosphere was tropically thick, too warm, choking in its density, and full of a sulphurous stench that coated the back of the throat. Towards the front a few of his congregation coughed, and their songs faltered.

'Brothers!' he called. 'Sisters! Be of brave heart, the Emperor walks with us! He watches us! Sing for Him! Sing!'

He pushed his way through them, making to the ramp himself. He had no battle pulpit or armoured preach-tank as his rank would permit, but wore a soldier's flak armour over his simple robe. He did not even have a helmet. He carried his chainsword and laspistol; they were oiled, primed, blessed and sanctified with fresh purity seals, but otherwise battered by long use.

His only concession to the dangers of Iax were the three armoured warriors bearing shields and swords that accompanied him, the mysterious warrior-ascetics of the Order of the Crimson Cardinals. They were his protectors, but nothing shielded him so effectively as his faith. As he approached the front of the hold, the fumes seemed to recoil, and the air become purer.

Fervour gleaming in his eyes, Mathieu shouted over the singing of his people.

'Fear not the pestilence of the false gods!' Mathieu shouted. 'It has no dominion over we, the faithful servants of the Emperor. Do not be afraid to breathe the tainted air of this world, for the Emperor protects, and will make it pure as the winds of paradise! We know, for we have witnessed Him at His work, and He is with us now!'

The ramp continued to clank downward, revealing more of Iax's polluted skies. Clouds tinged green blew on fever-damp winds. The view opened out, showing them the wide port grounds on the other side of the void shield shimmer: broad roads running between the knife-edges of the karst, warehouses clustered in huddled flocks, transit buildings, rail terminals, all the necessaries for interplanetary trade. Iax had been a beautiful world, but here was utility and hard grey rockcrete. At the port a subsidiary run of peaks had been truncated, topped with ugly artifice: scores of landing pads of various sizes set at varying heights. In concession to the planet's nature, the sides sported terraced gardens, but where vibrant colours should display, there were only drab browns and slime greens. The stagnant smell of dying plants joined the stench of sulphur.

The ramp touched down, its last decorations unfurling to display the Emperor's glory. Wan light glinted off gilt symbols of His divinity, and shone a little brighter for the touch.

Mathieu raised his voice further.

'In the name of the Emperor! In the name of His son, forward! Let us bring light back to this wounded planet, and succour to all His loyal servants who languish here in unholy sickness!'

The hymn swelled. In a huge mob, Mathieu's crusaders spilled down the stair-ramp to the pad the ship occupied, then down the grand stairway to the void port roadways. They were drawn from every world Guilliman's fleets had visited. They came from every ship within the fleets. Men and women who had slipped free of their mortal masters to better serve their divine lord. There were menials, ship's crew, bureaucrats and soldiers, even lords and ladies – deserters by some laws, but the officers who would call them so walked beside them, and more were coming to swell their numbers every day.

Singing hosannas to the dominion of man, the battle congregation walked fearlessly down the ramp, through the void shield and into enemy weapons fire. Dozens of them fell singing, but the rest stepped over the corpses, their faith making them fearless. Those that had ranged weapons opened fire, filling the air with las-shot and bullets. Still they died, still they marched, unstoppable, a tide of belief. They had total confidence in victory, yet the battle congregation was not the greatest of Mathieu's weapons.

As the throng poured down the steps of the lander, a piercing organ blast sounded in the darkness of the hold behind them, shaking the guts of all before it. Lights snapped on, yellow search beams fierce as the holy light of the Astronomican. There came the sound of engaged plasma generators, and the rumble of water tanks flash-boiling.

Screeching steam-damp music from towering organ pipes, the war train lurched forward. Great tracks clattered along the decking, shaking even the venerable frame of the lander. The train followed the throng of the faithful, its giant engine, forty feet tall, dragging battle carriages whose gun casemates were already jerking into life, the targeting lenses set into the faces of angelic sculptures burning a baleful red. Pilgrims ran to the steps on the sides, swarming up to man the fighting decks. The locomotive was an immense, mobile altar glorifying the Emperor, its every surface covered with gilded sculpture. Three massive chimneys on the engine vented scented steam. Upon its prow was an immense ram, above which an angel stood, outstretched arms and wings projecting a protective energy field. Sheltered behind it, an organ of a hundred pipes played by ten men hard-wired into their keyboards blared a mighty song. Behind that was an open command pulpit, but Mathieu eschewed it for now, wishing to put his sandalled feet upon the tainted soil, and claim it back by touch alone.

The engine dipped onto the landing ramp, and the congregation moved fearlessly around its crushing machinery. It ran down the stair-ramp, ground forward onto the landing pad, track units chewing up the ferrocrete surface; then it reached the stair leading to the roadways, and went into the enemy's fire.

The prow angel's shield sparked with a thousand impacts. The train struggled with the steep descent, and its brakes gave off a smell of burning metal. The carriages juddered as it picked its way down the stair, always, it seemed, on the brink of falling. Its tracks became red with the blood of the fallen. Traitor Guardsmen and civilians driven mad by Nurgle's gifts infested the void port. Though disorganised, they were almost as fanatical as Mathieu's followers, and more numerous. They turned their guns upon the train, hoping to cripple it while it was vulnerable, but potent warding technologies were installed within its cars, and their fury was turned aside, and all the while its holy, deafening music played.

The engine reached the road leading from the ziggurat, and the first car followed, then the second. When the third was on the level, the war train was no longer vulnerable, and it showed its worth. The faithful on the ground took shelter under its energy shields, and although some shots pierced the bubble, the slaughter ceased. On each carriage, armoured cowls rolled back. Racks of missiles elevated, each warhead painted with devotional scripts. The great guns mounted in the casemates opened fire, while the groups of crusading pilgrims manning the parapets added coherent beams of light to their shouted prayers.

Mathieu marched beside the train, his servo-skull dropping from the flocks above to buzz purposefully behind him. He had no strategy. He did not lead like a military commander, for who was he to plan when the Emperor would tell him what to do? But though he did not strategise, he did fight. He relied on the guidance of He of Terra to send Mathieu where he was needed, and when his target was ordained, he struck with righteous fury.

Now the whole of the landscape was revealed to him. Curiously flat plains studded with bladed mountains stretched towards the city of First Landing. The capital occupied the largest mountain, as proud as a fang, which thrust upward, a natural hive honeycombed with the warrens of mankind. Suburbs and satellite settlements clung to the sides of the peaks about. It too dripped with vegetation, and had been renowned as a place of great beauty before Nurgle's diseases had reduced half to slime.

Though the city remained in Ultramarian hands, renegades occupied the port. They were dug into the gardens spilling down the sides, from where they could rain fire down upon the roads. Guns shot from galleries in First Landing's lower-tier defences, targeting the larger concentrations of enemy. The gunfire of the loyalist forces mingled with the enemy's, both a risk to the battle congregation, but they went into the storm bravely, for they had faith as their shield.

There was little cohesion to the enemy forces; even Mathieu could see that. He set his sights on a heavy weapons nest three levels up on the nearest geoformed karst.

'I go to battle as the Emperor commands! Onward!' Mathieu shouted, and somehow he was heard over the great train's music and the clamour of battle. A group of the faithful joined him, and together they broke from the cover of the train's shields. His departure was marked by both sides; heavy stubber fire chased him across the road as he sprinted for the ziggurat's side, cutting down two of the soldiers who ran with him. From the train, his pilgrims poured suppressive fire onto the enemy targeting their prophet. The train rumbled on, its parapets level with the enemy in the gardens, then was past, and occupied itself with other foes.

By then Mathieu and his crusaders had reached the karst tower's base, and were racing up the stairs, his guardians angling their power shields to deflect incoming shots. More of his followers fell to lasguns wielded by once faithful men. A woman in a filthy blue uniform appeared over a terrace above and threw a chunk of rockcrete down. It bounced from one of the Crimson Cardinal's shields. Mathieu shot her dead.

Mathieu spared her only a brief glance when her body toppled onto the stair. She was a member of the Ultramar Auxilia, corrupted by the Plague God's influence and wandered far from the light. Yet Mathieu did not despise her. She had suffered, her hair was falling out, and her teeth were black.

'Rest in peace, sister,' he said, as he passed. 'Your pain is over.'

More men came from a door leading into the peak's insides. They were a mix of civilians and soldiers, much like Mathieu's battle congregation, but followers of an altogether darker god. Their skin was pasty grey. Their mouths were caked in sores. Their eyes were red. They smelled like the dead. One was massively obese, his throat swollen by bursting glands, his left leg fat with elephantiasis. Another was so emaciated he appeared to be a living skeleton, and his eyes swivelled madly in their sockets as if they sought to escape his torment.

'For the Emperor!' Mathieu roared, and his cry was taken up by his followers. Furious melee erupted on the stairs. Mathieu's chainsword roared. Blood and pulped flesh sprayed as he cut into the first traitor, casting him down. Mathieu shot the next through the head. Disruption fields crackled as the crusaders cut their way through the attackers. Mathieu's soldiers attacked with bayonets, his civilian followers with crude mauls.

'For the Emperor! For the Emperor!' they shouted. Clubs crushed skulls. Point-blank las-shots set clothing on fire. Mathieu's chainsword drenched him red. Flecks of diseased meat flew into his screaming mouth, but he had nothing to fear from the contagions of the enemy, for the Emperor was his healer and his guardian.

The flood of enemy pouring from the landing spire faltered, then reversed, and Mathieu's crusaders were falling over each other to chase the fugitives down. Mathieu shot one in the back. Others fell to bludgeons swung from behind.

'Forgive them!' Mathieu screamed, exulted by battle. 'You know nothing of their torments! Release them through death!'

Shouts receded into the ziggurat as the last few escaped. Mathieu had time to take one, blood-tainted breath before the tide of his little party dragged him up the stairs to the heavy weapons nest.

The Traitor Guardsmen manning the heavy stubber had not expected them, for they were still firing down into the press of the battle congregation. As Mathieu's party emerged, they tried to pull the gun from its tripod to swing it about, but they were too slow.

The missiles on the train fired, roaring up in staggered lines of three from the back of each car, and raced off into the sky. Accompanied by the rockets' deafening ascent, Mathieu's followers fell on the crew. They were frenzied, driven to the heights of bloodlust by their zeal, and they tore the luckless men apart.

The last few traitors on the terrace fled, firing as they ran. Another of Mathieu's men fell. His warriors followed, and Mathieu did nothing to stop them. They did the Emperor's work.

There was a further weapon in Mathieu's arsenal, and now it put in an appearance. The clouds parted around the drab-green hulls of Astra Militarum tank landers. Flights of Space Marine and Navis Astra strike craft dropped around them, their steep dives levelling out into strafing runs. Engines roared as the heavy transports set down on the summits all around the space port, their engine wash making the diseased gardens dance like the flags of a liberated people.

Colonel Odrameyer's regiment had come.

Mathieu grinned, his teeth white in a mask of blood.

'By the grace of His divine majesty, the God-Emperor of Terra, the void port of First Landing is ours!' He held up his weapons, and tilted his face to the heavens. Already, the air smelled a little sweeter.

'Praise the Emperor!' he roared. 'Praise the Emperor!'

CHAPTER ELEVEN

A HISTORITOR'S REQUEST

In the quieter hours, Marneus Calgar could almost imagine nothing was amiss. The defence laser batteries were silent while the Flotilla of Woe swung round the other side of the planet. There were no foes at the wall. If it were not for the smell of smoke, it could have been any day in Macragge's sadly infrequent periods of peace.

That high up in the Fortress of Hera, the smoke was thin, but it was persistent, and where the windows of the fortress monastery were open, the scent of fire was ever-present. If he went from his office, crossed the balcony to the balustrade and looked down, well, then there was no avoiding the fact that Magna Macragge Civitas was ablaze.

It was from there that he and Tigurius watched their city burn.

The conflagration had consumed all the grounds outside the ancient inner walls of the Murus Prisces. The city had spread since Guilliman's first life to cover over all the coastal plain, overcoming the great landing fields of the Heresy era and spreading out into the sea on artificial islands and flat strips of reclaimed land. Calgar had seen the maps; he had stood in this very spot with the primarch and heard him describe the way things had been when he was first alive. Not much of antiquity had survived the wars Macragge had seen. It seemed the same process of erasure was under way again.

Upon the Gulf of Lyceum, maritime habitats guttered like water lilies with fiery petals. Coastal arcology towers, their roots pushed deep into the seabed, were blackened, slumped skeletons of girders dipped into the water. The sea itself burned where promethium had spilled. There was the taint of rot on the air beneath the fires, hints of faecal matter and sickened bodies. Beyond the Murus Prisces a greater wall of fire climbed skyward, ever-dancing, angry red, eating at the heart of the Five Hundred Worlds. At night, it was reflected in the sky by the Great Rift.

'They will be here soon,' said Tigurius to Calgar.

'They will,' said Calgar.

He could see them out to sea: tankers, fishing vessels and cargo ships converted to troop carriers, bringing more of Mortarion's pestilential hordes to crash against the shore. As on the ocean, so in orbit, where the Flotilla of Woe crowded the void, an endless stream of plague hulks crammed with deluded mortals desperate to have their moment of violence. They had already overwhelmed the orbital networks. No matter how many ships the Ultramarines blasted from the heavens, there seemed to be more. Successful landfall was only possible far from Magna Macragge Civitas' formidable defences, and the hordes relocated to ocean ships for aquatic assault. They came in waves, regular, relentless and tiresomely predictable.

'You will not give the order to fire upon them? They are within the range of the slope guns now,' said Tigurius.

The two Space Marine lords stood side by side, looking out over the scene that was so neatly laid out before them it might have been a tactical hololith. The crowded plateau of the Fortress of Hera spread out from the mountainside to the great artificial cliffs of its walls. Beyond the rampart's plunge lay the inner civitas, then the outer ward and its burning buildings, and finally the sea.

'Not yet, Varro. Unless you recommend it.'

Tigurius sighed, and his eyes unfocused as he gazed into unknown futures.

'You are right to hold. Bombardment will make little difference as of yet. The hammer blow is yet to fall. This wave will not be the last. There is a greater danger ahead.'

'So we will open fire when they are closer. If there is to be an assault from another direction, I do not wish to have to hastily retarget.' Calgar spread the fingers of one of the Gauntlets of Ultramar across the marble rail. Blue ceramite rasped on stone. When fully open, the fingers of his gauntlets were big enough to cover the whole rail's width.

'We must be vigilant. Though the Librarius sense no impending daemonic infestation, and the warp is calm around Macragge, there are certain events in play.'

'Might we expect the Death Guard?' asked Calgar.

'No. These dregs are all Mortarion has to offer. His plans lie on Iax with our gene-father. There is another with designs here. He hides himself well, he knows I can sense him, so I remain ignorant of his nature or his plans. But be warned, something is coming. One of Mortarion's lieutenants, perhaps a daemon. Something with presence.'

'Will it come soon?'

Tigurius shook his head. 'I cannot see.'

'There we have it then,' said Calgar. 'A horde of misguided

mortals, no challenge for us at all. That is what Mortarion has for us, such is his contempt for our prowess. It offends me.'

'Do not place too much stock in his assessment of us. These dregs are meant to keep us from our gene-father's side. They have to be dealt with, so we stay to land the blow. It is an annoying strategy, but it is working,' said Tigurius. 'This is a tedious business. Mortarion has no chance of breaking the fortress.'

'If they are all that will come.'

'As I foresee, they will not be. That is why we must remain here. You and I cannot leave Macragge unguarded. If we rush to our father's side, it will fall. This I have seen. It is a certainty.'

Calgar made a soft noise in his throat. 'Even so, I am thankful there are so few of us on-world, and that the auxilia are sufficient to keep the dregs at bay. At least no more than a single battle company is tied down. It would be hard to justify sending others away, were they here. The question is, how much damage will the enemy do to the planet before they are destroyed, and what deeds that we might have performed elsewhere go undone?'

They watched blocks of troops moving neatly through the Civitas Vertus towards the inner walls. They marched along roads that bore the same names they had had in the primarch's day. Names were all that remained of his time. Within the inner walls, some semblance of normality reigned, save in those places where enemy munitions or energy beams had broken through the void shielding, and the graceful buildings had been thrown down, but as yet no fires burned inside the Murus Prisces.

'When we have the measure of them, we can wipe them out. I caution a little restraint, Marneus,' said Tigurius. 'The nature of the threat coming...' His eyes narrowed. 'There is something more, something beyond the fight here. A great peril to all. Something unexpected.'

'Until it reveals itself, restraint is my strategy. I am reinforcing the walls in case these vessels are not the only foes,' said Calgar. 'I trust your gifts, Varro, but I have five regiments of auxilia ready to move here from the interior if need be, and if the worst occurs, then we may call upon Tetrarch Balthus for reinforcement. The war is drawing to a close in the west, thanks to the aeldari. That is something.' Calgar rapped the stone with a mechanical knuckle. 'This is a poor situation. I cannot remain here much longer.' He shook his head slowly. 'Too many of us still fight at Vigilus. I should be there now.'

'This last decade has been difficult for you,' said Tigurius. 'I understand.'

'I think you are one of the few that do, Varro,' said Calgar. 'You have been wounded, and worn out, forced to sacrifice your brothers to speed me on through Nachmund. Both of us underwent the Rubicon. Our paths track each other.'

'And yet I think for you, it has been more difficult,' said the Chief Librarian. 'You have the burden of command of us all. You are the ruler of Macragge and of all Ultramar. There have been many changes. If I were in your position, it would be hard not to see the primarch's actions as criticisms. They are not.'

Marneus Calgar said nothing to that, but Tigurius read him accurately. He could not help but feel judged by their lord. In the years before Guilliman returned, Calgar had seen off tyranids, orks, the daemon M'Kar the Reborn, the Black Legion and the Iron Warriors. He had defeated every threat, until now. Each invasion had seen a little bit of Ultramar die, until this invasion of Mortarion's threatened to poison the whole realm.

The truth was he could not win the Plague Wars without Roboute Guilliman. If the primarch had not returned from the crusade, Ultramar would have died. The heart of it was dying now, and here he was fighting cultists and mutants, not daring to leave in case something befell the capital. The worst thing was, he knew it would make little difference to the war elsewhere if he did go. Guilliman cut across the stars like the Emperor's Sword, whereas Calgar's absence from the Battle for Macragge, the fourth such incident with the name in recent centuries, could prove disastrous.

Tigurius turned to look at him.

'Be at peace, brother. We both need to be here. This I know. This is our place.'

Calgar was not so sure, but hid his thoughts behind iron mental discipline. 'Days of primarchs warring,' he said, changing the subject. 'Does it not astound you?'

'It is as if legend lives again,' said Tigurius.

'Aye, but they are black times,' said Calgar. 'The end. Pagan tales of the death of suns.'

'You sound like the sons of Russ,' said Tigurius. 'There is hope yet. There are paths to salvation, though they are treacherous.' He went quiet again. Whatever Tigurius saw in the future troubled him. Calgar did not need to be a psyker himself to see that.

The ships approaching the coast neared. Their engines spewed black fumes from their smokestacks. Calgar activated his vox-beads.

'Slope gunnery, hear my order. Target and obliterate approaching plague fleet. Burn them all. Do not let their vitae poison our oceans.'

'*As you command, lord defender,*' the reply came. He hated that title, too close to that of his gene-father, as if he aped him, desperate for acceptance. As much as he thanked the Emperor daily for Guilliman's return, sometimes he felt suffocated by his presence in the world.

The wail of sirens rose all over the city, warning its inhabitants. The people of Macragge were disciplined, and could be counted on to look away. Not a single soul had lost their sight when the atomics flew.

The guns rolled out their god's tattoo. Shells whistled over-head. It took a surprisingly long time for them to hit their targets, but when they did, fission explosions obliterated the ships, one by one. The Space Marines' eyes and skin darkened immediately. Thus protected, Tigurius and Calgar watched the flotilla destroyed.

Nothing was left but fading mushroom clouds and columns of steam reaching up to support the sky. Calgar's sensorium registered a minor increase in radiation, but the shells were low yield; it would fade quickly, and the transient poisons of radioactivity were a small price to pay to rid themselves of Nurgle's diseases.

They were watching the bombardment tsunami hit the shore-ward districts and put out the flames when a knock sounded on Calgar's door.

'Enter!' he commanded.

The doors were wood, unpowered, ancient relics that were still not as old as their returned lord. They were opened by the two Victrix Guard that accompanied Calgar always. A member of the Praecental Guard, an elite unit of unmodified humans, stood in the door at attention.

'My lord,' he proclaimed. 'The Historitor Majoris Fabian Guelphrain and Sword Brother Racej Lucerne of the Black Templars Chapter petition you for an audience.'

'Guelphrain is still seeking entry to the Library of Ptolemy,' said Tigurius. 'I can feel his need to go within. Do not let him. There is some turbulence in the future around this desire. It will serve us all poorly if it is fulfilled, I am sure.'

'Do not fear, Varro,' said Marneus Calgar. 'At the primarch's order he is about to be disappointed again.'

The door to Marneus Calgar's private offices was shut silently by the Victrix Guard standing sentry. The hinges were well oiled.

The armour of the bodyguard was immaculate. The floor shone with polish. Everything on Macragge worked perfectly. The difference to the faded grandeur of Terra had astounded Fabian when he first arrived; now he found it extremely irritating. The whole realm was a glorious reminder of mankind's potential, but its efficiency meant there was no way round official obstacles. No little chinks to exploit. No men that might be paid to look the other way. When he was younger, he had dreamed of such a place as Macragge, where intention went hand in hand with action, and the lowliest Imperial servant was as upstanding as the highest.

That was before such rectitude had got in his way.

In short, when Marneus Calgar said no, he meant no, and he could not be circumvented.

'Throne damn it!' Fabian said, almost spitting. He stalked angrily from the doors through the anteroom, where various secretaries worked at high wooden desks. A couple looked up from their silent labours and frowned at his outburst. 'If he will not let me into the library, then why am I here?'

'I would remember where you are, if I were you,' said Lucerne.

He meant it kindly. Despite the stern reputation of the Black Templars, he was always in an equable mood. He strolled while Fabian strode in anger, and yet Fabian had to take four steps to match each one of his companion. Bent over, hands clasped behind his back, so hunched with annoyance he looked brittle, Fabian came up to the middle of Lucerne's black chestplate. So big was the difference in mass between the two, it looked like Lucerne could have comfortably stepped on Fabian and squashed him flat without noticing. They made an incongruous pair, but their body language was relaxed. Despite their differences, they were unmistakably friends.

'It is not Lord Calgar's doing, but the will of the primarch.

You should have patience. As I understand it, the lord primarch closed the library for largely symbolic purposes. I am sure he will let you within when he returns to Macragge.'

'Will he?' said Fabian, still angry. 'Did you see how Lord Tigurius looked at me?' He shuddered. 'He looks right through my soul.'

'He is one of the most powerful psykers in the Imperium,' said Lucerne.

They walked out of the inner office and into a long hall of scribes. From the level of organisation on display, it was clear Guilliman's hand was on everything, and it reminded Fabian of the Logisticarum, and the primarch's lack of patience with inefficiency, though on thinking that, Fabian remembered that Guilliman had established many of the original machineries of state that ran the Imperium, and what good had that done any of them?

'As soon as the regent gets back here, I'll be out of time. The crusade will be moving on, I doubt I will be staying here. I am one of the historitors majoris. With Viablo dead and Mudire and Solana on the other side of the galaxy, he'll want me with him when he crosses into Nihilus, I'm sure. I'm the only one to have been there before, he'll want me to continue my chronicle of what has occurred on the other side. Either that or we'll be packed off back to Vigilus, Emperor save me.'

'Probably,' said Lucerne amiably. He stood to one side as Fabian flung open a set of double doors. These too swung wide at the slightest touch, quiet as an infant's breath. 'It is a great hon–'

'My friend, I swear to you, if you tell me one more time that what I am doing is a great honour, I will grab the lip of your chestplate, haul myself up and punch you on the nose!'

'Fabian,' Lucerne admonished with mock offence. 'After all

the years I have known you, and you threaten me with violence? I am hurt.'

'I mean what, Emperor forfend,' Fabian went on, 'what if the enemy manages to break in here? What if they burn the library before I can examine it?'

'Now you are being melodramatic,' said Lucerne. He looked askance at the historitor and grinned. 'Besides, your choice of words there suggest that you wish to read the material. No enemy has taken this fortress, ever. It has been besieged, broken, breached and stormed. When the primarch awoke, the Black Legion were within the Temple of Correction. Are they here now? No. Did they burn the library? No. And nor did the tyranids, or the orks, the Word Bearers, Iron Warriors or any of the foes that have come against the Ultramarines and, I stress, been defeated.'

They were walking down the Great Stair now, out of the castella towards the plazas that made up the majority of the fortress. Ten Space Marines in differing colours, one from each of the Shield Chapters of Ultramar, stood at regular intervals down its length. They were so far apart each was a dot of colour to the others.

'I feel forgotten,' said Fabian. 'What we were doing meant something, the great aim of establishing history for all to see. I had a purpose. Not any more. All this war and fighting, and I am cast aside, ignored, when the primarch comes running home. I think he loses interest in the project. All the strife, the lives lost, for what? The Library of Ptolemy is one of the greatest repositories of human knowledge in all the Imperium. I have yearned to see it ever since I learned of it. Now I see the primarch for who he is. If what he commanded we historitors to do was that important, those doors would be open to us.'

'To you, you mean,' said Lucerne quietly.

Fabian didn't hear him. 'Instead, we're mired in endless struggles with the Inquisition and the Administratum on backward worlds where nothing but miserable collections of pamphlets can be found.'

'You're also opposed by the local authorities,' said Lucerne, 'and the Church.'

'Don't get me started on the Throne-cursed Ministorum!' snarled Fabian. 'I'd happily burn the lot down.'

'Come now, that's not worthy of you. You are being petulant, Fabian,' said Lucerne. They left the stair for another that led them to a small, heavily armoured postern. They waited as it cycled through its security checks.

'I feel petulant,' said the historitor. 'Every door I have opened has been forced wide by Guilliman's command, and yet he will not let me into his own bloody library. Why is that?'

'Perhaps he already knows what is in there, and wishes you to concentrate your efforts elsewhere?'

The door spirits chimed. It opened up, and let them into a corridor leading to an outer gate.

'Is that the best you can come up with, Racej? I thought the apotheosis of angels made you more intelligent than we mere men, not less.'

'It is a little feeble, I admit,' said Lucerne.

'This is outrageous,' said Fabian. 'I've never known Guilliman work like this before. Banning me! What has happened to him while I was away?'

'He is a busy man, and he did ban everyone, long before he established the historitors.'

'My behind. He just doesn't want me in his library. Do you know how long we've been in Ultramar? Months, and he won't see me. He didn't even summon me to see him when he was here.'

'You were the one who was too busy at your duties to attend his landing.'

'I don't recall being invited to that,' said Fabian.

'You are a historitor majoris. You could have gone. The truth is, you were sulking, and again you are taking this too personally. I said he is busy. The library will open eventually.'

'Will it now?' said Fabian. He slapped his palm against the glass locking plate of the outer door. It beeped and whirred, then ground open. Cold air blew in. The last light of afternoon was fading from the sky.

'You have to have faith,' said Lucerne.

'I leave that to you,' grumbled Fabian. 'I find mine a little lacking of late.'

'He values you, I know he does. Be of better cheer, Fabian.'

'Come on, Racej, think about it. He's hiding something. He created our organisation to uncover secrets. How many secret libraries and forbidden archives have we forced our way into, with bloodshed no less. These doors could simply part, but they won't. Why?'

'Fabian,' said Lucerne quietly. 'You are straying into dangerous territory.'

'Really?' said Fabian loudly, throwing up his arms. 'So you don't think that a man who has something of a track record for hypocrisy, from a certain point of view – with his non-Legions and his autocratic removal of High Lords who disagreed with him – might not preach long and hard about the truth, yet happily hide his own secrets?'

'I did not say that,' said Lucerne calmly. 'You are probably correct. He is a primarch. He will have secrets. That is what makes it dangerous.'

'Exactly. So, what possible thing could the returned primarch be concealing?'

'I would leave it there. We have good work to do elsewhere.'

'Lord Guilliman commissioned me to uncover secrets!' said Fabian. 'I'll not desist simply because some of those secrets are his.'

Booms rumbled high up in the mountains.

'They are firing. Again,' said Fabian, looking at the flashing clouds. 'It's only minutes ago that they stopped.' He scowled, and drew his cloak about him against the chill. 'It's so cold here. This damn world gives me a headache.'

'That is not artillery fire. It is thunder.' Lucerne looked up into the sky. 'It is about to rain. I would have thought that you would be able to tell the difference between war and the weather by now.'

Fabian turned around to face the giant Space Marine. 'How many times have you saved my life?'

Lucerne made a great show of thinking. 'Three, I believe, if we don't count that time on Gathalamor.'

'I wasn't going to fall in that hole! I was perfectly safe. You overreacted. You nearly broke my arm.'

'Then I have saved your life three times,' said Lucerne.

'Right.'

'Your point, my old friend?

'That saving my life...'

'Three times,' interrupted Lucerne.

'That saving my life three times doesn't give you any right to mock me,' said Fabian.

Thunder boomed again. A few fat drops of rain plinked off Lucerne's black armour.

'My, my, petulant doesn't cover it. I shall upgrade my assessment of your mood to sour.'

Fabian shivered, and suddenly his anger was spent. 'Yes. Yes, I am sour. Come on. Let's get ourselves to the Heran collection.

My catalogue is still not finished, and I've no desire to get soaked again. We might as well do something.'

They headed off across the great plazas of the fortress into the teeth of a downpour.

Getting wet did little to improve Fabian's mood.

CHAPTER TWELVE

DESCENT TO IAX

As Guilliman's diplomatic barque brought him down from the void, he had a large hololith of Iax projected into the transit lounge. As its name suggested, the barque was appointed for peaceful interaction, and so he watched the appalling damage to the garden world unfold over a deep carpet and fine, wooden fittings. As he took in what had been done to this jewel of his kingdom, his face set harder than marble, until he resembled completely the many statues that depicted him. Felix and the other aides attending knew this well as a sign of all-consuming fury.

Felix understood his gene-father's rage. He had felt similarly on visiting the worlds of the Eastern Tetra, and seeing the damage xenos had inflicted. What the Death Guard had done to Iax was worse.

The planet endured a living death. From the distant years of Felix's childhood right to the present day, Iax had had a reputation as one of Ultramar's most beautiful worlds, and it had only become more precious since its chief rival, Prandium, had been rendered barren by Hive Fleet Behemoth. Iax had stood for so long as an example of humanity's best, a world where mankind and nature lived in harmony. It was no bauble, no cultivated indulgence, but a productive world in its own right, an example to Ultramar and the Imperium beyond.

Mortarion had rotted it through and through.

Clouds blanketed both hemispheres in a drab, cirrhotic yellow. Iax had been known for its crystal skies, so this seemed a particular insult. Where the clouds broke, abused landscapes showed: seas choked with overgrowths of algae, forests decayed, marshlands spilling from their limits and gone to stagnant blackness, and its many waterways flowing with colourful pollutants and dammed by dead vegetation, so they overtopped their banks and spread illness over the land.

Iax's biomes had been sculpted by human hands. There were no true wilderness areas upon it, but every inch was gardened so skilfully it was said even the aeldari admired the work. From the least ecological niche the most was coaxed. Crops grew among ancient trees. Livestock lived alongside native beasts. Seas teemed with life that was exactingly husbanded, so that were mankind to depart, rather than being richer, Iax would have been poorer in life and diversity. Now everything was spoiled. Felix imagined seashores piled with skeletons, and woods where dying trees leaned upon the dead for support.

Atmosphere went from attenuated to resistant. The ship shook with friction and compression burn. The view below was obscured for a moment by bright fire, but the approach brought with it the sense of illness, as if the occupants neared the hospices of mercy where the aged went for peaceful death, and found there only indignity.

The ship braked. Sulphur-brown clouds streamed past the

viewports. As a ship descended into a gravity well, one expected increasing violence, but the atmosphere was lethargic, and Guilliman's shuttle passed through something more akin to a dead, plastek-clogged sea than air.

They pierced the lower cloud layer, and finally saw their destination coming up to greet them. Hundreds of horns of hard limestone upthrust from the land. First Landing occupied the largest; the others ran away from the city in lines of crocodilian teeth. Miles away, linked by tree-lined highways, the modest void port occupied multiple spires planed down to take landing grounds. The rest were less touched, those far out seemingly natural, though gun emplacements topped many, and on those nearest to the city were suburbs where large mansions occupied sharp-cut terraces. Throughout, garden and forest predominated. A hint of beauty lingered beneath the dying trees, and in the arrangements of the gardens now jaundiced with disease.

Whereas the other teeth were paragons of the horticulturalists' art, First Landing was the opus of sculptors, the stone pierced and carved through, as complex as a scrimshawed tusk. Giant walls girt it. A huge barbican protected its only gate, which opened up onto a wide plain crossed by a multi-lane highway. Between the grand hab-terraces and the three-tiered city walls there were more gardens. All were dead and what must normally have been a floral display was reduced to a sludgy hue.

Fires burned in the void port. A half-hearted exchange of fire was going on between the city walls and landing mounds.

A palace of rare splendour occupied the summit of First Landing, though this too made room for orbital defence batteries carefully hidden amid its architecture. They passed over, circled about. Felix looked into deep streets cut cleverly into the rock, and saw the inhabitants moving. But they, their draught beasts and even their cybernetic drones seemed torpid: not yet sick, but sickening.

Energy barriers along the walls registered in Felix's auto-senses, but the city had no void shields, which he did not regret, for the touch of the warp on his soul would have been nigh unbearable in that diseased place. The ship slowed further, coming to a halt over a small landing pad within the palace precincts. It turned a quarter, achieved the best fit, and set down. Engines fired and died. The ship gave a last shake. Chimes announced their arrival. Only then did Guilliman speak.

'Come,' he said. 'We will disembark immediately, and bring comfort to these people. This planet suffers by my brother's hand. I will make what amends I can.'

He said no more, but took his helmet under his arm and walked out of the stateroom, down the ramp and onto the languishing world of Iax.

Shadows from the highest minarets lay across the barque. The air was heavy and hazed, as if with pollen. Felix's helm gave a warning chime and his retinal displays alerted him to high concentrations of toxins, non-native fungal spores and viral fragments. The rest was smoke particulates.

Guilliman had gone down the ramp first, accompanied by four Victrix Guard, led by Sicarius. Felix followed after, Sergeant Cominus at his back. A number of other dignitaries and high officials from Fleet Primus accompanied them, most notably Fesrain Odos, Adiutor Principe to Isaiah Khestrin, and Maldovar Colquan, Stratarchis Tribune Actuarius, with a squad of his Adeptus Custodes. Felix was uneasy in their presence. He imagined what would occur should they learn of the interrogation of the daemonhost.

Nothing good, he thought. The images as he remembered the event were unusually vivid in his mind. He put them to down to contamination of his psyche, so ignored them as best he could.

There appeared to have been a breakdown in the normal

social order. The gardens around the palace were crammed with every manner of people, on cots under canvas shades. Despite the gulfs in station between them, they were all diseased. A line of Iaxian Ultramarian Auxilia held back those that could walk, and who had gathered to see the regent, with shock poles, clearing a path from the ship to the palace entrance, but still the crowd's hands reached through the gaps. They were desperate, risking a jolt of pain to call for Guilliman's miraculous touch.

Guilliman stopped in the centre of the path.

'Hear me!' he said, and his commanding voice quieted the crowd. 'I have no power as you think to drive your ailments from you. But I am here to help. We will remove Mortarion from this world, and return it to its former beauty. You have my word on that.'

Having spoken, he moved on, and their moaning pleas rose again. They smelled of sickness. Some were close to the end, dragging themselves from their deathbeds in the last hope of a cure. Felix was forced to harden his heart. He had seen faces like these on every planet in the star realm. Whether diseased, or starved, or mad with grief. He could not save them all. He could not save even a few of them.

'My lord, please! A blessing, a blessing!' a man cried at the tetrarch, but he marched onward, his eyes forward.

The shouts continued as Guilliman was greeted at the palace gates. Planetary Governor Costalis had come out himself for the meeting, though he too had a fever's pallor, and an aide waited discreetly near the back with a wheelchair.

'My lord,' he said, and struggled down to one knee. 'The honour I have in seeing you transcends the capabilities of human speech to convey. I can only give my humblest apologies...' His soliloquy broke into a rasping cough. He gasped in air. 'My humblest apologies for the poor state in which you find this most beautiful of all your worlds.'

'Governor Costalis, please, rise,' said Guilliman. When the man struggled to get to his feet, Guilliman himself bent to help him up. He looked into the man's watery eyes. 'By Terra, man, you should be with the medicae. Is that your chair? You, come forward.'

Costalis gave a weary smile. 'By that measure, we all should,' he said. 'Iax is a sick world.'

'Then I insist you at least rest before we take counsel. There is a battle to be finished in the heavens, and landings to be undertaken.' Guilliman put him firmly in the wheelchair.

Costalis nodded. 'Then please, follow me, I shall show you to the command suite for the auxilia here. It is yours, everything here is yours. I hope you will find my stewardship satisfactory.'

'It is a long time since I came to Iax,' said Guilliman. 'Even steeped in misery, it holds its beauty. Fear not, Costalis, this shall pass, as all sicknesses do.'

Costalis nodded miserably. 'I pray to your father nightly it is so.' He coughed again. A man in the uniform of the medicae dabbed at his mouth. His handkerchief came away red. Costalis sagged. 'My seneschal... My seneschal shall show you the way. I apologise once...'

'There is no need,' said Guilliman. 'Back to your sickbed. The Emperor commands it.' Uniformed men came forward, and asked the party to follow them. Costalis was wheeled away.

'He's a dead man,' said Colquan quietly to Felix. 'He has seen the last of his days.'

Felix could not disagree. Costalis' head was slumped on his chest, his strength used up.

'Emperor aid us all,' Felix murmured.

They were taken through corridors and staircases whose walls were carved with fretwork intended to let through the pleasant climes of Iax, but now admitting noxious smog and foetid winds. The smell of the planet's ailing was slight, but pervasive, and insidious, until after a short while it became unbearable, and Felix sealed his helmet against it. They looked out through hazy air, past the city, onto agricolae where crops stained with blights drooped into the dirt.

Presently, they passed a long set of windows looking down upon a large market square. A crowd gathered in an open area surrounded by boarded-up stalls. From there came a familiar voice raised high in prayer. The murmured responses of the crowd followed every phrase. It was a new prayer, one that praised Guilliman, and not only the Emperor.

'I know that voice,' said Guilliman. He stopped. Their guides looked up at him in puzzlement. Only one, a man with the rank insignia of an auxilia general, dared address the primarch. Although the primarch was looking out over the square, the general kept his eyeline above Guilliman's head when he addressed him, frightened he might capture his gaze.

'It is your militant-apostolic, my lord. We assumed you had ordered him to drive out the traitors in our void port. He landed half a day before you did. When he came into the city, he asked for the largest place of gathering. We showed him to the market square and he began to preach. The people are enraptured.' The man approved.

'I can see,' said Guilliman neutrally.

'We thank you for sending him. It is good to be reminded that the Emperor is with us in these dark times.'

'It is,' said Guilliman, and his words sounded dangerous. He caught the man's eyes deliberately. A shudder passed down the officer's spine at the contact, but he held, and looked back. 'What is your name?'

'General Tawik Ilios, my lord,' he said.

'And what is your role here?'

'I am general of the city defence regiment,' he said. 'It is my honour to be asked to escort you.'

Guilliman looked down at Frater Mathieu.

'Adiutor Odos, go to the command suite and establish contact with Khestrin. Have our staff begin preparations for assumption of command. Contact my equerry, Marius, and have him come down from the *Macragge's Honour*, along with divisio three of Primus' command staff. Colquan, send some of your Custodians with him. Make sure he is safe.'

'We are within friendly territory,' Ilios said.

'Nowhere is friendly territory any more,' said Guilliman. 'Colquan, Odos, about it.'

'As you command, regent,' said Colquan. He split a pair of Custodians from his squad.

'Yes, my lord,' Odos said and moved to obey, the golden giants following him.

'I can help them, if you wish,' said Felix.

'You are not my equerry any longer, Felix, leave Odos to his work,' said Guilliman. 'You will accompany me and the tribune to the market square. I wish to hear what Mathieu has to say. You should hear it too.'

CHAPTER THIRTEEN

A PRAYER FOR THE PRIMARCH

Ilios had his men clear the way down a covered stair to the market square, so Guilliman would not be seen. When he went down, he remained concealed from the crowd under the stair's exit. Colquan and Felix flanked him. The Victrix Guard spread out, Sicarius alert as ever for threats to his lord. In any case, it appeared to Felix that Guilliman would have had to step into the square's middle and announce himself, the crowd were so enraptured.

'What now?' Felix asked.

'We listen,' said Guilliman.

The party could not see Mathieu from where they stood, but they saw the faces of the crowd listening to him, their eyes alight with devotion and hope.

'…for is it not true that the Emperor came to the human race, and saved us from the tyranny of the xenos and the warlord?' Mathieu said. 'Did He not set out upon His Great Crusade and drive back the persecutors of mankind, and when challenged by the heresy of the Arch-Devil Horus did He not cast him down, and send him along with his eight fiends into the fiery pits of damnation? Even mortally injured, did He not take upon Himself the burdens of humanity's suffering, and ascend to the Golden Throne, where He bears the ills of this universe for us, and watches us, and keeps alight the great beacon that binds together His domains? Do His armies not strive tirelessly to ensure all the children of Terra can live and die in His light? Does He not protect us from the triple horror of the xenos, the mutant and the witch?'

'Yes! Yes!' said a voice in the crowd. 'He does!' said another, and 'He is our master!' These protestations of faith were mingled with the sounds of weeping, and coughing, and other signs of sickness, but neither hunger nor disease could dampen the crowd's fervour. Felix could almost feel it, coalescing over them into something solid.

'These are the truths of the faith,' Mathieu went on. 'They have always been so. For ten thousand years the Emperor has watched over us, and protected us.'

'The Emperor protects!' This shout came from several quarters.

'Yes, my brothers and sisters, the Emperor protects. He protects us because it is His will that humanity survives. Now He sends His last son back to us! What more proof do we need? And yet, not all believe! There are disaffected people in this Imperium of ours.'

Bitter laughter at that.

'Yes, yes, I know!' said Mathieu, sharing the crowd's irony. 'They say we are doomed, that these are the end times. They say that we have failed. That the Emperor has failed. This is blasphemy.'

'Burn them!' shouted someone, to a chorus of 'Yes!' and 'Bring them to the fire!'

'No, my brothers, and my sisters. We must be merciful. It has been a long time since the Emperor walked among us. Is it any surprise that doubt has worked its way into men's hearts? Best convince them. Be the bearers of good news, for there is a new truth.' He paused dramatically. 'The days of the Emperor's silence are coming to an end. The Emperor is at work among us, yes, even now!'

Now the crowd let out murmurs of disbelief, and of hope. Several calls of 'Praise be!' set off a ripple of the same.

'Praise be!'

'A new Great Crusade cleanses the stars, led by Guilliman, His only living son, returned to us by the Emperor's will and the Emperor's mercy. Think you that the Emperor has been idle all this time upon His Throne? I tell you all, He has not! He has a plan. He has a plan for you, and you, and you!'

Felix imagined him pointing at members of the crowd. A child shouted.

'Yes, even you, little one, especially you,' Mathieu said joyously.

Laughter passed through the crowd. Felix marvelled. Mathieu had performed an orbital combat drop, fought a battle, made his way across this dying land and was now delivering a sermon. Whatever faults his faith had, it made him strong.

'Through us, He works His will I have seen this with my own eyes. Through Guilliman, His holy son, He sets His plan in motion.'

Colquan took an abrupt step forward. 'This has gone on long enough.'

Guilliman put a hand on the Custodian's pauldron. 'Let him speak.'

'Can you hear what he is saying?'

'I can, and I wish to hear the rest. It is no more and no worse than what a hundred thousand preachers are saying at this very moment all across the Imperium. I shall rebut his opinion when he is done.'

'You plot a dangerous course, my lord,' said Colquan, but stepped back. 'He does not heed the warning you gave him. You must act.'

'I will not, and I cannot. So we will let him finish.'

Felix sent Colquan a request for private conversation.

'What has occurred between them?'

'You remember the day Guilliman spoke with Mathieu, after the Battle of Hecatone?'

'I do. I was set to watch outside. I remember he left the room in a towering rage. Not long after, I went to the east. He never told me what happened.'

'The primarch had a conversation with the good frater,' said Colquan. 'I will not betray Lord Guilliman's confidence, but I shall say that he was warned, and that he does not appear to have heeded that warning. They have not spoken since. Mathieu has gathered a horde of like-minded fanatics to himself, including the Cadian Four Thousand and Twenty-First Armoured Regiment. These are awkward developments. Mathieu all but preaches Guilliman's divinity, and Guilliman can do nothing to stop it. It is ironic, but his dilemma has deepened my trust of the primarch.'

'You do not trust him?' said Felix.

'Felix, I know you are not a naive man. My disapproval of seeing a primarch at the head of a crusade is known, and I have done nothing to hide it, though I serve him as well as I can. But lately, I find my attitude shifting. He believes in what he is doing, and if he finds himself on the path to the Throne, it will not be willingly taken. His belief in the old truths is unshakeable.'

'The light and the glory shines on us all!' Mathieu was saying now. 'There are more besides myself, those who have looked directly on the light of the Emperor, those who no longer need faith in Him, because we have *knowledge* of Him. They march with me now, on the Emperor's holy war. We do what we can, because for all the might and power the Emperor has granted the Lord Imperial Regent, he is only one man, and he cannot win all the Emperor's wars by himself! It is time, my brothers and sisters, to rise up, and seek service to Him, and to His holy son. Who even now, watches over you. Witness him, as I have witnessed His father!'

Mathieu had evidently pointed, for the crowd turned as one to look up the shadowed stair.

'Expected,' said Guilliman, and went to the bottom and into the view of the crowd, who when they saw him murmured, and began to cry out to him. Ilios' auxiliaries followed him, wary guns kept on the people.

'The primarch! The Ultramarines! The Emperor's guardians! We are saved!'

The shouting stopped suddenly, without warning. There was rustling, and a profound silence. Once again moving as one, the people in the crowd knelt, and prostrated themselves to their saviour.

There was a makeshift stage at the front of the market square where Mathieu stood, three large tuns roped together raising him well over the level of the crowd. Three Ecclesiarchy crusaders stood around it, guarding their prophet.

Guilliman swept his gaze over the people of First Landing. His face was stern, but he did not appear judgemental.

'Rise,' he commanded. The crowd did not move, but knelt with their foreheads pressed to the ground, mumbling prayers. 'Rise,' he said again, and picked his way through them. His boots were as big as men's backs, and he took great care not to crush the people there, who saw him approach and shuffled out of the way, still kneeling, still praying, with little sobs of terror.

'Give me your loyalty,' Guilliman said. 'Give me your service. Fight for the Imperium, for the Emperor, and for me.' He moved towards Mathieu. 'Give me your lives, your blood, your deaths. Give me everything, as I give everything, to protect Ultramar, and the Imperium. I will ask this of you and more.'

Felix saw him weighing his words, the endless struggle. The Adeptus Ministorum had proclaimed him divine, and he hated that. In the wrong mood, it would raise wrathful denial, but as he looked about the crowd, his gaze softened. These people were desperate. They needed him to be more than a man, more than a primarch. They needed the son of their God-Emperor, and Guilliman could not shatter their morale.

'But I will never ask for your worship,' he said softly. 'Look upon me, and you shall see that I am no god. Now rise! Rise, and be about your lives. I wish to speak with my militant-apostolic.'

Guilliman's commands allowed no disobedience. The crowd dazedly got to their feet. Most drifted away, and the market hissed to a hundred whispered conversations. There were many hopeful looks, and the need to speak with him, but the few that dared approach Guilliman were discouraged by Ilios' auxilia and the Victrix Guard.

'Seal the square,' Guilliman commanded.

'At once,' Ilios said.

The primarch neared Mathieu. Even with the extra height the barrels lent him, Mathieu was still shorter than Guilliman, so he looked like a child trying to match eyes with an ogryn.

Felix had not seen Mathieu for months. His robes were as worn and patched as before, if not more so, if such a thing were possible: the frater made a point of poverty. But his face had changed. Always zealous, he seemed now full of even greater purpose. It was no wonder people followed this man.

His resolve was not entirely his own. He borrowed authority

freely from the primarch, and when they met he looked upon Guilliman with open adoration. His expression concerned Felix greatly.

The crusaders guarding Mathieu presented their shields and swords to the primarch, giving Felix the insane impression they were saluting him before they attacked, and he felt his fingers twitch inside his gauntlet, but instead they wheeled smartly about on their heels, and stepped back, allowing the primarch to come close to his priest.

'My lord primarch,' Mathieu said, and bowed his head.

'Militant-apostolic,' said Guilliman. He glanced at the silent crusaders. 'You have new warriors to guard you.'

'They came to me one night unbidden. They are a gift from the Emperor,' said Mathieu.

'I recall they used to serve Geestan,' said Guilliman. Mathieu was not intimidated.

'I understand. You think I am being overly dramatic, but the men of the Crimson Cardinals only serve those they deem to be worthy,' countered Mathieu. 'I did not call them, they sought me out.'

Felix wondered what worth a dry old fossil like Geestan showed.

'Is this true?' Guilliman asked the crusaders. They were as statues, and did not respond.

'They have taken a vow of silence, my lord,' explained Mathieu. 'They will not speak unless the Emperor Himself commands.'

'I saw also a congregational battle train within the barbican. This too was Geestan's. You once spurned the trappings of your office, now you use them. What has changed?'

'Nothing has changed, my lord Guilliman,' Mathieu replied. 'As you say, Militant-Apostolic Geestan had many resources. The Emperor whispered in my ear, and told me to reject such an armoury on the grounds of principle was a foolish thing. Such weapons should not be left unused.'

'You have been busy, then.'

'The Adeptus Ministorum wages its war at your side, my lord. The Emperor has much work for me. I cannot hold back. You do not wish me to serve you directly, I must respect that,' he said, as if Guilliman were a young man asserting his first authority. 'But later the Emperor showed Himself at the Battle of Hecatone, and the faithful have been coming to me in greater numbers by the day. They need guidance.'

'So you now have an army.'

'I have a crusade, my lord! The Crusade of the Witnesses. Each one of these people has been touched by the Emperor's hand. Some of them have seen Him.'

'Impossible,' said Guilliman.

'No, my lord, it is the truth!' said Mathieu, and he stepped forward, a feverish light in his eyes. 'He is abroad. He is at work among us. Mankind is awakening to His glory. The foe thought to cripple His empire by opening reality to the warp, and now they reap His wrath. They call Him a corpse. They call Him carrion. But He lives and He is all around us. He moves, Lord Guilliman. Oh, He moves!'

Guilliman stared at him. Mathieu held his gaze, a look of rapture on his face.

'You have never seen or spoken to the Emperor,' said Guilliman. 'Only I have.'

'You told me this before, but there you are wrong, my lord. I converse with Him every day. I have seen His manifestations with my own eyes. Who do you think sent me to you? Who guarded me when the *Macragge's Honour* was captured, who guided you to choose me as your militant-apostolic? It was Him, it was your father. He told me I must open your eyes, and they are opening, I know.'

'Enough,' said Guilliman. 'You speak of things you know nothing of.'

'Do I? Am I deluded, or are you, clinging to your worldview when all the evidence points to the contrary?'

'You are a fanatic,' said Colquan.

Mathieu looked at the warrior. 'Am I? Your own kind say that something has changed. They say that the Emperor speaks to you again in dreams and in visions, after so long. How does it feel, when He touches your mind?'

'I repeat the lord regent's words. How can you know that?'

'Because the Emperor told me!' hissed Mathieu.

'We should kill him, lord regent,' said Colquan. 'He had his warning. He has gone too far. He has suborned an entire regiment to his cause. How far must this madness spread?'

'Will you shoot down your own people? Do you think the warriors and population of this world will rejoice to see men and women who wish only to fight at the Emperor's side cut down?' Mathieu said to Guilliman. 'You are His son. You would stop His servants doing His bidding by slaughtering them. How many more tongues do you wish to wag, and to say that the son would usurp the father?'

'Do not threaten me, militant-apostolic,' said the primarch.

'I am trying to help you, my lord,' said Mathieu, reaching out frustrated hands. 'When will you see that your father is god? When will you see that He is at work through me, through you, through everyone. The Emperor is with us. He stands at our right hand. You are His son. Accept your father's true nature into your heart. Acknowledge your own divinity, your power, and all your enemies will be as dust before you. You are a god, my lord, a living avatar of the one who sits upon the Golden Throne!'

'I warned you not to preach this.'

'I gave my word and I have not, even though it is the Adeptus Ministorum's official creed.'

'So you are also a hypocrite,' said Colquan.

'I am not. I cannot serve if I am dead,' said Mathieu. 'What use would I be then? I do not preach what you forbade me to preach.'

'Then why speak of it now, to me?' asked Guilliman.

'Because you and I must be honest with each other, if you are ever to be honest with yourself.'

Mathieu and Guilliman's gazes remained locked for half a minute, the mendicant priest, smirched with the dirt of poor living, his teeth blackening, his hair thinning, and the living son of the Emperor, tall, regal and inhuman. An angel and a pauper. To Felix's immense surprise, it was Lord Guilliman who looked away first.

'I have heard enough. Goodbye, militant-apostolic.'

'We will pray for you!' called Mathieu after Guilliman as he left the square. 'We will pray for you to see the light!'

'My lord,' Felix voxed him on a private channel. 'I fear Lord Colquan is correct. Something must be done about him.'

'Colquan is correct, you are correct, but unfortunately Frater Mathieu is also correct,' said Guilliman, and his voice was cold. 'That was no hollow threat he made.'

CHAPTER FOURTEEN

ATTACK ON HERA

The rains did not let up.

For day after day they washed the stones of the Fortress of Hera. Clean at first, iron-grey and cold like Macragge's seas, they became steadily more polluted. It was a gradual process, barely noticeable at first. A strange smell, a certain oiliness to the puddles sometimes, grit in them, or the odd wriggling larva that quickly expired, rare enough to be discounted. Some days these phenomena would not manifest, and the rains would run clean again, but each time the filth returned it did so a little stronger, and its effects persisted a little longer, until the sky wept poisoned slime and clean, cold water was a memory.

Fabian lay in his bed, awake. He had not slept for weeks. Although he'd become somewhat inured to the sounds of war over the last decade, and had slumbered soundly in trench systems under bombardment, and snored his way through void wars, these were the exceptions rather than the rule, times when exhaustion threatened to kill him before the enemy did. Fabian remained nervous at heart, and the conditions of siege exacerbated this tendency.

There was the endless waiting for something exceptionally bad to happen. Fabian would have preferred battle. That was over and done in moments, one way or another. One was either dead, or one was not. A siege was a limbo. He could deal with the terror and the bloodshed of a fight. He could not deal with waiting for it.

Then there was the unpredictability. The seemingly random times the great cannons of Hera's walls opened up, or the enemy would assay another of their doomed attempts to break the walls and the guns would bark and bark all night like packs of ravenous canids. Suddenly, it would be silent, nothing but the rain, but he would not sleep, for his ears would be straining to hear the sounds of doom coming for him.

Calgar grudgingly explained the situation to him. The enemy were feeble, and the Ultramarines could easily sally out, even with the low numbers they had present on Macragge, and wipe them away like dirt from the front screen of a groundcar. But the next day they would be back, and the process must be repeated, and maybe one or two of Calgar's men would fall. Not many, but if the same happened the next day, and the next day, then eventually there would be no one left, and they would lose by default. The same was true in the void. Every enemy ship downed was replaced. The Ultramarines could get out of their cities or off the planet, but they could not stay outside their defences long without being overwhelmed, while the enemy's troops were numerous but of too poor a quality to break any wall.

So the Space Marines sat in their fortresses and the enemy sat outside them, and they both waited to see how the war would turn out elsewhere.

It was torture. It was telling on Calgar too; Fabian had spent enough time with him on the far side of the Rift to know the signs. He and Calgar did not get on, which struck Fabian as a great pity, because he and Guilliman, he thought, had a good relationship. He could not even blame their mutual dislike on a recalcitrance at being watched. Calgar understood Fabian's mission all right, and had at first applauded it. What put them at odds was Fabian's personality. Calgar just didn't like him: he found him impatient, prone to complaint, too quick to anger, and despite the stoic, Macraggian demeanour they all affected here, the Chapter Master had come close to telling Fabian that to his face.

Or at least, that's how it felt to Fabian, late at night, lying in a bed that was too hard and too soft, too hot and too cold, his pillow wrapped around his head to shut out the endless, maddening rattle of water on the windows. Fabian could not get comfortable. He could not rest and he was too jittery to concentrate. Every crack of thunder made him think battle was about to start again. Every positive thought he had was fleeting, and at best damage control for his blacker ideas, which circled around and around his head.

Fabian groaned.

'I hate this planet,' he moaned. 'Even Vigilus was better.' He rolled over, found the position just as uncomfortable, then rolled over back to where he had been. That did not suit him either.

'Confound it!' he said, and threw his pillow aside. He sat on the edge of his bed, ground the heels of his hands into his eyes, then stood up with unnecessary force. 'Right,' he said. 'Work it is,' and he strode for the desk waiting for him on the other side of the room. The first thing he did was pick up the ewer of wine standing there, always full.

Fabian had to concede that the Ultramarines treated him well. His quarters were of a size and an opulence that the old him could not have imagined, albeit furnished in the severe Macraggian style. Soft fur rugs covered the stone floor. The furniture was beautifully crafted. But it was all like the wine of Macragge: well made, but sharp, and cold; like the planet, like the Ultramarines.

He poured and drank the wine nonetheless. He had yet to activate the lumens. Light from the fortress wall lamps shone through the rain coursing down the tall windows. Lightning flashed, revealing statues, colonnades and pinnacles otherwise hiding in the dark, and temporarily dazzled him.

He grumbled, opened his escritoire, pulled out his chair, ignited the lumen, sat down, put the wine carefully onto a round of stone to save the wood, and took out his latest notebook.

He found it hard to concentrate on his notes. It was dull stuff. The histories of Macragge and its surrounding worlds were recorded in meticulous, dry detail in the Chapter archives. His cramped hand condensed it down to a broad outline he thought to work into a tract if he ever got the time.

He would never get the time.

He snapped the book shut, and chided himself, and told himself it would be interesting if he did not know that only a few hundred yards from where he sat was a sealed library full of all manner of wonders. He imagined truly ancient works lurked in the Library of Ptolemy. Codexes from the Dark Age of Technology. The history of the settlement of this region of space. The writings of extinct alien species. The role of the Ultramarines in the Great Heresy War. Tantalising hints to what had befallen mankind's first stellar domain – another mind-blowing revelation, that the Imperium was not the first human empire to rise, a history so secret men had been killed for knowing it, all assimilated and mulled over by Fabian until it had become mundane.

Fabian knew so much that so few did, and yet there was always more to know. Human history was long and built of secrets.

'And the Library of Ptolemy is full of them,' he moaned.

The night rumbled. He listened attentively, assuring himself it was only thunder and not the guns beginning again. Greenish lightning flickered through the clouds, lighting up their roiling undersides. Rodded rain fell, as solid as a cloud of javelins. The grim countenances of Space Marine heroes of ancient days flashed bright, then fell back into darkness.

Thunder crackled again, fitful, angry, prowling across the heavens, a beast about to strike.

A little nervously, Fabian swigged sour wine and returned to his notes. He was engrossed awhile.

Tap tap tap. A noise at the window. *Tap tap tap.*

Fabian's neck hair prickled against his nightshirt, and he turned very slowly to face the source of the noise. All he saw was his own white, frightened face reflected back at him in the black glass.

Tap tap tap.

With shaking hands he reached for a candelabra, and touched the rune that lit the sticks. Flame burst from the wicks. He approached the window, haunted by his own reflection, face gaunt with lack of sleep, eyes hollow. Flickering lights danced in his eyes. He peered out into the night, but could see nothing

Tap tap tap.

The noise was coming from the base of the window. He bent low, searching for the source. Still all he saw was his own face and the glow of the candle flames in the glass. There were many lights on the walls, and where their beams fell the decorations of the fortress were visible. But Fabian's room was in a triangle of shadow, all the darker for being contrasted with the light.

He searched along the window bottom. His fingers touched cold glass.

Tap tap tap.

A flash of lightning blasted back the dark, and Fabian found himself face to face with a small, round creature peering in through the bottom pane. It had a wide spread of horns, and a broad, grinning mouth full of dirty teeth. It was only the size of a human infant, though so corpulent it probably weighed thrice as much. Having caught his attention it lifted a skinny arm and waved at him.

Fabian fell back, dropping his candelabra.

It was a plague imp. He'd seen them before, but not that close. Only a single thickness of glass separated him from a package of diseases that would kill him a thousand times over.

'Daemons. Daemons in the fortress.' He scrambled up to his feet. The little thing pushed its fat face against the glass, smearing it with unspeakable filth. He got a better look at it. It wore a hood. In its right hand it carried a short wooden staff with three branches curled into hoops. Its left arm carried a crop of subsidiary tentacles, and a second, gaping mouth. A third grinned in its belly.

It watched him with interest. It tapped on the window again. The primary face grinned, spilling maggots down its front.

Fabian kept his eyes on it, and scrambled back, his hand searching for the vox-bracelet resting on the table with his effects. He found it, held it up to his mouth, and depressed the alarm rune that should bring his escort running.

'Racej, we have a major problem.' He only half expected a reply, and was not surprised when none came. Often, manifestations of this sort were accompanied by all manner of disruption to the workings of things. Machine-spirits liked the supernatural as much as men's souls, and recoiled from it.

He considered what to do. Should he run for help? Racej Lucerne's quarters were a hundred yards down the hall. There was nobody else nearby in that part of the Chapter monastery. The Fortress of Hera was huge, and the Ultramarines, even at full Chapter strength, could not fill it. He might be lucky, and stumble across one of their Praecental Guard, auxilia or other mortal servants on patrol, but they too were spread thinly. He risked losing the creature if he took his eyes off it, then it might slip away and do any amount of damage.

They were not defenceless. The failure of vox would be logged. The reason detected. The alarm would be raised. How long would that take though? That was the question.

'Emperor,' Fabian said. The imp was still watching him curiously, as if he were a specimen in a xenological garden. Now he knew where it was, he could make out its position by the glimmer of malevolent eyes. They blinked, and it disappeared a moment, then returned.

'Don't move,' he said, to himself more than to it. 'Just wait there.'

He grabbed his clothes, pulling his trousers on, and his boots. He left his underwear and his socks off, tucked his nightshirt into his trousers, pulled on his braces, and buckled his boots up.

'Stay there, stay there,' Fabian said. 'Just stay there, Throne damn you!'

The little imp showed no signs of going anywhere, but cocked its neckless head and watched.

Fabian slowed now, for he was reaching for his weapons belt slung over the back of a chair, and did not wish to startle his visitor. His laspistol hung from the belt in its holster. His sheathed power sword rested horizontally on a wooden frame nearby.

He pulled his belt tight, slowly drew his pistol, and pointed it at the tiny daemon.

'Got you, my friend,' he said.

If anyone had suggested to Fabian back in his Administratum

days that he would become a good shot, he would have laughed in their faces at the idea of him even touching a gun. But he was a good shot. Heated air cracked and a flash of coherent blue light punched a neat round hole in the glass.

He blinked after-images away to see the edges of the glass were a cooling orange. A curl of smoke rose from the hole. The little nurgling looked down at its belly, where a corresponding wound was already squirming shut. It pouted at him disappointedly, shook its head, then skipped off into the dark. Fabian raced to the window and pressed his face against it, trying to see around the corner. A flash of lightning illuminated the imp bounding through the puddles away from Fabian's room, onto the wider plaza.

'Shit!' he said. It would take him two minutes at least to make the nearest exit. Two minutes too long.

'Racej!' he shouted as he went for his power sword, drew the ornate weapon, and threw the scabbard aside. 'Racej!' He thumbed on the generator switch. Miniature skeins of lightning crackled over the blade. His reflected face lit blue in the window. 'Calgar is not going to be happy about this,' he said, and ran at the window.

His sword bit through the glass. Fizzing bits of dissolving matter spattered over the rugs, setting them alight. Fabian didn't slow, but followed his sword blade through the casement in a blizzard of glass shards, and found himself outside in the rain. Fire was licking behind him. He ignored it and raced into the downpour.

The little creature was fifty yards ahead and moving fast despite its bulk and stumpy legs.

'Alarm! Alarm! Daemons in the fortress!' Fabian shouted.

The storm swallowed up his voice. Rain ran into his mouth, salty as fluid from a blister, with a strong, acrid taste. He spat, and shot again at the creature. It leapt to the side from his las-beam and his shot scored the paving, sending a line of steam up into the rain.

'Warp take it all,' Fabian cursed. 'Daemons!' he shouted as loudly as he could. 'Daemons in the fortress!' He discharged his gun into the air twice. The crack of the beam heating the air was a feeble imitation of the thunder. 'Daemons!'

The imp looked behind itself, chortled, waved at Fabian and ran around the corner of a monumental statue podium.

Fabian pounded after it, rain soaking him and crackling in the power field around his sword.

'Daemons!' he shouted, and fired above his head again. The thin wail of an intruder alarm began somewhere down the walls, closely followed by others. Giant search lumens began snapping on with noises sharp as the breeches of guns closing. 'Oh, thank Throne for that,' Fabian said. He half skidded around the corner, sending up a curtain of water, and ran directly into danger.

A gangling creature waited half in shadow, its horned head bowed, a black sword dangling from its arm so that the tip rested on the floor. Where the lights of the fortress lit it, he saw glistening skin rent with open wounds. The sword gleamed with deep-green highlights, and a milky fluid wept from its edges to mingle with the rain.

The nurgling pattered past its larger cousin. Fabian came to a faltering stop.

'Plaguebearer,' he whispered.

Hearing itself named, the thing lifted up its head. Long, lank, patchy hair ran with the downpour. A huge eye, white and bulging as a peeled egg, stared at him. The daemon hissed, a croaking exhalation that formed a single word.

'*One,*' it said.

To its right the skim of water on the stones bubbled. A horn rose up from it, and a head, then shoulders puffy with a drowned man's skin. The first plaguebearer pointed at the second with a palsied finger.

'*Two*,' it counted, and turned inevitably to its left, where another of its kind was also rising from the ground.

'*Three*,' it said, and took a step forward.

Fabian let out a wordless shout, raised his gun and opened fire.

The plaguebearer stepped forward, its soft feet plashing in the water. Fabian hit it with every shot, punching hissing, cauterised holes into its stinking hide, but it took them without complaint and, its eye fixed on him, came forward, one leaden step at a time. It was close enough that Fabian could see the flies bobbing lazily around its head, the maggots in its wounds, the threads of worms squirming on its black gums. Its brethren came with it, flanking it, counting out the impacts of Fabian's laspistol on their leader's flesh.

'*One, two, three*,' they said, keeping pace with the first.

Fabian's shots vaporised an ear, brought fluid from swollen intestines hanging from an opened belly, destroyed the leader's elbow.

'*Four, five, six*,' they droned.

New wounds overlaid old. Maggots fried in a weeping sore. A hit to the face destroyed its cheek, bouncing black teeth across the plaza.

'*Seven...*'

Fabian took careful aim, breathed, and squeezed the trigger. His shot burst the plaguebearer's eye. It tottered forward, and he put a second shot into the same place, blasting out the thing's putrid brains from the back of its skull. It fell down dead, black fumes rising from the corpse as its sorcerous flesh unravelled. Unfortunately for Fabian, there were two more.

'*Eight…*'

They were fifteen feet away. They plodded forward at the same, maddeningly slow pace. His eighth shot clipped the shoulder of the next closest. Then his gun ran dry. He had no spare power pack.

'*Eight? Eight,*' gurgled the plaguebearers, affirming the number of shots between them. They raised their swords.

'Racej!' Fabian shouted again. He looked to the heavens. 'Oh Emperor, if you have ever had the smallest inkling that I exist, I pray that you look upon me now and protect me, because I'm going to need your help.'

He holstered his gun. His weapons were gifts from Guilliman and he wasn't about to cast them aside, even if he was going to die. He presented his sword in a high guard. The pouring rain made the blade flash and pop with sundering molecules. Hydrogen liberated from the water went up in tiny spurts of flame.

'Oh Throne,' he said. 'Oh Throne.'

Together, like automata, the plaguebearers raised their black swords, and came at him, their turn of speed surprising.

'*One,*' the first said, bringing its sword down.

Fabian parried it.

The second swung its sword into the space left by Fabian's turning of the first blade. '*Two,*' it said.

'*Three,*' said the other, bringing its sword in for a second strike.

Fabian parried them one after the other, his blade flashing through the air with such precision it would have made his trainer give one of his rare, wry smiles.

He was forced back. The daemons attacked mechanically, each strike counted off by their giver. Fabian's blade was longer and he was faster, and he blocked them all. But they would win. Though the daemons had the frames of famine victims, they were taller by a head than he, and ferociously strong. Their blows jarred his arm. They did not need to wound him gravely to kill, either; one touch of their claws or blades and he was a dead man. He was probably infected by proximity alone. He couldn't help think that with the higher parts of his mind, while his subconscious took over the business of survival. Years of training dictated his blows and counter-attacks so that it appeared to Fabian that another person wielded the blade.

Finally, he saw his opportunity, and struck. His power sword cut into the side of a plaguebearer's neck. It hit like an axe going into wet wood. The weapon seemed disturbed by the contact: the effusion of its disruption field was muted, and the pla-steel of the blade dulled. A hot pain raced along the weapon, squeezing Fabian's hand with a fever's aches. He gritted his teeth, but though he clung on his grip was loosened, and when the creature hissed, and pulled back, its uncanny strength wrenched Guilliman's gift from his hand.

Fabian faced the monster weaponless, clutching his arm, dodging the blows of the thing's fellows.

'*Nineteen,*' it hissed. '*Twenty.*' The pass of its sword splattered him with its poison, and Fabian's skin burned.

He moved back. They followed. He could hear gunfire down the parapet, shouts and distant counting voices. Alarms wailed all over the fortress.

The plaguebearers raised their swords.

'*Twenty-one…*' they said.

Their blows never fell. A vox-amplified voice roared out of the night.

'Fabian, get out of the way, get out of the way!'

Fabian threw himself backwards as three bolts streaked through the air trailing fire, thudding into the plaguebearer wearing his sword. They detonated almost simultaneously, blasting stinking viscera everywhere, a large quantity of which splashed all over Fabian. Incredibly, the daemon still stood, though its torso was hollowed out and its sword arm was lying twitching on the floor.

Sword Brother Racej Lucerne came out of the night like a runaway heavy hauler, slamming the tottering plaguebearer off its feet. It lifted clean into the air, and came down twenty feet away with a hard smack. Offal slid out of its open torso. Fabian's sword hilt hit the ground, and the weight of the daemon landing on it as it came down turned it, neatly cutting off the creature's head as if it were the top of a spoiled fruit.

While Lucerne barged the first back, his own power sword cut clean through the second. Larger than Fabian's weapon to the point it looked ridiculous, Lucerne's sword didn't so much bisect the daemon as obliterate it. The disruption boom stung Fabian's ears. The top half of the creature lifted clean into the air. It too was dead and dissolving back into nothing by the time Lucerne brought himself to a stop and went to his comrade.

'Are you all right, friend Fabian?' Lucerne asked. He let his pistol swing from the chain holding it to his wrist, and reached a night-black hand out to help up the historitor. Rain plastered his tabard to his legs. The templar's crosses of his livery gleamed in the wet.

'I am better for seeing you,' said Fabian. Lucerne did not move at all as Fabian put all his weight onto his arm. 'Come on,' said Fabian. He retrieved his sword from the bubbling mess of the dead plaguebearer. He sneezed, and cursed.

'You should report to the medicae,' said Lucerne. 'These unclean Neverborn carry all manner of pestilence.'

'We'll let the Emperor decide if we'll succumb, shall we?' Fabian said.

'Do not mock my faith,' said Lucerne.

'I'm not,' said Fabian. He hunted about through the sheeting rain for the fugitive nurgling. 'Look, these things don't have much purchase on reality. Their bodies are already dissolving. If I were going to die from their illness, I'd be dead already.'

'You can't rely on–'

'All right! I'll get myself to the medicae,' he said. 'Just help me first. I'm looking for–'

'That?' said Lucerne. His battleplate stablight snapped on, ringing the nurgling in a hard round of light. It was in the process of exaggeratedly creeping away, and it froze.

Undaunted, it turned to look at them. It held up a finger to its lips, the tentacles around its left arm wriggling, and pointed with its right hand through the storm towards the mountainside. Fabian strained his eyes into the dark, trying to see what it was pointing at.

'I condemn you to the Emperor's fires, unclean thing,' said Racej, levelling his bolt pistol.

'*Uh-oh,*' squeaked the nurgling.

Lucerne fired. The nurgling burst like a squeezed cyst, splattering all over the paving.

'What was it pointing at?' murmured Fabian. He shuddered. His skin felt unbearably hot.

Gunfire barked nearby. A trio of Ultramarines approached, shouting call-and-response litanies of cleansing. Two were white-helmed First Company veterans. Their leader was Tigurius.

'Sword Brother Lucerne,' said the Chief Librarian.

'Daemons,' said Lucerne. 'This section is clean, I think.'

Tigurius nodded. 'You speak rightly. They have gone. We have contained this outbreak, for now. But they will come again. This is only the beginning. It is this rain.' He looked up into the downpour, then down, his eyes gently aglow with his psychic might. They alighted on the bubbling remains of the nurgling, and he bent to pick up the thing's wand between thumb and forefinger.

'A lone nurgling, my lord,' said Lucerne.

Tigurius stared at the little staff, which was proving resistant to reality's efforts to banish it, remaining solid, steaming but a little.

'Something worse, much worse. It appears one of the Plague God's favoured servants has noticed us.' His eyes flashed, and the little staff vanished with a miniature thunderclap. 'This was a minor avatar of Rotigus. I can feel its touch all around this place.'

'Who?' said Lucerne.

'A greater daemon,' said Tigurius. 'According to our books of lore, one of the Plague God's most exalted.'

Fabian was only half listening to the transhumans. He walked in the direction the nurgling had been pointing. He saw something. A gateway in the rock.

His muscles convulsed, and he fell, Guilliman's sword clattering from his hand. The impact of the hard stone on his knees made him gasp, but he could not get up. He hiccuped, short of breath; his head spun.

'He has been exposed,' said Lucerne.

'Summon the Apothecaries,' Tigurius told his men.

'Fabian?' Lucerne said.

The historitor looked up at his guardian, but could not find him. 'I cannot see,' he said, and his voice sounded far away.

'We need to get him inside,' Tigurius said. He continued to speak, but all Fabian heard was a roaring in his ears, and he felt a tightness in his chest. He tried to speak himself, to tell them what he had seen, but the words remained locked in his head.

The imp had been pointing at a subsidiary entrance to the Library of Ptolemy.

CHAPTER FIFTEEN

GUILLIMAN SPEAKS

Diamider Tefelius was not quite feeling himself. He waited at attention with his fellow officers, his lasgun held out in front of him in an awkward position that made his arms shake. His ceremonial uniform was uncomfortable, hot in the cloying afternoon.

The officers of the Iaxian Astra Militarum Ultramarian Auxilia lined the stairs leading from the Spiral Way to the Palace of Flowers. The palace's name was well earned, for in normal times it was covered in blooms of all kinds, a colourful, living architecture; but it was sick like everything else, and all the colour had died upon the stalk, leaving stringy black slimes to dribble from the planting boxes. Yet even streaked with ooze the palace was magnificent. In fact, Diamider thought, as he looked out over his aching arms, beneath the shining peak of his helmet that restricted his view, it looked better like that, as if the stains accentuated the glory of what was, and what might one day again be. It was symbolic, he thought, of the eternal wheel of death and rebirth, and how the works of mortals could not hope to stand against entropy...

Then he thought, *What by the Throne am I thinking?*

Trumpets blew down the stairs. The voices of auxilia captains stationed at every landing barked orders to present arms for the primarch. Feet stamped. Entire troops praised him. The trumpets neared, the voices neared, and behind them came the heavy tread of armoured gods.

When it was Tefelius' turn to shout out the order of welcome he almost missed it; he would have, had his cornet not elbowed him forward before he put his lips to his silver trumpet. The trumpet blasted in his ear. Shocked out of his fugue by the sound, Tefelius stamped his feet, and bellowed in his best parade-ground voice.

'Present arms for the Lord of Ultramar! All hail the Lord Commander. All hail the Imperial Regent!'

His troops turned on their heels to face the last living primarch, and stamped, shaking the stairway. They thrust out their weapons before them in presentation of arms. The position of his fellows and the high plumes of their dress uniforms obscured everything but the bobbing forest of standards coming up the stairs behind the primarch. They were magnificent in their profusion and variety, representing every part of the Imperial military.

All to be tarnished. All to be cast down, Tefelius thought, to his own alarm.

As Guilliman climbed towards them, the officers stepped back and swivelled into their prior positions, pulling in their guns across their chests, then shouldering them, for which the aching arms of Tefelius were profoundly grateful.

'All hail Lord Guilliman!' they shouted. 'All hail the saviour of Iax!' though he had not saved the planet yet. That was Costalis' idea, giving thanks for a gift not yet given. The Imperial commander had been almost pathetic in his enthusiasm for the primarch's arrival.

Again Tefelius was taken aback at his train of thoughts. Why was he thinking this? He had nothing but respect for Costalis. Sweat trickled from under his helmet. He felt faint. He feared he would pass out before the regent came.

The procession was on him, a confusing mass of people in robes of all kinds, priests at the head, administrators after, then Lord Guilliman himself, huge and impatient among these scurrying rodents, yet obliged to keep to their pace. For a moment Tefelius beheld him, this son of god, this titan in blue armour, and in that moment he felt a raw and unbounded terror that was not his own. Something squirmed in the back of his head.

He just about managed to stay upright as the primarch swept on, and other voices and other trumpets higher up welcomed him, while a long train of mighty lords and the Angels of Death tramped by.

Tefelius slowed his breathing. After today was done, he was going to have to see the medicae.

'Captain? I say, sir? Are you all right?'

He blinked. His colour sergeant was speaking out of the corner of his mouth at him. Tefelius had not a clue for how long.

'You're supposed to join the other officers in the procession, sir, is that not correct?'

A long tail of Iaxian officers were heading up the stairs. Tefelius should have been at the back of them.

'Yes, yes,' he said, and hurried to join them, wondering what in the Imperium was wrong with him.

Tefelius' troops were to serve as ceremonial guard ringing the Palace of Flowers, and though he was due to stay with them before heading to the primarch's briefing, missing Guilliman's address to the wider people, Tefelius did not remain there for long. There was a squirming urgency in him, as he remembered from being a youth – those times when he wished to act but did not know why or what he wished to do. He told one of his lieutenants to take his place, and hurried off.

The Palace of Flowers was a large, round building, with many arches in stacked rings making up the sides. Those above the ground floor were filled in with brick, and hung with horticultural boxes, all full of wilted stalks in those difficult days, and with recessed niches from which trees grew, these also mostly dead. Stumps filled many of the recesses where cultivators had removed them.

The lower ring of arches was open, so that the Palace of Flowers perched on many columnar legs so finely made it appeared to float. Tefelius went through, and came to an inner ring of similar arches, these all barred with iron. One was gated, and the way was open, leading to a fantastic hall of inlaid stone lit by ornamental lumens: the palace's main entrance. A huge door of Macraggian pinewood closed the way into the Great Hall, but through it he could hear the rumble and boom of transhuman voices, and his heart quickened.

The gate was held by warriors of the gubernatorial guard, pikes crossed to bar the way, and that day they were supplemented by a pair of Space Marines. Tefelius knew his heraldry, recognising them as members of the Doom Eagles and the Aurora Chapter. There was a certain degree of fear engendered by their presence – Astartes Dread, some called it. They were enormous, heavily armoured and bred to kill, but chiefly his feelings were usually of religious awe, and safety, for though dangerous they had been made to protect men like him.

Just then, though, he felt utter terror, and he faltered, unable to process why he was going within. He stood, mouth agape, and began to sweat again.

'Captain Tefelius?' one of the guards asked, for he was well known in the city.

'I...'

'What business do you have in the hall, sir?' asked the second guard. 'Are you not to walk the perimeter?'

Tefelius caught a slight movement in the corner of his eye, and realised with growing worry that the Doom Eagle had turned his silver helm towards him, and was regarding him with pitiless, glowing eye-lenses.

Sweat poured down his neck.

'The primarch,' he blurted. The words came from that place at the back of his head, the place where his fear spewed uncontrollably. It was his mouth that moved, and his tongue that flapped. The voice was his, familiar as breathing, but the words were not his own. He felt something rearrange his face into a grin. 'The lord of all the Imperium is here, excepting the Emperor Himself.' These last words hurt somehow, and his grin stretched uncomfortably, feeling more and more transparently false. 'I wish to go into the observer's gallery, and see him. A minor abuse of privilege, I admit. I volunteered to stand guard, but having seen him, I cannot let the opportunity pass.'

The Doom Eagle spoke up.

'Why did you change your mind?' he said. His deep voice shook Tefelius' bowels, threatening to open them.

'With respect, my lord angel,' said Tefelius, standing taller. 'I am among Iax's most celebrated officers, and have fought with Lord Agemman himself. I bear his medal, and have the rank to make my entrance permissible. I would never dream of entering such a place were it not allowed. I am due to attend the briefing in the strategium after the address. What harm is there to see him speak now, when he only wishes to raise our spirits?'

There was a click inside the Space Marine's helm. Tefelius saw the telltale flash of retinal laser writers, suggesting the warrior was recovering files on the captain.

'What you say is true,' said the Doom Eagle. 'His clearances are valid. Let him through.'

'You may pass, captain,' said the human guards, and uncrossed their pikes.

'Thank you,' said Tefelius.

He stepped forward. An armoured hand grabbed his shoulder, gentle as a mother's touch, but there was strength waiting there to crush his bones. The Aurora Marine.

'Wait,' he said. 'You are sweating.'

'These damned illnesses that come among us from the enemy's camp,' said Tefelius. 'It is nothing. A mild fever. Half the population is ill here at any time.'

The Aurora Marine looked at him carefully. 'Make sure you are examined by a medicae at the first opportunity. We have experience of the Death Guard's diseases. The most minor of symptoms can be a sentence of death.'

'Yes, yes, I will, I promise,' said not-Tefelius.

'You may go now,' said the Space Marine.

Sweating more heavily than ever before, Tefelius saluted them all and went within.

He did not approach the great doors, for these were guarded by an entire squad of Ultramarines, but walked up the stairs to the second floor observer's gallery. He passed men from his own regiment standing guard on the stairs, and they saluted him. On the thick carpet his booted feet made no sound. The doors to the upper gallery were equally quiet, and he slipped inside.

The Great Hall of the Palace of Flowers was a giant, circular auditorium arranged around a stage. The centre was hollow, and vast. Multiple, thin circular galleries looked down upon it. The seats were arranged to match the building's curve, and set steeply above each other so that everyone within had an unobstructed view. The place was full of military officers and administrators. The hall was used for performances, but it suited as well for oratory, and Guilliman's voice carried clearly throughout the building, raising equal parts devotion and terror in Tefelius. The primarch's voice made him feel unsure on his feet, and he grabbed the nearest seat, not checking to see who occupied it. The man leaned forward when Tefelius sat, and squinted at him in the gloom.

'Hello, captain, I thought that was you,' he whispered.

'Colonel Etander?' Tefelius' heart skipped a beat, and he had the ridiculous notion he had been found out.

The colonel leaned in close. 'I'm surprised to see you in here. A few weeks ago, you were adamant that you wished to guard the exterior – you didn't trust anyone else, if I recall. You rather put Dius' nose out of joint suggesting you were the better man than he.'

'Well, I am,' said Tefelius.

The colonel shifted in his seat and sniggered. 'Ah, you always were bold, Tefelius, just the right mix of arrogance and duty. A man like you goes far. But you couldn't resist could you, when it came down to it, coming in here to see him?'

The colonel looked down on Guilliman with a look of pure devotion. Guilliman stood upon the central stage in gleaming blue and gold lit by startling lumen beams. The stage turned slowly so all in the audience could see him. His guardians surrounded him, scarcely less intimidating than their lord. Flocks of cyber-constructs whirred through the air, some recording the occasion for posterity, others watching for threats.

'Yes,' said Tefelius' new inner voice through his mouth. 'I wanted to see him before the briefing. Do you mind?'

'Is there someone in your place?'

'Lieutenant Tethermere,' he said.

'A good man. No, I don't mind. I'll let it go. I understand.' He smiled. 'Magnificent, isn't he?'

Guilliman was speaking of brotherhood, victory and new beginnings.

'We will win with him on our side,' whispered the colonel. 'Mark my words, a new era is coming for the Imperium, whether Iax recovers or not. It is worth the loss of our home to know our species will rise again.'

'Yes,' said Tefelius, dazedly, while his inner passenger seethed. Guilliman's words were naught but platitudes for the masses, nothing of worth at all.

They listened in silence as the primarch spoke his rousing, empty speech.

'He's not giving much away, is he?' said Tefelius.

'This is just the appetiser,' said the colonel. 'We will see him closer. You are due to attend the briefing?'

'Yes, I am.'

'Then you may accompany me if you wish. There'll be an informal meeting afterwards, which you may attend with me. You're going places. I don't mind acknowledging that. It's time to let people know. You've earned it.' Colonel Etander smiled. 'And if I may, it makes me like you more now I know you're not so upright all the damn time.'

The something in the back of Tefelius' head did tiny somersaults of joy.

'Yes, colonel,' Tefelius said. 'I would like that very much.'

CHAPTER SIXTEEN

A STRATEGY BETRAYED

Piloting the human was boring. The Tattleslug had an eternity of experience parasitising other beings, and could manipulate them without paying much attention to their stupid limbs. There was something about humans it found particularly objection-able. Probably because there was so little potential there. No challenge. They were already halfway damned the moment they were born. Where was the fun in corrupting something already corrupt?

What a dullard this Tefelius was. No great passions apart from his love-mate and his dreary duty. But Tefelius would realise he'd betrayed the godling, the Tattleslug would make sure of that. That would have to do for fun. There'd be a little delicious despair there, before its host died.

Tefelius-Tattleslug followed the colonel from the auditorium to the governor's strategium. From the grumbles of disapproval of the altered humans, it assumed this room was not an impres-sive example of its kind. Personally, the Tattleslug had little idea.

It had seen so many variations on the theme of strategic conference areas, from damp caves to living, networked brains the size of moons, that they were all unimpressive to it.

Guilliman took the only seat big enough to accommodate him, at the head of the room's large central table. The most senior of his advisors and the planet's government were permitted to sit at the table with him. Otherwise, the room was the same design as the auditorium, round and clean and boring. This task was not half as much fun as the Tattleslug had hoped. It was only doing this to elevate itself in the hierarchies of Nurgle.

It snickered to itself. Elevation was the reason it did everything! Its giggles came out of Tefelius' mouth as a burp he only just managed to cover.

Careful now, Tattleslug, it told itself. There were several powerful human witches in the room. Their souls tempted it with their brightness, but it must not venture close, oh no, for if it did, it would be seen, and that would provide a less than optimal outcome for its mission.

The Tattleslug had chosen well. Tefelius and his master were important enough to be in the room, but not important enough to sit close to the godling, and they took seats right at the back, far away enough from the primarch and his daemon-killing friends that the Tattleslug almost felt safe.

Almost, it reminded itself, was not as good as certainty. It must be cautious. There had been more like it once, hatched from the same magic-blasted corpse. Its siblings had not been cautious enough, and it was one of a few left. Mortals didn't like spies, and it was not impossible to kill a Neverborn. One of the witches in the room would see to that. Then there was that terrible sword…

It tried not to look at the sword.

Wriggling a little closer to the front of Tefelius' awareness, the Tattleslug settled in to listen.

Guilliman made a few acknowledgements of those present, picking out the more powerful men and women in the room to flatter them, the Tattleslug thought; the officials of this world, people who clung to the idea of Iax while Pestiliax was already born.

The Tattleslug fidgeted through the introductions and the platitudes, causing Tefelius to cough. He struggled to hide it with his fist, chest heaving, face reddening. The host was strong, but soon enough it would succumb to the gifts of Nurgle. It was always the way. The frailties of mortals limited the Tattleslug so much.

Guilliman finished his opening drone, and turned to the matter at hand.

'My lord Planetary Governor Costalis, lords and ladies of Iax, I will not coat what I must say in sweetness, for the truth of it would be unpalatable even were I to do so.'

He looked about the room, his brow beetling, so serious, so stern. The Tattleslug rolled Tefelius' eyes.

'Iax is in danger of falling into the warp and all of Ultramar with it,' said Guilliman. 'I have come here to prevent that from happening.'

A pretty picture sprang into being above the table. The Tattleslug recognised it as a map of Ultramar, and though many of its stars shone with a less healthy, more pleasing light in real life, this was not reflected by the cartolith. Faint, globular glows marked the boundaries of Imperial systems, which were isolated by dark wilderness. Presented that way, with its borders lit up, Ultramar looked imposing. In truth, it was thinly spread and vulnerable, a few hundred systems in an area of space that supported tens of millions of stars. These creatures were fools for believing themselves masters of the galaxy. Even this limited reality was beyond their reach to encompass. They were doomed, like so many others before them.

'Mortarion established a sorcerous network across our domains, corrupting the minds, souls and bodies of Ultramar's subjects as much as its worlds,' Guilliman continued.

Across the map a web spread, tinting each star system it touched with a lurid green. The tendrils between split and spread further, fracturing the void. The Tattleslug approved of this greater accuracy.

'This web of power stretched from world to world,' Guilliman went on. 'Each centred upon a nexus point of potent corruption.'

A number of clocks appeared in succession next to the map, each exquisitely ugly.

'We have destroyed many of these throughout Ultramar. The network is disrupted. Peace returns to our worlds. Civil disobedience provoked by the corruptive effect dwindles. Plague is on the retreat.'

Some of the stars flashed. The network shrivelled away from Parmenio, Espandor, Drohl and dozens of other star systems, leaving the remaining web broken into stringy pieces.

'But the central point of this network is here, on Iax. For Mortarion to be finally defeated, the heart of his web must be torn out. When it is finished, be hopeful, my people, that Iax can recover.'

Guilliman did his signature trick of looking at all the most important people in the room again, as if he were relying on them personally. The Tattleslug thought it transparent pantomime, but it was glad the primarch did not look its way.

'There will be a source to the infection, a nexus point. A physical artefact from which all the ills that bedevil us stem. It was my intention to destroy this thing, as we have destroyed all the others. I have committed the considerable resources of my fleet to finding it. The machines of the ancients, Archmagos Cawl's new devices, and the abilities of our most powerful psykers. However, all locations within the most afflicted areas of the world are uncertain. Neither technological nor esoteric means can discern the artefact's location.' He paused meaningfully. 'Therefore, we have no choice but to concentrate our efforts here, at First Landing. We will fortify this city, and issue open challenge to Mortarion. I will face him, and kill him, and that will be an end to it.'

Governor Costalis raised a shaking hand. Now there was a man well blessed with Nurgle's gifts, thought the Tattleslug.

'Speak,' said Guilliman.

'My lord commander and regent,' said Lord Costalis. His voice was weak, his skin the colour of whey. 'The initial infection of our world took place at a medicae hospital in Hythia. From there, all afflictions spread. Why not...' He took a gulping breath. The orderly accompanying him brought up an oxygen mask to his face, and he breathed hard a moment before waving it away. 'Why not strike there?'

'Can you locate this facility now, Lord Costalis?' Guilliman asked.

Costalis looked uncomfortable. 'We know where it should be, my lord.'

'Yet your auguries suggest it is no longer there?'

'Yes, my lord.'

'This is because Iax has become a place upon the borderlands, Lord Costalis,' said Guilliman. 'It is no longer wholly within the bounds of the materium. The warp taints it. We can no longer assume geography is as it was.'

'The very stones are corrupted,' Costalis said. 'Disease comes first. Crop blights, and plagues upon the trees. Animals suffer next, then when we are in despair to see our home sicken, pestilence strikes the human population, now the placing of things is disturbed. What manner of war is this?'

'An unholy one,' said a Space Marine the Tattleslug recognised as Tetrarch Decimus Felix.

'Then how can you win, my lord?'

'The acquisition of strategic points is of limited interest to the fallen primarch,' said Guilliman. 'Mortarion's armies fight in a manner that is superficially difficult to predict, but he does have a strategy. There is a pattern here. You must only think like him.'

Guilliman looked at the interlocking patterns of epidemic, livid on the cartolith of Ultramar like the marks on a plague victim's skin.

'Mortarion follows a strategy designed to feed his god's ambitions. It is obvious, once one takes his viewpoint. To a mortal mind, this war may appear nonsensical, hard to predict, impossible to counter. But that is a false theoretical. It is a ritual, and rituals are predictable.

'In provoking me to come here, Mortarion has revealed his own weakness. Once the nature of the war as a ritual is understood, the pattern may be unlocked,' Guilliman said. 'Ritual warfare is one of stricture. For it to succeed, it must be successful at every juncture. It is not like mundane war, where setbacks may be overcome by fresh strategy. Ritual war is rigid, and therefore, it is easy to counter.'

'Did he goad you to come here, my lord?' asked a general of the planetary defence regiments.

'He did more than that,' said Guilliman. 'At the climax of the Battle of Hecatone, on Parmenio, he challenged me to face him on this world.'

'Then he must have had some purpose,' said the general.

'Indubitably,' said Guilliman. 'This is a trap. He intends to kill me.'

'Then you are at risk, my lord primarch.'

'I shall decide the level of risk that is acceptable for me to take, and currently I judge it low,' said Guilliman. 'This is an example of what I mean by the limitations of ritual war. My death is one of Mortarion's goals, but is not his ultimate aim. I would venture with some confidence that it is only a stage in his ritual, a sacrifice to ensure success of his overall strategy. Having examined his actions throughout Ultramar, and after consultation with the Concilia Psykana, I have concluded that he intends at least a lasting corruption of our realm, and most likely the opening of a new warp rift as we have seen on other occasions through the greater war. My fallen brothers show a desire for territorial acquisition. I believe Mortarion desires Ultramar for his master, and whether his intention is to take it entirely into the warp, or to create a plague-ridden materium-immaterium overlap as he has done at the Scourge Stars, the result will be the same for our people – a living hell of decay and disease, with no release, and no succour.

'However,' the primarch went on. 'His desire for territorial acquisition means he is beholden to two competing sets of demands – of the mundane, or the territorial, and the esoteric, meaning the ritual. Both have limitations, and these limitations multiply one another. He is therefore more restricted than I, for I must only disrupt his actions in order to remove his chance at victory. That is, I note strongly, not the same as our victory. Victory for us is the total removal of these threats, the prevention of material-immaterial corruption, and the restoration of our holdings to their previous state. As lasting corruption is a result of my brothers' presence, we can at best hope to limit the damage. It is easier for us to cause him to lose than it is for us to truly win, if those terms are still applicable to a war of this kind.'

Again he looked so sternly at these cowed men and women who worshipped and feared him. The Tattleslug longed to introduce them to its own master, who was far less demanding, and altogether more generous.

'I am here. Mortarion is somewhere on this planet. I will not go to him. He could have taken this world weeks ago, but he wants me. Doubtlessly, he has left this city alone in order to encourage me to wait for him here. I will oblige. We will fortify the city, and fight him. He has become arrogant. In this way, by exploiting his plan, we shall triumph.

'In summation, our first goal is to ensure Mortarion does not succeed. Our second is to destroy the web of corruption underlying Ultramar. His power is waning. Mortarion is failing. We have news that a large part of Mortarion's Legion have departed Ultramar. His plans are unravelling, much as his network of filth. We will drive him out. Once accomplished, the rebuilding of Ultramar can begin, as can its fortification against further attack.'

The cartolith shifted, zooming in to the position of First Landing.

'There are unknown quantities that we must anticipate, including but not limited to Mortarion's daemonic allies, and the true strength of his void forces in this system or close to translation from the warp.'

'Mortarion controls eighty per cent of the world,' wheezed Costalis. 'But there are other hold-outs. What about these other civitae? Some of them are in a poor state, and could perhaps be abandoned, but those nearby are as little touched as First Landing. We cannot leave them to their fate.'

'I have accounted for this,' said Guilliman. 'Mortarion will come against us here, because I am here. But he will attack elsewhere in order to provoke me into rash action. I do not wish this to happen. I want him to be forced to commit more assets than he intends to the battle here. Our armies in the system are large. Accompanying me are three full battle groups. The crusade has reconquered subsectors with fewer resources than I have at our disposal. Therefore, each of the surviving towns will receive a garrison to hold them. These will be of sufficient size to discourage opportunistic attack, Astra Militarum with a core of Adeptus Astartes and Adepta Sororitas, with Mechanicus support. They will be well supplied with decontamination crews, psykers and medicae personnel.'

'Our citizens will still be at risk,' said Costalis.

'That is why we shall concentrate our efforts on material protection only. All civilians are to be evacuated, commencing tomorrow. As you all will be,' said Felix.

A little uproar then, from men and women who had resigned themselves to dying in defence of their city.

Felix raised his voice. 'There is space in the fleet for all from First Landing. We will take what others we can manage. Standard humans will stand little chance in this battle. You must leave the defence to us, or you shall perish to no good effect. If we fail, you shall live to serve the Emperor elsewhere.'

The Tattleslug took the moment to reflect. *So*, it thought to itself. *Guilliman does not know about the Godblight, or about the cauldron. He is going to fail.* It permitted itself a quiet titter, hiding the smile on Tefelius' face with a clumsily puppeted hand.

It felt a cold, hard gaze upon its host's face.

Tefelius looked up. The Tattleslug shrank back in terror, fleeing into the warp to report to Ku'Gath. It left Tefelius confused, with a pounding headache, and a deep sense of unease at the Space Marine Librarian staring straight at him.

CHAPTER SEVENTEEN

KU'GATH'S TRIUMPH

Lightning flashed in angry skies. It was only appropriate.

Bells tolled around the plague mill. A host of daemons worked within. A line of plaguebearers passed sodden wood from hand to putrescent hand, fuelling the fires beneath Nurgle's Cauldron. Great Unclean Ones watched from a safe distance, while nurglings capered madly, driven to the heights of excitement by what was going on, running to and fro, and getting under everybody's feet.

Ku'Gath ignored them as best he could. He could afford no distraction. What bubbled in the cauldron could conceivably kill him. Unusually for a daemon inured to all forms of disease, Ku'Gath wore a protective suit made of slimy human leathers stitched together in disturbing tessellation, so the skins appeared to be flat people tumbling like leaves in autumn. For the moment he had the hood back, flopping about on his back. Soon he would have to don it.

With utmost care, Ku'Gath Plaguefather prepared to harvest

his latest, and finest, concoction. He stirred carefully, his practised eye examining each swirl in the liquid, each popping
bubble. He tasted the mixture, looked upward a moment as
he judged the quality, then stirred it again three more times,
each swish of the paddle exactingly performed. He knew it was
done when a little plume of steam burst up, sending a froth of
bubbles skating over the surface. The steam formed a death's
head that hung agape before parting and wafting away.

'Silence, my pretties! Silence!' Ku'Gath called. For once, he
was obeyed. Everyone went quiet, from the most garrulous mite
to the most cantankerous plaguebearer. All eyes were on him.

'At last,' he whispered, lest too much volume disturb the brew.
***'The Godblight is nearly ready. There is but one ingredient left
to add.'***

All knew their roles. Without prompting, several plaguebearers shuffled onto a pier of black wood jutting out from the
broken floors of the plague mill. Ku'Gath backed up to them,
and with a great deal of moaning, the plaguebearers dragged his
hood up and pulled it over his head. More cursing followed as
they wrapped up his antlers and tied off all the many slippery
sinews required to keep the daemon safe. When it was in place,
Ku'Gath's eyes were protected by bottle-bottom lenses and his
nose covered by a long beak stuffed with foul-smelling herbs.

'Careful now,' he muttered. *'Careful. A blight to kill gods will
slay a mere daemon such as myself with ease.'*

The plaguebearers wisely shuffled out. The nurglings, too feeble-
minded to comprehend the peril they were in, watched on.

Ku'Gath peered about him, then reached into a rusting bank
of lockers that served him as an ingredient rack. He flicked a
door open, ferreted about beneath the dank leaves inside, and
with a pair of delicate tweezers pulled out a small glass phial
no bigger than a human thumb.

'The primarch's vitae!' he said, with not a little drama, for the moment demanded it. The blood was still disgustingly clean. He had been relieved to stash it in the box for a while, for touching the glass, even through his skinsuit, made Ku'Gath feel ill, and not in a good way.

'*Oooooh,*' said the nurglings. As the plaguebearers departed in an increasingly hurried shuffle, more and more nurglings came waddling in. They all wanted to see, the fools.

Inside his suit, Ku'Gath sweated. The next part was dangerous, the part that came after more dangerous yet. He had to be careful.

With an even tinier pair of tweezers, he removed the stopper from the bottle, letting it dangle from the fine chain that kept it tethered to the phial. Some of the purity of the blood got into the air, and the nurglings closest hugged each other and whimpered.

'Now, the risky part,' he said to himself again. Ever so carefully, he took hold of the opened phial with the larger pair of tweezers, and using the smaller to keep the lid free of the bottle, gently tipped the vessel over the cauldron. The ruby drop ran along the inside, and poised at the lip of the neck.

Ku'Gath put aside all tremors and other infirmities while he performed this task. His hands were as steady as a surgeon's. With a very gentle twitch, he sent half the blood falling through the air into the cauldron, flipping the other half back into the phial, which he deftly shut.

The blood vanished into the liquid, the single splash of crimson quickly swallowed by glowing green. It appeared as if nothing had occurred, but Ku'Gath was too wise to believe that. He took a step back, and secreted the precious blood back in the box. He would hide it under his skin again later.

Then he waited.

Still nothing happened, but it would, he knew; he had brewed this blight to perfection. Ku'Gath stayed stock-still, staring at the mix. The nurglings, not knowing any better, tiptoed forward. They crowded the walls and the gantries around the pot, making cliffs of eyes about it.

Final synthesis started as a simmering in the liquid. This became rapidly more violent, splashing over the sides from bubbles that burst with gurgling pops, until the whole cauldron was shaking, rattling about on its three pegs, and sending cascades of sparks out in all directions from the fire. Thick wells of fluid spilled down the sides, frothing and noxious, hissing onto the logs and causing waves of stinking smokes and steams that made the nurglings shriek.

The fly symbols stamped into the sides of the cauldron glowed bright with Nurgle's corpse lights. The cauldron rattled harder. A twist of wind turned around it, wrapping itself into a tight vortex that lifted higher, and higher, tugging at all around it with violent currents. Where Ku'Gath's suit was a little loose it bellied, while nurglings were sucked screaming from their perches into a growing tornado that reached up and up. Above the plague mill a great gyre was turning, sucking at the clouds until a blackness appeared that was not of the void. Within it, a scaly eyelid opened, and a yellow eye peered curiously down.

'His eye is upon us!' Ku'Gath shouted, and pointed. 'Grandfather sees!'

With a great roaring, the liquid burst up in a straight spout and punched through the vortex. It seemed to climb so high it tickled the eye of the Grandfather himself. There was a peal of thunder that sounded almost like laughter, the vortex ceased, the liquid fell back to earth with a mighty splash, and nurglings rained all around.

The lid of clouds closed again. The great eye in the sky was gone.

Ku'Gath leaned over the cauldron. Where a sea of green had bubbled there was a dirty test tube sealed with a bung of crumbling cork. Inside was a pint's worth of liquid that swirled about as if alive, turning from glowing green to purple as it performed its perturbations.

'Oh ho ho, success!' Ku'Gath said, though he did not completely believe it. He leaned on the lip of the cauldron, strained to grab the tube, could not reach, so rocked the cauldron. The tube rolled back and forward in the dregs left in the bottom, but still Ku'Gath could not catch it.

'Drat,' he said, and rocked harder.

Suddenly, the cauldron tipped over, and Ku'Gath pitched forward, his covered antlers clashed against the lip, and he fell down. The cauldron rolled. Ku'Gath snatched frantically for the tube as it dropped towards the ground, only just grabbing it from the air.

He let out a long, slow breath.

'Oh, oh. This must be handled carefully. Oh, very carefully.' Cradling the phial as if it were his most favourite of all nurglings, he got up, crooning over it, whispering his love and his pride.

'I've done it. I've done it!' He reached up and tore free his hood, then frowned. *'But, oh my. What if it does not work?'*

He looked at the nurglings ranged around him. They looked back. A few of the brighter ones widened their eyes, turned around and began to quietly waddle off.

'Just wait there a moment, my pretties. I have something for you.'

He reached for his tweezers, and plucked out the cork from the tube.

The panic spread among the nurglings, and they were all running, tumbling over and trampling each other. A few popped like blisters, and they were the lucky ones.

Ku'Gath stretched his arm out as far as it would go, shielded his face with his other hand, and allowed a single drop of the tube's contents to fall to the floor.

The effects were instantaneous. A smoky, circular wavefront blasted out from the point the liquid hit the ground. Every nurgling it touched was reduced to a sticky black smear. Their tiny souls screamed back into the warp, already corroding to nothing under the blight's supernatural effects. From the goo left by their demise, a secondary infection spread, skittering in all directions. Nurglings sneezed. Mucus filled their eyes, blinding them, and they ran into each other, spreading the disease further. They coughed up their guts before melting like slugs exposed to salt, wailing as they died. For Ku'Gath, who had been greatly irritated by nurglings since he had ceased to be one himself, it was the sweetest sound he could imagine.

The devastation spread quickly, overtaking all but the fastest nurglings, until everything around him was covered in stinking ooze.

He squinted, looking with his daemon sight into the warp, and saw not one of the souls of the dead imps had survived.

'It works,' he whispered. 'It really works!' He danced about, his covered feet slapping in the remains of his servants.

For once, Ku'Gath Plaguefather allowed himself to smile.

It didn't last. He remembered himself soon enough, put back on his scowl and corked the tube. Already, giant snails were slithering into the room to slurp up the nurglings' remains.

'Mortarion,' he said. 'I must summon him. He must come here personally!'

With a little pride and a little hurry, Ku'Gath went to contact his ally.

CHAPTER EIGHTEEN

THE CRUSADE OF
THE WITNESSES

A few days passed, and preparations for the battle against Mortarion's warriors were well under way. The towers of First Landing shook as ship after ship laboured overhead, hauling the city's frightened inhabitants out to the relative safety of the Fleet Primus battle groups, and others came down, bearing Space Marines and tanks and the battle automata of the Legio Cybernetica. For much of this time, Guilliman was closeted with his warlords, and it was during one of their many discussions of strategy that a banging came upon the door of the strategium. Quiet talk among the Custodians, Space Marines and groupmasters came to a close, and Guilliman ordered the doors opened. None but his Victrix Guard had permission to knock so.

A mortal messenger was admitted, and came before the primarch, trembling with fear at the news he must deliver.

'This had better be significant,' said Colquan. 'There are standing orders in place that the primarch is not to be disturbed.'

'I am sorry, my lords,' said the messenger. 'But the news I bear is most important. Tetrarch Felix bade me come.'

'Then spit out whatever it is you have to say,' said Colquan. 'We have a war to win, and you are delaying us.'

The man shook under the hostility of the Custodian, but managed to speak.

'Militant-Apostolic Mathieu is attempting to leave the city.'

Guilliman looked down with such concentration the messenger looked like he might dissolve into a puddle of sweat.

'Is he now?' said the primarch. 'Where is Felix?'

'At the Evergreen Outlook, my lord, above Puscinari's Barbican.'

'Now he goes too far! Let us put right our error,' Colquan said. 'I'll wring that scrawny preacher's neck, I swear.'

'You will do nothing. None of you will. You will all remain here,' Guilliman told his generals. 'I shall deal with this myself.' The Victrix Guard standing at the door made to come with him, but Guilliman stayed them with a gesture. 'Myself, I said.' And he left.

Guilliman went out from the Palace of Flowers on a quick route through crowded alleys to the edge of the city. He took steps carved for mortals five at a time, scattering people queuing to leave the city as he went. Those nearest recoiled from him, overwhelmed by his presence, terrified by his might, but away from him cries went up, and crowds gathered to see.

He came to the Spiral Way that curled round the city, headed down, and stepped out onto a broad platform cut into the top of one of the city's cliffs at the third-tier defences. A macrocannon squatted silent in the middle, its stoppered muzzle poking out from under a tarpaulin. The platform tapered to a point overlooking the plains, and budding from the side of that, like a tree clinging to a cliff face, was an observation post. This was

sized for humans, and so Decimus Felix watched from the parapet instead.

A heavy hauler grunted into the sky from the space port near
the horizon.

Guilliman went to stand by the tetrarch, causing the soldier
manning the post to almost drop his magnoculars in surprise.

'Decimus,' said Guilliman.

'My lord Guilliman,' said Felix. 'You see our problem?'

Guilliman nodded. The city's only gate was two thousand
feet below. A cliff face of statues, palaces and defence points
carved directly into the living rock descended into the haze,
and halfway down was the second-tier wall, but even through
all that he could see Mathieu's war train and his assembled
host. They crammed the barbican projecting from the mountain, a vast sub-castle that occupied a square mile. The walls
rivalled those of the Fortress of Hera, and the towers of the
gatehouse were monstrous things, cruel as spearpoints, and
well provided with guns.

'It seems the militant-apostolic wishes to liberate the world
himself,' said Felix.

'That is not all he wishes to liberate, Decimus,' said Guilliman.

Felix gave his gene-father a quizzical look. 'I do not understand, my lord.'

'He wishes to liberate my soul,' said Guilliman softly.

'What are your orders then? The city guardians have the militant-
apostolic detained. He is trapped. The gates are locked.'

'What is his reaction?'

'Silence,' said Felix.

'And what does he want?'

'For the gates to be opened, nothing else. He tells my men that
he has been given a holy task, and that he must take the fight
to the followers of the Plague God.' Felix paused. 'My lord, he

has thousands of the city folk with him. They have joined his crusade. He is delaying the evacuation. He is insane,' said Felix.

'A subjective judgement. He thinks the same of me,' said Guilliman, still staring down.

There was a whir as Felix upped the magnification of his eye-lenses. 'Colonel Odrameyer's regiment is with him. Several units of the Adepta Sororitas also. Others. There are many people in his host who have deserted their posts for him.'

'Then he may stand a chance,' said Guilliman, still staring, still speaking softly. His hands clenched a little, then relaxed as he thought.

'Then you mean to let him go? He is taking many men with him who would best be used elsewhere.'

'What would you have me do, Felix?' said Guilliman. 'If we oppose him, he will fight. He was correct, the damage that would do is incalculable. He has outplayed me. I must remain content that he is on our side. He may achieve something, and although he and I may disagree on the origin of the phenomena we have seen in this campaign, there is no doubting their reality.'

'Then you wish to let them proceed?' said Felix.

Guilliman nodded. 'Open the gates, let him out. The men he takes with him would have been evacuated anyway. He is not weakening our defences much. We can spare him a few Battle Sisters.'

'They will all die, my lord,' said Felix.

'Is that so?' said Roboute Guilliman. 'Why do we not let their faith prove itself. I decree that their fate shall lie in the hands of my father, for I will have nothing to do with it. Give the order.'

Felix did as he was told. Guilliman walked away, but Felix stayed to watch the gates to First Landing open wide, and Mathieu's battle congregation set out in a singing column around the war train.

Once it was clear, Colonel Odrameyer's tanks swung out around it to form a rolling cordon through the fields either side of the highway. Felix was angry at such defiance of the primarch's will, but Guilliman had commanded that Mathieu be let free, and so let free he was.

He did not intend to stand there so long, but Felix watched the column until it had vanished into the polluted mists, and for a time after. He thought upon the primarch's reasons for allowing the preacher out. *Theoretical*, he thought, *Guilliman is at genuine risk from the Church.* There was undeniable truth there. The Adeptus Ministorum was all-powerful, everywhere, influenced everything, from the hopes of the smallest child to the operation of the grandest organs of state. But he did not believe that the Ecclesiarchy's pervasive influence and Guilliman's need to treat it carefully was all that was going on here. There was another, far more troubling possibility.

Theoretical, he thought, but slowly, hardly daring to consider the idea.

Theoretical, Roboute Guilliman is beginning to believe his father is a god.

Diamider Tefelius stumbled through life as if it were a thick, cloying fog. He could hardly speak when spoken to, concerning his wife and worrying his subordinates. Only bursts of anger orchestrated by his passenger kept the medicae away. He wondered what was happening to him, why his hair was falling out and his teeth hurt so much, but every time he considered taking himself off for an examination, the Tattleslug would tweak a synapse here, or pull a ganglion there, and the idea would be replaced with a dread of doctors.

The Tattleslug recognised the signs well enough. Time was running out. It was careful with its diseases, but it was a daemon of plague and no amount of restraint on its part would stop its host from suffering. Tefelius would die soon.

Tefelius had no notion of any of this. Once again he found himself somewhere he had not expected to be, swaying slightly upon a ledge with nothing but spore-hazed airs between himself and the ground thousands of feet down. From there, he had a clear view right into the heart of Puscinari's Barbican around the gate. A large military force was leaving the city. Some part of him buried way back in the rear of his skull seemed to find the sight very interesting indeed, so interesting, it let go a little of its hold on Tefelius.

The captain blinked, a sick man waking, not quite sure where he was or what was happening. Then his sluggish brain caught on to his situation, and he gasped, nearly fell, and spread his arms wide upon the stone behind him. He looked to left and right. He knew where he was: a little nook in the city at the dead end of an obscure path, round and furnished with benches, open to the sky but protected from the drop by a tall wall pierced by three unglazed windows, one of which he must have climbed through. It was distant from the main thoroughfares, and often deserted, a place frequented by lovers looking for privacy, and the occasional suicide.

He had no wish to join that second category. The problem was, he was on the wrong side of the wall, his feet balanced on a ledge.

His heart in his throat, he inched along. The ledge was an architectural flourish, barely three inches deep, and crumbly with age. Grit from the stone rasped under his soles. He dared not lift up his feet, but shuffled. Growing up in First Landing tended to blunt a man's fear of heights, but this was too much.

His hand hit an empty space, and he forced back a rush of panic. It was one of the windows. Shaking with fear, he turned himself around, one hand gripped tight to the window's edge, and pulled himself through.

He sat there shivering, sweat pouring down his face. He had to get himself to the medicae.

There was that strange movement in his head, damping down his concerns, making him quiescent.

'What's wrong with me?' he wondered aloud. His breath stank. His tongue was sore.

'A question I would very much like the answer to,' said a deep, transhuman voice.

Eye-lenses lit up eerie blue at the back of the little hideaway. A curtain of vines over a stone pergola obscured the seats there, pink-leaved and vibrant before Mortarion, now stringy as hag's hair. There were still enough dead stalks to conceal the Space Marine within.

The warrior came out, ducking to avoid destroying the beams holding up the vines. His battleplate was a deep blue, covered with esoteric markings. His left shoulder pad was green, and bore the badge of the Aurora Chapter.

'I saw you, in the strategium.' Tefelius' shaking was getting worse. His stomach boiled with acid.

'You did. I am Codicier Donas Maxim. I am an advisor to the primarch.' The Space Marine planted his staff carefully upon the ground. 'You are unwell.'

'It is nothing,' said Tefelius. He got up to his feet, hardly able to stand, a combination of illness and fear making him weak.

'It is something,' said Maxim. 'I have been watching you. I have listened to your thoughts. You are not yourself. You have a passenger.'

A squirming, awful fear flooded Tefelius, and only part of it was his own.

The Space Marine levelled his staff at Tefelius' chest.

'No, my lord, wait, please, I–'

'I will try to save you if I can,' said Maxim. His eyes flashed bright, and a pulse of lightning burst from his staff into Tefelius.

Tefelius' muscles locked. He fell down. He got up on his knees, and tried to crawl away. Maxim moved in front of him, blocking his path as surely as a tank.

'I am sorry,' the Librarian said, and pushed another burst of psychic power into the captain. 'What is within you must come out, and it must be slain.'

Tefelius began to retch, whole-body-shaking convulsions like those made by an ailing canid. He felt something inside him, huge, too big to fit inside, and yet it seemed to be coming up out of his throat. Maxim had his staff couched under one arm like a feral worlder's lance, his other hand out, crackling with sparks of warp power as he drew out the poison in the captain.

The thing moved up, squeezing stomach acid into Tefelius' gullet and searing it. Impossibly, it seemed to be coming from out of his head and his gut at the same time. Tefelius' neck bulged. His airways were closed off. He choked on something indescribably foul. Vomit churned in his oesophagus with no way to be released.

Maxim closed his hand. 'I have you now, Neverborn,' he said.

Struggling against eviction, the thing was drawn out further. It stuck in his throat, soft and wriggling, pushing against the back of his jaw. Pain, terrible, awful pain, consumed Tefelius, and he tried to scream, but could only moan deep in his chest. It became worse, and worse, until with a sudden click, his jaw detached, flapping wide on his chest, and the thing inside him plopped onto the floor, steaming and vile. A buzzing blackness cast itself over Tefelius like a hood, but still he was conscious.

Tefelius had time to get a good, long look at the monster that had been hiding inside him; to see its stubby arms, the slug-like body, its insect's wings beating feebly as it tried to escape, before Donas Maxim pinned it to the ground with the horns atop his staff, and blasted it from existence with a pulse of warp-born power.

Unable to speak, clutching his dislocated jaw, Tefelius collapsed into a puddle of blood and vomit on the paving slabs.

'I need a medicae team at my position, now, in full protection gear,' Tefelius heard Maxim say, then the blackness closed tight around him, and he was spared further pain.

CHAPTER NINETEEN

KU'GATH'S GIFTS

Before Mortarion arrived, Ku'Gath prepared himself. He stripped off the leather suit and rolled it up to eat, slurping it down in one, long noodle of hide. Then Ku'Gath took a size that would not outdo Mortarion, whose form was fixed owing to his half-mortal nature. The primarch would find Ku'Gath modestly occupying only the height of the plague mill's first two floors, and not towering through the broken roof. He had the cauldron shrink too, and set it back on its feet, with a fresh fire prepared beneath, though this he left unlit.

Ku'Gath was tiring of Mortarion. His moods, his arrogance, they oppressed him, and if there was one thing Ku'Gath's spirits did not need, it was more oppression. He regretted his alliance with him completely. Still, it had to be seen out to the end, and there was no need to be rude.

The primarch flew in on silent moth wings, but his armour gave out a series of coughs and splutterings, and his respirator was so loud Ku'Gath could hear him well before he saw him.

Mortarion circled the plague mill once, dragging out the fumes of the Plague Guard's campfires as he passed through them, then came down in a rush of smoke and odour, followed by an entourage of nurglings that plopped down from under his cloak and waddled across the floor as if they owned the place. A few of them had wings, and they carried some of the chained censers that hung from Mortarion like a lady's train.

He brought with him his own fogs, and these mingled with the mists of the marshes.

'*I have come, Ku'Gath, in answer to your summons.*'

'*My lord primarch,*' said the Great Unclean One, and inclined his mighty head a little, forcing out his goitre so that it inflated like the throat of a toad.

Mortarion gave him a perfunctory nod, then paced around the ruined hospital, using his enormous scythe as a staff, looking up at the broken floors, poking into the weed-infested rubble, crushing dirty glass under his heel. With the toe of his boot he turned over a skeleton livid with fungi and hissed appreciatively.

'*So pleasing,*' he said. '*So right, to see the feeble cut down. Mankind requires culling. All these places of healing should be destroyed. They encourage weakness.*'

'*Quite so, my lord,*' said Ku'Gath. '*Grandfather is most generous in decimating them so they may become stronger. They are so numerous that a lesser god would have become bored, but our Grandfather always did have the virtue of persistence.*'

'*And this, this is his cauldron?*'

'*It is, my lord. A part of it, anyway,*' said Ku'Gath proudly. '*A manifestation of the eternal whole.*'

'*That's why it is so small. I expected it to be bigger,*' said Mortarion dismissively. Ku'Gath's own coterie of nurglings giggled and blew raspberries, while Mortarion's looked at him with an air of insufferable superiority. Ku'Gath battled to keep his spirits up.

'It is bigger. It can be smaller.' Ku'Gath clicked rubbery fingers, and the cauldron shrank down to the size of a coin, fire and all. *'Or larger.'* There was a flash, and both it and Ku'Gath filled the space, monstrous as the gods themselves.

Mortarion remained resolutely unmoved.

'Do you think I am entertained by these theatrics?' he said, staring up at Ku'Gath.

Ku'Gath shrank back to his previous stature. *'Perhaps, then, you will be impressed by this.'* Keeping his yellow eyes firmly fixed on Mortarion's cataracted orbs, he thrust his hand under a loose flap of skin, pushing aside fat and muscle tissue as a man might rummage in his pocket. From it he drew out the plague phial, and held it out to the fallen primarch between thumb and forefinger.

'The Godblight,' he said quietly, full of awe at his own achievement, though his mood fell immediately when he saw that Mortarion did not share it.

'Is that it? A dirty glass full of poison?'

By now, Ku'Gath was feeling thoroughly irritated by Mortarion's manner, and for once he dared to show it.

'And what would you have, my lord?' he said acidly. *'A spiked trinket like those you wear?'* He gestured at the censers and thuribles hanging from Mortarion's armour. *'The poisons in them might kill half a world, but this...'* He thrust the phial forward. *'This will kill a god.'* He tightened his grip. *'If I were to crush this glass and cast this liquid into your face, then you would die. First, that part of you that was fashioned in the mortal world would perish, in some delicious agony, but that would not be the end, oh no. This disease would chase you into the warp, and eat at your daemon's soul. It would consume a mortal essence*

in a trice. It would take a little longer for you, but it would end you. It would even kill me. There is no cure for it. No way to stop it beyond the exertion of the greatest amount of sorcery. Once it is released, the mortals will flee. They would have to destroy this world to prevent its spread.' He peered lovingly at it, his tongue flopping messily from his mouth. *'It is bacterium, phage, virus, rogue protein, parasite, cancer, mutant gene-code and more all in one. It is alive as you are alive, aware as we are aware. It thinks, and all it wishes is to infect, infect, infect. The Destroyer Plague is a nothing compared to this. The Rot is a sniffle. It is my finest creation.'*

Mortarion reached for the phial, but Ku'Gath drew it back.

'You must be careful when you administer the dose,' said Ku'Gath. *'Prick him. Inject him. It must go into his body. If it is exposed to the air it will afflict you as well.'*

'Understood,' said Mortarion.

'And stay clear of any secondary effusion his body may give, or you will also die.'

'A mighty gift.'

Ku'Gath nodded. *'Perhaps its concoction will please Grandfather, and he will finally forgive me. He was watching me, you know, when I finished it. A great eye in the sky!'*

'As I hear it, you are his favourite,' said Mortarion, who could not keep up his sourness now the promised weapon had been revealed, and sounded almost impressed.

'Then perhaps I can finally forgive myself for the error of my birth,' said Ku'Gath. *'With this disease, I have earned my name. I am the Plaguefather, well and truly. So you see, it needs no fancy container to accentuate its value. Anything like those,'* Ku'Gath gestured at Mortarion's adornments again, causing the primarch's nurglings to stick their noses in the air, *'would only diminish its glory.'* Ku'Gath shook the test tube, causing little

motes of light to dance around in the greater glow of the plague. *'This is a fitting vessel. Simple, dirty, effective, as all Nurgle's best gifts are, and I am giving it to you.'* Ku'Gath extended the phial towards Mortarion again. *'So I will have a little more respect. Please.'* His voice was level and firm. Despite his exalted rank in the hierarchy of pestilence, it took all his will to stand up to the daemon primarch so.

Mortarion took the Godblight, weighed the phial in his hand, then tucked it away. *'Understood, oh father of plagues. You have aided me well, my ally, and soon we shall both reap the rewards of Nurgle's pleasure.'*

'Well,' said Ku'Gath. *'We'd best be swift. If we can conquer Ultramar, it will garner us much glory in the garden, but if we fail, and we also do not heed the horns of war calling all back to the Scourge Stars, then we shall both suffer for it.'*

Mortarion's change in humour was instant and terrifying. Before Ku'Gath could gather what was happening, Silence was whistling through the air in a double-handed sweep. It came to a stop a particle's breadth from Ku'Gath's nose, where it quivered with the force Mortarion was obliged to employ to arrest its progress, the metal of its yards-long blade humming.

'Speak not to me of this new war,' he snarled.

'But Lord Mortarion, Nurgle himself commands that we...'

The small chainblade attachment on Silence's tip whirred into motion.

'Do not speak of it,' hissed Mortarion. *'Does Grandfather think I cannot defend my own holdings? Typhus returns with the First Plague Company and more besides. No daemon army can stand against him.'*

'He does not go at your command, my lord, but at Nurgle's. You delude yourself. Typhus heeded the call, so should we. Nurgle's bounties are endless, and he is inclined more to generosity than wrath, but he should not be crossed, not ever!'

Silence moved infinitesimally closer. Close enough that Ku'Gath wondered if his Neverborn soul would survive contact with it.

'You chose to serve me to advance yourself. Do so, or I shall kill you. Or bind you to my will. There is space in the scythe to house another daemon,' Mortarion said. *'We finish this war. We win it. Then we attend to the other. Nurgle shall be pleased with us. There shall be no other outcome. I do as I want. I am no one's slave. Not the Emperor's, and not Nurgle's. You chose to aid me, so aid me. Understood?'*

Ku'Gath's eyes went to the brass censer at the head of the weapon. In there was another being much like him, trapped. Ku'Gath did not doubt Mortarion could enslave him also. He swallowed. His tongue was suddenly, awfully dry.

'Understood,' said Ku'Gath.

Mortarion held Silence perfectly still in front of Ku'Gath's face, then pulled it back, and set the butt back down upon the floor.

'I am pleased we have an understanding. Do not worry, Plague-father,' Mortarion said, without anger. *'All goes to plan.'*

'Perhaps I can aid you there,' said Ku'Gath, keen to regain favour.

'How so?' said Mortarion scornfully. He did not rate Ku'Gath as much other than a brewer of ailments.

'I have information.'

'What information?'

Ku'Gath gave a conspiratorial wink, rather spoiling things as his loose eye popped free of his face. He hastily stuffed it back in.

'It was the Tattleslug who told me, do you know it?'

Mortarion gave Ku'Gath a withering look. *'Should I?'*

Ku'Gath pursed his lips. *'I should not be surprised, useful though the Tattleslug is. It is a little thing, very lesser, of no consequence to the likes of you or I,'* he said, waving his hand airily around, *'but that is much to its advantage, for it passes unseen and unnoticed. Its abilities as a spy are marked.'*

'This Tattleslug brought you news?'

'It did,' said Ku'Gath proudly. *'I told it to. I sent it to First Landing, where it overheard the Anathema's son, erm... your brother,'* Ku'Gath added quickly, *'laying out his strategy. It has performed many valuable services for me over eternity, and reported to me shortly before I finished the blight.'*

'Then bring it to me, so I might question it closely.'

Ku'Gath's face became more miserable than ever. *'Alas, my servant is dead, slain by the Anathema's witches. The Tattleslug has tattled its last.'*

'Then,' said Mortarion, *'what use is anything it said?'*

Ku'Gath raised fat, puffy-skinned hands in placation. *'Oh lord of unparalleled puissance, I ask you, please be calm. It told them nothing before it died. How could it, when it was fried to a crisp in the fires of their sorceries? I felt it die, it gave me a most pleasing heartburn. I promise you they learned nothing, whereas I,'* Ku'Gath licked his black lips, *'I learned everything.'*

Mortarion's aura flickered with energies black and purple, like flames they were to Ku'Gath's eyes, and in their dancing he saw the Lord of Death's renewed desire to strike him down.

Oh Lord of Death, Ku'Gath thought, *your assumed name tells all – you shall never be as mighty as you could be, because death is but half Grandfather's bounty. Without rebirth, what use is death? This is why you fail.*

He did not relay this thought to the half-daemon.

'Shall I tell you, or shall I not?' Ku'Gath said into the full force of Mortarion's glare.

The Lord of Death relaxed a little, hunching over, cadaverous and weary. *'Do so, then I shall decide upon the merits of your information.'*

'Guilliman has only part of the tale. He is aware you intend to kill him. He knows Pestiliax is the centre of your efforts, and suspects you wish to steal the realm from under him. He apprehends also that there is an artefact here that serves as the lynchpin to your web of decay.'

'It is self-evident he knows this. He is Roboute Guilliman, a primarch! He is my brother, he is not a fool!' snarled Mortarion. Angry plumes of vapour jetted from his respirator.

That does not, thought Ku'Gath, mean that genius runs in the family.

'Ah, now now,' said Ku'Gath. 'There is what he does not know, and in that we can find our road to victory!'

'And what, pray tell, is that?' said Mortarion. He turned his back and took station by the cauldron, and was peering into its empty belly.

'He does not know we intend to unleash a plague the likes of which has never been seen before. He does not know that what we have here is not some...' He chose his next words carefully. 'Cunningly contrived clock, but a living echo of Nurgle's own cauldron.' He rapped his knuckle upon the side of the rusty iron and it boomed. 'He is unaware of the power we hold against him. We have him at a great disadvantage. Indeed, he is so unsure that before it perished, my spy reported that he will hold at First Landing to await you. He will be easily trapped there, and the plague delivered.'

Though they stood at the cauldron together, Mortarion's face was still obscured from Ku'Gath, and at that point the Plaguefather saw that the primarch's shoulders were shaking. He took it first for an ague, but no, it was laughter, huffed out through his respirator with clouds of stinking, acrid fumes.

'You daemons are so narrow-minded. You are a fool, you are all fools!'

'*I am sorry?*' Ku'Gath said, taken aback.

The Lord of Death turned to look at him. '*Of course he will know. He plays with us. Do you think such an effort as creating the Godblight can be undertaken without his knowing? Mortals are not blind, Ku'Gath, and we primarchs are the mightiest among them.*'

'*I did not mean to…*' Ku'Gath began. Mortarion hissed at him, and stepped in close.

'*Guilliman has his sorcerers, his Librarians and his slave-aeldari seer. His eyes are everywhere. The warp floods the universe with raw power, and though it benefits us more than our enemies, they use it against us.*'

'*Ah, I see, I had not thought of that.*'

'*No, you hadn't, and he has something you discount.*'

'*And that is?*' said Ku'Gath, who wished that Mortarion would just go away.

'*He has his mind! He will have anticipated all of this. Do you think he would come down to a planet we have partially dragged into the Garden of Nurgle already and spout his plans for all and sundry to hear? Whatever this Tattleslug heard, it will have been* meant *to hear. No, I have no doubt Guilliman wishes to provoke me into open battle, as I wish to provoke him the same. Both of us desire to set the stage of our confrontation, but this is not the only consideration.*' Mortarion looked skyward. '*There will be others on their way here, do not doubt it. They will strike at the cauldron, because he will know, one way or another, that within it rests the wellspring of our power. If he destroys it, our web of decay will be dealt a fatal blow, and all will be lost. There are two ways we can lose. The loss of the cauldron, or my death. I think you are the weaker target.*' Mortarion gave him a beady stare. '*You must prepare for battle.*'

'*Me?*' said Ku'Gath, who was not fond of battle, and had had enough to last a millennium at the plains of Hecatone. '*Here?*'

'Yes, you. Yes, here. They will come. They will attempt every means to deprive us of Nurgle's Cauldron. Look to the skies. Look to the warp. Guilliman will not attempt a full-scale ground assault. It is not his preferred manner of war, certainly not under these delightful conditions you have provided about the mill. You could expect an orbital drop or bombardment, and he will try these things, but he will suspect, as I know, that neither of those things will work.'

'Then I am safe?' said Ku'Gath, adding hurriedly, 'The cauldron, I mean.'

'Oh no. There are other ways, other means. They could come from the land. They could come from the warp. I would guess he will send the Emperor's Talons after you here. The null maidens, the Emperor's own guardians, perhaps the Grey Knights.' Mortarion said this last with a scowling mien, and hunched deeper, remembering the insult done to his heart by the warriors of Titan. 'All his finest daemon slayers, you can be sure.'

'But... but... my Plague Guard is ravaged,' said Ku'Gath. 'Many of my best warriors were slain on Parmenio, and await rebirth. My lieutenants dream in their pods in the garden. Why, Septicus Seven endured the true death!'

'Then if you do not wish to enjoy the same, find yourself more warriors, and quickly. They are coming here. Make no mistake.'

'Will you send your Plague Marines to help me?'

'No,' said Mortarion. 'Guilliman's forces here are immense. If he commits the majority to First Landing, I will need all of my Legion that I can muster to attack him.'

'Release the plague now then!' said Ku'Gath. 'It will cross the planet, and kill him, and we can be away.'

'No.'

'No? No?' said Ku'Gath shrilly.

'I must see him be infected. I have to see him suffer.' He turned away. 'He has to understand why I did what I did,' he said quietly.

'*Your hubris will kill us all. You cannot be overconfident. We have the advantage now, use it!*'

'*It is not hubris, though I wish to best him, I cannot deny, and I wish even more to see him die. It is practicality. Release it now, and he has the chance to escape, and to burn this world to cinders from orbit, your plague along with it. He suffers the same strictures, too. He wishes to make sure I am dead. He needs to know for certain the cauldron is destroyed. The gaming pieces mirror each other exactly. All that must be decided are the strategies we choose, and I think we will the choose the same. King against king, but first he will attempt to sweep the board of pawns.*'

The very tone and content of Mortarion's speech sparked such a fury in Ku'Gath it was all he could do not to strike the primarch down right there. A pawn, was he a *pawn?*

'*Well. Right,*' said Ku'Gath frostily. '*Then I shall begin a muster.*'

'*You should. There is another thing we must take into account. In the creation of strategy, we must consider what Guilliman actually knows, what he professes to know, what he intends to do, what he knows of our intentions, and what he conceals of all of these things.*'

'*Naturally,*' said Ku'Gath irritably, for he was reckoned no mean general in his own right.

'*Be warier still, there is a further factor.*'

'*Which is?*' said Ku'Gath, who had never thought like a mortal and never could.

'*There is that which he does not know and does not intend.*'

'*Surely that is a good thing.*'

'*Perhaps,*' said Mortarion with a shrug of his broad wings. '*But in my experience, when fighting my brother, it is these unseen circumstances that work against me. I hate to give him credit, but he was always a more flexible tactician than I, so let us limit his options. If you wish to give me a true gift, Ku'Gath, brew*' *me up a storm. Pull in the rot and disease of this world, and weave about Pestiliax a shroud. There will be no aid for Guilliman from his fleets once battle commences. We have him where Grandfather demands he be. Let him not spoil it for us. Let this be a contest of brothers, not of armies.'*

'Oh, so you have an unparalleled plague, and now you want a storm?' said Ku'Gath huffily.

'Yes.'

'A warp storm.'

'Is there another kind?' With that Mortarion spread his wings. His coterie of imps squealed, recognising the signs of departure, and ran to grab his boots. *'Just do as I say, Ku'Gath.'* A single, silent beat sent the primarch powering into the air, where he vanished into the clouds.

'Do as I say?' Ku'Gath gritted black teeth. There was a pitiful squeal, and he looked down. A single one of Mortarion's nurglings had failed to grab his master's boot, and remained behind. Its pride had departed, and it looked quiveringly to Ku'Gath for mercy.

'Not so haughty now, eh?' Ku'Gath said, and drove his foot down hard upon the nurgling. For good measure he ground his heel into its remains. *'Guilliman is not the only one who may perform the unexpected,'* he said, thinking of the half-drop of blood in its bottle, hidden under another fold of flesh. He looked to the sky a moment longer. It was decidedly calm. Then he turned about and waddled away.

'Sound the drums, blow the horns,' he grumbled. *'Make ready our beasts and our nightmares!'* He shouldered his way through a crumbling wall, bringing most of it down. Already a clamour of music, shrieks and droning counts was rising around the plague mill. *'The Plague Guard must war again,'* he growled.

'Brew me up a storm,' he mimicked, addressing the marshes

as if they might console him. *'Who am I, his butler?'* He sighed. *'So be it. Someone fetch me water! Light the fire!'* he bellowed angrily. *'Apparently I still have work to do.'*

CHAPTER TWENTY

TESTIMONIES

The column of the faithful took the First Landing-Boonswell highway, which ran close by the capital, for it, unlike the hydroways Iax relied on for much of its transport, could accommodate the war train's majesty. After travelling all afternoon, through the evening and into the dark, they stopped in the ruined town of Argardston, some fifty miles from First Landing, where they passed the night full of the confidence only faith can bring. Joy was on every face, though the rations were poor and death certain at the end of the road. Argardston was entirely deserted, most of it burned to the ground, the whole of the population having relocated to the safety of First Landing. There were few signs of the enemy there, and the damage to the town had been done by the townsfolk themselves, who sought to deny their possessions to the foe.

They rose early, ate in the predawn, and set out again at first light of the sun. To speed their progress, half the pilgrims jogged alongside the Cadian tanks and the Ministorum war train, the other half riding every perch upon the vehicles. They changed over at hourly intervals. Few of them were natural runners, many had lived difficult lives. But the strength of the Emperor ran through them, and they ran with glowing faces, and they did not complain. The Sisters of Battle sang hymns in pure voices that never ceased, but folded one into the other in ever-increasing complexity, while preachers standing atop tanks in pulpits made from empty ammo crates and scrap metal gave fiery sermons as the train's organ played. In these ways did they maintain their strength, and kept up a steady pace. No sickness troubled them, and none of the enemy appeared to inflict more direct harm. Not in the beginning.

At first, the carefully manicured landscapes of Iax seemed merely troubled, as if by drought or passing pestilence. Wilting forests and agricolae lined the highways, but life prevailed; indeed, there was if anything too much of it, for the fields were choked with weeds that blotted out the light from the crops, the canals thick with algal blooms and the woods were tangles of strangling creepers. These plants had no place on the garden world, and were sinister looking, but were not noticeably unnatural in form, though their nocturnal rustlings had the sentries gripping their lasguns tightly, and the faithful were warned from venturing off the road.

After three days of travelling, they were still within two hundred miles of First Landing, and by then the grip of Nurgle tightened with every league they advanced. By the dawn of the third day, the trees were rotten, pulpy sticks, whose leaves lay black around their roots. The turbulent sky was visible through their black skeletons, and no animals or aviforms called out. Even the creepers succumbed, hanging dead in slimy tangles from their hosts, while the fields of the farms were plains of musty straw. The congregation knew their first sickness, though they were careful to boil and treat their water before use, and all they consumed was blessed by priests. A malady of the gut took hold in several groups, and thereafter spread rapidly. For most, the symptoms were unpleasant rather than deadly, bestowing upon the sufferers cramping pains and loose bowels, but it was sufficiently dangerous to kill, and the weak succumbed. A few of the more firebrand preachers declaimed that they were lacking faith, and despite the intervention of Mathieu's presbyters, some of the pilgrims were cruelly abandoned. Others pleaded to be left behind so as not to slow the procession.

The mountains of the Loann moved up over the horizon, the tallest of their sharp peaks well over six thousand feet high and impassable on foot, but the highway headed directly for them, and passed through a huge cutting cleaving the range in two. One morning as they approached the mountains, before the train gave off its steam and the march continued, a group of some two hundred came to Mathieu. Shamefacedly their elders spoke, and told him that they were going to turn back. Among them were those too afraid to continue, and although their stated intention was to gather up the ill and take them back the way they had come, it was patent that cowardice was the cause.

There were rumblings of treachery and denunciations then, but Mathieu calmed them, speaking of the Emperor's individual plan for each man and woman. that some were intended to fight and were given the courage to do so, and others were to perform other roles.

'This is not a failure of heart,' he told them, 'but a realisation of purpose. They go with the Emperor's blessing.'

The group of dissenters left in peace, though it was smaller than the crowd who had come to ask permission to leave, for a full half of them had their spirits revived by the words of Mathieu, and the only soldiers that left with them were those too sick to fight.

They stopped a further night before the wall of the mountains, and kept watch closely there, for the dark was close and cold, and the voices of strange beings tittered from the mists.

Damp wood snapped in the fires, driving back a little of the night's chill. Mist rose from the soil in tendrils that searched through the air. The faithful round the fires talked in a hush, not wishing to call the fog to them, or whatever things might lurk in it. But vile though the land had become, there was a sense of confidence around the camp. The pilgrims were staunch, and though they were wary, their spirits remained high. Righteousness guarded them.

Watchful pickets walked the perimeter. Everyone took a turn. The sense of comradeship was strong, their faith making a coherent whole from many disparate parts. But the Cadians provided the backbone. They were the ones with the most experience. They had the greatest discipline, and it was their tanks that sat farthest out, targeting lenses staining the rising fog red as their weapons swept back and forth.

Colonel Odrameyer walked the line himself. His weather-beaten face, bristling eyebrows and moustache were famous, and the patrols saluted him as he passed. He stopped to tell a group of Naval deserters how to keep a better watch, advising rather than rebuking, and moved on. The fog was getting thicker and thicker. The congregational war train had been perfectly visible when he'd set out from his command vehicle, but only its smokestacks were above the vapours now, and every time the mist rolled over them, they appeared in a different place to where they had been before.

No fog would defeat them. The pilgrims had set their fires so that they were visible to each other. It was beautiful, thought Odrameyer, surprising himself. He'd not thought anything beautiful for a long time.

He passed a pair of his soldiers. He didn't know their names. Despite the fact his regiment was much reduced, there were still too many names to learn. When it came to the corpse-gathering after a battle he saw faces of those he did not know, and it saddened him that was so.

There was a younger one, and an older one. The older wore the marks of a squad second, a sergeant in waiting.

'Good evening, sir,' he said, full of respect.

Odrameyer nodded in response.

The younger was cockier. 'Nothing good about it, Dedlin. I'm freezing! I thought Iax was a warm world, sir.'

'Nature says it is,' said the colonel. 'Right now it's whatever they want it to be.' By 'they' he meant the enemy. The great foe that no one dared name. The sanction against acknowledging Chaos had become unworkable in most places since the Rift, but old habits died hard. 'We'll make it right, son, by His will.'

'His will,' the boy replied. The older soldier nodded and hurried his cohort along. Odrameyer continued to where he thought the train to be, and the pair disappeared into the mist.

Ten frustrating minutes passed. The fires began to give out, and the mist beyond was thick and blank. He reached the pla-steel wall of a Leman Russ standard variant, and realised he'd crossed the entire camp. He turned back, determined to find his way without asking for directions, not willing to admit he'd gone awry in the fog. He was lost again in moments, and turned about hopelessly.

A bell tolled. He heard singing. The train's organ began to play gentle hymns. He listened a moment, sure he had the direction fixed, and headed towards the sound.

As the singing went on, the mist thinned, and in a few minutes he was at the war train. Mathieu was standing in a weapons cupola up on the side, using it as a pulpit to deliver a sermon.

He was reaching the end of the First Homily, and Odrameyer got down on his knees and bowed his head. Dirty water soaked his trousers, but he bore the unpleasantness, letting his mind fix on his desire to serve the Emperor's will.

'For He of Terra,' the prayer ended.

'For He of Terra,' the crowd responded.

'Rise, my brothers, my sisters,' Mathieu said. His voice cut through the mist, when every other sound was muted. 'Do not fear this fog, though the enemy sends it to confound your senses. Do not fear what creatures wait beyond the light of our fires, though the enemy sends them to slay you. We are followers of the purest light of all, the light of the Emperor, which resides in us all, and that light will penetrate the darkest night, the thickest fog, as it penetrates the empyrean to guide our ships to port. There is a candle in every heart in this camp, each a small fire that might be stoked into a roaring blaze!'

Cries of affirmation rose from the congregation. There were hundreds present. Mathieu gave sermons every hour and a half, and the pilgrims never tired of them. Odrameyer had been a gruff man who practised his religion quietly, when he did so at all. He was an occasional blasphemer, and a sometime doubter.

That had been before.

'Many of us were there, at Hecatone, when the Emperor showed Himself to us, and brought the fiends of the Great Enemy low!' Mathieu said.

'Yes!' the crowd shouted. 'The Emperor!'

'Many of us have seen His hand. I myself witnessed His glory before, when the crew of the *Macragge's Honour* were in bondage to the Red Corsairs, and I was their priest. He came to me then, and set a boy free from the touch of the warp!'

'Praise be!' shouted the crowd. The mist quivered and shrank back. The train went from a single, visible stretch of wall to a huge shape, solid in the fog, and the more solid it became, the more the mist recoiled from it.

'Perhaps more of you might share your testimony?' Mathieu asked. 'Perhaps more of you will reveal what you have seen, and help us spread the new truth of the Master of Mankind?'

Voices called from the crowd.

'I saw Him on Monaeth Moti, before the last hive fell!' called one.

'He came to me in a dream, and told me not to go to the rations booth. The next day it was gone in fire.'

'The tarot has not lied to me since the Rift opened in the sky. I feel His eye upon me.'

'I saw Him, in the dark, the day that Drohl was attacked. He showed me the way to escape, and He guided me to save a hundred others.'

'Yes, yes. He is watching us all!' Mathieu shouted. 'He is at our side. Is that not so, Colonel Odrameyer?'

Mathieu was looking right at him.

'Would you care to share your own experience, colonel? For those who have not heard it? It is a most uplifting tale.'

Uplifting was not the word that Odrameyer would use. He sweated despite the chill night. He was used to commanding thousands of troops, dealing with the worst alien horrors, and the most powerful men in the galaxy, but Mathieu unnerved him. Part of it was embarrassment – he did not like to retell his story – but that was not all. There was something behind Mathieu's eyes that was terrifying. He could barely believe he could be scared of so slight and unkempt a man, but he found it hard to look into the militant-apostolic's face.

He could not say no. He opened his mouth to speak.

'No, colonel, come here,' said Mathieu. 'Join me, join me so that all may hear what you have to say.' He beckoned.

'Very well,' said Odrameyer gruffly. He walked to the side of the train. Mathieu's silent bodyguard stepped aside from the staple ladder leading up to the weapon's cupola. His servo-skull hovered down and followed him up the side. Odrameyer scaled the vehicle. Mathieu welcomed him in.

'Please, colonel,' Mathieu said to him, as he clambered over the rail mount for the cupola's heavy stubber. 'Leave nothing out.' He then turned to the crowd. 'Colonel Odrameyer, of the Cadian Four Thousand and Twenty-First Armoured Regiment!'

There was a scattering of applause, and shouts of 'Welcome, brother!'

'Remember, tell them everything,' whispered Mathieu.

'We were on Parmenio,' he said, and immediately faltered. His voice echoed back at him from the mist, and he did not know how to go on. Hundreds of expectant faces looked up at him from the congregation. He was acutely aware they were waiting.

Throne, he cursed inwardly, *get a grip of yourself, man.*

He started again. 'I have never been an overtly religious man,' he said. 'I have always believed in the Emperor, and His protection of mankind. But to me, He was distant, an ideal. I was lax in my following of the rites. I attended fewer of the regimental services than I should.'

He paused. He expected opprobrium. None came.

'Forgive me if this makes me seem faithless. I was not. But Terra was far away, and the Eye of Terror was close. I have trained since childhood to fight the Emperor's wars, and though the Emperor was always there, He was a talisman, a statue, His light shone over Terra, not Cadia. The light of my lasgun was closer, and mine to wield.'

He looked down at his fists. They were shaking, and clenched so tightly his knuckles showed white against his skin.

'When the enemy came, and Cadia fell, my faith wavered

more. The talismans seemed useless, the Emperor further than ever. I never stopped believing, as some did. They thought we had been abandoned. I did not, but I will not lie to you. I considered the possibility. We fought in many wars. My men fought on fifteen worlds in the last years, so many they blur into one, a picture of fire and death. My faith did not die, but it guttered low, and never any lower than on Parmenio.'

What could he say about Parmenio? It had been saved, but it was a wasteland of mud and sickness, like this world was becoming. He remembered the rot and the death. But he also remembered the light, and though the night pressed coldly close, he spoke loudly, unafraid.

'We came from outside. We were not part of Fleet Primus, but an early vanguard reinforcement, sent to Ultramar to hold the defences. When we arrived, we were asked to stop Parmenio falling while the lord commander, Emperor's blessing be upon him, marshalled his forces and set his strategy into motion. We waited weeks for reinforcement, and we were tested every day. On Parmenio the dead would come in waves, young, old, civilian and soldier, all with that dreadful grin of death, and eyes that lived in rotting flesh. I...' He faltered. 'I cannot bear to recall the look of terror in them. They were aware of what they had become. I am certain of it.

'There was an enemy breakthrough at our command post. I and my staff officers were obliged to fight at close quarters. The dead were everywhere, but I remember well in particular one young man, in an apprentice colonus' garb. His teeth grinned through green flesh, open at the cheek. His arm was a slime of flesh held on by stinking sinews. He came for me, trying to scratch at my exposed face. One wound from those nails is enough to induct you into their ranks. I thrust my sword into his chest. I have a power sword. I am an officer of rank. I was lucky. The blade laid him low. Several of my men were killed, but it is not their screams that haunt me – it is the eyes of that youth, rolling in horror, pleading silently for an end. I…' His voice cracked under the strain of remembering, and threatened to desert him entirely in front of these people, but they had to hear. They had to understand. He forced himself to continue. 'Thank the Emperor I was able to give him release.

'Every day we killed them and we killed them, and the day after there would be more, and some of those would wear the faces of comrades who had fallen the day before. Some of my men went mad, and there was not one of us who did not despair. We waited to be relieved. Every day I begged to be informed of the primarch's plans, and when we might see the Angels of Death fighting alongside us. They would not tell me, it would have been tantamount to informing the enemy themselves, but I needed to know. Nearly two months passed before the Adeptus Astartes were in place.

'We survived, we men. There are many in this galaxy who give thanks to the primarch, but I do not. I would like to say it was all down to our training, and our grit, had I not experienced the effect that world had on our minds and on our souls. We were corroded, inside and out, by relentless horror. We would have died, some of us clawed down by the impossibly living dead, but the rest of us would have died from withered spirits. First our faith, then our hope, finally our sanity would have deserted us. I have seen this happen to men, many times. Then we would have died in our bodies, given up, or perhaps lost our will altogether and prostrated ourselves in front of the foe and begged to be spared. I have seen this happen too. We would have been lost, were it not for one of our regimental preachers who, in his death, showed us the light. Were it not for the intervention of the Emperor Himself.'

He fell silent. The mist was thinning, and he could see the fires closest to the war train properly now, not only as will-o'-the-wisps in the murk, and he could see the people below the train – faces of every type and colour turned up to him, from dozens of worlds, hanging onto his words. Soldiers whose own homes had burned, and in one sense they were the fortunate ones, for many more endured endless fears for their loved ones. A soldier rarely got news from his people once enlisted; now there was none for any of them.

He looked over them, and he felt pity, an emotion he had once only had small stores of. There were far more listening than he thought, drifting even now from the comfort of the flames to hear him speak his testimony.

'His name was Frater Othis.'

A light sliced across the crowd. Odrameyer looked up into the face of Iax's larger moon. As if it were a sword blade, the moonbeam cut the lid of cloud, and stars, cold and pure in the dark of the void, shone upon the sickened land.

Murmurs went through the crowd. Odrameyer's heart lifted a little. Once, he had not believed in signs. He did now.

'When the Adeptus Astartes arrived, the enemy's attacks became larger, more desperate. On the day we were relieved, the largest attack came. The sky turned black with clouds of flies that fell biting on my regiment, so thick that when flamers were turned against them, the air seemed to burn, and then filled again. Under the cover of this assault, the dead attacked in a horde so vast, I cannot put a number on their multitudes.

'We people of Cadia are bold, raised to be warriors from birth, and yet that day I saw many men and women who I knew to have courage in them tremble with fear. There were tens of thousands of the dead coming at us, moaning and snapping their black teeth. The flies surged around them, bleeding our las-fire of its strength and obscuring our aim. Our big guns took a toll on them, but we were poorly supplied with artillery, and our tanks' magazines were empty of shells. Before we knew it, they were on us, biting and clawing, falling in an avalanche of rot into our trenches. Scores of us fell in those first moments, hundreds in the minutes afterwards.

'I remember my moments of terror in shame, for a Cadian officer should have no fear, and yet I did. I feared to die. Moreover, I feared to become like the dead, and be made a slave to the very beings who would destroy all we value. I called a retreat, but my voice was not heard, for my vox-operator choked upon the swarm of insects, his body putrefying in front of me as they packed his mouth with their bodies. There was a blast of plasma as my gunner unleashed his gun, and another, greater wash of heat when his weapon exploded. In his panic, he did not purge the firing chamber, and the cooling vents were clogged by the flies. The rest of my command squad died, blasted apart by the sun gun's failure. I was flung clear, scorched, but alive. It is my great dishonour that I lay there and watched our colours burn in the mud.

'The dead were coming closer, I could hear their moans, and I prepared to die, yet then another voice came to my ears, that of Othis, and that is when I saw the Emperor at work.

'Othis advanced calmly, his pistol held up, his chainsword inactive. No temporal weapons did he deploy, but he wielded the word of the Emperor. He sang the great hymns of Cadia, and his voice was loud with his faith, full of a heavenly music, and the power of elemental forces. The flies dropped from the sky around him, little more than flecks of blackness trodden underfoot. The dead swung towards him, their dark masters sensing his holiness and his light, and desiring above all things to douse it. But when they approached, they fell down, truly dead, and they did not rise again. I watched him go, alone, the flies falling around him, the dead stumbling to a final halt, and then he was gone into their midst.' Odrameyer's voice was strong again, swollen with the wonder of what he had seen.

'My soldiers, in full retreat and close to the edge of breaking only moments before, stood amazed, their weapons hanging from limp fingers. They stared after Frater Othis, into the gap he had pushed into the dead and the swarms. I scrambled up to my feet, my fear forgotten. I took up the standard pole of my colour sergeant, paying no heed to the burn of the hot metal as I brandished it over my head, and shouted.

'"He is with us! The Lord of Mankind watches over us, sons and daughters of Cadia! He is with us! Attack, attack, for the Emperor, for Terra, for Cadia!" There was no strategy, only a desperate charge into the teeth of death. By instinct, we formed a wedge, ragged at first, then firmer and deeper as the regiment gathered together, and poured up over the trenches. Everyone. Infantrymen, artillerymen, tank crew who had lost their mounts, staff officers, the hale, the injured. Every tank still running. Every person on that battlefront who could hold a gun. Support auxilia abandoned their crates of powercells and took up the weapons of the fallen. Our medicae put down their stretchers and drew their pistols.

'"Onward, onward! For Cadia!"

'We ran into the foe. They fell before our fury and our faith, their strength denied them by the power of the God-Emperor Himself, and we slaughtered them. Their return blows were feeble, their protective shrouds of flies faded away. I caught one last sight of Othis. Though far ahead, the path he had pushed into the enemy had not closed, as if they could not cross the ground he had walked upon. I saw him hold aloft his holy symbol – a heavy, golden, barred letter I. I had often thought it beautiful, but I did not understand the power of that symbol until that day.

'There was a blinding flash. I threw up my arms to protect my eyes, but then I saw the light did not hurt my eyes, and the blast front that followed touched not a single one of my warriors, nor did it stir even a hair on their heads. But where it touched the dead, it was another matter.

'They exploded into ash, showers of it, soft and fine as snow, and they fell to nothing for a mile around. The light tore the heart from the horde of the dead. I looked up then, and thought I saw in the pillar of holy flame touching the sky, a great giant in golden armour, our god come to save us.

'Then He was gone, and the light was gone, and the sky was clear of toxic cloud, but blue and pure, and the trails of Space Marine assault craft were grey across it. We were saved, by the Emperor. By then we were too exhausted to do anything other than watch the fire trails of their drop craft. No one cheered. There was no celebration.

'Of Frater Othis there was no sign, only a blackened circle some hundred feet across at the heart of the enemy horde, surrounded by the ash of the dead.

'After the battle, I reported what I had seen to Lord Guilliman's corps of logisticators. They showed no interest in what I'd witnessed. But I heard rumours of similar happenings, and of what happened on the plains of Hecatone. I thought never to see the light of the Emperor again, though I felt blessed to have done so, and would have died happy having seen it, until Frater Mathieu sought me out, and questioned me about the battle. I saw the same light in his eyes. That is why I pledged my regiment to the Adeptus Ministorum, before we could be inducted into Fleet Primus. And so here we are.'

Odrameyer looked to Mathieu, who nodded. By now the

clouds had fled, and the sky was full of stars. The planet was on the far side of the sun to the Great Rift. It had turned its face from Chaos' horror, and the night sky was the untouched void. Up there, the great ships of Guilliman's crusade looked placidly down, metal gods in their heaven.

'I have nothing more to say,' said Odrameyer. 'This is my testimony. The Emperor protects.'

CHAPTER TWENTY-ONE

KILL-TEAM

Not long after Mathieu's crusade set out, psychic storms began growing over the planet. They affected the upper orbits first, intensifying the effects of Mortarion's spells, and dashing the last slender hopes the Imperial forces had of hunting out the artefact from orbit, but occlusion works both ways. Two Overlord tank lifters ghosted through the poisoned atmosphere towards the surface unseen.

In their loading clamps the Overlords carried armoured vehicles of the Novamarines in quartered bone and blue. The lead bore a Repulsor main battle tank, Executioner class. Behind its brutal block of a hull was slung an Impulsor grav-transport, no less hard in outline, though a little smaller. On the benches in the rear of the Impulsor, six Primaris Space Marines in Phobos plate faced one another across the open-topped back, feet mag-locked to the deck, armour systems bracing them in position. The trailing Overlord carried two further Impulsors, both fully occupied, Assault Intercessors in the first, ranged Intercessors in the second. There were but five Space Marines of the ranged group: Justinian Parris' squad, four of whom occupied the transport compartment, the other driving. The sixth position was taken up by Magos Fe, a member of the Adeptus Mechanicus, who wore badges proclaiming his allegiance to Mars and the Adeptus Astra Telepathica. Justinian had the honour and responsibility of keeping him alive.

The tech-priest was not enjoying the ride down through the atmosphere. Through the clear faceplate of his environmental gear, his features were locked in a rictus, teeth clamped so tightly together they looked like they might break.

'Relax,' said Maxentius-Drontio, Parris' second. 'We will be down soon.'

'I will attempt to,' said the priest. He had a small, delicate head, a characteristic exaggerated by his brutal augmetic limbs and his heavy helm and chestplate.

The vox clicked in Sergeant Justinian's earpiece. Maxentius-Drontio opened up a private channel. 'Probably wishes he could have ridden down in the Executioner, but his equipment's worth more than he is. Got to keep them separate, in case we lose one.' He was in good humour, and found the tech-priest's discomfort amusing.

Maxentius-Drontio switched back to open frequencies. 'It will be fine, just hold on,' he said.

The tech-priest was pressing as hard as he could at the bench with his robotic hands, helping brace himself against the backrest. 'There is no provision for such an action,' he said, half strangled by fear. 'Nothing to grasp.'

'Take it up with Cawl,' said Maxentius-Drontio. 'These are his designs.' He patted the seats. 'You're a tech-priest. You know him, yes?' His lack of seriousness was lost on Fe, who managed a frightened shake of his head.

'No, no, I have no personal connection with the Archmagos

Dominus. But if by the will of the Machine-God I ever meet him, I will submit a respectful request for a pattern alteration to the templates of these machines.'

The ships were coming in at a shallow angle and low speed, energy emissions restricted, to lessen their chances of detection. Not that Justinian expected to be seen. The atmosphere was a greenish soup. Blinking runes on his retinal display warned of corrosive elements. Warp lightning crackled in the skies, and where the bolts went ghostly faces grinned.

'I would not want to breathe this air,' Justinian said to Maxentius-Drontio.

'We might not get much choice,' said his second. 'This stuff will eat through our seals eventually.'

So much had changed in such a brief space of time. A few months had passed since their battle aboard Galatan. The Sixth Auxiliary Squad had been permanently attached to the Third Company and redesignated as Fourth Battleline. They were now serving under Lieutenant Edermo in the second demi-company, who despite Justinian's somewhat cold first meeting with him, had been impressed by Squad Parris and sought them out.

Not that there was much left of his squad. Only three of them had survived the attack on the Crucius Portis II, Achilleos being the other besides he and Maxentius-Drontio. He wore his bionic left arm as a mark of honour, leaving his armour off to display the gleaming chromite of the limb. Mechanical fingers curled loosely around his bolt rifle.

The other two were still relatively new to the squad, and they were not like Justinian and the others, who were Mars-born all. One, Orpino, had been a Scout who had experienced the apotheosis of Cawl's Gift rather than the older process of trans-formation, whereas the other had been a firstborn who had undergone the Calgar Procedure and crossed the Rubicon

Primaris. He was not alone, for although all were Primaris brothers in the group of twenty-six, nine of them had been firstborn, including Apothecary Locko and the lieutenant, whose own near death in the attack had forced the issue for him.

Following Chapter Master Dovaro's death, the depletion of firstborn ranks on Galatan and the arrival of more Primaris tech with the crusade fleets, conversion from the old type of Space Marine to the new had been enthusiastically embraced by the Chapter. They were rapidly moving from being one of the Ultramarines primogenitor Chapters with the fewest Primaris Marines to one with the most. That they all shared exactly the same physiology made it a little easier for Justinian to feel brotherhood with them, but only a little. The cultural gulf between Ultramar and Honourum remained.

His helm vox pinged. The lead Techmarine pilot was opening up a communications channel to the whole recon force.

'Prepare for release in three minutes. Activate grav-engines on my mark.'

In the driver's compartment, Pasac, the fifth and final member of Justinian's squad, responded. *'Instructions received. Awaiting activation order.'*

There was no difference Justinian could see, just the same thick clouds all around them. He imagined then falling through them forever, and never hitting the ground. But the engines were changing pitch, the Overlords were braking. The underslung tanks shivered.

'Surface soundings positive. Three hundred feet and closing. One hundred feet altitude required for safe insertion. Approaching. Activate.'

The Impulsor's engines came on. A wave of contragrav bleedover passed up through the tank from the protection baffles and shook the transport.

'Engines active,' Justinian's driver announced. Identical responses came from the other three tanks.

The lead Overlord dipped suddenly.

'Insertion position reached. Tank one, away.' A pause. 'Tank two, away.'

The lead aircraft pulled up into a steep climb, flashing past the nose of Justinian's transport. Their own Overlord dipped low, a bird hunting insects over water.

'Tank three, away,' their pilot said. The carry arms holding the Impulsor in front of Justinian's sprang open, and it vanished into the fog. Then it was their turn.

'Tank four, away.'

Justinian's tank fell quickly. The Overlord disappeared, and for a second they were alone in the green murk. Then they reached a height where the contragav could bite, the thrum of the engines changed in pitch, and they came to a cushioned stop. Water bulged up and washed away from them.

Boot locks disengaged. The Intercessors got up, presenting their bolt rifles to the fog. Fat droplets swirled about them. Their world was restricted to a sphere ten yards across. Magos Fe remained seated, barely less terrified than before.

'I can't see anything in this,' said Maxentius-Drontio.

'Lieutenant Edermo, can you hear me? Provide location pulse,' Justinian voxed. He got nothing but silence in return. 'Brother Pasac,' he ordered his driver. 'Slow search sweep.'

The stablights on the front of the tank came on. All they did was fix two cones of light into the fog. Mud-brown water stretched in all directions. The tank turned slowly around, the thump of its contragav twitching the water's surface like a drumskin.

'Looks like the hydroways have overflowed,' said Justinian. 'But where are we?'

'I see something,' said Achilleos. He braced his bolt rifle on his thigh so he could point with his augmetic arm. 'There.'

Justinian followed his gesture past the antennae of the orbital comms array atop the driver's compartment. There were a number of shadows off to the left of irregular shape, but they could have been anything. His suit's sensorium was as useless as his own eyes, the retinal display and the augur screen embedded in his vambrace both crawling with nonsense alphanumeric runes.

'Ten degrees left, Pasac, fifty yards ahead,' Justinian ordered. 'Let's see what we have here. Maybe we can use it as a landmark to guide the others in. Brother Orpino, get on the iron storm.'

'Yes, brother-sergeant,' said Orpino. He went through into the driver's compartment. Justinian got a glimpse of Pasac in the dark, surrounded by shining screens, before the door slid shut again. A moment later, Orpino emerged from the compartment hatch, and took hold of the pintle stubber attached to the ring.

They coasted forward, lights only dazzling them, still lost. The shapes grew, and suddenly resolved into a copse of trees of no mortal species.

'What by the Throne…?' murmured Maxentius-Drontio.

The trees were tall, oddly pyramidal in shape, covered in slick bark that wept rivulets of slime. Huge, globular flowers quivered on top of the squat trunks, sticky yellow pollen puffing out of them at odd intervals. But it was their mouths that gave away their true nature: like those of sea beasts, huge slits lined with teeth that ran most of the way up the trunk. They sighed and whispered. A fat pink tongue lolled out of one and splashed into the water as the tank passed by. Their branches twitched like fingers, and reached out to touch.

'Stay clear,' said Justinian.

'Where by the primarch are we?' asked Achilleos. 'My cartograph makes no sense.'

'That's why we need him,' said Maxentius-Drontio, nudging Magos Fe with his boot. 'Isn't that right?'

'I can do nothing without my machines,' said the tech-priest touchily. 'Where are the others?'

'We have no fix on them,' admitted Maxentius-Drontio.

They coasted on at minimal speed. Dozens of the trees crawled out from the fog, and then buildings, submerged up to the top of their ground-floor doors. These too proliferated.

'A civitas,' said Achilleos.

'Yes, but which one?' said Maxentius-Drontio.

'Any sign of Lieutenant Edermo?' Justinian asked Pasac.

'*Negative, brother-sergeant. No signum, no vox. Nothing.*'

'Then head for the centrum. Carefully, and slowly.'

The buildings grew in stature as they neared the middle of the town, dead plants hanging off their sides. The patterns of roads and canals emerged, each one lined by daemon trees.

'Hiastamus,' said Orpino. 'Look, brothers.'

He pointed up the side of a seven-storey building covered in judgemental statuary, all now smothered in grey moss. A sign proclaimed it to be the local Administratum office of the Hiastamus sub-district.

'That makes no sense. According to the planetary data, and our landing point, Hiastamus should be on the other side of the world.'

'At least we know where we are now,' said Achilleos.

'How long will that remain the case?' Justinian said.

Past the office, they came to the town's central square, also inundated by filthy water. In the centre a gargantuan tree towered over everything, and its branches were heavy with terrible fruit.

From the end of each twig a hanged corpse dangled, smothered in thick growths of fungus of a startling orange, recognisably human nonetheless.

'Remind me why we volunteered for this mission again?' said

Maxentius-Drontio. He turned to Justinian. 'Maybe we should topple this, it is an abomination.'

'We cannot afford to make too much noise,' said Justinian. 'If we are detected, then our mission will have failed. It is as simple as that. Pasac,' he said, 'move on.'

They hovered over the water, passing the face of the tree where three mouth slits pumped out washes of vomit and sighed sad words of self-comfort.

'Can it see us, that is the question,' asked Achilleos.

'It will be aware,' said Magos Fe, speaking up for the first time. 'These plants are a form of daemon, but I doubt they are sentient enough to see us as a threat, or have the means to report it.'

'Are you sure?' asked Maxentius-Drontio.

'I am a magos of the Technii-Psykanum, and a valued servant of the Adeptus Astra Telepathica. It is my role in life to know such things,' said the magos.

'Well, I do not like it,' said Maxentius-Drontio.

They finished circling the tree, and came to another exit from the central plaza. Justinian ordered Pasac to take it. The civitas was small, and soon they were cruising back out of the town limits into the flooded lands beyond.

'Nothing but water, and mud,' said Achilleos. The flotsam of the town bobbed sadly past, pushed into sudden motion by the passing of the grav-tank.

'Hiastamus was a coastal town,' said Justinian.

The driver's compartment door opened, and Pasac turned back to look out into the carrying bay.

'Brother-sergeant, I have signum lock on Lieutenant Edermo.'

'Go to him, now,' said Justinian. 'The sooner we can get the magos' machines up and running, the quicker we shall have this done.'

'Look sharp, magos,' said Maxentius-Drontio. 'You are up soon.'

CHAPTER TWENTY-TWO

MOUNTAIN OF FLESH

Mathieu led his war congregation towards the cut through the Loann Mountains, riding atop the principal pulpit at the feet of the protective angel above the organ. All around the train marched the hordes of the faithful, those who had witnessed the greater miracles lit up by their experiences, those who had not seen such things drawing faith from those who had.

Odricus' Cut loomed ahead, the wound in the planet so deep the rock was still bare and weeping four millennia after it was made. It was a wound that was now infected. The shadows of the hills fell over them, chilling them with a fever's touch; the air was hot and close, yet they shivered in that shade. Black fluid ran down the stone walls in place of water, clogging the drainage systems with its thickness, so that awful slicks of matter gathered in the gutter heads sloping down to the plain either side of the highway's embankment and choked the hydroway canals running either side. From Mathieu's vantage, he could see all the way down the man-made canyon, whose walls grew so close through perspective that they seemed to touch. A thin stripe of green sky watched them.

The column came to a halt before the cut. Mathieu searched the cliffs and their high tops for signs of ambush. The land all about was deathly quiet. The noise of the Witnesses was subdued by the devastation they found themselves traversing, and further attenuated by Mathieu's height over them, so that he existed in a quiet world. The waiting engine throbbed beneath his feet. Behind him stood Odrameyer's liaisons, his own presbyters, the headmen of various militias and the Sisters Palatine of the Adepta Sororitas, all hanging on his word.

He narrowed his eyes. If he were the enemy, he would stage an attack here. He would crowd the edges of the slot with fiends and toss in explosives to slaughter the faithful. He would fire on the Witnesses from these positions of impunity, and he would emerge triumphant with minimal casualties to show in the ranks of his infernal army.

'I am not a man of war,' he said to himself, then let his voice rise to a shout, and the words boomed down the length of the cutting. 'I am a man of faith! We go forward.'

'Most holy father,' said Odrameyer's chief lieutenant immediately; he had been waiting to object. 'If we go here, the enemy will inflict on us a terrible slaughter.'

'This is our chosen path, shown to me by the Emperor,' said Mathieu. 'We take it under His protection.' He turned to look at the assembled leaders. 'The Emperor protects,' he said.

'The Emperor protects,' they responded, though a few of them could not meet his eye.

'Fear not,' he said. 'Forward.'

With a titanic hiss of steam, the war train lurched into motion. The high, dark stone of Odricus' Cut closed overhead.

* * *

The journey through the pass was fraught, but done quickly. Seven miles lay between the two sides, and not a sign of the foe did they see. However, upon gaining the far edge they found a very different scene, the mountains having formed a bulwark against the corruption of Iax, keeping it from the provinces closer to First Landing. On the far side, Chaos ran rampant.

The hills swept down to lowlands that had once supported a mix of arboreal plots and well-organised farms. These gave way to the pasturelands of Hythia, and the large marshes the province was dominated by.

Against all logic and fluid mechanics, this was all gone. An upwelling of Stygian waters had overtaken the land, filling the lowlands as far as the eye could see with shallow lakes. No goodly living thing could be seen, only their remains: rotting woods, greened skeletons of livestock lying in puddles, all vegetation black in death. Things were alive there, but only of a malevolent sort. Clouds of insects hovered over the water, some unnaturally large, and the surfaces of the pools rippled with hidden motions. Where the land rose, small islands persisted, and buildings protruded over the dank expanses. The great highway too stood proud of the meres, its embankment now acting as a dyke, but all else was still water: dark, stagnant and noisome.

A thin, yellowish mist scudded over the lakes, ripe with scents of decay and death, restricting visibility to a few miles at most, less where the fume gathered thickly.

'We go carefully from here,' said Mathieu.

The train's reactor trembled like the heart of a frightened beast as it drove out onto the plain. The mountains dwindled behind them, until they were a low mound on the horizon, the corpse of a giant who had laid down in despair and died. The marshes stretched on forever. The clouds were an awful green. A storm crackled lethargically in the distance, filling the louring sky with traceries of anaemic lightning. When rain fell on the column, it stank of sulphur, and burned the skin. The Witnesses sang louder to quell their fear, and the skies rumbled warningly in return.

After a time, hideous trumpeting blasted over the inundated farmlands, and a lookout cried out, and pointed to the south-west, where a gargantuan, pale shape disturbed the fogs. The shape resolved as a mountainous beast, come heaving across the landscape obliquely towards the road and the Witnesses. It bellowed mournfully, and a cloud of flying things swarmed around it.

The foreparts came first: a head like a hill, bearing the features of a mammalian creature, though juvenile in form, as if an infant rodent had been made massive. From its slobbering mouth lolled a tongue dozens of yards long, yellow eyes blinking along its length. The beast's face, by comparison, seemed blind; the two depressions it had either side of its face that hinted at eye sockets were covered over with slack and pustulating skin. Rodent's teeth jutted from its upper lip, yellow and black with cavities as large as caverns. There were sockets for a lower pair, but these were bloody and pus-filled, their rawness revealed by the creature's drooping lip. It keened as it moved, a cry of despair and pain that came close to the sound of a woman weeping. The noise of its woe filled the plain with a palpable misery, like a poison gas that, though invisible, has enough density that it might be felt on the skin before it kills. More than a few in the army watching succumbed to its sorrow, and wept.

Drool poured from its mouth, the stink of it vile even from so far away. Floods of it ran over the stumpy, cancerous limbs it used to drag itself along. Stands of sparse hair quivered over skin that was otherwise pale and naked, the covering thin enough that the watching army could see parasites large as men lurking in the deeper thickets.

Odrameyer had come up into the command pulpit for a while, and he signalled to his master voxman, whispering to her as if the beast could hear what they said, though it surely could not, so loud were its wails, and so distant it was.

'Have our armour units move up. Give me some prognostications on range, number of rounds we may be able to fire before it is on us, and whether we might be able to kill it.'

'Yes, sir,' the woman said. When she had gone to her task, Mathieu placed a hand on Odrameyer's shoulder. The colonel suppressed a little shudder as he felt the strength of the Emperor pass into him.

'I would let it be,' said Mathieu, and he did not hide his voice. 'We are in no danger.'

The creature presented its flank to them. The belly rested on the ground, rippling to drag it over the land. Its spine was high and arched, lifting up the back in a crooked ridge. In the flesh-faces of this peak, small orifices twitched, sphincters unwinding in sinewy spasms and gushes of fluid. Rushing out upon these falls of slime, wriggling sacs were birthed. From afar, compared to the huge size of the creature, these seemed small, and yet they were not. They knocked free the mountain-beast's parasites where they rolled over them. When these offspring hit the ground they did not burst into ruin, despite the great height they had fallen, but the sacs split with more explosions of foulness, and frill-headed monsters struggled out, shook off sprays of slime, and went gambolling after their giant parent. They followed, yipping happily, gathering in large packs that grew larger even as Odrameyer and Mathieu watched. Odrameyer took out a pair of magnoculars to watch some as they bounded past a ruined domicile.

Ranging runes pulsed on the magnified view.

'Emperor alive, those things are fifteen feet long!'

They pushed through the water easily, and when they fell into areas that were too deep for them, they paddled like whelps until they could surge out, delighted.

'Do not fear them,' said Mathieu. 'The Emperor shields us.'

'Then you are sure it has not seen us?' asked Odrameyer. He did not believe it could be so, for the eyes on the tongue looked in all directions, and the train was obvious upon the raised highway.

'Have faith, colonel,' said Mathieu, his calm voice a balm. 'Whether it has or has not seen us, it will not come against us,' said Mathieu. 'It stays upon its course, and neither it nor its offspring look in our direction.'

This much was true, Odrameyer admitted, though he remained concerned. The beast came nearer, and would soon cross the highway, but it stayed true to its path, and it did not deviate towards them. Still, Odrameyer had his tanks fan out either side of the war train, four squadrons of them, closely packed on the road, but such was the beast's size they could easily elevate their cannons, fire over each other, and still hit it.

'It is going for the end of the mountains, where it shall turn west and head for First Landing. All the apostate traitors will gather there,' said Mathieu. 'Lord Guilliman gives open challenge to the fallen devil Mortarion. That is where the final battle will be.'

'And the fate of Iax decided, if not all Ultramar.'

Mathieu smiled. 'You think it is the primarch who will save this realm? That is our role in this, brother. The battle might be won or lost at First Landing, but it is by the Emperor's will working through us that this war shall be decided. He has a great task in store for us.'

The beast reached the embankment. It paused a moment as its rotting bulk encountered shaped earth and hard rock-crete, gave out a dispirited howl, then heaved itself up the slope, gouging out a deep trench as it did so. Crash-fences buckled under it, long ribbons of metal crumpled like dry grasses dragged under and along with it, ripping out at the posts. It crushed the central safe zone between the two sets of four lanes, toppling the troughs that had once held floral displays and fine examples of trees, now only containing a stinking black slop.

The thing's exertions caused its flesh to undulate, squeezing its orifices and forcing a rain of the monsters free from their birthing canals. They exploded on the hard rockcrete of the highway. Even those that did not meet this fate failed to hatch, for they were premature and small, twitching feebly within their sheaths of mucus.

The beast straddled the highway, its faeces-streaked hind-quarters hauled up the bank, gushes of dung squirting from the rear, the smell of it so rank it caused the Witnesses to gag. Its paddle forelimbs pushed up ridges of earth and stone, and with a last mournful bellow, it slipped down the far embank-ment. The rest of it followed, the overstretched skin on its belly tearing with the effort, its arrival sending out a slow wave of mud and filthy water, before its progress resumed the stately, painful manner of before. Its children swarmed up and over the bank, skidding gleefully through the trails of filth their parent left behind. They skipped and squirmed, all the while baying like hounds. By the hundred they slithered their way over the obstacle, and back into the new marshes.

The stream of its offspring slackened, dwindling from a herd to groups of a few dozen, then to individuals. The last bounded over the embankment, and paused halfway across. It sniffed at the air, and turned to look at the column.

Odrameyer tensed. 'Prepare to open fire,' he said.

With an idiot's grin plastered over its face, the creature waved a bloated, damp hand at the Witnesses, then raced after its kin. The giant beast moved on, and presented its back to the highway. It gave out another mournful booming, and was swallowed by the mist.

Odrameyer looked over the road. The creature had carved a furrow into the hardtop some fifty yards across and at least twenty feet deep. It was filled with a noxious mix of fluids that was only slowly running into the marsh.

'This will slow us down,' said Odrameyer.

'You have bridge-building equipment accompanying your armoured units?'

'Yes, frater, as you requested, I made sure to find some.'

'The Emperor guides me,' said Mathieu placidly, 'and I guide you. I suggest you bring the mechanisms up from the rear, and make good this gap. It will come to pass that we must leave the road, but that time has not come yet.'

CHAPTER TWENTY-THREE

A MOMENT OF REFLECTION

Felix was patrolling the mid-tier eastern walls of First Landing when he encountered Donas Maxim.

A chance meeting was not unlikely. There were dozens of Chapters of Space Marines at the city. Each had their roles to play, their routes to walk. Only Guilliman knew everything, and Felix, who was influential but outside the organisational structure of any Chapter, was free to do as he wished. So he walked the walls alone.

The haze that shrouded Iax had thickened to a brown fog. The heavens rumbled with barely contained power. By chronomark, it was just before dawn, but the sun had ceased to rise and set, and a constant, dim light suffused everything. No ships could land and none could depart. There was no contact with the fleet, but Felix had no concerns. He trod his lonely path, thinking of the future, and the many tasks he must perform to secure his tetra of Ultramar. War was only a part of that.

The mid-tier wall clung to the cliffs in ripples like those of underground flowstones. Above and below him were the delicate towers of the city, surrounded by their dying gardens; outside it, the flat agricultural plains that so incongruously interspersed the karst towers. To save himself from the miasma choking everything, he kept his helmet on, and set to hard-void protocols. His breathing echoed in his ears. His mask was clamped tight to his face. Occasional notification chimes of incoming data or systems events overlaid the hum of his reactor and the cumulative whine of hundreds of fibre bundles contracting and stretching. Cawl's armour marks were quieter than the old. He had met Space Marines whose battleplate practically growled with every step they took, but he was glad the Gravis type was not silent, for he had come to find the clicks and hums comforting – womblike, he supposed. The sound's similarity to that made by the machines that had kept him prisoner aboard Cawl's ship did not bother him much. His armour was a machine he controlled. It was his protection. His ally. He could discard it or not as he pleased. He was not at the mercy of another to take a breath of free air.

He was feeling a little guilty. He should not have come here, leaving his given realm for this fight. He wondered why he had. Was it only his need to confront his gene-father about the path he was taking, or did he simply want to see him, to draw reassurance from his presence – inspiration perhaps, or strength, to perform the impossible task he had been given?

Any and all, he thought. *Any and all.*

He stopped at a point where the wall's sinuous curve embraced a gun platform. A portable missile system in Silver Templar colours tracked back and forward with mechanical diligence, exactly the same speed, exactly the same arc. All the way to the north-east, where it gave a clunk and a little jerk, as its servo-motors turned it back and it made a turn to the south-east, where the clunk and jerk were repeated and it returned the other way. A single, rounded glass eye stared out from the centre of the quad launchers towards the horizon. There were armoured ammo boxes nearby full of spare missiles. He saw the hulking shapes of two servitors, both offline, both with retrofitted hazard robes over their organic components. They were completely still, waiting for the voice of their machine master to call them into action.

Felix walked to the wall and looked out, unconsciously following the movement of the missile system.

'An endless watch, tetrarch,' said a voice Felix knew. He turned about and met the gaze of another Space Marine.

'Codicier Donas Maxim,' he said, and let his pleasure at seeing the man show in his voice. 'I have not met with you in some time. It is good to do so again.'

They clasped forearms as warriors did, wrist to wrist, ceramite vambraces touching.

'Good to see you too, tetrarch.' Maxim stood by Felix.

'You have undergone the Calgar Procedure,' Felix said. 'When?'

'Two weeks ago. It only seemed right,' said Maxim. 'I thought that here was a way to make me better able to serve the Imperium. I had no right to turn down the chance. The risks were commensurate with the gain.'

'I am curious to know what effect it has on the firstborn. How do you feel?'

'Bigger,' said Maxim.

Felix snorted.

'I mean it,' said Maxim. 'It is strange to grow suddenly. I was one shape for three hundred years, and now I am another, though I think what I like best is your wargear,' he said. He opened one gauntleted hand and examined it. 'Superior in every way. It should be made more widely available.'

'I sometimes think Cawl refuses to manufacture his weapons

to suit the firstborn in order to tempt them to cross the Rubicon,' said Felix.

Now Maxim gave a brief laugh. 'Perhaps. I am sure the real reason is far more practical. The firstborn are a dying kind. Why waste resources on them? I suspect that is closer to the truth. I for one appreciate my new form, and the strength it gives.' He paused. 'It was worth the experience of having my bones melted from the inside out, anyway. And I am told the residual pain will pass.'

'You have fought much, since I saw you on Macragge, I understand.'

'The primarch has had me busy,' said Maxim. 'After Mortarion's challenge to him at Hecatone, he summoned me back from my Chapter, and had me join his Concilia Psykana. After a few months of that, I began to consider crossing the Rubicon. The things I have seen and done...'

Maxim was not an overly emotionless sort, Felix thought, but a little strain crept into his voice.

'I understand. I was there three weeks ago, remember, at the interrogation.'

'How could I forget? That sort of thing is the least of it. I've faced my fair share of warp peril in my time, but these years have been unprecedented. There are daemons everywhere, while the number of psykers climbs ever higher. The universe is saturated with the wickedness of Chaos, tetrarch.' He stopped. 'Enough of my woes, how goes it in the east?'

'It goes,' said Felix. 'Oftentimes I think the task given me is beyond my ability, but I persist.'

'In that we share something,' said Maxim. 'This is why you walk the walls without your Chosen? It is why I roam tonight.'

'It is,' said Felix. 'That, and the wait before the battle is always the worst of times. The anticipation of slaughter, the possibility of death. I admit, I have come to enjoy the resolution of disputes that do not require a bolt rifle.'

'I am sure you have. Whereas I long for troubles simple enough to be solved by a gun.'

They fell silent a moment, enough time for the missile system to makes its traversal three times. *Clunk, jerk, whirr.* Magical lightnings raced through the sky. The planet was being smothered by the warp.

'I heard you found a spy, a daemon of some sort,' said Felix.

'You are not the primarch's watcher now,' said Maxim.

'Yet I would still like to know,' said Felix. 'Will you not tell me?'

'I will tell you. I rile you a little for my own amusement,' said Maxim. He took a deep breath, rasping in his helmet. 'It was a plague imp of some sort, of a kind I have never seen before, and its manner of control over its host was unusual. Not a possession, more of a parasite. It had hold of a captain of the Ultramarian Auxilia. I drove it out.'

'Terrible,' said Felix. 'I commend the poor man's soul to the protection of the Emperor.'

Maxim glanced at him. 'Oh, he's not dead,' said the Codicier. 'Though if I were you I would have guessed the same. No, the poor fellow yet lives, I've been told. What will happen to him now is unsure. I read his soul, and the corruption done him by the thing's touch was minimal, and though his body is full of cancers, they are curable. He is a staunch man, a true believer in the Imperial Cult. It may be that preserved him from greater harm.'

'Perhaps. Or it was the imp's work. A rotting corpse or screaming mutant hardly makes a good spy.'

'Indeed not,' said Maxim. 'His relative purity will not help him, I expect. He will be away to the shrivers of the Ecclesiarchy, and their mercy is limited. We cannot afford kindness. We must instead think of what he has been used for. He was in the initial briefing. I felt something coming off him, so I tracked him down. In all likelihood Mortarion knows of our plans. I should have acted sooner.'

'I would not let that disturb you,' said Felix.

'You are not concerned?'

'Lord Guilliman anticipated spies. He told the assembled officers of this world enough so they could perform their role. Not the whole plan. He has concocted some scheme with the aeldari that is not widely known. Even I am privy only to the half of it.'

'I would expect nothing less,' said Maxim. 'Still, even knowing what we are to do here gives Mortarion an advantage.'

'Or it will pull him into a trap,' said Felix. 'Little by little, the primarch lures his brother in. This storm keeps out our orbital support, but bars any aid for him as well. All the forces he can commit are here on this world. He may summon up his daemons, but there will be no more Death Guard to come. Guilliman will wait until the last before calling out the fallen primarch. And though we may appear weak, we are not. To win, the artefact that supports all this effort of Mortarion's to steal Ultramar away must survive, and it will not. He will have anticipated an attack on the cauldron, and diverted some forces there. But how many, how much will be enough? These questions will have taxed him, and divided his armies. When the time comes, Mortarion's eyes must be firmly on this place.'

'Guilliman has managed to locate the artefact, then?'

'I do not know,' said Felix. 'There are elements in play, a trusted force, the wild card of the militant-apostolic. Natasé assures us of victory if we follow the right path.'

'The aeldari,' said Maxim. 'It sickens me that we must put so much faith in his scrying.'

'What else should Lord Guilliman do? Lord Tigurius might match the farseer in prophetic ability, but he is far away. There are no others with such strength of foresight in our forces here. All weapons must be used. The trap is set, brother. We must hold our nerve.'

'I can see now why Guilliman chose you for one of his tetrarchs,' said Maxim. 'Yet I for one still misgive. What of this disease? How can he counter that?'

'As I said, I do not know everything.'

Felix stood up straighter, alert.

'Something's changed,' he said. He turned to the missile system. It had ceased its steady sweeping of the horizon, its single eye staring out over the plains. The light was getting brighter, but the fog thicker, and so everything was soaked in a sickly glow.

From far out over the plain came the tolling of a sorrowful bell, then another, and another. Thunder boomed. The clouds shone purple and gold, like spoiled sides of meat.

Maxim held out a hand. 'I sense daemons, and Traitor Marines. They are coming.'

A distant firecracker ripple announced the commencement of bombardment.

'The battle begins,' said Felix. 'Fight well, Brother Maxim.'

They departed to their stations.

CHAPTER TWENTY-FOUR

COLLATERAL DAMAGE

Reconnaissance Force Edermo stopped again to calibrate Fe's machine, and find their way through the nonsense landscape of corrupted Iax. They found a few dozen acres of muddy ground rising over the flooded plains, and set up there. A dead olive grove spread contorted limbs into the fog, the carefully tended paths between them treacherous with fallen leaves.

Justinian guarded Fe while he tinkered with his machine. It was a strange thing when opened up, all tubes of glass and coils of copper; it looked like a still, though there was nothing in this universe that would convince Justinian to drink the contents. He had been born in less superstitious times, and to him technology was not the work of magic many in the 41st millennium took it to be, but even he knew this particular machine for sorcery when he looked inside it.

'How does it work then?' asked Maxentius-Drontio.

Fe was fishing about inside with a fine silver spanner. He was finding it difficult to work with his vision limited by the environment suit and he gave out a little noise of irritation.

'Your unpleasant attitude towards me would suggest you are only feigning interest in order to mock me,' said Fe. 'Emotional degradation by mockery among Adeptus Astartes is common upon apotheosis from standard *Homo sapiens* stock in order to build unit cohesion. Advisory – if you wish to be informed of the secrets kept by others, attempt, if you will, to be friendlier to non-Space Marines.'

'Talkative, aren't you, when you're not falling out of the sky?' said Maxentius-Drontio. 'My apotheosis has little to do with it. I incline to surliness, that is all. I am one of those people who finds life overwhelmingly sad, and therefore protect my delicate soul by being dismissive of nearly everything.'

'You see?' said Fe. 'Your vocal patterns, though suggesting truthfulness, show heightened indicators of insincerity. Conclusion – I shall tell you nothing of my craft.'

'Come on, I mean it, tell me, how does it work?' said Maxentius-Drontio. 'I am interested, and not just because I am bored.'

'Hmm, calculating potential for targeted, induced social embarrassment.' The magos stopped, stock-still. Something clicked in his chest. 'Risks acceptable. Bond with me. Pass me that size nine molecular manipulator, please, in order to initiate emotional pairing,' said Fe.

Maxentius-Drontio pulled out a tool from the box. It was very small, but he managed to pick it up. 'This one?'

Fe took the manipulator. 'Thank you for your care in retrieving my article and rapidity of response to my request.' Fe made an adjustment, and shut the casing. Closed up, it looked like an ornamental cylinder of bronze. Three feet high, featureless, abstract art. 'Are you aware of a witch-finder device?' asked Fe, his little face serious.

'No. But I believe I can figure out what it is,' said Maxentius-Drontio.

'Some ordos and adepta employ mechanical detection devices to supplement their human psykers. They are temperamental, hence the dual deployment alongside organic search mechanisms. All warp tech is temperamental. To operate a witch-finder of this kind in this environment is extremely difficult. But bringing a psyker here, to a place saturated with and opening up to the warp, would be dangerous to us with a potential of discovery nigh on one hundred per cent. It would be tantamount to announcing our presence by open vox-hail, and singing a little song.'

'What?' said Maxentius-Drontio.

Fe blinked mechanically, though his eyelids were entirely organic, as far as they could tell. 'You see, I too am capable of performing humour.'

'Right. I suppose you are,' said Maxentius-Drontio.

'We are forced to use this alone, for the sake of safety and concealment. However, the source of warp energy we are seeking is so powerful that it is relatively easy to lock on to, and it gives us a true location we may aim for among all this uncertainty.' He looked down at his machine with an obvious sense of pride.

'I know all that. How does it work?'

'I do not cast aspersions upon your advanced intelligence. You are Astartes and better equipped for comprehension than most Terrans, but you would not understand,' said Fe. 'I will humour you a little and explain as much as I calculate you can take in. It is mostly a fluidic construct. Positively polarised blackstone particles in suspension, mixed in with a little cerebrospinal fluid from harvested psykers. It is a compass, in effect. An esoteric one, but the principle is the same.' He tapped a dial set into the top of the cylinder, the sole feature on the casing. One half of the needle was red, the other white. A hand-painted dial was divided into quadrants. 'Follow the red indicator. That is the totality of necessary action.' He stopped suddenly, and went to pack up his tools into his box.

'Charming little man, isn't he? Typical magos, never get a straight answer out of them,' said Maxentius-Drontio to Justinian.

'Would you have understood, if he had explained?'

'I might.'

'It is not the habit of the people of this age to question the functioning of things,' Justinian said.

'It wasn't in mine either,' said Maxentius-Drontio. 'But I always have.'

'Then that makes you very special, brother,' said Justinian.

Maxentius-Drontio gave a short noise of mirth. 'I am glad you noticed, brother sergeant.'

They walked together away from Fe, to where Edermo and Locko were by their parked tanks. Men manned pintle weapons on the Impulsors and, along with the Executioner, kept watch over the island, while Sergeant Vasilon of the Infiltrator squad was busy with the orbital relays carried by all three Impulsors.

'How goes it?' Justinian asked.

Vasilon shook his head. 'Even in linked series I do not know if we will be able to contact the fleet, and when we are in combat we will not be able to link them anyway. Not by hardline. There is an unnatural silence lying on this world that stifles everything. The warp storm.' He gestured upward. 'I guess it will only get worse.'

'Keep trying,' said Edermo. 'Our whole purpose is to get loc-data for bombardment and potential teleport assault. If we cannot broadcast, we are wasting our time.'

'I shall do what I can,' said Vasilon. 'I am getting some communications from central command, but I cannot gauge our own uplink capability without revealing our presence. It will be a test of the hour whether the equipment will serve or not.'

'Well,' said Maxentius-Drontio. 'It is either that, or a glorious death. I know which I would prefer.'

'He lacks gravity, your second,' said Vasilon to Justinian.

'My apologies,' said Maxentius-Drontio. 'I shall attempt to mediate my natural tendencies the better to follow the example of Honourum.'

Vasilon grunted again.

'Lieutenant,' said Fe, joining them. 'I have recalibrated the machine to provide optimal directionality.'

'Do you have a location?' asked Locko.

'I regretfully provide a negatory response to your query. I may provide non-specific data in so much as' – he pointed in a direction that could have been any direction at all – 'that way.'

'Very well. Recon force, mount up. We depart–'

'Movement, on the ridge,' said Maxentius-Drontio. He brought up his bolt rifle. A shadow was disappearing through the mist. 'Too slow,' he said. 'Permission to begin pursuit?'

'Wait, brother,' Vasilon said. He put his finger to the extended vox-pickup attached to the side of his helm. 'I have notification of energy signatures and life signs on this island. Triangulating with other members of my squad. A moment.' He gave clipped commands to his warriors, ordering them to spread out, consulted his instruments again, then looked further up the hill. 'We are not alone.'

'We should investigate. We may have been sighted,' said Edermo. 'Squad Vasilon, Squad Parris, with me.'

'And I thought today was going to be boring,' said Maxentius-Drontio.

Two more of Vasilon's squad appeared from the mists to join them. Their Phobos armour was completely silent, and the first indication of their presence that Justinian got was the thin lines of their targeting lasers attached to their bolt carbines: shorter ranged than his squad's weapons, with a smaller, less penetrative bolt, but exceedingly accurate, and easy to handle.

'Over there,' one of them said. 'There's a temple building. Gallio and I read seven-plus devices, light power draw.'

Justinian looked downslope. Over the haunting shapes of dead olive trees, he could see what might have been the outline of a building. 'Civilians?'

'A possibility,' said Vasilon.

'Then we should leave them be,' said Justinian. 'Get out of here before they notice us.'

'We may have been seen already,' said Vasilon.

'Not maybe,' said Maxentius-Drontio sadly. 'We definitely have been.'

A young woman was pointing at them, waving on an old man who leaned heavily on a stick. Both were filthy, ill looking and thin with hunger, but their faces were lit up with joy.

'I told you, I told! she said. 'I saw the angels, they have come!'

Tears brimmed in the old man's eyes. 'Praise Lord Guilliman. We are saved!' He struggled through the muddy ground. When he reached them, he cast his stick aside extravagantly and threw himself down before them.

'My lords, oh my lords, you have come for us.'

'How long have you been here?' asked Vasilon.

'A hundred days. More. We have lost count.'

'Get up,' said Vasilon. He moved forward to haul the man to his feet. The girl took a frightened step back.

'Do not be alarmed, child, these are our saviours!' He looked at them anew. 'You are not Ultramarines.'

'No. We are of Lord Guilliman's line, however. We are Novamarines, a Second Founding Chapter,' said Edermo. 'Honoured primogenitors.'

'I have heard of you.'

'How many are you?' asked Vasilon.

'Sixty-three,' said the man. 'We have been hiding in the temple. Its holiness has kept us safe. We've been living off nothing but jarred olives. Terrible, I–'

The Space Marines' vox-net clicked to private, cutting off their words from their external voxmitters.

'Maybe these two, save the rest,' Edermo said.

'I would rather not,' said Maxentius-Drontio.

'…I shall call the others out to see you, they will be full of joy,' the man was saying.

'Do not do that,' said Vasilon. 'You must come with us. You and the girl.'

'Yes, my lords, but I must tell my people. It will take only a moment.' He got up and turned around. 'My people!' he shouted. His voice rang out loud.

'Be quiet. Be quiet now!' said Vasilon. His voice was aggressive, commanding, as the voices of all Space Marines were, qualities accentuated by his armour, but the old man was too addled or scared to pay heed, and what would have reduced a normal human to weeping only encouraged him to shout louder. 'They are here!'

'Silence him,' said Edermo.

Vasilon obeyed immediately. His gun stock whipped up and caught the old man hard under the chin. His head snapped round, too fast, his neck breaking with a crunch.

The girl stared at them in utter terror, screamed, and ran, still screaming, down the hill to the temple.

'Throne curse it,' said Vasilon. He lifted his bolt carbine and drew a bead on the girl, twin laser dots fixed between her shoulder blades.

Maxentius-Drontio knocked his arm, sending his aim wild. The bolt skimmed past the girl's head.

'What are you doing?' Vasilon snarled.

'I did not come here to shoot little girls,' Maxentius-Drontio said.

'It is too late for such qualms,' said Edermo quietly. 'The alarm has been raised.'

The girl had gone into the temple. Its bell began to ring.

'Emperor, no,' said Maxentius-Drontio.

Edermo hefted his shield up out of the muck and looked at his men.

'What we must do now will be hard. There are daemons in these mists. All it will take is for one to find these people here and our mission will be over.'

'They have not been found yet,' said Justinian.

'Sergeant, this mission is supposed to be a secret. It will remain so, even if I have to slaughter half a planet to ensure it. The fate of all Ultramar depends on our actions here. A few civilians are a small price to pay.'

'I will not do it,' said Justinian.

'Nor will I,' said Maxentius-Drontio.

'You will. I order you.' Edermo took a step towards Maxentius-Drontio.

The Intercessor stood taller.

The lieutenant's hand went to his sword hilt. 'You will do it in the name of the primarch and of the Emperor.'

The bell continued to ring. Maxentius-Drontio and Lieutenant Edermo stared at each other. Justinian wondered what to do if they came to blows. Who would he aid?

In the end, the decision was taken from Justinian's hands. Maxentius-Drontio shook his head, flicked off the no-fire catch on his gun and set off down the hill.

'You know I am right,' said Edermo. 'They are dead anyway.'

'Let's just get this over with,' said Justinian. He turned away down the hill after his second, his head bowed. The others followed.

A few minutes later the raucous sound of boltguns cracked through the mist. There were a few screams, and then silence descended again.

CHAPTER TWENTY-FIVE

FIRST LANDING ASSAILED

Shells pounded remorselessly against the second-tier wall. Felix watched the battle from the observation jetty of a plasma battery. Only half the enemy rounds were solid-shot munitions, the others carried deadly loads of chemical and biological agents that would have slaughtered the civilian population had they remained. But the Space Marines were not safe there either, for shells crashed in waves of fire against the cliffs of rock, bringing down ornate buildings in avalanches of rubble and opening the hollow interior to perilous miasmas.

The Death Guard deployed weapons so dangerous that they fought as a Legion only, without their hordes of deluded mortal followers. Only their daemons accompanied them, and for the time being those were few in number. Felix wondered if this was how it was upon the walls of the Imperial Palace, when Chaos reached the apogee of its tide and the dream of Imperium nearly died.

Out on the field, cohorts of Plague Marines advanced in huge squares behind siege engines. They defied the Imperial guns to slay them. Bolts, missiles, cannon shells and energy beams ripped into them, but on they came, protected as much by their own astonishing resilience as they were by the buzzing energy fields of the mantlets they pushed ahead of their formations. Though Mortarion's army was primarily composed of infantry, as was his preference of old, there were hundreds of fighting vehicles in support. Packs of Predator tanks fired at maximal range, hull down, dug into positions to the enemy's rear. Land Raiders waited far out for a breach in the wall to be made. Rhinos snorted along behind the infantry, ready to snatch up squads and redeploy them at a moment's notice. All the vehicles were rusty, covered in filth and mouldering fetishes, but serviceable nonetheless. Daemon engines of peculiar design roamed the battleground. Flights of bloat drones attempted to attack the higher levels of the city, but were driven back. Squadrons of blight haulers ran in support of the foot blocks, shrouding them in obscuring fogs. There was a preponderance of medium, self-propelled artillery pieces, coughing shells into high parabolas that came moaning down over the walls.

Having been concerned with the trickier battles of planetary diplomacy for the last few months, Felix saw Mortarion's sons with fresh eyes. This form of war was an insanity to him, a mixing of the magical and the mundane that still seemed impossible. It was carnage, it was chaos. Energy screens on both sides thrummed and popped. Enemy artillery blasted ancient buildings to rubble. In return, Imperial guns gouged holes in the Plague Guard ranks. Swarms of flies passed over the battle, thick and sudden as squalls of rain, obscuring everything in sight until they passed on. Where Mortarion's force had come from was hard to discern. Mortarion had no ships in orbit. More warpcraft, surely, Felix thought, and wondered if more awaited to be disgorged upon the dying earth.

The storm raged. Unnatural colours filling the sky raced and burned. Still no contact could be made with the fleets. No message went up and no orbital support came down. It was as if the stage had been set for a game between rival deities, where the champion primarchs of the Emperor and the Plague God would face each other to decide the fate of worlds.

That was yet to come. There was no sign of Mortarion. For all the battle's fury, they yet endured the opening phase. Felix led his ten Chosen of Vespator and a demi-company of Silver Templars, honoured for their battles on Talasa Secundus. He had limited experience of the Chapter, but they were renowned as steely warriors, duellists all, and they were as impatient as him to fight.

Down by the lower-tier wall, guns boomed and flashed from both sides as the Death Guard attempted an escalade and the Space Marines repelled them. Ladders on rusty carts were swung into place by hand-cranked drums, only to be targeted by melta weapons and collapse as sagging, molten wrecks. A shell got through one of the parapet energy screens protecting the walls, hitting the crenellations and lofting up the great stones as if they were made of card. All along the wall the shields were visible as bands of light. They glowed bright, the invisible made visible by strain. A generator exploded, fire roaring out in a dragonfire plume from the reinforced plasteel tower holding it. A section of the wall shield went dark, and was immediately targeted, cannon fire smacking into unprotected masonry.

Felix's aural dampers increased their effect, cutting out the screaming whoop of the plasma casters he stood between. The vox announced itself. Cominus' rune flashed in his vision.

'I would wager a quart of good Ardium Red that you are staring down there so much because you want to get into it, my lord,' he voxed. He was only fifteen feet away, but if they spoke aloud together, they would not be heard.

'Our orders are to hold the second tier, brother-sergeant, priority-one protection of this battery.'

'They are indeed, but who among us likes to watch a battle and not be involved?'

A triad of bloat drones attempted a run on the battery. Clunky-looking cylinder grenades bounced from the Imperial gunshields. The plasma cannons continued to fire long, blinding streams of energy while their attackers took a hammering from iron hail stubbers and Icarus lascannons. All were downed in a matter of moments. One detonated, spraying pus; the second lost an engine and crashed into the wall; the third was chased off and gutted of its daemonic components from behind, the bleeding metal shell plummeting into the fury of the fight on the lower wall.

A long, mournful wail sounded out on the plains. Fog, smoke and gas cut vision down to a few thousand yards, and Felix struggled to pick out what made the sound between the blades of the karst.

The cannons' machine-spirits caught sight of it first, all four of them pivoting as one to lock on to their new target. Daelus, one of Felix's Techmarines, was directing them from a control console platform bolted to the side of the second gun's turntable. He discharged them in series, their emissions taxing the ability of Felix's helm to protect his eyes and broiling the air to a dangerous heat.

They burned out the vapours as they speared their target, exposing it to the world.

'Throne of the Emperor,' Cominus said. *'That is not a sight I ever thought to see.'*

A rot-fleshed hulk two hundred feet high lumbered towards the city, moaning and howling. The plasma beams blasted its forequarters into steam, and it screamed like a thousand people dying in pain. Still it dragged itself forward, though one shoulder was charred down to the bone, and the flipper limb beneath folded under it, but it moved with a certain determination, like an aquatic beast heading for its breeding ground on shore.

As it neared, it was possible to see the weeping orifices that covered the body. From these, cocoons squeezed out, slipping to the ground and unleashing the daemon-form designated beasts of Nurgle. A seemingly endless stream of these things galloped around the flesh mountain, as eager as pups at play. They bounded through the Death Guard's lines, upsetting their formation and bowling some of them over in their enthusiasm, though the Plague Marines were unaffected by the poisons the beasts exuded, and clambered up, grumbling, once they had gone.

More guns had turned to target the hill-sized monster, for should it reach the first wall, it would surely crash through it. Further down the second tier, the sleeved barrels of macrocannons recoiled. Groundcar-sized shells thwacked into it, blasting giant craters in its body that filled with watery blood. It lowed mournfully, and reared up, exposing an underside mottled with scabs and rashes, and the beginning of its muscular, slime-dripping mollusc's foot. Guns from all over the fortress fired, opening its chest and belly. An explosion of fluids saturated all in front of it, and it crashed down, dead, its tiny children sniffing and mewling at the corpse.

A cheer went up from the walls, audible even over the din of battle. Felix was spared the heat of the plasma discharge a moment as Daelus vented coolant from the dorsal slots, drenching them all in white steam.

When it cleared, Cominus spoke again.

'A small victory. The enemy come still.'

CHAPTER TWENTY-SIX

THE PLAGUE MILL

The highway became impassable on the crusade's seventh day. For some time, the road had exhibited signs of decay. The surface cracked. The embankment scalloped with landslips. Plasteel signs and traffic direction measures were lumps of corroded matter. The land around was waste. Every living thing was dead, become a black slime that coated everything. Strange mutant things had taken the places of local creatures, similar to true animals at a distance, but when examined closely shown to be far from natural. A cloud of gnats trilled awful songs from shrivelled human faces. Herds of bovids lumbered by screaming, encumbered by fronds of useless limbs. A flock of caprids sped past, lashed into stampede by tentacles growing from their spines. Where the ground was not covered by water, it was a barren, reeky mush. When the mists parted it was possible to see unnaturally far. The remains of small towns, farms and other facilities stood in the desolation, naked as bones, so clear they might be touched with an outstretched hand, before the mists swallowed them again.

The crusaders still sang. Although their voices were swallowed up in the perpetual gloom, their hymns drove back a little of the blight, and fewer of them succumbed to disease than even the most optimistic expected, and they spoke excitedly among themselves of the Emperor's grace.

The days darkened. The nights were full of terrible cries and stenches that wafted up from hidden hells. Those that breathed the fumes woke choking, eyes red, blood leaking from their noses. Or they might not wake up at all. The paint of tanks bubbled with rust, until it flaked off, and revealed sores of red, orange and brown beneath that spread before the watchers' eyes. Only the war train was left unmarked. Equipment failed. Lasgun power packs lost charge. Propellant in bullets degraded, producing slow fizzes of flame when firing pins fell on them.

And then they came to the end of the road, and the situation grew worse. The highway suddenly disintegrated into a series of islands with no evidence that they had ever been joined, like a child's sand sculpture on a beach broken up by the incoming tide. Utterly flat spaces divided them, patched with a froth of bubbles, like the spawn of amphibious creatures. Out to the east was a plain of flesh, where a hill remade as a giant daemonic face watched them greedily.

They did not delay or pause in fear, but under the militant-apostolic's watchful eye, descended from the highway, following his directions to the north-east, skirting the flesh plain, where his heart told them their target lay.

Reality was losing its grip on Iax. The days and nights ceased to hold to normal lengths. Sometimes, night would last an hour, or a moment, day coming as soon as the sun set. Other times it would persist for hours at a time, and the crusade would be haunted by noises coming out of the dark. They did not stop. When the sky was clear of lightning and painful colour, which was rarely, they looked on alien stars, no sign of the giant crusade fleets holding orbit over the planet, or of Iax's moons. Most of the time fog clung to the ground and the crusaders walked in human chains, arm to shoulder. Still some of them vanished, never to be seen again.

More weapons failed. More people died. The air thickened, becoming toxic. Equipment provided no safety. Only faith seemed to protect them. Iax left no room for doubt.

They reached another flooded land. Stands of dead reeds suggested it had always been waterlogged, but it too was much corrupted. Strange fungi pulsed and glowed amid dead trees. There were green shoots pushing up through the water, but all of them were grotesque caricatures of real plants.

'The Plague God mocks the cycle of life and death,' Mathieu explained to his followers. 'We have seen death, now we see his idea of life. This is more dangerous to us, yet have faith, and we shall pass unharmed.'

Overhead the storm wailed and crashed, raining spit from fanged maws, and lightning erupted from transient eyes. They saw armies battling there, and visions of times past and future. Sometimes the storm ceased, and inimical faces stared at them in utter silence.

The pilgrims slogged on through the swamp. When they rested, their legs were covered with black leeches. Many of them became sick. The water deepened. They took refuge on their vehicles, packing the upper fighting decks of the train. Those denied space were forced to cling to the side of the war train, or ride upon the tanks. With every mile, Odrameyer lost another vehicle to mechanical failure. Oil congealed in engines. Promethium denatured. But the train pushed on, sucking up the waters of the swamps to drive its pistons without harm, emitting them as purified white steams.

By the time Mathieu called upon his column to halt, half his followers had perished, and it was a much reduced crusade that looked upon their goal.

They were deep in the swamps. The mist cleared a little from the higher airs, and though it clung to the water's surface they could see some distance. Ahead, on a rise of hills rotted black, were the broken walls of a large institution. About it burned thousands of smoking fires, and the slopes were thick with daemons.

What the institution had been, Mathieu could not tell. It was in no way exceptional. They had seen other ruined places of its type, many warped and made bizarre. But Mathieu knew, right to the iron core of his being, that it was there he must go. It was not an inner knowledge, no personal revelation that rose up unbidden from his secret self. Mathieu was wary of such impulses. Instincts could betray. They masqueraded as divine guidance. There was no better deceiver than oneself, and so on earlier feelings Mathieu had shocked himself with his auto-flagellator and prayed for the Emperor to guide him towards the truth. Sometimes he was right, and his instincts were false, poisoned by arrogance. Other times they were not.

This was nothing like that. He did not need to ask. A pillar of brown smoke climbed from the roofless central building, braided with lightning, boiling with screaming faces. It whipped back and forth, but remained anchored at the bottom in the ruin, and at the top where it fed the storm. When he set eyes on that there was a certainty that came from outside, as sure as an angel stooping from heaven to whisper in his ear, that the place he saw was a medicae hospital, that it was the source of all evil upon Iax, and that it must be destroyed. This was not an intuition. No prayers for clarification were required. This was a divine command.

As if in response to his certainty, huge, fat-bellied fly-beasts rose up from the horizon and droned towards them in formations of three and seven. These were not truly insectoid, but a nightmarish combination of maggot, fly and pachyderm beast, some with huge trunks that slobbered steaming spittle, others with needle teeth in tiny jaws, and eyes that shone with the moist light of otherworldly fevers. Upon their backs daemons rode. The swamp belched black gas. Ripples disturbed the surface.

'The enemy are coming,' Odrameyer said. He gripped the rail on the train's pulpit hard. Leather gloves creaked. 'We must prepare for battle. Where should we make our stand, your holiness?'

'We do not stand. We must advance,' said Mathieu. He pointed to the institution. 'Set course for the medicae building, full speed,' he said, suddenly knowing exactly what it had been, and exactly what it had become.

'But the creatures, your holiness, we may be better to take them here at the full range of our guns.'

Mathieu shook his head slowly, like someone lost in a dream. 'Advance. Take up the sword of righteousness, colonel. Go to your men, lead your tanks and kill them all. The Emperor commands it.'

CHAPTER TWENTY-SEVEN

BATTLE JOINED

The landscape changed before the grav-tanks. Dead farm-land gave way to low, bleak hills. The Space Marines skimmed onward, ever alert for signs of the enemy. When strange beasts winged their way through the sky, they hid in black copses, casting out shrouds of electromagnetic interference and clearing their minds of thoughts. These periods of blankness lasted as long as death. When Justinian came round from them he was reminded uncomfortably of his millennia in slumber, and recalled the burn of methalon cold.

The hills topped out in a series of stinking bogs: black sludge, spiky with half-dead shrubs. Wary, the task force halted at the edge, and stepped down for a few moments, guns ready, while Magos Fe set up his witch-finder. Turret and pintle weapons on the tanks panned restlessly over the land.

'Do you have a positional?' Edermo asked Magos Fe, for what must have been the thousandth time.

The little man gestured off to the south with his huge limbs.

'Proceed on current approach vector. Psi-concentration remains in our southerly quadrant, no significant deviation from current course.'

'None?' asked Edermo.

'Two point zero-five degrees. Not significant. I hazard we are close.'

'I will believe so when we see the target,' said Edermo. 'This world is plagued by the effects of the warp.'

Justinian agreed. 'The lack of movement of the target is suggestive of a trap.'

'Or some other madness,' said Edermo. 'Brother-Sergeant Vasilon, do you have any readings?'

'No broadcasts upon any vox range. Electromagnetic activity is beyond all known scales, and erratic. I could not signal another company of our Chapter if they were only a mile distant.'

'Will you be able to get a teleport locus?' Edermo asked.

'Negative. Interference to auguries and psy-augury is exceptionally high. Non-accurate positional information is the likely result,' responded Fe. 'Teleport insertion will fail.'

'I concur,' said the Infiltrator sergeant. 'We will not be able to call down reinforcements either via teleportation or by orbital landing. Nothing short of a miracle will enable that.'

Vasilon paused, consulted his wrist cogitator, and looked up, staring through some display of sines and interference peaks projected within his helm.

'I calculate that we should be able to get enough of a data-burst up to call down an orbital strike, but we will have to call it down practically on top of us, and they will struggle to target anything accurately.'

'So then,' said Edermo. 'We find the target. We call down the fury of the fleet.'

'Orbital fire may prove inadequate,' said Fe. 'What we seek is known as an empyrical manifestation of rare power. Weaponry that functions according to the laws of the materium may be insufficient to destroy it. As previously stated, I calculate a near one hundred per cent certainty that we will require the Talons of the Emperor to complete this task.'

'Then we move on,' said Edermo. He cast his eyes over the bog. Lazy bubbles popped, releasing hisses of mephitic gas. 'I do not like the look of this. It has a fell air.'

'It will take too long to go around,' said Justinian.

'That is why we cross directly,' said Edermo. 'Move out. Keep your wits about you.'

The bogs widened as soon as the tanks began the traversal, until they were seemingly without end, the sludge blending with the mists at the limits of the Space Marines' sight. Auspex pulses suggested the mud to be shallow, but this did nothing to blunt the Novamarines' vigilance as they skimmed the surface. They were certain they were watched.

'Movement,' Achilleos reported. 'Quadrant four. Position one-three, six-two.'

'Got it,' Maxentius-Drontio responded, moving to the back of the Impulsor and training his gun behind them. Orpino swung the iron hail stubber around. The Space Marines shifted to allow it a clearer firing line over the transport deck. Fe scuttled to the driver's door access and crouched out of the way, looking like a child amid the Novamarines' armoured legs.

Justinian had his helm provide an enhanced view, and scanned over the indicated quadrant. Lumps of sod turned over with eructations of marsh gas. His displays clicked, and discarded each movement, until they alighted upon a slithering in the bog, as something breached the surface and slipped away out of sight. The threat indicator in the top of his sightline flickered uncertainly through severities of rune.

'Marked,' said Justinian, data-casting the information to the whole group. 'Lieutenant, something follows us.'

'Contact acknowledged,' Edermo said.

The Executioner's heavy turret rotated back. On the other tanks, the Space Marines prepared themselves. Bolts racked into firing chambers. Brothers knelt so those standing behind them could fire over their heads. Their boots locked to the deck. At Edermo's command, the vehicles increased speed. Grav-motors thumped. Fans of black mud sprayed behind them, splattering the Novamarines' already dirty armour with sticky clods.

Ahead, the edge of the bog came into sight: hillsides clad in disintegrating grass and trees rotted to wet sawdust, rocky ridges stripped of cover standing naked, shocking as an exposed spine in a flensed back. The mist was shredding, giving way to a green light. A sail of fog brushed past over the ground, and Justinian saw for a moment a wavering pillar of lightning-filled smoke, climbing to a vortex in the clouds that was as raw as an open sore.

The mist closed over the sight, and he returned to scanning the rear, so he missed the movement that came in from the side, and the impact that flipped one of the Impulsors. He heard it well enough, a huge bang followed by the warble of damaged impellers. He turned back in time to see the upset vehicle ploughing a deep, wet trench in the bog, and its contra-grav shove up a tall wave of mud that half swamped Squad Vasilon's transport, forcing it to scud out of the way.

It was Squad Drucellus' vehicle, the Assault Intercessors. Two of them were thrown free, slapping into the ooze. The others went under when their Impulsor rolled over and sank.

'Enemy contact!' Maxentius-Drontio roared. He opened fire, his bolts thwacking into the morass and exploding pathetically. Justinian restrained his own fire, searching for what had hit the tank.

An Assault Intercessor surfaced like a cork released at the bottom of a pond. Under him came an obscure thing, coming up as if from great depths, though the mud's modest thickness could not possibly contain it. It was as big as the Repulsor – bigger, maybe – covered in flailing tentacles and breathing tubes that pumped filthy water. A mad thrash of limbs gripped the Space Marine, and lifted him high by the legs. The warrior could not get his chainsword to start, and so hit at the limbs holding him with a quiet blade, but his blows skidded ineffectually from the beast.

Justinian opened up, planting red craters in the creature's flesh. It shrilled horribly from several mouths that opened all over its ball-shaped body. Eyes were studded randomly between them: red, yellow, and human blues and browns.

He saw human arms too, and human legs flopping from the sides, as if there were people stuck head first inside that were trying to run away.

'Squad Parris, clear!' Edermo ordered. Pasac flung their Impulsor into a steep turn, dipping the right-hand side into the mud like a sailing ship leaning from the wind.

The Executioner's laser destroyer discharged, sending out a beam of light so bright the Space Marines' lenses dimmed. A wall of steam erupted from the bog where it hit, and when Squad Parris' Repulsor levelled off, the thrum of its impeller arrays cracked vitrified soil into shards.

The mutant roared, and flung the Space Marine in its tentacles at the Repulsor tank. He clashed off the side. The Repulsor fired again.

The beam hit the mutant square-on, evaporating a cylinder of flesh and cooking more for several feet around it. Pus slopped out, bright yellow, mingling with the mud. The Repulsor's coaxial gatling cannon tore into it, bringing forth more squirts of vile fluids. Justinian had Pasac bring their own transport around. Vasilon was on the other side, both squads pouring bolt-rounds into the creature. Its mouths snapped closed, and it dived beneath the peat, leaving a slick of ichor atop.

Bubbles popped. The mud sagged inward.

'Clear!' said Justinian. No sign of the beast appeared on his sensorium. Vasilon went to the stricken Impulsor. As his Infiltrators were dragging the Assault Intercessors out of the bog, the beast returned.

It shot up into the air. What they thought had been the body was merely the tip of a long, muscular stalk, studded with gasping human faces. Ragged skin cloaked it, covered in boils and cancers. It remained above the surface long enough only to scream, then crashed back down, taking the wrecked Impulsor with it out of sight, the vehicle's signum giving a depth reading of hundreds of feet before blinking out, in a place that should have been far into Iax's bedrock.

They retrieved the survivors. Two had been lost, pulled down with the tank. The Space Marine hurled at the vehicle, Brother Mantello, was injured, though not badly. They watched the skies and ground carefully as they reached the edge of the bog.

'We must have been heard,' said Maxentius-Drontio, but there was no indication that they had been.

They crested the bony ridges, and a new landscape opened before them. Mile after mile of marshland, full of burgeoning growth, spread across the land. The strange fronds pushing up through the water thickened towards the east, further along the hills, where Justinian once again saw the smoke and the vortex – and, this time, broken roads leading to the ruins of a facility.

'The medicae,' he said.

'Target located,' said Magos Fe with undisguised satisfaction.

Just then, the rippling peals of heavy gunfire sounded. The

Space Marines turned their sensoria towards the noise, and spied a column of tanks engaging a great host of daemons. At the centre rode an Ecclesiarchy war train.

'This is unexpected,' said Edermo from the turret of the Repulsor. 'The militant-apostolic is here.'

'Did the primarch plan it?' asked Achilleos. 'I thought our mission unique.'

'The preacher has a history of defiance. He probably set out on his own,' said Justinian. 'That war party of his makes a mockery of our stealthy approach.'

'No doubt he would call it divine providence that we come to him,' said Maxentius-Drontio, taking in more of the daemons. 'They are struggling. The question is, to what do we ascribe this meeting, and what do we do in the light of it?'

Edermo fell into silent thought long enough that Justinian was compelled to ask him what his orders were.

'We move out towards the primary target,' Edermo said. He fetched out his massive storm shield, and unsheathed his sword. 'Vasilon, relay our coordinates to the tribune, if you can. Prepare to request orbital bombardment on our mark. We are close.'

They turned their grav-tanks to the south, and the fighting.

CHAPTER TWENTY-EIGHT

PTOLEMY OPENS

Fabian awoke from delirious dreams weak and ready to pass out again. He sensed a presence, and lifted a head on a feeble neck to see a towering figure in black standing at the end of his bed. His vision swam, and at first he thought that death himself had come, but then Lucerne spoke.

'Fabian, I was told you may wake today. I am glad to bear witness to it.'

'Racej.' Fabian let his head fall back onto the plastek-covered pillow. The touch of it, both slippery and tacky at once, was unpleasant on his skin, but his neck felt as strong as a thread of string, and he would not have been able to lift his head again if he had wanted to. There were pipes in his nose. In his arm he felt the pinch of buried needles.

'The one and the same,' said the Space Marine. He moved closer, and his features sharpened from imagined skull to concerned face. Excepting his bare head, he was fully armoured, his battleplate covered in dust and scratches, his helm clamped under one arm. 'It is good to see you.' He smiled. 'Though you look terrible.'

Fabian groaned. 'Why did I have to be assigned the one flippant Space Marine in all of Fleet Primus?'

'It is only joy in my heart at the Emperor's truth that makes me greet everything with a smile, my friend, for I know of mankind's glory.' Nevertheless, he frowned. 'I was worried about you.'

'It's my fault. It's not a good idea to get too close to a plague creature like that.'

'Indeed not.'

'I was stupid.'

'I would say brave.'

'That doesn't make me feel any better.'

'Well, pay heed to my truth. Your bravery will be needed again,' said Lucerne. 'We've been under attack for days. You have been unconscious for most of it. Daemons manifest out of the rain within the fortress. The heretic mortals have finally mounted their assault and have shown some tenacity. The remains of the Neverborn do not fade away when killed. Lord Tigurius says the warp is leaking into reality here, and that is interesting to learn, but the reality of it is grim, for when the daemons are slain their diseases remain.'

'Is it that bad?'

Lucerne made an equivocal face. 'It is that bad, but we've seen worse, you and I, and Macragge is no stranger to invasion. Marneus Calgar is one of the great heroes of the Imperium. We will prevail.' He shifted his helm under his arm. 'How do you feel?'

'Bloody awful,' said Fabian. His eyes could barely stay open. 'Disgusting. Like I've been squashed and left to dry out on a stone, and then been embalmed in dung.'

'A colourful turn of phrase.'

'Words are my craft. I do not wish to disappoint,' said Fabian. His throat was dry as sand. 'But I am alive, thanks to you.'

'I would give your praise to the Emperor,' said Lucerne. 'His role was greater than mine.'

'Can you get me some water?' said Fabian. The brief exchange had exhausted him. He was close to passing out, but he had such a powerful thirst he had to drink before unconsciousness claimed him again.

'It shall be my honour.' Lucerne clamped his helm to his thigh, poured a glass of water from a ewer, and presented it to Fabian. When the historitor tried and failed to take it, Sergeant Lucerne lifted his head ever so gently. Armoured fingers that could have crushed his skull like an egg cupped it with a mother's tenderness. He held up the glass to Fabian's lips with the other hand, and the historitor sipped at the water greedily.

'Enough?' Lucerne asked when Fabian turned his head away.

Fabian managed a weak nod. Lucerne lowered his head back to the pillow. He was unconscious before his weight had settled.

'Sleep well, my friend,' Fabian thought he heard Lucerne say. Then the dreams returned.

Fabian woke again the day after, and felt well enough to get out of bed and set himself on the road to recovery. The medicae were good to him, feeding him cocktails of nutrients and vitamins, and he surprised himself by how quickly his strength returned. Within three days he was well enough to pass the day awake, within five to walk about. By the end of the week he was able to help the medicae staff with small tasks, insisting he be given something useful to do, for the facility was full of the wounded and the sick, the majority of them civilians, and the staff were overworked. So it was he found himself running messages up and down the wards. The facility was built into the face of the mountains of Hera, straddling the ancient wall that had once divided the Chapter monastery into two parts. The windows were shuttered against the war, but he could hear at all times the thunder of guns, the rumble of distant explosions, and the crackling screeches of void displacement as incoming ordnance hit the fortress' aegis. What he did not hear, he felt, for the rock shook.

He heard nearer battles occasionally, the shocking banging of bolt weapons and inhuman voices counting, when daemons managed to penetrate the city's psychic wards again and manifest inside the fortress. He thought the medicae may be at risk, but he was assured that as yet, the creatures had not managed to take material form within the buildings of the fortress, only outside. The static feel of arcane tech buried in the mountains tickled his gums, and when the feeling surged he knew the Neverborn were coming. *Not inside,* he told himself, *not inside.*

Occasionally, he would find himself by an unshuttered window or an open loophole, and then he would stop and look outside, as he had stolen glimpses of the Palace on Terra long ago. It was dark all the time. Artillery firing made the sky flash. Energy weapons cut painful after-images into his retinas. Magna Macragge Civitas was ablaze from end to end. Only the fortress was free of flame. It was disturbing, but he supposed it had been burned before and risen, and so it would rise again.

Fabian had lost muscle tone, so spent what time he could training with his weapons. After another week, he requested an armoured environmental suit. It arrived quickly, the emblems of the Logisticarum and the Logos Historica Verita already applied to its plating. He kept it in his room, open and ready to don. He had no desire to be helpless when the need arose.

The time came soon enough: in the middle of the night, predictably. Wailing alarms woke the whole facility. Fabian's room was lit up by flashes of red and the loud booms of landing shells. Grit bounced onto him from the ceiling. The lights were out. The power had failed. The shutter over his window had opened. The maddening dental itch of warding machinery filled his mouth as thoroughly as if an entire colony of ants had been packed in, from the brood mother to the least significant worker.

Daemons were coming.

He scrambled out of bed, and was already sealing up his carapace when soldiers of the Praecental Guard came running down the corridor, banging on every door.

'Prepare to evacuate!' they were shouting. 'Prepare to head into the deep shelters!'

Fabian, his movement restricted by his half-donned suit, waddled to the door, and shouted after him.

'What's happening?'

One of the men turned back. When a man of Fabian's rank asked a question, it was answered.

'An escalade. Mortal traitors at the inner wall. Daemons manifesting on the plazas. Heavy bombardment is taking down the shields. This is it.' He was already running away, banging on more doors. 'They'll be going for the anti-orbital guns next, to attempt a landing in the city, perhaps within the Fortress of Hera itself.'

Then the man was away, hallooing and hammering on doors like a pranking youth on Sanguinalia night.

'Emperor,' Fabian said. Grit had fallen into his boots but he had no time to empty them out. A second of tainted air could cost him his life, perhaps his soul, so he ignored the discomfort and brushed at the suit fastenings, for fragments of rockcrete had gone into these as well, and they had to be clean to make a good seal.

Undersuit first, trouser cuff connected to boot, spats over boot top and trouser. He zipped up the front, pressing down the soft sealant strip and praying he'd got all the muck out. He left the gloves off while he attached laminated hard-carbon plates to magnetic fastenings on his shoulders, shins and lower arms. The joined breastplate and backplate went on next – he paused before he put it on over his head to blow the debris from the ceiling out of the helm ring, then struggled it on. It was awkward, and heavy, and had to sit right to seal properly or it would be of no use at all. Backpack next, with its air and water recycler, then gloves, locked with a twist to the wrist, and lastly the helm, which he lowered over his head slightly out of true, then twisted into place hard as if he were breaking his own neck.

He snatched up his weapons. A moment of cursing while he adjusted his belt to take account of the suit's additional girth, then he was out into the chaos and noise of the medicae facility.

People were screaming. The inhabitants of Macragge were inured to war and redoubtable by character, but the hospital shook with the impacts of shells punching through the failing voids, and that was enough to terrify anyone. The beam of the stablight mounted on his shoulder danced around madly, lighting on faces in moments of terror, cutting dusty tracks through falls of debris. There were soldiers there of the Praecental Guard and the Magna Macragge Civitas Auxilia. They were doing their best to direct the patients and staff down passages into the mountain. Heavy blast doors, until now shut tight, stood open. Lines of crimson flares marked out the way into the rock.

'Move, move, move!' an officer in blue shouted, his face sweating under his helm mask. People streamed down the corridor into the mountain, away from the violence, where the silent mass of stone would surely keep them safe.

Fabian found himself among a crush of patients and pulled

along. He did not know where he was going, only that he went. Perhaps he wanted to join the battle, or to find Lucerne. He realised he was heading west – was he going to the library, he wondered? He could have forced his way through, but he reined in his urge to shove, and began to help, supporting the feeble, pushing invalids in chairs, handing them off to orderlies who hurried them into the shelters.

Something big hit the exterior of the medicae building, making it rock. The tremors subsided, only for another impact to succeed where the first had failed, and blast a hole in the side. He turned to see the outer wall collapse, as if disaster were tapping on his shoulder to make him see what it did. The wall rushed down in front of him, taking the floor with it, rubble gathering speed to collapse the floor beneath that, then the one below that, each slamming into the next like a tower of cards knocked down. He saw this through a whirl of dust and flashing as he fell back. Somehow, he kept his feet, when all about him were thrown down or slain, and when the clouds of dust blew out of the breach, the way back to the east had gone.

For a hundred yards in that direction the medicae had been stripped right back to the bare rock of the mountain, and its innermost rooms exposed like the hewn cave dwellings of a lost tribe. A wide slope of rubble slanted up from the plaza, mottled with splashes of white. From above they looked like fallen blossom, and not the corpses of the sick that they were.

There were lights down there. Fighting. Blue, ruby and orange flicking back and forth, a deadly light show of bolt and bullet, las-blast and plasma stream.

The aegis flashed, and he looked up through hideous patterns of purple. He'd been told the enemy flotilla had very few true warships, with only a handful of direct ground attack weapons among them. Evidently something had changed, for he saw the explosions spreading over the energy skin, their fury bled into the warp.

People were groaning. Dust and grit soaked up pools of blood. Limbs were scattered around like litter. He went to help, only to find the woman he reached first was dead. He was dizzy, confused – shocked by the blast, he realised – but events had no pity, and fate was not done with him.

'They're coming! They're coming!' A soldier was running from the west. Gunfire chased him.

The words of Sergeant Hetidor, the Catachan Guardsman who had trained him, came back to Fabian.

'There are two options when faced with battle,' Hetidor had said, probably spitting down in Fabian's face after he'd thrown him to the gymnasia mat for the hundredth time. 'You can run, or you can fight. But there is only ever one outcome. Either way, one day you will die. Cowardice might spare you awhile, but time will not, and old men serve the Emperor badly in a fight.'

Hetidor had reached down, grasped his hand, and pulled him to his feet. In Fabian's dazed state, it was as if he now reached out of the past and dragged him towards the enemy. He reacted automatically. His pistol was in one hand, his drawn sword in the other, field buzzing in the sooty air. He strode past the soldier, who was kneeling and snapping off bright blue beams of las-fire down the corridor. Fabian raised his pistol and waited for a clear target.

They came out of the smoke.

They were men who had turned against reason. Dressed in ragged uniforms, cult symbols half visible under the accumulated dirt of war, they were at once savage and pitiful, undernourished, diseased, a sham army. They behaved without mercy, bayoneting the wounded with bestial shrieks of triumph. Fabian aimed his gun at the nearest, and fired. The upper two-thirds of the man's head vanished. The las-blast wasn't enough to cauterise the network of blood vessels that had, until a micro-second before, been feeding the man's brain, and he fell down pumping vitae high from his neck, like an exclamation, or a celebratory pyrotechnic.

The man behind opened fire on Fabian straight away. The historitor ran into the spray of stubber bullets, totally uncon-cerned that were his undersuit nicked, he would likely die of disease. Bullets ricocheted from his armour plates. One skated, hot and urgent, off his helm's armaglass. Fabian's second shot felled the man, then he was among the others and set to work with his power sword.

Fabian had been well schooled in sword technique, but in the close press of the corridor there was room for only butch-er's work. In that kind of situation the warrior with the best weapon won, and Fabian's blade was fine indeed. His power sword cleaved rifles in twain as bayonets sniffed for his vitals. His following strokes ended the lives of their bearers. The sword was sharp, but with power weapons it was the field that did the damage, undoing atoms like clothes fastenings and spilling the wet contents of bodies onto the floor. The men he hit were not cut, but exploded, his sword strokes wide furrows rather than delicate slashes in flesh.

Over a decade of fighting, and he'd never got used to the adrenal rush of it. The fear, mostly, that amazed him with its intensity every time. But there was also exultation.

Before he knew it, he was through the group, and then chasing the last few as they broke and fled. He ran screaming after them down a stairwell, emerging onto the higher plaza of the fortress proper. The cultists scattered, and were blown apart by boltguns fired from unseen places.

Suddenly, he was alone in a world of fire. He needed to piss badly, but the discomfort registered only distantly, as if it were someone else's. He was near the Library of Ptolemy's main gate, its domed mass rising over the violence disdainfully, as if it were morally above it all.

It was then he noticed that the door was open. Battered in, in fact, shreds of gold-plated wood hanging from their hinges. For some reason, its multiple defences had not engaged, and the creature that had done the damage was forcing itself through the gap free of harassment.

Fabian opened his vox, and tuned it to the Chapter command frequencies.

'This is Historitor Majoris Fabian Guelphrain,' he said. 'I need to speak with Chief Librarian Tigurius immediately.'

Fabian supplied order codes of the highest potency, and the mortal manning the other end of the channel complied without demur. When he reached Tigurius, the Librarian was angry, and he was fighting. Fabian could hear the sound of gunfire in the background.

'What are you doing on this channel, historitor?'

'Listen to me. I am not going to be oblique and pretend I don't know what a daemon is. You know what one is, I know what one is. A very large one has just broken down the main door of the Library of Ptolemy, and has headed inside.'

'What of it, they are everywhere.'

'It looks like the imp that was in the fortress that night. A minor manifestation of Rotigus, you said.' The very name tasted disgusting on his tongue. 'Believe me, that might have been minor, but this is a major one.'

There was a long burst of boltgun fire. Then Tigurius spoke again.

'I am on my way. Do not follow it. Do not engage it. Only the warriors of the Librarius can meet this threat. If you can, keep everyone else out of there. Do not enter the library!'

But Fabian was already moving forward. In later years, he could never decide if he followed the daemon because he wished to stop it. If that were so, then he was not entirely to blame for what followed, and he felt a little less guilt. But in his heart of hearts, he knew that he had gone in because the Library of Ptolemy was open. He had been denied it for too long; he wanted to see it, he wanted to know what was in there, and damn the consequences.

Yet it was he that was damned by his actions.

CHAPTER TWENTY-NINE

SOUL GRINDER

'Assault on second-tier wall under way, Battery Nine Theta. Daemon machines inbound. Requesting immediate reinforcement,' Felix voxed First Landing command, and got no answer. The storm had intensified, the vox was useless, and in the sky every flash of lightning threatened to reveal some awful vision hidden just out of sight.

The first tier wall had fallen, breached in half a dozen places Death Guard and their machines poured into the city. Felix found his own position under attack from artillery moving up from the rear as the front shifted. Now the second-tier power fields were failing, and shells crashed down all around him, weakening the walls and turning buildings into rubble.

He spotted the daemon pack as they came through the first-tier breach, and guessed they would come up against his battery, even before they had reached the cliffs and dug curved claws into the rock.

'Soul Grinder pack ascending. Estimated contact, five min-utes,' he reported.

They were massive things, great corpulent bodies – seemingly of flesh, but in truth composed of the nothing energies of the warp – sat atop motive carriages fashioned like metal arachnids. The bodies wobbled with flab and were covered with Nurgle's usual festering display of disease, but beneath their rotting exte-riors muscles of iron worked, pulling them up the rock face quickly.

'Line the parapet!' he commanded, his vox squealing with inter-ference from the firing of the plasma cannon. Silver Templars and Chosen of Vespator took up position, weapons aimed down.

'Concentrate fire on the lead,' he told his men.

Bolts flew unerringly into the plague hulks. The first had a pair of grinning heads that were half melted into one another. Stringy organic matter joined them. It possessed a pair of ape-like hands, both knotted with keratinous mutation, and used these to help pull itself up the climb. A shoulder-mounted weapon twitched upon a gimbal, half of steel and half of exposed bone. Behind this projected the mouldering hilt binding of a sheathed sword.

The following two bore strange physical attributes of their own. One had a head out of proportion with its slack-bellied torso, and a trio of hairy spider's legs waggling experimentally at the air from its left-hand side. The other limb was a giant mechanical pincer. The third Felix only saw briefly, for it took a hit from a reversed wall gun on the lower defences that blasted one of its rear legs free and knocked it off the cliff. In a welter of oil and steaming ichors it fell into the melee below, crushing combatants from both sides, before staggering off, smiting every-thing that came within reach of the wriggling metal tentacles that sprouted from its shoulders, its belly and its mouth.

The remaining two drove their taloned limbs into the living

stone with piston-assisted might. When they reached the area where masonry and cliff blended at the base of the wall, they tore blocks free in their hurry to gain the top.

Boltgun fire did not slow the things at all. The lead machine's front was a mess of craters, from which issued a storm of flies that beat themselves to death against the Space Marines' helmets, spoiling their aim.

'A few more steps and it will be over,' voxed Cominus.

'Fall back,' Felix ordered. 'Silver Templars, bring your Hellblasters to the fore. Daelus, abandon the guns.' The line of Space Marines leaning out over the parapet ceased fire and fell back over the broad Spiral Way leading up to the city pinnacle, taking up position against the foot of the next cliff, where collapsed buildings and broken cellars provided plenty of cover.

'If you would give me a moment...' Daelus said. He was still bent over his machines. Three of the four cannons were still functional and firing.

'Now, Daelus,' Felix commanded.

The first of the Soul Grinders emerged over the parapet, twinned faces gurning, huge hands ripping free a run of the crenellations as it hauled itself over the edge. Daelus' forge bolter swivelled of its own accord on his servo-harness, and filled the daemon engine with large-calibre rounds. It roared and raised its shoulder to shield its faces as the missiles exploded all over it, reached up behind its back and pulled its sword free. The weapon was fifteen feet long, rusted dull, more a bludgeon than a blade.

'Hellblasters, fire!' Felix commanded.

From behind a pile of broken brick and timber, a demi-squad of Silver Templars seared the dust in the air to glass with plasma weapons on maximal fire, targeting the creature's foremost leg. It went from rusty brown to brilliant white heat in an instant, and exploded in a shower of bouncing metal sparks.

The Soul Grinder roared, staggered on its remaining three legs, then braced itself with its fist to knuckle along, scattering debris before it. It charged at the Hellblasters, sweeping aside their barricade with one blow of its sword. Poisonous liquid sprayed from its shoulder weapon, catching one of the Silver Templars and melting him alive. His plasma gun exploded as the bile ate through its powercells, mercifully killing him. The others were spotted with the liquid, but fought on, armour smoking, as it ate its way through their ceramite. Three Hellblasters fired. The fourth cast his gun aside, plasma jetting from a ruptured containment chamber, and drew his pistol.

The second Soul Grinder came over the edge, ripping out the plasma cannon from under Daelus' feet with its pincer as it clambered onto the parapet. Daelus attempted to jump free, but was overbalanced by his servo-harness and fell with a loud clatter on the paving. He managed to get onto his back, loosing off most of his ammo when the Soul Grinder came for him, blasting off the spider legs and making it roar in anger. The additional limbs on his harness moved with mechanical precision, and he was back on his feet before the machine could recover, his Omnissian axe crackling in a double-handed grip.

'Silver Templars duellist squads two and four, aid Brother-Techmarine Daelus,' Felix commanded, and turned to confront the other machine.

The battle was confused. The squad transponder signums of his Chosen gave him little idea where his bodyguard actually were. The fighting was a mess of small melees and desperate rushes to plug gaps in the defence. Flying daemon engines exploited the Soul Grinder attack, dipping down to spit thick liquids from their guns. Felix registered all this as a series of micro-realisations harvested from his strategical inputs in the time it took him to cross the road.

A Space Marine struggled on the creature's blade, impaled through the gut, his armour plates shattered by the blow. He pushed at the rusty metal with the flats of his hands in an attempt to haul himself off. The daemon backhanded one of his squad brothers into a wall, bringing it down in a tumble of blocks and dust. Its plague sprayer let out fans of liquid seemingly at random, sluicing down the broken buildings, and where fires burned it sizzled like hot fat poured into water.

Felix ran at it. No war-hymns issued from his voxmitter; his heavy Gravis armour crushed rubble to dust beneath his feet. He let off a burst of fire from his boltstorm gauntlet to catch the thing's attention, aiming for the pair of bubbling flasks that fed the plague spitter from its back. The filthy glass splintered, and one of the flasks shattered. Acidic toxins coursed down the daemon machine's torso, causing it to roar in agony. Felix drew back his fist to strike as it began to turn. His power sword would do little against the armoured carriage; indeed, he risked breaking it, so he left it sheathed. The boltstorm gauntlet's power fist was another matter.

He hit the daemon's left back leg as it turned to face him, putting all his momentum and all his weight into the blow. There was an explosion of shards that scored his battleplate, and the heavy joint snapped. The leg collapsed under the weight of the daemon machine as it was rearing up and coming round, a nightmare centaur of diseased flesh and metal. Now both its left legs were destroyed, it fell sideways heavily, throwing out its arms to catch itself. The sword, still with the Hellblaster impaled upon it, flew from its grasp.

The giant was brought low, eye to eye-lens with Felix, yet it still was not dead, and as Felix levelled the underslung bolter of his gauntlet at its faces it swiped at him, sending his shots wild, and grasped him about the waist. Its hands looked soft with rot, but they were strong and they squeezed hard. Warnings chimed in Felix's helm. Ceramite creaked. His legs were crushed together and he could not move them. Flashing red runes warned of imminent armour failure.

The thing snarled at him with a mouth full of yellow tusks. Felix raised his gauntlet, and fired wildly into its chest. The thing shrieked, and slammed him down against the floor. Felix drew out his sword, but the thing wiped him across the ground like he was a rag, and the weapon went clattering away across the stones. It heaved itself over on broken limbs, bringing its shoulder-mounted gun to bear upon him.

Felix's head rang. Ooze dripped from the gun's barrel. Time seemed to run slow. Details leapt to the fore in confusing clarity. The black veins in the thing's conjoined faces. Little scabs and pustules, the pattern of rust on its mechanical parts.

Behind it was a light of fire like the rising sun, shining brighter until it filled the sky.

A wall of flames descended. The daemon screamed – not a roar of anger, but a cry of genuine fear. Felix fell down, and saw the daemon's arm had been severed at the elbow. The primarch was in front of him, the Emperor's Sword roaring. Guilliman blasted out all the creature's eyes with the Hand of Dominion, and as it blindly tried to drag itself away, Guilliman stepped in and beheaded it with a single blow. Beads of fat ignited under the heat of the sword, and the beast fell down, truly dead. No spirit would emerge from its corpse to go back into the warp. Another iota of spiritual poison had been cleansed from reality.

Felix managed to prise apart the dead fingers of the monster. Guilliman reached down to him with the gauntlet, the disruption field going out. Felix took it with his own powered fist, the weapon he bore seeming so dainty compared to that carried by the primarch.

'I heard a call for assistance from this position,' said Guilliman, as he hauled the armoured Felix to his feet. 'I am glad to bring it.'

'Thank you, my lord.' Felix was forced to shout, for two dozen Space Marines of all types had surrounded the second Soul Grinder, and were blasting it methodically to pieces. Daelus gave a triumphant Martian war cry to see such a blasphemous construct brought down, and finished it off by burying his axe in its head.

Guns barked everywhere. The sound of battle receded. Reports crackled into Felix's helm.

'Now, Felix, please join me.' Guilliman set off down the Spiral Way. His men flowed after him.

'You go to draw Mortarion out?' Felix followed, sending a wordless data-pulse order to the Chosen to remain at the battery.

Guilliman nodded. 'All his army is committed. It is time to sally from the city and bring him into battle. He will meet me this time, because as far as he is concerned, everything is set to his plan. I am going to enjoy surprising him, and when his god's favour is taken from him, I shall destroy him.'

'What if the recon force has been detected and destroyed? What if the artefact remains whole? What then?'

'It will be destroyed because it has to be, Felix, or all is lost. Have faith in your brothers. Let me worry about Mortarion's schemes. Natasé assures me this is the best course to follow for victory.'

'But how likely is it?'

Guilliman looked behind him, and did not answer his question. 'If you can avoid getting yourself killed, I will be pleased. Having to choose another tetrarch so soon after reinstating the institution will make me look foolish.'

He turned back to look out over the plain. They were descending the Spiral Way rapidly. Warriors were moving into position from all over the city. In the barbican, tanks were preparing to move out.

'We gather our men,' said Guilliman. 'We go out. The true test is out there, not behind these walls. There the final moves shall be made.'

CHAPTER THIRTY

LAST CHARGE OF THE
CADIAN 4021ST

'Tanks, echelon right, advance!' Colonel Odrameyer gave the order for his regiment's final charge.

Ahead, hordes of daemons arranged themselves into formations fit more for a battlefield of spear, axe and shield than a war of shell and las, but Odrameyer had faced daemons before, and knew any confidence he had in technology was misplaced. Sure enough, when his Leman Russ opened fire, its shell vanished into the swamp, and produced only the sorriest spout of filth. The plaguebearers were hardly inconvenienced, jostled a little by the wave the explosion produced, and none fell. The three heavy bolters the vehicle carried alongside its main armament fired a burst that would have obliterated a hundred mortal men arranged in ranks like that, but only a couple of the fiends succumbed. The rest absorbed the bolts and their subsequent explosions with looks of mild irritation.

His other tanks did little better. A few holes opened up in

the daemonic army, but for all the fire and thunder unleashed, Odrameyer gained little advantage. The tanks forged on regardless. His sole aim now was to live long enough to keep the enemy from the war train.

He turned back and looked behind him through fogging lenses. The breathing kit he wore was sweaty. The seal irritated his skin. The difficulty of drawing breath through the tube leading to the filtering unit made him feel forever on the verge of suffocation. It was a panic that could not be completely suppressed, but he took heart that Mathieu's engine pushed on through the swamp like a ship in a shallow sea. It seemed brilliantly white against the browns and virulent greens of the corrupted marshland. It was an island of purity. In its progress Odrameyer saw the will of the Emperor manifest. For was it not so that its formidable weaponry was taking a toll on the daemons, where his did nothing? That its blessed beam weapons and lascannons were cutting paths of clear air through the clouds of flies that swarmed around the foe? He was half convinced that he saw angels riding the lightning of its voids, holding up shields of gold to turn back the sorcerous blasts hurled by the enemy.

His tank bounced, bruising his thigh on the hatch ring. He turned back to the front. His war machines were pushing through the swamp, toppling rotting trees and bursting through groves of soft, unnatural growths. The water was unevenly deep. Where he rode, the filth only grazed the bottom of his tank's side armour, yet a hundred yards out to his left, Leman Russ tanks pushed through ooze that washed over their glacis, clogging the barrels of their bow guns. None had yet become mired, but it was only a matter of time.

The landscape only added to the danger posed by the daemonic host. They were all suffering from the rotting effects of the creatures. The hull of his tank was rusting before his eyes and the engine wheezed with mechanical maladies.

There was a cough and bang. A Chimera in the back line came to a shuddering halt.

They would not last long. They must press on and make every second count.

'Onward, brothers and sisters of lost Cadia! Now is the moment for vengeance! Now is the time for redemption! In the name of the Emperor, onward. He is watching us now. Do not fail Him!'

Odrameyer believed this as fervently as he believed he was about to die. He had seen the Emperor act in the living world, moving His servants to defend mankind. He knew no fear, but instead experienced a holy ecstasy at what he must do. He would die joyfully.

Over the roar of the engines and the thunder of guns, he heard a doleful tallying, endless conflicting counts performed in misery. A desire to stop it seized him. It was not a noise that could be silenced by the likes of him forever, but he could interrupt it awhile, and by the Emperor he would.

He banged on the tank's roof. It accelerated. He didn't need to give any orders to the other machines. The tank crews seemed to intuit his desires, increasing their own speed not in response to his acceleration, but along with it in perfect, God-Emperor-ordained simultaneity.

They hit the ranks of the plaguebearers a moment later. His tank ploughed into them, and then the creatures did fall, crushed under the tracks or blown apart. The heavy bolters fired so much they glowed red with heat. Daemonic faces burned on them as they pivoted about, raking everything flat within their field of fire. Daemons were obliterated into puffs of rotten matter that lifted up to swirl away in the fog.

Overhead, the storm grew, as if angered by the Imperial advance.

Lightning raced in all directions from the medicae building. Thunder growled.

The tank charge crashed through the first five ranks of the plaguebearers. Odrameyer grabbed the handles of the tank's pintle storm bolter and sprayed more rounds into the foe. Carpets of lesser imps crowded the feet of the daemons, and these exploded most satisfyingly. Streams of energy leapt between the corpses of the Neverborn, their souls raging, constrained by the storm their master had set about the planet, making them powerless to escape.

Odrameyer was singing the first verse of 'Cadia In Eternum', the most rousing part of the song, over and over again. When his storm bolter's ammunition was used up, and he reached for fresh drums of bolts from the boxes tied down to the turret, he heard the words sung back at him over the vox, as the entire regiment gave voice. He reloaded, and recommenced firing, singing so loud now his throat hurt and his eye-lenses were entirely fogged up. But the enemy were so packed he could not miss. The tank slewed from side to side as the driver rammed his sticks back and forth, using the tracks as weapons to churn the daemons into the soil. Still, the charge was slowing. The enemy were crowding them, hooking leprous arms over the sponson guns to slow their traversal. Severed heads thumped into the tank, bursting like spoiled fruit, but none came near him, and though their loads of vermin turned plasteel into dust, he remained unharmed.

Blades of rusted steel, diseased bone and noxious crystal scraped on the tank, injuring it and poisoning its spirit, but it was indomitable, infused with the will of the Emperor as much as the men of his regiment were, and it heaved against their restraint. Another tank drove past, swinging out its heavy bolter and blasting the left side of Odrameyer's Leman Russ free of attackers. Momentarily released, it surged forward, knocking its assailants sprawling.

The echelon forged on, cutting through the daemon horde as a mower fells a crop. Chimeras followed the battle tanks, their weapons creating brilliant cross-hatchings of light all across the battlefield. It was too perilous for infantry to fight on foot, but they manned the lasguns that bristled all along the fighting vehicles' flanks, adding to the harvest.

Then they were through the leading enemy regiments, into a gap between the first and second lines.

More horrors awaited. More blocks of droning infantry. Greater beasts, more hideous Neverborn. Odrameyer remained stalwart. He had faced them all before. They could be killed.

'Forward!' he shouted. 'Forward!' The tanks accelerated again, weapons blazing.

Flights of horse-sized flies flew overhead, the beat of their wings a buzzsaw dirge. To his right, a Leman Russ exploded spectacularly, its turret lifted high on a pillar of bright flame. To his left, another died under the stabbing plague blades of daemons, its armour corroded through and engine rusted solid. One of the larger beasts made passes through the air with its staff, and a pulsing mist descended on a Chimera, engulfing it a moment. When the mist rose, the transport's shape was a vague suggestion under a crowd of fungi, the largest of which bore the screaming faces of the crew. Feeble-looking Neverborn killed armoured vehicles with blunt blades. Vomited maggots burrowed through plasteel like it was mouldering cheese.

The charge continued into the second line, but the numbers of the Cadians were dwindling fast, while the daemons seemed never-ending. Odrameyer looked back the way they had come. It seemed such a short distance, for the war train was still large nearby, and yet a part of the enemy's force was diverted from Mathieu. The train was close to mounting the hill, and he comforted himself that it had made significant progress towards the facility. The deaths of his men, his death, would mean something.

Now into the reserve blocks of the enemy's army, the Cadians' progress slowed. Odrameyer had his tanks re-form into a spearpoint. By dint of sheer weight of fire, they gained the base of the hills, and hauled themselves out of the quagmire. By then there were only a dozen left, and they were attacked on all sides.

Something huge was wading towards them. It held a great flail over its back, and a hooked knife in the other hand. A toad-like head with three yellow eyes and a single greening horn glowered at him from a cushion of chins. Strips of diseased skin hung like epaulettes from its shoulders. It was hugely fat, the preceding belly crushing its own troops when they were too slow in moving. A tiny replica of its head snapped and giggled on the end of a long, muscular tongue that danced in the air with serpentine menace.

'Bring it down!' Odrameyer ordered, just shouting, unable to use his data-net, hoping he would be understood.

A lascannon scored the daemon's flank, and it grumbled, turned aside, and vomited a stream of bile towards its aggressor. The liquid dissolved the front of the tank, caving it in and carrying a torrent of worms inside.

The tank came to a stop, a smoking wreck. The giant daemon giggled so that its jowls quivered, and turned its eyes upon Odrameyer.

'Oh, ho ho! If it isn't Colonel Odrameyer! Your name is whispered in the garden by the singing, biting things. The coward of Kasr Balyn, they say, who fled the world of his birth. Judgement comes for you, the judgement of Torpus Spleenbelch!' It barged its way forward, squashing plaguebearers beneath its belly. Unlimbering its flail, it began to spin it around its head, the hooks on

the ends of the chains moaning through the air as they built up speed. *'Treacher. Craven. Deserter,'* it crowed. *'Know what you are before you die.'*

Odrameyer's tank was jammed in by milling plaguebearers. The facility was five hundred yards away. Mathieu's war train was approaching with murderous purpose.

'I am no coward,' Odrameyer said. 'We fought to the last. We watched our world die and we wished we could have fought a little harder to save it.'

He said his piece with hushed conviction. The daemon heard him nevertheless.

'Only cowards flee their responsibilities.'

A worm of doubt twisted and niggled at the back of Odrameyer's mind, but he crushed it. They had been ordered to evacuate, and though it was a knife wound to his heart, he had obeyed.

'If I am a coward, then the Emperor will let you strike me down.'

The beast neared. Its reek penetrated his breathing apparatus somehow, making him heave, but he spread his arms and looked to the heavens.

'Emperor! Look upon me now!' he called.

'He cares nothing for you. Enjoy the next stage in the great cycle, in the garden.'

With a grunt of satisfaction, the daemon flicked its flail forward. The hooks sang.

Odrameyer prayed.

'Oh Emperor, protect me! Oh Emperor, guard me!'

His prayers were answered. The air shimmered. A veil appeared to be drawn aside, giving him the briefest impression of a landscape both glorious and terrible. In that place were gods, and one reached out to him, to wrap him about in His protection.

Or so it seemed.

A brilliant flash of light shattered the flail into spinning chunks of metal, none of which hit the colonel. Odrameyer was left blinking, rapturous, mumbling pieties. The Great Unclean One stared in puzzlement at its sundered weapon.

Odrameyer's crew were quick to take advantage.

Rusting bearings squealing, the battle cannon swung round, the barrel already depressing. It opened fire before it had finished moving, and the shell sank into the monster's gut like a stone hitting thick mud. The daemon looked from its flail down at the wound, a comical expression of surprise on its face, then the shell detonated, exploding the thing and scattering it to the four winds. Wide flaps of rotting hide slapped down on the tank. Garlands of intestine sizzled on the bolters.

Odrameyer was covered in disgusting fluids. They clogged his breathing filters. The sense of suffocation became unbearable, and he tore off his mask, exposing himself to the toxic airs. The pain as they ate into his lungs was immediate. And yet he endured it without fear.

He stood high on the turret's inner step, and drew his power sword.

'The Emperor is with us! The Emperor is with us!' he called. 'Praise be to He of Terra! Praise be! Forward!'

Guns blazing, tracks churning, the last women and men of the Cadian 4021st Armoured Regiment advanced towards their target.

Edermo urged the Novamarines into the battle without hesitation, not even pausing to ascertain why the militant-apostolic was there.

'*Prepare to engage,*' he voxed them, his voice clipped. '*Vasilon, get the fleet on the vox by whatever means possible.*'

'Who are these people?' Maxentius-Drontio asked Justinian.

'They are allies, brother, that is all we need to know.'

'I like simple answers,' said Maxentius-Drontio approvingly.

'*Recon Force Edermo to split*,' the lieutenant commanded. '*Squad Parris to engage the enemy, contact the militant-apostolic, find out why he's here. All other squads, prepare to attack the facility.*'

'The lieutenant has not asked me to confirm the artefact is present,' said Fe, somewhat aggrieved.

'Is it?' asked Maxentius-Drontio

'Why, yes!'

'Then be silent, tech-priest, and pray to your machine-god you live out this day.'

The grav-tanks swept down the slopes towards the medicae facility, coming in from the north. This path took them through the back of the plague horde's rear lines at an angle, and as they passed they spied Astra Militarum tanks mired in huge mobs of daemons.

'*Lend them a little aid*,' Edermo ordered. '*Targets of discretion.*'

Without slowing, the Repulsor's turret swivelled, sophisticated machine-spirits keeping the barrel level, and locked on. A spear of brilliant light flashed across the blighted land, connecting with a greater daemon's weapon and blasting it to fragments. It panned efficiently on a few degrees, putting another shot through the skull of a beast covered in matted fur and twigs. The gatling cannon whined up to firing speed, and mowed down dozens of lesser daemons. The things were soon in range of their bolt weapons, and the guns of the Impulsors. All the tanks kept on firing as they sped by, cutting apart the horde from the rear. The threat to the Cadians diminished as the pressure of the back ranks of daemons reduced, and the Astra Militarum tanks hauled themselves forward. Edermo voxed out a few orders to them, ordering them to link up with the Space Marines at the facility.

'*With such weapons as these, mankind will rule the galaxy forever*,' said Pasac.

Justinian looked at Maxentius-Drontio. He gave a shrug and reloaded his bolt rifle.

'The reborn get a little excited by all these new guns,' Maxentius-Drontio said.

As they neared the wrecked facility, the Repulsor Executioner veered off, disgorging a squad of Eradicators close by the wrecked medicae building. Vasilon's squad jumped down. Justinian had his Impulsor slow enough to drop the remaining Assault Intercessors off, before racing on and down towards the war train while the other two tanks recommenced firing on the horde.

'Patch me into the orbital relay. Let's see if it can boost our vox enough to establish communication with the war train,' Justinian ordered.

'*As you command, brother-sergeant,*' Pasac responded from the driver's compartment.

A painful squeal of overtaxed electronics blurted into Justinian's ears, then levelled off to a continuous rasp.

'Adeptus Ministorum war train, respond.'

They were moving at top speed now. Flies became smears across the hull. The train grew rapidly. A huge crowd of daemons of all sizes and kinds were mobbing it, attempting to prevent its progress further up the hill, but its racks of weapons burned them to ash, and its great mass would not be held back. As slow and inevitable as Imperial retribution, it ground up towards the corrupted facility. The fighting decks were crammed with people, most of them armed with simple weapons, and hardly any wearing any kind of protective equipment. And yet they breathed the toxic air, and they fought off the swarms of flies and aerial daemons attacking through the voids. Men and women on foot advanced alongside it, though they were falling fast.

Achilleos saw this too. He ceased firing a moment in amazement.

'They should all be dead,' he said.

'They will be soon,' said Maxentius-Drontio. 'Look, the war train's shields are failing. It cannot stand long.'

As they watched the last void collapsed. Airborne daemons fell on the defenders, reaping a terrible toll. The train was moving slowly, and plaguebearers on foot began to press at it, and clamber aboard.

Orpino was shaking from the iron hail's recoil as he raked the daemons. The tank bounced on its grav-cushion, a strangely soft sensation, when it ran down the foe. Achilleos and Maxentius-Drontio knelt on the transit bay benches, guns resting on the raised sides. Pasac fired the storm bolters mounted in the forward sponsons. For such a small vehicle, a fully crewed Impulsor put out a tremendous amount of fire, and they opened up a corridor, for although the daemons they faced were resilient ordinarily, some quality of the train made them weaker than could be expected, and Maxentius-Drontio especially grunted with satisfaction at each daemon felled.

'Adeptus Ministorum war train, I am Brother-Sergeant Justinian of the Novamarines. Respond with status and tactical objectives.'

There was a broken series of sounds, then clear, calm words.

'Well met, by the light of the Emperor, brother,' Frater Mathieu replied. 'If you value humanity at all, you will help me get into the medicae building.'

'Be advised, orbital bombardment imminent,' Justinian said. 'I suggest you hold position.'

'If the fires of the Emperor Himself were to scour that place to dead rock, still I would go there,' said Mathieu. 'The Emperor calls me. You are His angels come to lead me. Take me to my destiny.'

Maxentius-Drontio looked to Justinian. The sergeant nodded.

'Do as he says. Fall in with the train and escort them up the hill.'

* * *

Ku'Gath looked out at the bothersome mortals forcing their way into the mill. They were making quite a dent in his followers, and he hesitated a moment. Could he leave the pot?

'*It might boil over,*' he mumbled. '*Then where would the storm be?*'

The pot bubbled with vicious enthusiasm, buffeting his soul with the negative energy it poured into the atmosphere. He was proud of his alchemical abilities.

'*What I have done here is not easy,*' he grumbled. '*Brew me up a storm! He makes it sound so easy, but to gather all this potential and violence, to prod decay into energy? Not. Simple,*' he said. He shook his great head wearily. '*Keep them out, my Plague Guard!*' he shouted, but he lacked conviction. There were none of his lieutenants nearby. The Great Unclean Ones he had roused from the garden to replace his old generals were not of the same calibre, and he had only a few, one of whom, he glumly noticed, had just managed to get himself banished. '*No mortals. No Plague Marines. No shuffling afflicted. Only daemons.*'

Will it be enough? It should be enough, he told himself. He sighed.

'*But it won't be enough, will it?*'

It was all so wearily predictable.

He felt the orbital attack before it hit, for he was intimately connected to the cauldron. The cauldron made the storm, and the bombardment came through it. Bits of his soul were spread through the atmosphere. The incoming lance fire tickled his gut with an unwelcome cramp. He burped, then looked up.

'*Oh dear,*' he said.

Rains of las fell through the skies. A lot of it fizzled out, the orderly transference of energies disrupted by Ku'Gath's magic, and that made him happy. The Corpse-God's vessels were flinging the energies of stars at the cauldron, but it would not be so easily destroyed. What made him less happy was that beyond the shield over the cauldron, a fair amount of fire was getting through, incinerating his Plague Guard by the score.

'*They certainly are being reckless,*' Ku'Gath said, as a lance strike slammed into the ground close to the war train, sending up a cloud of steam into the sky. Boltgun fire and the revving of chainswords were coming closer. He looked into the cauldron again. He did not enjoy fighting, as a rule.

'*But sometimes we have no choice,*' he grumbled. '*You, you, you – get up here and stir.*'

The indicated plaguebearers shuffled up the slippery wooden scaffolding around the cauldron. Ku'Gath relinquished his stirring spoon to them. It was twice the size of any of them. Only by a complex rig of straps and ropes could they drag it around the mixture, and they argued dolorously about who should wear the harness.

'*Oh, do get on with it,*' Ku'Gath snapped. He waddled over to his great sword, propped up against the wall, and took it up. By then, the plaguebearers were pulling the spoon around.

'*Slower!*' he snarled. '*Slower! It's a tempest, not a tornado.*'

Shaking his head, he wandered off in the direction of the shooting.

He ambled down a long corridor, his antlers scraping the remains of the sodden plaster from the high roof, his sword dragged behind him, ripping up plastek floor tiles. He went out into one of the medicae's grand entrance halls. Ku'Gath had little use for the space, and had not actively remodelled it, but his mere presence ensured it was dank, streaked black with mould, and the floor covered over with tumorous flesh and stands of dying weeds. The ceiling had caved in across half the room, showing the nauseously churning sky.

'*Halllooooo?*' he called, one hand to his mouth. '*I hear you down here, little men. Come out! Come out now!*'

By way of answer, a fusion beam roared out from a side arch, and hit him square in the belly. Ku'Gath looked at the wound with a scowl. His attacker sheltered behind a pillar of dulled marble, and wore some sort of quartered design.

'This is my house, and you treat me with such ill respect?' he hooted. *'How impolite!'*

Another fusion beam blew out a chunk of his guts. A second and third of the warriors were approaching from the other side of the room, all armed the same.

'Ouch,' he said. He brandished his sword. *'A little ambush, eh? Not good enough. Do you know who I am?'*

He strode forward, and smashed down his plaguesword into the first Space Marine. Blue-and-bone armour went black. It cracked into a thousand perished pieces, and the man inside was rendered into stinking oil, black as midnight.

'I am Ku'Gath Plaguefather, first in Nurgle's favour,' he said. The other Eradicators shot him again in the back, so Ku'Gath whipped out his long, frog-like tongue, and wrenched one from the ground, tossing him into the air. As he flew, the warrior underwent a process of rapid mutation. By the time his decay-racked body burst against the wall, it was a collection of mismatched limbs with its guts worn on the outside. *'I am no weak-willed pox-pusher, but a master of disease!'* Ku'Gath scolded. *'There are few things in this universe strong enough to beat me.'*

Bolt-rounds thumped into him from all quarters. Other Space Marines were coming in, sighting down short carbines.

'Oh, more of you, is it? Do stop it,' he said. *'I am rather ticklish, and apt, when provoked, to tickle back.'*

The Space Marines continued to fire at him. Ku'Gath turned around. They circled him.

'This is not fair, so many against one. I will even the odds.'

Where the walls were covered with delightful growth, they rippled and bubbled.

Ku'Gath grinned. Plaguebearers emerged from the shadows behind the Space Marines. The bolter fire eased off.

'*Now,*' Ku'Gath said, grudgingly admitting to himself that this was rather fun. '*Who is going to fight me?*'

'I shall.'

One of the Anathema's toy grandsons strode out of the dark, pompous as a nurgling on a dung pile. He hefted a shield fronted by a bound skeleton, and carried a glowing sword of some size, though it was a lot smaller than Ku'Gath's. He was disgustingly clean and healthy looking. It would be a pleasure to cut him down to size.

'*Oh, you'll do,*' Ku'Gath said with relish. '*You'll very much do indeed.*'

CHAPTER THIRTY-ONE

A LIBRARIAN'S DUTY

Fabian went alone into the darkness. The main doors opened directly onto a long flight of steps leading down below the fortress plazas. The Library of Ptolemy's outer building was immense, but it had existed for thousands of years, and the collection it housed had long ago outgrown the original structure. Subsequent delving into the bedrock of the mountains had expanded the library tenfold, so that its stacks stretched on so far underground that Fabian could imagine them going on forever. Even in the entrance hall, the walls were crammed with books. Five storeys of brass balconies served by hundreds of ladders on wheels, left where their last users had put them before Guilliman had closed up the place.

All the lumens were out. There were still piles of data storage media on side tables, and a few personal effects, coated with years of dust. Fabian got the impression that Guilliman had chased out the scholiasts without warning.

It was quiet in there, and cool, even in his armoured suit. The noise of the assault was muffled by more than the library's thick walls; sound seemed suppressed by the weight of knowledge. There were thousands of years of history within the place. The violence of the moment was nothing to that, and the library treated it with the contempt that it deserved.

Fabian crept along silent halls, his breath echoing around the close confines of his helm.

'What by the Throne am I doing?' he muttered to himself. The monster he tracked was far beyond him. He shouldn't be there, for a whole host of reasons. Guilliman's ban was only one of them. The gun he held so capably would probably elicit no more than a titter should he shoot the creature. Just looking upon a greater daemon would probably kill him, and yet he pressed on. The truth was, the temptation to tread those forbidden halls was greater than his fear.

The daemon was not difficult to follow. Where it had passed, slime crawling with parasites puddled the floor, streaks of blood and pus adding dashes of colour. Footsteps were marked by dissolving stone. Brass fittings were tarnished, steel and iron rusted. On the shelves above Fabian's head, certain runs of books were furred with colourful moulds, as if the daemon had run its fingers carelessly among them, decaying with its touch. Curtains hung shabby, full of holes. Clumps of odd plants grew from mulched volumes, and pasty flowers huffed out spores that glimmered in the glare of Fabian's stablight.

The thing had got ahead of him far quicker than Fabian expected and was nowhere to be seen, though it had seemed so huge and so slow when it had pushed its way through the door, as if Fabian would find it a couple of yards ahead, breathing laboured and flab wobbling. He had to remind himself that it was no mortal creature he followed.

He tried his vox and got nothing but expectant silence, as if the books were waiting to see what would happen next. There was not so much as the hiss of an open connection. His world was the soft glow of his helm instruments, the long cone of his stablight. He supposed he should feel afraid, and yet he was not.

The slime trail headed deeper into the library, passing under cyclopean arches from the time the library was first extended. The stacks reared up higher, becoming multi-storey edifices. All manner of data storage was contained there, not only books, but scrolls, crystals, picts, paintings, holodiscs and tapes. The daemon had headed straight down the grand hall, right into the mountain. Fabian followed, finding its trail had gone left down a narrow side way. Shelves of books pressed in from either side, so that he was in a narrow defile of knowledge, though all those the daemon had come close to had rotted to unreadable trash, as if the space had been used to dump cast-off ideas nobody wanted any more.

More turns, more twists. He found himself going from grand arcades into lower ways, where books imprisoned in mesh cages looked sadly upon freedom. The roof lowered substantially. Flaps of skin hung from the ceiling where his quarry had scraped the plaster. Where the beast had steadied itself against the book cages they were pushed in, and their dampened contents covered in mushrooms.

Shortly after this, the signs of destruction and decay lessened. The slime dwindled. The parasites became dead brown lines in shrinking puddles. Fabian had to bend over to follow the trail, until he was peering at the floor.

A small, fat shape awaited him in the middle of the corridor. The imp from the rain.

It stood with its legs spread, fists on hips, its many chins jutting up, striking as heroic a pose as any actor on a stage.

It held this position when Fabian's light fell on it, just so he would see, then stuck out a blistered tongue, blew a rasp, and skipped off giggling. Fabian levelled his gun, thought better of it, and ran after.

That night it had wanted to show him something. What, he needed to know.

It skidded around a corner and into a low, hexagonal room domed with stone blocks. Its huge armoured door stood wide open. Six shelving units lined the walls. Five of them held books, the other a mixture of what seemed to be odds and ends and sheets of thin brass. All of them were chained in place, behind fretted silver screens.

The little imp was climbing up one of these in self-conscious parody of a mountaineer, making a great show of huffing and puffing. The silver went black where it touched, long runs of tarnish spreading. Plasteel furred. Books crumbled.

The nurgling reached its destination, leaned out on one hand and pointed with the other at an innocent-looking volume nestled among all the rest. It looked no less ordinary than the others, being the height of two handspans, and a few inches thick. The leather binding looked dry, its age hard to judge. It could have contained the details of anything.

The nurgling let go with a trill of delight and plopped onto the floor, then it ran across the room into a patch of shadow.

There had been nothing in the room besides Fabian, the books and the imp. Now there most assuredly was something else, huge and rotting. A wave of stench hit him. The Great Unclean One he had seen enter the library, the thing he had chased all the way down there, stepped forward. The air shimmered around it, as did the walls. Although there was insufficient space to hold it, somehow it fit. The imp clambered up its folds of flesh, using loose muscle fibres like ropes, until it reached the monster's enormous hand. It squirmed inside the palm, and the greater daemon began to pet it.

The beast looked down on Fabian with a face from a nightmare, yet it appeared bizarrely good-humoured, almost benevolent. Like the imp, it had two other mouths, one in its belly, the other in its left arm. All three of them smiled.

'*Hello, historitor,*' it said with a voice like a knot of snakes hissing. Its mouth was full of churning maggots, and when it spoke they fell out in twos and threes. '*I am Rotigus the Rainfather, second in Nurgle's favour. It is my great pleasure to meet you.*'

Fabian raised his gun and fired. The las-beam hit it right between the eyes. The creature peered up at the smoking mark, pupils crossed.

'*That was a little rude,*' it said, and returned its gaze to Fabian. It grinned, and more maggots pattered to the floor. '*I will take no offence. You know nothing of me apart from the lies your kind tell. I only ask that you hear me out.*' It lifted its right hand away from the imp's head and waved it above, as if gesturing to another presence. '*I mean you no harm.*'

Fabian was overcome by terror. He sought some heroic rejoinder, the sort of declamation a Chapter Master might make before laying into this thing with his power fist, but could think of nothing. He swooned, close to passing out.

'What do you want of me?' he croaked.

'*I want to give you something,*' it said. '*My god is a generous god. He brings gifts, gifts of life and gifts of death. He is the lord of rebirth, and the end of suffering. What I have is not quite so dramatic, but you will like it just the same.*'

As the beast spoke, Fabian could feel his suit perishing. The rubberised fabric tightened, threatening to crack. Delaminated carbon flaked from its armour plates. The power indicators on his laspistol dimmed, one after another. He should run, but he could not.

'*If I were you, mortal,*' Rotigus went on, '*I would read that book there.*' It extended a long black nail towards the volume its minion had pointed out. '*I would reach it down for you, but, you know, if I were to do so, you would not be able to read it.*' It sniggered, and each heave of its chest spilt maggots from its mouth like grain falling into a hopper.

'Why would I do anything you suggest?' said Fabian. 'I have read of your kind. You tempt and you corrupt. That is all you do.'

'*Is that so?*'

'All your gods are evil.'

'*All gods are gods. They are neither good nor bad.*' The mouth embedded in Rotigus' belly licked its split lips. '*Nine of your primarchs turned from your god to the Great Four. They were men far above you. If they did so in their wisdom, do you not think the offers of Chaos are worthy of consideration?*'

'No,' said Fabian. He backed away. The air twisted, and suddenly Rotigus was behind him, blocking the door, and there was no way out.

'*I'm not done with you yet,*' it said. '*You pursue knowledge, do you not? That is your purpose. That is your drive. I can see your thoughts, mortal. I know that as much as you revile me you are curious about what I say, so thirsty for knowledge you are. You are thinking, why this book, why is this monster showing me, tempting me, what knowledge is in there?*' Rotigus gave a one-shouldered shrug. '*You justify this to yourself. You are wondering what I might be giving away. What power the knowledge could give you against my kind, and whether it would be worth the sacrifice of your soul. "Fabian the hero", part of you thinks, and it is tempted. Another part of you is tired with war, and despairs. "This is a way out", you think. But we both know that*' *those thoughts are only half true. The real reason you want to look into that book, is because you just want to know. You have always just wanted to know. It is why the Anathema's son raised you up, and it is why you will be his undoing.'*

'I will not betray Lord Guilliman!' Fabian shouted, choking on fear. He brandished his weapons impotently.

Rotigus laughed. *'How delightful. Well then, ask yourself this, if he is too pure to betray...'* It licked its lips and gave a knowing look. *'Why would your lord lock away this book? Why would he lock this whole library against you and all other scholars, when he chose you specifically to uncover knowledge and reveal the truth? Just for one book. That book, right there.'*

'It's symbolic.'

'Rot, and you know it.' Rotigus held up a finger. *'I'm going to tell you why. In that book is a truth that the primarch does not want revealed.'* Rotigus leaned forward. Gas puffed from holes in its guts. Its face was inches from Fabian's. *'Hypocrite,'* it whispered. *'So take it, and know what kind of being leads your race towards extinction, and this reality to dissolution. Go on.'*

Fabian hesitated. He stared into the daemon's eyes, knowing he would never ever be able to get the thing's face out of his mind as long as he lived. He polluted his soul for a moment of defiance. It seemed worth it.

'No,' he said. He drew and activated his power sword. Against all the odds, the powercells caught, and the disruption field ignited.

Rotigus sighed. *'Very well,'* it said. It passed its hand in a wide circle, and all the books in the room collapsed into sodden dust. Then it reached with its right hand for Fabian, still cradling its pet in the left.

'Let's see how you fare in the garden,' it said, but Fabian moved back, and struck hard with his sword, cutting deeply into the thumb of the daemon.

The fist and tentacles on Rotigus' left hand closed reflexively, crushing the nurgling purring in its palm.

'Ow!' it shouted, snatching back its hand. Dark ichor sprayed from the wound, and it sucked at it. Maggots wriggled into its flesh from its mouth. It wiped the remains of its pet down its side.

'Look what you made me do,' it said, staring at the mess in its palm. A shadow gathered about its right hand, forming into a short staff topped with three circles of living wood that glowed with dangerous light. *'You'll pay for that. Perhaps a little change here and there will make you more pliable.'* He grinned. *'Body of a slug? A maggot's face? Ever-running bowels? A combination, perhaps. Then you'll listen.'* Rotigus raised up its wand. Pale ghost lights played around its triple rings of living wood. *'Something to prettify you in the Grandfather's eyes...'*

'I told you, historitor, not to follow this thing down here,' came a loud voice.

Heavy, clanking footsteps approached. Rotigus turned to look, moving a little, so that Fabian could see past it down the corridor. Chief Librarian Tigurius was coming towards them, his helm ablaze with psychic power.

'You may flee if you wish, spawn of Nurgle, and save me the time of sending you back to the warp.' He sounded annoyed.

'You have faced none like me,' said Rotigus. *'I am not going to run from you, little sorcerer. You should be running from me!'*

'I am a Librarian of the Ultramarines. I run from nothing. Protecting this knowledge is my duty. This is my library, and I command you to go from it forthwith.'

Tigurius levelled his staff. Rotigus punched its forwards. Surges of energy burst from both, crashing into one another halfway between the two with a force that threw Fabian back into the room and made the halls shake.

Blazing with arcane power, daemon and psyker fought.

Fabian's gaze was drawn upwards. The imp was back, and peering down from the shelf. Out of all the books in the room, only a single one survived.

It put a finger to its lips, and pushed the volume from the shelf. It landed with a thump on the floor a few feet from Fabian.

Hesitantly, he reached for it.

CHAPTER THIRTY-TWO

TWO BROTHERS

Maldovar Colquan stood on the command deck of the *Macragge's Honour*. Colquan held his tall helm one-handed by his side. A servitor waited behind him, carrying his guardian spear. Hundreds of people worked with a tense efficiency all around him.

Isaiah Khestrin was firmly in command, occupying the primarch's command dais rather than his own, rather more modest throne. Runners bore scrips of parchment from station to station. Servo-skulls transported data loads from one side of the deck to the other. Servitor choirs sighed nonsense words interspersed with technical information. Tech-priests from every common specialisation worked among human crew. Ultramarines stood guard around the back.

Colquan was a golden presence in their midst, unmoving as a block of stone, face set. The crew paid as much attention to him as they would a crag.

Fleet Primus encircled Iax. Nothing could leave its surface. The Imperial fleet was unopposed. There were few forces that could take on three full battle groups of the crusade. Even Mortarion's Legion, fully assembled, would have been hard-pressed to prevail against them.

Fractured reports of a large force moving on First Landing came from the surface, but proper numbers were lacking. The Lord of Death commanded one of the greatest, most coherent threats to the Imperium, and yet he had wished to take on Guilliman practically alone.

It made no sense. Colquan was aware that Guilliman and Mortarion were operating on a level even he would struggle to process, but taking that into account, neither strategy of the opposing sides seemed appropriate.

In the battle groups were hundreds of thousands of men, a quarter Titan Legio, aircraft, tanks, warriors from every branch of humanity. Guilliman had not deployed them. The ground was difficult, Colquan agreed. Large war machines would be easily outflanked in the karst landscapes round First Landing. Plague put less durable strains of humanity at risk, that much was true, but what about the Adeptus Mechanicus, or Colquan's warriors of the Ten Thousand? Surely they had a role from the start, not hanging back to act as executioners. Guilliman had told him no.

'These primarchs play a dangerous game,' he said to himself.

He feared Guilliman had underestimated the threat of Mortarion's plague. He feared this would be the end.

He did not approve of this plan.

He was tense and he showed it. Khestrin wanted him off his bridge. The fleetmaster would have preferred Colquan to wait in the teleportarium with his men, for the time his part of the battle came. He had no authority to order Colquan away, so the tribune stayed. Currently, they studiously ignored each other.

'Give me status on the bombardment of the plague nexus,' Colquan said suddenly. A strike group slightly detached from the fleets were punching columns of lance fire through the atmosphere.

'No return on bombardment effectiveness, my lord. We are firing blind,' an officer responded.

'Keep up lance bombardments on the Novamarines' mark. Prepare main batteries for firing should clarity impose itself. I want this over with as soon as possible.'

Khestrin glanced up from the report he was reading and addressed the tribune.

'Are the Ten Thousand ready for teleport strike, tribune?'

'We are.'

'Then perhaps you would like to join them?' he said, a little tautly.

'When a locus lock is provided,' said Colquan. 'There is no point in us descending to attack the artefact until its location is properly determined, and the secondary attack site shall only be engaged at express order of the primarch or tetrarch.' He remained steadfastly where he was.

He did not trust this human to win the battle. A dozen ships waited in reserve, the most potent weapons the Imperium had in its arsenal ready for launch, all pointed at the planet; Guilliman's insurance against Mortarion's victory. Colquan thought such power should not rest in the hands of mortal men. The consequences if Khestrin launched them at the wrong time were unthinkable. As much as Colquan wished the primarch gone, if he died then the Imperium would go with him.

A squalling message from the surface screeched out of a vox-horn. It took tech-adepts several passes with their filtering equipment to make sense of it. When they were done, a clarion blew, announcing a priority communique.

'The primarch sallies out. The battle enters the second phase.'

'Is the pre-lock still valid?' Khestrin asked his gunnery chief.

'Yes, my lord.'

'Then fire upon the predesignated target immediately.'

Colquan's grip tightened on his helm. 'Mortarion will make his move soon. We enter the most dangerous phase of the battle.'

The main gate of Puscinari's Barbican swung open. The enemy responded slowly. You could see the ripple of realisation spreading through them like waves in oil as ten thousand decaying helmets turned towards the gate.

Gunfire blasted out from every corner of the barbican. The north-facing guns still active on the first and second wall tiers joined the batteries on the third, and those on surrounding peaks, targeting the field before the gate. They scoured the ground of foes, monster, man and Space Marine, melting the rockcrete of the highway leading away from First Landing to a viscous lava. Flights of Inceptors burst from concealed positions and dived down. After two minutes of ferocious, world-shattering bombardment, the wall guns cut out, and Guilliman's force sallied forth.

They came in Repulsor, Gladiator and Astraeus grav-tanks, many dozens of them of them in a score of Chapter colours, pouring through the gate, already firing their main weapons before they had cleared the arch. They powered forward and spread, blasting apart everything that came against them. Inceptors and Suppressor squads roared ahead, clearing the enemy from the sides of the advance while the wall guns continued to fire, gridding the battlefield further out and annihilating the foe square by square.

The sally was fiercely opposed, and after only a few moments of disarray, the Death Guard reorganised themselves, and turned their medium-range guns onto the path of the advance. Shells hammered into the vehicles, blasting many to pieces, yet still they went on, driving straight into the enemy. Siege mantlets were targeted from behind by Gladiator tanks jinking through the narrow gaps between, blasting out field generators and leaving the warriors sheltering behind them at the mercy of the wall guns. Repulsors formed spearheads that crushed traitors into the dirt with their pounding contragrav.

To the foe, the primarch's gambit must have seemed reckless. There were many tanks, but the Legion of Mortarion outnumbered them greatly. It seemed a doomed charge, and would have been, if a simple charge had been Guilliman's intention.

The tank formation split, then split again. A large arrow of tanks peeled off to the left, heading around the base of the walls, where Space Marines leapt out and attacked Plague Marines already pushing into the city.

Another portion of the tanks drove to the east, pulling the attention of the foe's left flank away, while the central formation broke in two, and circled the middle of Mortarion's army. Several were blasted to pieces, or bogged down and overwhelmed in melee, but enough fulfilled their objective, shepherding Plague Marines by fire and grav-pulse into a dense mass a mile across.

The sky rumbled. A point of light appeared overhead.

A single shell fired from the *Macragge's Honour* fell through the atmosphere. It was a munition of rare manufacture, warded against the effects of the psychic storm by the remains of human pariahs salted into its metal, and its guidance system was locked on to a psy-beacon buried beneath the plain.

Roboute Guilliman watched it descend, a cacophony of voices in his helm reporting successful completion of manoeuvres. The tanks raced away, still shooting.

'A display of weakness can be a strength,' Guilliman said. He turned to Felix, who stood at his side. Behind him were the entirety of the Concilia Psykana. 'You know what to do, tetrarch.'

'Remember,' Natasé said. 'The sword is the key. Draw on your father's power, or die.'

Guilliman nodded, then walked out of the gate towards the enemy alone as the star fell from the sky and exploded.

Roboute Guilliman headed into its false sunrise.

The descending torpedo carried a single magma warhead. The use of such weapons was intended for Exterminatus-grade actions. They were planet killers, not tactical devices.

At four hundred feet above the surface of Iax, the warhead's servitor brain detected optimal airburst height and detonated. High explosives erupted in a sphere around a core of potent isotopes, crushing them. Atoms fused, releasing vast amounts of energy. Condensed gas metals around the warhead core were vaporised instantly, creating a cloud of plasma that raced out far in excess of the speed of sound. The shockwave hit the ground, reflecting back into itself, intensifying the effect. A compact firestorm roared in the heart of Mortarion's army, obliterating traitors who had plagued the Imperium for centuries.

Guilliman walked towards this nuclear starburst, his post-human physiology protecting him from the heat and light. The ground rose up beneath as the shockwave passed towards the city through the earth. Troops were flung off their feet, then blasted by a roaring front of superheated gas. Guilliman's tanks fled as quickly as they could, though some were caught. Mortarion's army were far less nimble, and hundreds of them died instantly.

Guilliman leant into the gale, the wind stripping colour from the Armour of Fate and discolouring the rare alloys of its decoration. But he did not stop.

The fading wavefront hit the city. Buildings weakened by the battle collapsed. Fires kindled in flash-dried gardens.

Guilliman walked on.

Through a field of corpses and wounded men the primarch

continued. A few miles out from the walls, a cloud of vaporised matter crawled skyward, lit bright beneath by the glow of molten rock. The destruction was immense, but it had no real military purpose.

Guilliman intended it only as a provocation.

'Mortarion!' Guilliman shouted. 'Mortarion! You wanted to fight me, I am here! Mortarion!'

Guilliman was three miles from the city now, a good distance for what he intended. He slowed and drew out his sword. Flame burst into being along its length, and he held it aloft.

'I have come to Iax as you asked. I stand once more upon the field of battle, and once more I call you out! My fleet stands ready to obliterate your army, as you have seen. Do me the courtesy of bravery, and face me. It is what you want. It is what I want. Let us cease this tedious chase, and settle this brother to brother.'

Smoke and fumes blew away from the primarch, clearing the air a little. He stood with his arms raised in open challenge, and considered the probability he had made an error. He would never do this against one of his more calculating brothers. Perturabo would have seized the opportunity to blast him to pieces from afar. Alpharius would have had some convoluted trick to undo him. Lorgar would have tried to convert him. But Mortarion needed to prove himself. Guilliman was relying on his brother's insecurities.

He smiled beneath his helm. If he was wrong, it was going to be a very short duel.

Roboute Guilliman was rarely wrong. Smoke stirred beneath the beat of mighty wings. Mortarion descended from above.

Guilliman sent a coded signal. The Concilia Psykana set out in a fleet of transports, circling the ground Guilliman occupied while his armoured columns kept the enemy back.

Huge, armoured feet crunched into the battlefield's debris. Mortarion shook out his wings and fixed Guilliman with blind, white eyes.

'*Hello, brother,*' he said, his sepulchral voice loud in the burning land. '*You accepted my invitation.*'

'I never turn from a fight,' said Guilliman. 'Do you?'

Mortarion chuckled. '*And you know this is a trap for you, and I know you have laid a trap for me. Our game goes on.*' Fumes billowed from his respirator. '*You don't really have the capability to target my Legion, do you? The storm sees to that. You used a beacon, correct? That was an expensive toy you used there. I doubt you've got many of those.*'

'I have you now, right where I want you.'

'*That is amusing, Roboute,*' said Mortarion. '*I could say exactly the same about you.*'

He gripped his scythe and gave it a couple of experimental passes. Silence hissed with anticipation through the air. Toxic smokes trailed his strokes.

'*Shall we?*' he said.

Guilliman got into a guard position, sword up, feet apart.

'I hope you are not going to run away from me again,' said Guilliman. 'I would hate to see your cowardice proven twice over.'

'*Oh, definitely not,*' said Mortarion. '*Fulgrim's already killed you once. It's my turn now. I intend to do a better job.*'

'Halt!'

Felix's Impulsor came to a stop. All around the ground where Mortarion and Guilliman met other vehicles drew up. Twenty in total, each one carrying Space Marine Librarians.

The crash and roar of combat still echoed over the land between the razor-edged mountains. Space Marines and daemons fought everywhere, but the nature of the fight had altered, broken up by the sally and the magma bomb into smaller battles. Data streamed in from every quarter, and although it was corrupt with scrapcode and stymied by vox-disruption, Felix had enough of a clear picture to feel concerned.

'We do not have much time,' he said to Donas Maxim and Illiyanne Natasé. 'Mortarion's forces will regroup. As soon as they realise what we are going to do, they will target our positions.'

'The skein is set,' said Natasé. 'We have done all that we can to prepare the most favourable conditions for victory.'

'This has all been your doing from the start,' said Felix. 'Allowing the spy to see our briefing, locating the artefact.'

'Your mind is not so dull as you imply,' said the aeldari. 'You knew these things. You have known what my role was in all this, tetrarch. Trap against trap. In these subtleties we aeldari excel where a human would blunder to his doom.'

'Then I know who to blame should my father fall.'

'I have told Lord Guilliman what the futures hold, but the plan is his. I swear to you. You must trust to him to save himself now. I have done what I can. You do not trust me, but know that his death is not my intention.'

'Still we must win,' said Felix.

'Yes,' said Natasé. 'Your Space Marines must find the artefact and destroy it. Guilliman must weather Mortarion's plague. Many other things could go awry. Victory is far from certain.'

Felix had his eye-lens magnification up to maximum. Through shimmering air, he watched Mortarion approach his brother. Guilliman was so small compared to his twisted sibling. It was impossible to imagine they had once been the same, had fought side by side, spoken as equals.

'We could lose. We could lose him.'

'We could,' admitted Natasé. 'The future is not your friend, nor mine. All we can do is align ourselves with the best course that fate has to offer. Do not fear, Decimus Felix. My people have long practice in this art.'

'We shall try our utmost, tetrarch,' said Maxim.

'Then proceed,' said Felix. 'Waste not one more second.'

Natasé laid out a cloth of shining black patterned with the geometric sigils of his kind. He sat cross-legged, and pulled rune after rune out of a cloth bag at his side. These floated about him, giving out a wan, blue light. Natasé settled into meditation.

'You may begin, Donas Maxim. Lend me your power.'

Maxim nodded. He gave the signal to his brothers of many Chapters, and held out his hands. Bright power collected there.

Mortarion passed his scythe through the air. Guilliman gripped his father's sword. *How can he beat that?* thought Felix, and wished he was at the regent's side.

Mortarion saluted his sibling as he had on Parmenio, scythe haft pressed against his forehead.

'Hurry, they are about to begin their duel,' said Felix.

'All will be as it will be,' murmured Natasé, and a cold luminescence crawled across the sky. 'We can do no more. The fate of Ultramar is in Roboute Guilliman's hands, as it always has been.'

The aeldari's runes glowed with a brilliant light. The dome of force enclosed the duelling ground.

The primarchs charged.

CHAPTER THIRTY-THREE

EXTERMINATUS

The brothers moved together.

There was a split moment when they locked eyes. A pressure joined them, heavy enough to compress time. When they attacked, they did so without thinking. Abilities woven into their gene-code at the dawn of the Imperium saw to that.

Mortarion had the greater reach and struck first. Silence swept around in a reaping cut. Guilliman halted its seemingly unstoppable swing upon the quillions of the Emperor's Sword. Thunder crackled from the blow. Fire mingled with noxious smoke, burning poisons away. The daemon spirit of Silence gibbered in fear as the flames licked its brazen cage.

Mortarion cocked his head. Guilliman nodded in acknowledgement. Mortarion stepped back, and round, disengaging his weapon's head from Guilliman's block and turning in a circle, using his height advantage to stay clear of the burning blade. Silence whistled round through the air, built up to blurring speed. Guilliman stepped away, hewed one-handed at the weapon, jarring it hard. Flames roared up from the Emperor's Sword again. Mortarion jabbed with Silence's wicked back hook, and this too was diverted with a ringing of unearthly steels. Mortarion turned his weapon slightly, and yanked back hard, seeking to trip his brother. Guilliman jumped over the head, the buzzing chain tip passing an inch beneath his feet. He struck out, catching the cage of bones around Silence's top, breaking them.

The daemon screamed. Mortarion hissed. Smoke boiled up over Guilliman from the censer built into Silence's head. It ate into his softseals, penetrated his breathing grille. He coughed, tasted blood in his exhalations. A heaviness afflicted him.

He staggered back. The Armour of Fate's machinery whined into a higher activity, purging his body, and the weakness receded.

Guilliman swung the Emperor's Sword about in a figure of eight. Fire roared.

'You rely too much on unclean gifts, Mortarion. You never were much of a swordsman.'

'You were always bad at boasting,' he said. *'Such a tedious little paragon.'* He yanked out the Lantern from its holster, aimed and fired in a single movement. But Guilliman reacted fast, a hail of bolts from the Hand of Dominion exploding around the weapon and Mortarion's wrist, knocking it from his hand. The energy beam carved a trench of glass into the ground.

'Let us keep this blade to blade, shall we?' said Guilliman.

The regent leapt forward, his Emperor-given strength working in tandem with Cawl's miraculous armour to launch him at his brother. Fire blazed as he brought the Emperor's Sword down, cleaving through the links of a chain holding one of the many censers Mortarion wore on his armour. The fallen primarch jumped back, wings spread, and took to the air. Guilliman landed; the point of the sword angled down, missing its target, and blasted a glowing crater into the earth.

'*Temper, temper, Roboute,*' said Mortarion. He looked overhead, where the fine skin of energy put out by the Concilia Psykana was glaring in his warp sight. '*I see your witches are at work. So let me show you my power in return.*'

He threw out his hand. A bolt of yellow leapt from the palm. Guilliman swung up the blade to intercept it. The bolt slammed into the weapon, where it was absorbed. Mortarion pushed forward, still venting the might of the warp from his hand, but Guilliman stood firm, though he shook with the effort and the flames on the sword dimmed. He shouted, and pushed back. The energy stream curved in on itself, and exploded, and Mortarion was pushed away.

'Where is the warrior who stood before the assembly at Nikaea and denounced all use of the warp?' said Guilliman. 'You are everything you purported to despise.'

'*I opened my eyes, brother,*' said Mortarion, circling Guilliman in the air. '*I saw the lies our father spouted for what they were. I found a better master, and I became stronger than you.*'

'You are a slave.'

'*So are you.*'

Mortarion folded his wings and dropped suddenly, clashing with Silence. Guilliman turned to the side, bending under the whistling blade. Silence caught the decorative halo mounted on Guilliman's power plant, wrenching it free. Guilliman staggered, and Mortarion pressed his advantage, bringing the bottom of Silence's haft up in an underhand blow. Iron-hard wood smashed into the Armour of Fate's chestplate, scoring it with ugly marks that wept poison. Guilliman was spun around.

'Fool,' Mortarion gloated. '*Look at me. Look at how much power I have. I am far more than you could ever be, I am–*'

Guilliman raised the Hand of Dominion and fired straight into Mortarion's face. Bolt-rounds exploded all over his front. He raised his hand to shield his eyes and turned away with a metallic cry of pain. Guilliman leapt forward and attacked with the Emperor's Sword.

Mortarion blinked to clear his rheumy eyes, still managing to block Guilliman's blows.

'I thought you wished to keep this to blades, brother? I see you abandon your sense of honour when it suits you.'

'There can be little honour in a battle between us, Mortarion.'

'Very true,' said the daemon primarch. He aimed a blow at Guilliman that was easily evaded, but then Mortarion turned his motion into a kick. His heel connected with Guilliman and sent him several yards back through the air. He landed heavily on his back. Sparks spat from a severed power line.

'This is wearisome, my brother. You are no challenge at all.' He threw out his hand, and a gale of poisonous mist engulfed Guilliman. The sword flared and burned it away. *'Even with our father's weapon you cannot beat me. I am the best of both material and immaterial worlds. A master in either medium. You are a leftover. The rusted tool of a dying god.'* Another flaring bolt of psychic power arced from his palm, striking Guilliman in his chest as he tried to rise, knocking him back down to the ground. *'A dead man, brought back by means you would otherwise decry, had they not saved your miserable soul. Xenos magic, and wicked science. You carry it around with you. It is in your blood, and you have the gall to tell me I am corrupt?'*

Guilliman rolled onto his side, reaching out with the gauntlet to fire again, but Mortarion whispered words of power, and ammo feeds corroded. The metal of its guns dulled. In Guilliman's helm alarm runes flashed.

'You are nothing, my brother,' Mortarion hissed. *'The last shreds*

of our father's dream, clung on to against the face of reality as they break into nothing. You are not even a memory, but a relic falsehood.'

'You betrayed us,' said Guilliman. 'You and the others.'

'I did not,' said Mortarion, coming to stand over his sibling. *'For how can one betray a lie?'*

'It need not have been this way,' said Guilliman. He tried to stand again, but Mortarion pinned him to the ground with a massive foot. Guilliman punched at it with the Hand of Dominion, but it did no good, and Mortarion leaned his weight upon him.

'It always has been this way, brother, for it could not have been any other.'

Guilliman struggled, but could not shift his brother's massive weight from bearing down on him. Mortarion bent down and pulled off Guilliman's helm. The loyal primarch's nose and throat burned with the gases coming from his brother's wargear, and the stench of his body made his stomach lurch.

'You were disappointingly easy to beat,' Mortarion said. *'For all your scheming and your plans, when it came down to it, you were no match for me. Not any longer.'*

Mortarion reached up and took hold of one of his many pendants, a small, dirty phial, and yanked it free.

'I have a gift for you, a gift from Nurgle. Take it willingly, and see his glory.'

'You will never turn me.'

'Then that is your loss.'

Mortarion pressed the dirty tube into a greening brass syringe. Careful to keep it well clear of himself, he bent low and jabbed the needle into his brother's neck with a deep sigh of satisfaction, just above the scar Fulgrim had given Guilliman.

Immediately, Guilliman gasped. He spluttered. Veins turned black and his eyes went red as a tide of filth washed through his veins.

'*That's right, brother,*' said Mortarion, laughing, stepping back and casting aside the syringe. '*Take your medicine.*'

Toxins boiled into streamers of gas that raced out from the primarch's mouth. Where they touched the dead upon the field, they collapsed into revolting clots of matter. Their wargear corroded instantly to unidentifiable remnants that looked as if they had been excavated from a thousand-year interment.

The nurglings around Mortarion coughed and squealed, dropping and dying on the ground, where their bodies bloated, sank inward and decayed in an instant. The daemon primarch was careful to remain untouched by the wisps of toxin, turning them aside with his psychic might. Nevertheless, he took several more steps back from his afflicted brother while the Godblight did its work.

'*Ku'Gath told me this disease would be deadly to both of us,*' said Mortarion, and his voice betrayed his struggle keeping the plague at bay. '*I can well believe it, my brother, looking at what it is doing to you.*'

Guilliman's skin had turned black. In places it deliquesced, running from his skull, exposing bone that gleamed before going a rotten brown.

'*Don't struggle,*' Mortarion said. '*This is only the beginning of your suffering. I'd save your strength if I were you, or how else will you savour it?*'

Felix watched helplessly as Mortarion beat the primarch to the ground and stepped on him, holding him in place. He stood in total indecision, then made to go to his side.

'No, tetrarch!' said Maxim through teeth gritted with effort. 'You must let events follow their course.'

Gas of a hideous hue raced out from the two primarchs, occluding Felix's view. The psychic shield flared over the battlefield when the gas hit, rolling up, doubling back on itself in a wave of screaming, insubstantial faces. Maxim grunted. Natasé's runes were shining so brightly Felix could not look upon them.

Felix took a step forward. He stared into the fog, looking for his gene-father. The vapours swirled and gathered like live things seeking escape from a cage. When they cleared enough for him to see to the centre for a moment, he clenched his fists. The two primarchs were flickering in and out of sight, as if they only partially occupied realspace.

'What is happening?' he asked.

'The disease is a thing of the othersea,' said Natasé. 'Should it succeed in killing your lord, it will pull his soul into the realm of Nurgle, and thus be the trigger that drags all of Ultramar into the warp. It is time for the second phase. If you would save your men, begin your withdrawal.'

Alarms whooped across the bridge of the *Macragge's Honour*, and the cry went up.

'The primarch has fallen!'

The news raced round the command deck.

'Hold,' Colquan commanded. 'Hold your nerve!' He swept his gaze about, silencing all. 'Is this true?'

Vox-operators listened hard to messages shredded by the boiling of reality.

'Unknown,' said one of them, eventually. 'Tetrarch Felix reports Lord Guilliman and Mortarion are in a state of warp flux.'

A nervous, calm silence fell. All faces turned to the fleetmaster and the tribune.

'Perform your roles. Stand your ground.' Colquan turned back to the oculus. 'This is nearly over.'

'Lord Felix has given the order for the evacuation,' said a woman manning one of the logistics desks. 'Communications are at almost complete break-up.'

'Empyric indices are climbing on every scale,' reported the psy-augurum.

Vast networks of energy raced around and around Iax. Faces leered from the clouds. The planet seemed to flicker, as if it were no longer really there.

'The storm is growing worse,' said Khestrin. 'Warp interface imminent. Status on the artefact?'

'Actual position unknown,' responded an officer. 'Reconnaissance status unknown. Bombardment effect unknown.'

'You should heed the tetrarch, launch the evacuation ships,' said Colquan.

'We stand to lose them all, if that storm is not broken,' said Khestrin.

'Better to risk a few ships' crews if there is a chance loyal Space Marines might be spared.' Colquan looked at the fleet-master directly. 'I do not like it. The Adeptus Astartes are flawed weapons, but they are the best we have. Bring them back, whatever the cost.'

Khestrin considered a moment.

'Very well. Launch all evacuation ships. Begin fleet withdrawal from the planet. If the veil does collapse here, I will not have my ships pulled into the warp.' Khestrin took a deep breath. 'And begin preparations for Exterminatus.'

'You would destroy Iax?' said Colquan.

'I would not, but I will if I have to,' said Khestrin. 'We must understand that this is the final battle of this campaign. Mortarion's defeat and the purging of his corruption must be accomplished, or we will lose all of Ultramar, and more beyond. This is the stark choice we face. I will not commit any world to the fires of Exterminatus lightly. But those were the lord regent's express orders. Things go against us. The artefact remains active. The planet fades from reality, and the primarch has fallen.'

A black bell began to toll. At the rear of the deck, hooded figures went to work. One came up, slow and solemn, to Khestrin's dais, there to take the rod of activation from him, which was handed over with due, if brief, ceremony.

'How shall it be done, my lord?' the man intoned. 'By Provisio Primus – sterilisation by virus bomb. By Provisio Secundus – sterilisation by atomic fire. Or by Provisio Ultrus – planetary annihilation by crustal disruption?'

'All of them,' said Khestrin crisply. 'I want all of them. Nothing can escape this planet. If that damn aeldari witch's predictions are correct, we cannot allow this disease to get off Iax.'

'I say do not be hasty,' said Colquan. 'The witch made another set of predictions. We must trust those will come to pass.'

'I command it to be done,' said Khestrin to the hooded adept. 'I speak on behalf of the primarch.'

'Whereas I speak with the authority of the Emperor Himself,' said Colquan.

'So then, Custodian, do you claim to follow the religion you have long despised, and say He speaks to you now?'

'No,' said Colquan. 'But we must wait. We are not finished yet.'

'Why do you believe so? All the signs are against us,' said Khestrin.

'Because nothing can stop the Avenging Son,' said Colquan, his eyes fixed once more on the planet below. 'I know, for I have tried.'

CHAPTER THIRTY-FOUR

A GOD TO FIGHT A GOD

'Throne curse it,' Maxentius-Drontio said. 'The bombardment is not getting through to the facility.'

Lance beams stabbed repeatedly at the landscape. Most went wide, and those that were on target halted a hundred feet over the hospital, their beams dispersed into fizzles of weak sparks.

'They are firing blind,' said Achilleos.

'That storm would make a mockery of a true shot even if they were not,' said Justinian.

'*Sergeant Parris.*' Edermo's voice was faint behind atmospheric interference and energy discharge. '*The orbital bombardment is proving ineffective. Teleport lock impossible. We must attack the artefact ourselves. All assets to reinforce at our position. We have engaged and will occupy the enemy while you advance.*' He was fighting. Justinian heard the strain in his voice and the explosive crash of weapons against his storm shield.

'We have to go in,' Justinian said.

'What about the militant-apostolic?' said Achilleos, pointing back at the war train. 'He was insistent he be delivered to the hospital, and it seems there is some effect around the priest that somehow keeps the daemons at bay. He could be useful.'

'Oh yes,' said Magos Fe. 'Faith! A powerful weapon. Some say the living blade of the Emperor.'

'What do you mean by that?' said Maxentius-Drontio.

The magos shrugged. 'It takes a god to fight a god.'

'I am not so sure about the efficacy of prayers over bolts,' said Maxentius-Drontio. 'The war train is being affected now. It is rusting. Look.'

Corrosion had appeared over the train's armoured plating and its pistons were catching, on the verge of seizing up.

'Better to have all possible weapons. Edermo requested all assets, so we are going to take the militant-apostolic in,' Justinian told his squad. 'Perhaps he can weaken the daemon's hold and open the artefact to the fleet weapons.'

'If he cannot?' said Maxentius-Drontio.

'Then we will do it your way, brother, with knives and bolts, but for now he comes with us. It appears an escort will no longer suffice. We must fetch him. Brother Pasac, bring us around. Make this quick.'

The Impulsor swept back towards the war train, manoeuvring thrusters sending it into a tight turn. It blasted its way through the daemons shambling about on the hillside. There were many left, but their organisation was shattered. The war train's formidable armament had banished thousands of them, taking out their leaders with well-placed beams of plasma and las.

While Brother Orpino and Pasac mowed down the foot-soldiers with the vehicle's armament, Justinian had his men pick out the last remaining specialised daemons from among the masses. Those bearing scrolls, standards, instruments, the ones capering madly to encourage the rest. Their heralds and sorcerers, what passed for an officer class among them. They executed them at range where possible, felling them with hails of bolt rifle fire without getting too close, for the diseases of the stronger ones were dangerous even to the Adeptus Astartes.

The battlefield was among the most chaotic Justinian had ever experienced. Orbital fire slammed down from the heavens at random, flash boiling the clouds, shuddering the sky with artificial thunderclaps of superheated air, ionising the atmosphere and spreading spectacular displays of lightning from horizon to horizon that seemed to physically battle with that of the storm. They were lance strikes exclusively, and this along with the nature of the dispersal pattern told Justinian the fleet had no accurate targeting data despite the recon force's broadcasts. As they sped back down the hill, they were lucky they were not hit themselves.

'Frater Mathieu, can you hear me?' Justinian signalled. He bellowed over the roar of the stubbers and bolters, hardly able to hear himself. His vox was spitting, as if the components were on the verge of failure. 'Frater, prepare to evacuate.'

'I do not think he can hear you, brother-sergeant,' said Achilleos.

He was probably right. It appeared to the Space Marines that there was an intelligence working against the train, bringing evil magics to bear on its fabric, for though it had resisted the accelerated decay at work everywhere in the zone, now it succumbed it did so faster than anything else, and there was a heaviness around Squad Parris when they moved into the train's forward arc, as of a baleful attention. Something seemed to emanate from the ruined facility and press at reality, flattening it, threatening to smooth out the creases of individual lives into homogenous entropy. Their helm displays flickered. Power levels in their armour dropped.

'I have never felt something this wicked,' said Maxentius-Drontio. 'The warp is strong here.'

'The warp!' said Magos Fe with a mad laugh. Lights gleamed from his pendants and detection devices. 'This is not just the warp. We witness the influence of one of the Great Powers. The Plague God is fixed on the priest!'

He sounded terrified. Justinian, too, felt disquiet for the first time in years.

'Well, if he is going to all that trouble, it suggests he is a threat,' said Maxentius-Drontio.

Justinian hammered on the driver's hatch, no longer trusting his vox-systems. It struggled to open, shedding flakes of decaying ceramite when it did. 'Get us out of this area,' he said to Pasac. 'Approach from the side or it will undo us as well.'

Manoeuvring jets fired and the Impulsor skidded sideways. The train groaned. There was a hollow, metallic noise, and something gave at the side. A jet of steam a hundred yards high shot out at a steep angle. Its guns were grinding to a halt. As Justinian watched, a plasma cannon's bearings rusted right through, and the weapon dropped free. Plasma vented in all directions, washing up over the fighting decks and searing pilgrims from existence. Screams joined the faltering hymns and the counting of the daemons.

With a grunting clatter followed by a great and weary sigh, the train came to a stop.

They ran down half a dozen daemons and halted at the train's flank. The Impulsor's engines were making an unhealthy sound. The train trembled with accelerated decay. Above, the songs of the last pilgrims were becoming anguished moans.

'Wait here,' Justinian ordered. 'Turn about. Keep an escape corridor free. I'm going to fetch him.'

Justinian leapt up the side of the train, climbing hand over hand up its heavy decoration. This was disintegrating even as he went past the first gun ports, angels' faces becoming formless blobs, their wings falling off. He reached a subsidiary fighting deck, and saw the pilgrims there were dying in puddles of their own rank fluids, the dead already like corpses left a week out in the sun. He ran through the mess, towards a staple ladder leading to the command pulpit. There were a pair of daemons moving about, mumbling numbers, and pawing at things with curious incomprehension. He gunned them down and hauled himself up the ladder, felt a touch on his boot; looked down to see the dead crusaders getting up, rictus grins on their faces, grasping for him. He kicked down, obliterating rotten skulls, and climbed.

His armour was suffering more now, the systems displays giving off plaintive peeps and whines. The coolant in his back-pack was losing efficiency. The fluids around his polymer muscles were drying, and his warplate's machine-spirits fought their own battle as he climbed. The train shook, and he guessed the reactor bonds were failing. The fires of its fusion core were going out. Rust ate through foot-thick armour in moments, quick as a time-lapse vid. One of the staple rungs came off in his hand, and he nearly fell.

He reached the top. A screaming daemon mounted atop a gargantuan fly dived at him. He shot out the mount's soft belly with his bolt rifle, and it smashed hard into the deck. There were bodies everywhere, most killed not by violence but by disease. A few people moved weakly, afflicted by a dozen ailments at once. The angel and its command pulpit were ahead. The train shook beneath him as it underwent centuries of rot in moments, collapsing into itself. His armour was wailing now, running out of subsidiary systems to reroute its power flows through as circuit after circuit failed.

When he rounded the angel's cast bronze robes, he did not know what he would see in the pulpit. He was genuinely surprised to find Frater Mathieu standing in perfect serenity while all around him the other leaders of the crusade deliquesced. His crusader bodyguard were piles of rusted armour and mildewed robes. Fungus and pallid plants that looked like drowned men's fingers were growing rapidly from the remains. Knots of worms squirmed their way out of disarticulated jaws. But Frater Mathieu was untouched. He stood with an expression of rapture on his face, clutching his inactive servo-skull and stroking absently at the bone.

'He is with me. He is with me,' he was saying, over and over again.

'Militant-apostolic,' Justinian said. 'You must come with me. This vehicle is no longer viable.'

Mathieu turned to him, as if he thought Justinian had been there the whole time. 'Yes, I must. I must go there.' He pointed to the facility, now so close. 'Take me.'

'Then let us go.'

The man did not move. There was an odd light playing around his eyes, and Justinian's doubts as to Mathieu's usefulness grew.

'I don't have time for this,' Justinian said. He dropped his bolt rifle, went to the priest, and picked him up. From the command pulpit it was a sheer drop of forty feet to the Impulsor, where it hovered in wait, still shooting. Achilleos and Maxentius-Drontio had disembarked, and were firing on full-automatic into the daemons.

'Pasac, get out a little from the edge,' he voxed. 'I am coming down directly.'

Trusting that his squadmate had heard him, Justinian took a few steps back, then ran at the parapet surrounding the pulpit, his armoured weight shaking the disintegrating structure. When he reached the edge, he jumped, his armour's strength-boosting capabilities lifting him easily. He pushed off the wall as he flew over it, and arced down through the air.

The Impulsor rushed at him. He hit the centre of the transit deck. The vehicle sank into its contragrav field, then steadied.

'Get back in,' he ordered his men, putting Mathieu down. 'Brother Pasac, get us into the medicae facility now.'

Achilleos and Maxentius-Drontio clambered back up onto the transport deck, gunning down monsters that attempted to follow.

Grav-engines howling, the Impulsor raced back up the hill, slaughtering daemons as it went.

CHAPTER THIRTY-FIVE

A LIGHT IN THE GARDEN

For a moment, there was nothing but blackness.

'Do you feel it, brother?' Mortarion's voice was a gloating hush that came from nowhere. *'Do you feel the warp?'*

Pain returned and Guilliman roared. His skin was on fire. His bones felt like ice. His organs were a hundred stab wounds. He was falling, tumbling over and over, into some nameless darkness.

'Do not fight it, my brother,' breathed Mortarion, and his voice seemed to be right by his ear. *'Accept it, and Grandfather will spare you. You could join me. Together, we could overthrow our other brothers, cast down their false gods, and bring the galaxy the endless renewal of death and rebirth.'*

Guilliman could not reply. Pain attacked him on every level, each part of his being suffered.

'It hurts, yes?' said Mortarion's voice. He sounded almost regretful it was not he who was afflicted.

Guilliman dug deep inside himself, to some small corner that the pain had not yet found.

There was a light there. He fled into it.

His awareness shifted, and he was two people, two versions of himself at two different times.

The gate to the throne room was before him.

'This is interesting,' said Mortarion's voice. 'This is a memory you hide in. You went to see father? You want Him to protect you now? How touching.'

Guilliman, still tongueless, lipless, wordless, could only relive what he had seen. Trajann Valoris bade the great doors open. His words were a jumble, broken by time, his movements a fan of overlapping images in terrible shades of gold.

But when the gates opened, and the light came out, that was pure.

Mortarion gasped in discomfort, and Guilliman felt a little hope.

He remembered. He relived. He had gone in to see what his father had become. Guilliman had been thousands of years dead. He had spent subjective years lost in the warp to come to Terra, only to find an empire of ruin laid starkly before his disbelieving eyes.

All building to this fateful moment.

There was light and fury, a radiance that passed through the bones and burned at the soul. Endless sound that filled eternities.

There were the wordless screams of the psykers drained to feed His terrible majesty.

There were visions of gods, and demigods, of a brown-skinned man of calm expression. Clad in skins. Clad in mail. Clad in clothes of all colours and bewildering variety. Clad in armour of gold. He had many faces, all proud, all betrayed. He saw Malcador in him, the first regent. He saw his brothers.

A million ideas battered him, memories from tens of thousands of years of existence. Random, circular trains of thought, obsessions, predictions and fears. So many voices, all the same, all different, none coherent.

He saw a dusty room, titanic in scale, crammed with machinery of awful purpose, the living dying in relay to sustain this monstrous thing. The centre was a machine of gold, shrouded in the dust of broken dreams. A skull-faced cadaver, all life gone, perched within its seat – but then the vision flickered, and he saw a king of infinite power, resting awhile upon His throne to think, only lost to His subjects for a while, and when done with His meditation He would rise, and rule justly. He saw a tired man who would be his father, giving him grave counsel he could not hear, telling him what he must do. Again, his view changed, and he saw an evil force to rival the great powers of Chaos. He saw sorrow, triumph, failure, loss and potential. There was no one face among all the faces, no one voice, but a chorus, a cacophony. The Emperor's presence was a hammer blow to his soul, a tremendous scouring of being. He could not stand before it, and fell to his knees, though Valoris remained silent by his side as if nothing had happened.

He was in the dust of a corpse-king's court. He was before a resplendent Emperor for all the ages.

'Father,' he said, and when he had said that word, it was the last time he had meant it. 'Father, I have returned.' Guilliman forced himself to look up into the pillar of light, the screaming of souls, the empty-eyed skull, the impassive god, the old man, yesterday's saviour. 'What must I do? Help me, father. Help me save them.'

In the present, in the past, he felt Mortarion's wordless presence at his side, and felt his fallen brother's horror.

He looked at the Emperor of Mankind, and could not see. Too much, too bright, too powerful. The unreality of the being before him stunned him to the core. A hundred different impressions, all false, all true, raced through his mind.

He could not remember what his father had looked like, before, and Roboute Guilliman forgot nothing.

And then, that thing, that terrible, awful thing upon the Throne, saw him.

'My son,' it said.

'Thirteen,' it said.

'Lord of Ultramar.'

'Saviour.'

'Hope.'

'Failure.'

'Disappointment.'

'Liar.'

'Thief.'

'Betrayer.'

'Guilliman.'

He heard all these at once. He did not hear them at all. The Emperor spoke and did not speak. The very idea of words seemed ridiculous, the concept of them a grievous harm against the equilibrium of time and being.

'Roboute Guilliman.' The raging tempest spoke his name, and it was as the violence a dying sun rains upon its worlds. 'Guilliman. Guilliman. Guilliman.'

The name echoed down the wind of eternity, never ceasing, never reaching its intended point. The sensation of many minds reached out to Guilliman, violating his senses as they tried to commune, but then one mind seemed to come from the many, a raw, unbounded power, and gave wordless commands to go out and save what they built together. To destroy what they made. To save his brothers, to kill them. Contradictory impulses, all impossible to disobey, all the same, all different.

Futures many and terrible raced through his mind, the results of all these things, should he do any, all or none of them.

'Father!' he cried.

Thoughts battered him.

'A son.'

'Not a son.'

'A thing.'

'A name.'

'Not a name.'

'A number. A tool. A product.'

A grand plan in ruins. An ambition unrealised. Information, too much information, coursed through Guilliman: stars and galaxies, entire universes, races older than time, things too terrifying to be real, eroding his being like a storm in full spate carves knife-edged gullies into badlands.

'Please, father!' he begged.

'Father, not a father. Thing, thing, thing,' the minds said.

'Apotheosis.'

'Victory.'

'Defeat.'

'Choose,' it said.

'Fate.'

'Future.'

'Past.'

'Renewal. Despair. Decay.'

And then, there seemed to be focusing, as of a great will exerting itself, not for the final time, but nearly for the final time. A sense of strength failing. A sense of ending. Far away, he heard arcane machines whine and screech, close to collapse, and the clamour of screams of dying psykers that underpinned everything in that horrific room rising higher in pitch and intensity.

'Guilliman.' The voices overlaid, overlapped, became almost

one, and Guilliman had a fleeting memory of a sad face that had seen too much, and a burden it could barely countenance. 'Guilliman, hear me.

'My last loyal son, my pride, my greatest triumph.'

How those words burned him, worse than the poisons of Mortarion, worse than the sting of failure. They were not a lie, not entirely. It was worse than that.

They were conditional.

'My last tool. My last hope.'

A final drawing in of power, a thought expelled like a dying breath.

'Guilliman...'

It felt to Guilliman like his mind had exploded. There was a blinding flash, and the king and the corpse and the old man overlaid and overlapped, dead and alive, divine and mortal. All judged him. Guilliman staggered from the throne room. Valoris stared into the heart of the Emperor's light unflinchingly a moment longer, then turned away and followed.

They emerged days later, though only seconds had passed. Guilliman could not be sure of anything that had happened. When asked later, Valoris said he saw nothing but light, and had heard nothing, and that nobody had heard anything from the Emperor since He had taken to the Golden Throne thousands of years before, but he said he had seen Guilliman speak, as if deep in discussion, and although Valoris could not hear what was discussed Guilliman seemed serene and firm. That he had not seen him fall, or plead.

Every time he remembered, it was different. Was any of it real? He did not know. He would never know.

The moment fled back into the past where it belonged. Guilliman's body slammed into wet soil. He was dying again. His soul clung on, but that too was being eaten alive by Mortarion's plague.

Footsteps halted by his head. There was a poke on the breast-plate of the Armour of Fate. Guilliman heard Mortarion speak, but he could not see, and he could sense nothing else but pain.

'*Do you see, Guilliman, you follow the wrong master,*' said Mortarion. '*He is a cyst, a pus-filled canker surrounding a dead thing lodged in the fabric of reality, like a thorn, or a piece of shrapnel. It must be drawn out for things to heal. Do you understand now, that this is what you follow?*' Mortarion grunted in amusement. '*Of course, you can't answer. I doubt you understand, anyway.*'

There was the sound of Mortarion shifting his stance. A wistful tone entered his voice.

'*We will soon be in the Garden of Nurgle, my brother. The veils are parting. I can see it already. Once you are dead, this world will fall within it, and become a jewel of decay. You have damaged my network, but not by enough, and at the coming of your death, one by one each of your worlds will pass from this place of cold void and uncaring stars into the Grandfather's embrace.*

'*I wish you could see it. It is beautiful, full of life and potential. There are trees here, and plants of amazing variety. It is not barren. It is not like that cold light you showed me. Not like Him. It is not like the materium at all, with its pointless struggle against inevitability. Here nothing ever truly ends, but is reborn and dies and is reborn and dies, over and over again. Everything here is given many gifts. Nothing, no matter how small, is overlooked, and all share in Grandfather's bounties. There is no pain, and because there is no pain suffering is borne gladly. Now tell me, brother, compared to the hell our father has inflicted upon the galaxy, does that sound so terrible?*' He took a deep breath, a man sampling country air on a fine day. '*I wish you could see it,*' he said again.

The pain still raged through Guilliman, but it was diminishing.

'If only you would turn. You are nearly dead. Soon the pain will be over.' Mortarion knelt beside his brother, and rested his hand on his chest. *'Don't you want that, for it to be done?'* He began to stroke, like he was soothing a feverish child. *'Hush now, Roboute. Hush. Go to the Grandfather, and you will see, he will make it all all right. He will take the pain away forever.'*

CHAPTER THIRTY-SIX

THE CALL OF HONOURUM

'*You are a most troublesome gnat,*' Ku'Gath said. It whirled its huge sword around its head and struck.

Edermo moved aside, and the weapon missed him, carving down through a wall. Crumbling brick exploded everywhere. The daemon advanced on him.

'*How do you think you can win this fight?*' it said. It swiped a diseased paw at Edermo. The lieutenant slashed at it as it came, cutting a deep gash in its thigh. The strike exposed him to the daemon's sword, but it was worth it to see the thing's outrage.

Edermo took the return blow square on his shield. Lightning burst all round him. Thunder boomed from the interface of magic and technology. A little kinetic overspill got through, and the daemon forced him backward, its sword blazing with energy where its edge pushed on Edermo's power field. Edermo waited for the right moment, and stepped around, parrying the greatsword. The weight of it was monstrous, and he was forced to put all his strength into it to push it aside, but the daemon wielded it like a kitchen knife.

'Stop. Moving. About!' the daemon shouted angrily.

Edermo glanced behind him. Their fight had demolished a good part of what was left of the medicae facility, opening up dank, filthy rooms to the sky. He glimpsed the artefact, a huge, round-bellied cauldron pockmarked with rust and steaming foul vapours. There was a rickety gantry around it, which three lesser daemons used as a walkway to push a gargantuan spoon round. From this action a triple braid of lightning streamed upwards in constant motion, fuelling the great vortex in the sky and the storm beyond it. The essence of it was nothing but the purest evil, and its baleful touch reached out to him, weakening his limbs, and diminishing the efficacy of his wargear.

'Sergeant Parris, target the daemons by the cauldron. This is a priority order,' he voxed.

Justinian's reply was obliterated by another mighty strike from the daemon. Edermo lifted his shield over his head, where again the power field took the brunt of the blow, but this time the overspill drove him hard into the ground. His knees banged into his chestplate. The top of the shield rang off his helm, making him bite his tongue. He swallowed blood.

Come on, Parris, he thought. A clumsy leap threw him backwards to avoid the daemon's next swing, and he staggered.

'You're getting slow. You're getting sloppy,' chuckled Ku'Gath. *'I shall try to spare your form. Destroying you would be such a waste of good meat. A million phages could feast on you, and spread their gifts from your corpse. Such a pretty little package of pestilence you would make.'* The sword went up again. With arms numbed by repeated impacts, Edermo raised his shield to cover his body.

Bolt-rounds coming in from the right distracted Ku'Gath.

'Lieutenant, get back.' Vasilon and two of his men were coming at the daemon, bolt carbines on full-automatic. Black fluid glopped from the creature's monstrous body with every impact.

This is a private affair!' gurgled the daemon. It drew in breath, and exhaled, spraying them with a torrent of filth. Vasilon was driven back. One of his men went down, devoured by frenzied maggots when the bile melted through his armour. The other was snatched up by Ku'Gath's tongue and dashed against the floor. Two deaths rang out their mortis runes in Edermo's force roster, but for a moment, Ku'Gath had its back to Edermo.

The lieutenant took his chance. He dropped his shield, reversed his sword and ran at the daemon, leaping high. He drove down with his sword, catching the daemon in the side under its shoulder blade and punching the point into the thing's body like a nail, sinking it up to the hilt in the blubbery flesh. He hung from it, using his weight to drag it down. The disruption field did the rest, annihilating Ku'Gath's false body. Bones cracked apart, rancid meat caught fire.

Ku'Gath roared in outrage and agony, throwing up its arms in an attempt to swat its tormentor. Down Edermo slid. Flesh peeled, half cooked, from Ku'Gath's back. Edermo came past the cage of the daemon's ribs, and the sword slid faster through soft guts. Ropes of entrails poured out and engulfed him.

Still screaming furiously, Ku'Gath groped for the source of its pain, caught Edermo by the leg, and tossed him away. The wheeling Space Marine crashed into and through a wall, then another, then into a pillar, breaking it in two as he bounced from it and hit the ground.

He tried to rise, but could not. He could not feel his legs. The power had fled his battleplate. Residual energy powered his retinal display, and it showed him damage all over his wargear. His power pack casing was cracked, forcing it into emergency shutdown. He brought up his pharmacopeia overlay, and saw, in blinking, final red, that his back was broken.

He let his head bang on the floor. The ceramite rang. He looked around, left to right. His sword was nowhere to be seen, but from where he lay he could see straight into the heart of the daemon's domain, for he had come to rest by an arch that led into the cauldron chamber. Though that close the cauldron burned his soul, with some relief he saw that Justinian and his squad were advancing within, guns blazing. He saw the recent initiate Orpino go down, three rusty plagueswords stabbing him, but there were few daemons left within now. They had a chance.

A heavy tread approached, and the scrape of steel on stone. Ku'Gath came barging through the walls Edermo had holed, sending them crashing down. It too was injured, severely so. The daemon had reached round with one fat arm to hold its back shut, but did a poor job. Its intestines slithered over the ground behind it. Its liver slipped out and back in with every step it took, like a mischievous tongue. Its left leg dragged. The right hand still held the sword, but awkwardly, letting it trail through the black muck coating the paving, as if it had become too heavy to lift. One of the daemon's eyes hung on grey muscles from its socket.

Edermo looked towards Justinian, wondering why they were not killed instantly by the power of the cauldron. Then he saw, behind Squad Parris, the priest moving as if through a dream, and Edermo was sure that he too would be slain; but when a daemon came for him, he held up his hand, and the thing disintegrated. There was nothing left, no residue, no blood, no body. Not even vapour. Then Edermo understood.

Protected by the priest's faith, Justinian was moving on the three daemons pushing the paddle around and around the cauldron; the source of the storm.

Edermo began to laugh.

Ku'Gath came to a lumbering stop by the lieutenant. It panted hard, dragged up its greatsword, and leaned on it.

Edermo spat a mouthful of blood into his helm. 'I hope I hurt you.'

'*You did,*' admitted the Plaguefather. '*And so what? I am eternal. You are not. You wounded me, I am going to devour your soul.*'

'I give it gladly in the service of the Emperor.'

'*No, no. You fool, you idiot! It's not going to your Emperor.*' Ku'Gath leaned forward and sneered. '*It's going to go to Nurgle.*'

'I say who is the fool?' said Edermo. 'You are too late. You have lost.'

There was a sudden roar of boltguns. Ku'Gath looked up.

'*No!*' it gasped.

Justinian's men filled the plaguebearers with bolts. They jerked and spasmed, even their unholy vitality not enough to save them from the hail of micro-warheads detonating in their bodies. They were comprehensively blown apart, the chunks falling into the cauldron.

The spoon fell, clacked on the metal, and slipped under the surface.

'*This will not do!*' screamed Ku'Gath. '*Stop!*'

The lightning dancing over the mixture cracked, reignited, then went out. Above, the clouds ceased their boiling. A fresh wind blew from the west.

'We win, daemon,' said Edermo.

'*Then you die!*' roared Ku'Gath. It lifted its sword and stabbed down, impaling Edermo on the tip, breaking his aquila and his hearts. It crushed him under one foot to pull the weapon free. Yet Edermo lingered long enough to savour the taste of victory.

He began the hymn of sacrifice. He had time, as he gasped the sacred words through bloodied lips, to see Ku'Gath lumbering, distraught, towards the cauldron. Time to see the priest look at the daemon, a terrifying light in his eyes.

'My pretties, my pretties! To the spoon! Stir! Stir! Or all is lost!' the daemon shouted.

Deep inside Edermo's altered body, the Belisarian Furnace ignited, trying to save his life, but it was already slipping away.

The battle faded from his awareness. Somewhere, nearby, he could hear freezing winds keening over the moors. He smelled sharp mountain streams lapping young rock. A grey light grew, and as if through a mist, he perceived stone titans holding weapons defiant against a cold, wet sky.

Honourum called.

CHAPTER THIRTY-SEVEN

THE CAULDRON OF NURGLE

The last of the Cadian 4021st closed on the mill. Five tanks alone survived of their glorious charge. The rest littered the ground all the way back to where Odrameyer had given the order. Most were now so decrepit they appeared to be part of the landscape, relics of forgotten wars rusted into place by time and decay. Some were covered in vegetation, little islands of vibrant growth in the filthy swamp. Others had succumbed to Chaos magics, and had become hideous amalgams of machine and crew that wailed for death's release.

'All for the Emperor,' Odrameyer said. 'All for the Imperium. I have seen Him at work. I serve His purpose.'

The remaining vehicles groaned, drive wheels crunching on dying bearings. Their guns were dry of ammunition or had seized up, gummed with sticky algae, platelets of flesh or worse things.

They still had their bulk. They still had their heft.

'Onward!' Odrameyer shouted. His throat was hoarse. His

breath was short. Lungs exhaled blood-tainted air. The war train was a dead hulk. The pilgrims were dead. His regiment shattered. But the orbital bombardment continued, blasting daemons back to the hells whence they crawled, and within the medicae facility he could see the flash of gunfire, and hear the crackle of bolt-guns. A couple of tanks in bone and blue held back a tide of plaguebearers at one side of the hospital. The Adeptus Astartes fought on. Odrameyer was dying, but he would serve until the end. Victory was still within their grasp.

The tanks drove on, mowing down daemons beneath their tracks. The enemy were much reduced in number, and seemed to have lost coordination. Their great blocks had broken up into directionless knots that stumbled about. Still they were dangerous. One then another of Odrameyer's tanks was stopped, and rotted to pieces by the daemons' fell touch.

'Onward!' he cried. 'For the Emperor! For Cadia! For the Imperium!'

The wall of the medicae facility was ahead. Odrameyer gripped the edges of the turret as they drove right at it.

Plaguebearers erupted from everywhere at once. Justinian and his last Space Marines joined with the remnants of the task force and fell into a circle around the priest, blasting at anything that moved. Justinian's armour was no longer breaking down. His bolt pistol fired smoothly. There was a light at his back, coming from the priest, blazing from the eyes of the skull he took everywhere with him, and shining around his head.

'Stay by the priest,' Justinian commanded. 'He shields us from harm.'

'The Emperor shields you,' said Mathieu, his voice distant. He clutched his servo-skull. 'Take me to the cauldron. The Emperor commands it.'

'Do as he says,' said Justinian. He believed it, for he had no other choice.

The cauldron was only a few yards away, but plaguebearers pushed at them from every side, pouring in through the broken walls and sagging doors in something approaching panic.

'I am out of bolts.' Maxentius-Drontio threw down his gun, drew his pistol and his combat knife. He blew out the bulging eye of a daemon, and it collapsed like a sack full of offal.

Soft hands reached for them. Black swords swung at them slowly, easily parried, but too many to stop all of them. They pushed in against the ring of Space Marines. One of their battle-brothers fell.

Mathieu was muttering prayers.

'Oh Emperor! I give myself to you to use as your instrument, to break this most wicked vessel of pestilence, and to release Iax from its suffering. Oh Emperor, deliver me to where I may best serve you!'

The press of daemons thickened, though they recoiled from Mathieu, and whatever psychic power the priest was manifesting weakened them, and protected the Space Marines from their fiendish maladies.

But plaguebearers were not the sole threat the Space Marines faced.

The jostling of the plaguebearers lessened, and they parted. The cauldron was close, not quite within touching distance.

Justinian thought they would not reach it.

The Great Unclean One who had slain Edermo lumbered towards them. Though it was gravely wounded, it was still deadly.

It brought up its sword. It was panting. Black blood leaked from its mouth; nevertheless it scowled.

'I would ask that you step back, mortals, from the cauldron of Grandfather. There's good fellows.'

The Space Marines answered with gunfire. Bolts smacked into the body of the daemon. Its scowl deepened.

'Unwise choice,' it said, and vomited a torrent of slime, maggots, bile and half-digested bones at them.

'Oh Emperor, oh Emperor, watch us now,' Mathieu murmured.

The daemonspew hit an invisible force surrounding the Novamarines, and vanished into wafts of cold vapour free of taint.

'Fine,' said Ku'Gath irritably. *'Let's just do this the physical way then.'* It hefted its sword.

'Split!' shouted Justinian, and he grabbed the priest and hauled him forward, smashing down a muttering lesser daemon with his pauldron. The daemon's blade hummed through the air, and hit Vasilon, crushing rather than cutting him, and leaving him dead.

'One down, seven to go. How apposite,' said the daemon.

Justinian turned, forcing the priest behind him, firing until his bolt pistol clicked dry. To his dismay, the wounds Edermo had inflicted on Ku'Gath were closing up.

'You next, little spawn of the Corpse-God,' the daemon said, and pointed a warty finger at Justinian. *'You're far too feisty.'*

'Get back!' Justinian said, shoving the priest towards the cauldron.

The sword came up. Justinian reloaded and continued to fire.

His preparations for death were rudely interrupted.

The outer wall of the cauldron chamber burst in. A Leman Russ battle tank bearing the personal heraldry of Colonel Odrameyer roared through the wall and straight at the Great Unclean One. Before Ku'Gath could react, the rusting cannon barrel speared the monster right through the chest, and the tank reared at the impact, shoved the daemon off its balance and carried it backwards, the treads ripping swathes of foul, rotting flesh free before they bit into the paving slabs. Ku'Gath was pinned to the wall, its fat head wobbling and gaping in a manner that would have been comical in any other circumstance.

Black filth poured over Odrameyer's tank. It was simultaneously falling to pieces and mutating under the touch of Ku'Gath's blood. Patches of it throbbed as plasteel transmuted to sore flesh. Puckered orifices opened below the turret and belched moans of stinking gas. The power of the warp was on it. A heavy bolter fell and hit the floor mount with a soft thump, turned soft and began to crawl away. The engine coughed black smoke and died. Streaks of rust and fleshy growths spidered over it, running up onto the colonel himself.

Justinian and his men were firing. Plaguebearers were dying. Odrameyer pulled free his hand, ripping flesh that was melding to the metal. His skin was running like wax, but he crawled doggedly on, leaving crimson streaks of blood behind.

He got to his feet, somehow, and stared into Ku'Gath's remaining eye.

'*My, my, my, what do we have here?*' said Ku'Gath, and ichor sheeted down its chins.

'A loyal servant of the Emperor,' said Odrameyer. With the last of his strength, he thrust his power sword into Ku'Gath's empty eye socket. A final burst of power from the failing generator cooked Ku'Gath's brains.

'Praise be,' Odrameyer whispered, then he died.

With a sorry sigh, Ku'Gath's soul fled back to the garden and his Grandfather's disapproval.

The plaguebearers wept to see their lord banished, but fought the harder. Maxentius-Drontio was beset, Achilleos nearly dragged down.

On hands and knees, Mathieu reached the cauldron. Even he, guided as he was by his faith in the Emperor, could not resist its power so close, and his skin blistered under its evil magic, yet he dared reach out to one of the great artefacts of the Plague God.

'For you, my Emperor, I perform my final service,' he said.

His words cut through the tumult of war. Justinian turned to see him touch the iron skin of the cauldron.

Mathieu screamed in ecstasy.

Light engulfed him. His servo-skull shattered. From everywhere came soul-rending shrieks. The plaguebearers evaporated in the face of the light. The Space Marines were flung away from the cauldron as if caught in the overpressure wave of a macrocannon shell.

Justinian hit the wall hard.

He fell down, and saw Mathieu and the cauldron disappear behind a wall of shocking luminance. For a moment he thought he saw a golden giant bringing down a flaming sword onto the cauldron, his eyes full of sorrow, yet his face determined.

There was a tolling of a great bell. A sense of release tore out from the epicentre of the psychic maelstrom. The sensation was close to deadly, but pure, and carried away before it every manner of corruption, and thereafter all touch of the warp ceased.

Overcome, Justinian's mind fled for the safety of unconsciousness.

Upon the command deck of the *Macragge's Honour*, a young officer leapt up from his station, voice excited.

'My lords, psy-augurum indicates dropping levels of warp interference with the realspace frame of Iax. The storm is disrupted.'

Colquan leaned forward a little.

'Invoke main tacticaria displays, now,' said Khestrin.

Above the central hololithic pit, an image of Iax's polluted globe formed. It seemed uncertain at first, almost coy, as if hiding. Then it shivered, and undecided continents took on solid form. Lightning burst away from a central point. Howling faces dissolved, becoming nothing more threatening than clouds. The churning of the atmosphere quietened.

From the vox-centre and the strategic command nexus, from Khestrin's command dais and the gunnery control, from every quarter rang out a cacophony of voices, chimes and target locks. A rash of data spread across the globe. Around First Landing, in Ephoris, Arteria and other places, Imperial signum transponder signals gathered thickly.

'The artefact is destroyed,' said the chief magos of the psy-augury. 'Repeat, the artefact is destroyed. Massive reduction of warp overlap registered, and decreasing.'

'Did we hit it?'

'Negative impact, my lord,' gunnery command reported. 'It must have been the Space Marines. I have transponder signums coming through now.'

'Whatever did it, it is gone, praise be to the Golden Throne,' the psy-augurum officer added.

A massive cheer went up across the deck. Khestrin smiled openly at Colquan.

The tribune nodded slightly.

'Increase evacuation of all Imperial forces. The way is open,' said Khestrin. He stood straight, some of the tension slipping from his shoulders. 'Exterminatus command, stand down.'

'What of the primarch?' Colquan asked.

'No news. His signum is erratic. Force dome holds,' said a strategic officer.

'We finally have teleport loci,' said Khestrin.

'Your hint is received and understood,' said the tribune. He put his helm on and sealed it, and took his guardian spear from his attendant servitor. 'I shall lead relief forces to hold back the Death Guard and speed retrieval of our men. Stand by for full planetary bombardment on my mark only. This battle is halfway won. Try to resist the temptation to blow up the primarch's favourite world while I am gone.'

Colquan left for the teleportarium, leaving behind a frantic exchange of coordinates as Fleet Primus prepared to wipe Mortarion's army from existence.

CHAPTER THIRTY-EIGHT

FOR THE EMPEROR

He sensed the cauldron's passing as a tolling, as of a bell's ring felt but not heard.

The garden shook with an earthquake. The strange daemon creatures that dwelled there set up a cacophony of cries and moans. On the areas of Iax that it overlaid, reality trembled and reasserted itself, and the garden began to fade.

'*Impossible,*' Mortarion whispered.

The corpse of his brother twitched. The Armour of Fate was a corroded shell, but somehow its power pack restarted, and lights blinked on systems all over it.

Guilliman's blackened face turned up to look at him. Mortarion felt something huge and dangerous moving through the warp. Something he had not felt for a long time.

Guilliman's back arched. The armour was humming now, giving off a psychic signature as arcane mechanisms within it powered on throughout.

The earth shook again. A second toll of the unseen bell sent the denizens of the garden into panic. Trees cracked as they dragged up roots and attempted to lumber away. A million kinds of daemon-fly buzzed up from the corpse-grounds and flew off in gathering swarms. Nurglings shrieked and waddled as fast as their little legs would carry them.

Mortarion stood hurriedly, raised Silence and made to bring it down, to destroy Guilliman finally, take his soul as a sacrifice to the great god Nurgle even if he could not take his worlds.

But he could not move.

Guilliman's eyes were glowing with pure, white power. The last slimes of his decayed flesh burned away, and a network of feathery capillaries spread in their place, bearing new blood unsullied by the Godblight. The metal of the Armour of Fate shimmered, impossibly remaking itself. Bright decorations appeared as tarnish cracked and fell away. Wires grew and reconnected as surely as Guilliman's skin was growing back.

The neverground of the garden shook hard. Daemons large and small were screaming, emerging from their hiding places and fleeing in riotous stampede. Away in the distance, ever visible wherever you went in the garden, Nurgle's Black Manse shivered, and Mortarion felt another presence, as powerful as the first, looking at him from behind its ever-shuttered windows.

The ground cracked and broke. Glaring whiteness blazed from the crevasses. Guilliman's corpse rose up, and hung in the air, supported by a pillar of radiance, and slowly turned so he was upright. He reached out, and the Emperor's Sword appeared in his hand, and burned with the fires of a thousand suns.

'He speaks to me, brother,' said Roboute Guilliman. 'Does He not speak to you?'

The unbearable radiance enfolded Guilliman, so glaring Mortarion threw up his hands.

'*Father?*' Mortarion said, and his voice quailed like a little boy discovered in the course of some small but unforgivable crime.

'I am His right hand, brother,' said Guilliman. 'I am His general, His champion. I am the Avenging Son. By His might am I preserved.'

The landscape flickered between the blasted battlefield of Iax and the Garden of Nurgle. The ground of the garden was rolling.

'*This is impossible! You should be dead!*'

There was the creak of a door, faint but portentous, coming from the manse. The doors never opened to Nurgle's house.

Mortarion turned very, very slowly, and looked to the great house. A single, tiny shutter on an insignificant gable was open, a square of deeper blackness in the black wood.

'*Forgive me, Grandfather,*' he quailed.

Guilliman looked past him, and something looked through him, seeing all worlds at once. Eyes as bright as the centres of galaxies stared at the black, forbidding house.

'You are a traitor,' Guilliman said, in a voice that was not quite his own. 'You have brought low all that could have been, but you are as much a victim as a monster, Mortarion. Perhaps one day you might be saved. Until then, you must go back to the master you chose.'

'*No!*' Mortarion cried, but it was too late. Some force reached for him, and yanked hard. He flew back, over and over through the garden, towards the black house of the Plague God. He felt a moment of perfect terror before he flew in through the open portal, and it slammed shut behind him, trapping him with an altogether more awful god.

Nurgle was displeased.

Guilliman looked over the Garden of Nurgle. He was between two worlds. The warp was a shifting thing, never constant.

The garden was a collection of ideas. It had no true form, and through it he could see a million other worlds that underpinned it, the dreams of souls living and dead, and past that, as if glimpsed through banks of glittering sea mist that evaporated before the morning sun, the battlefield of Iax.

'Hear me!' Guilliman's voice boomed through eternities. The sword blazed higher, until the fire of it threatened to burn out time. 'I am Roboute Guilliman, last loyal son of the Emperor of Terra. It is not your destiny to end today, God of Plague, but know that I am coming for you, and I will find you, and you will burn.'

He gripped the Sword of the Emperor two-handed and raised it high. Rising waves of fire ripped into the garden. From the great manse a cry of rage sounded, as a wall of flame hotter than a million suns devoured everything in its path, finally breaking and receding within yards of the black walls of Nurgle's house. Its infinite halls shook. Mossy tiles fell from the roof. Sodden timbers steamed.

'This is a warning. The warp and the materium were once in balance. For too long, you have tipped the scales. Understand that it is not only the warp that is capable of pushing back. This realm is not real. Only will is real. And none may outmatch my will. Be assured, Lord of Plagues, and convey this message to your brothers, that I do not speak for myself.

'I speak for the Emperor of Mankind.'

Then he was falling, falling, falling forever until his knee hit the ground, and he woke into reality once more.

Guilliman opened his eyes. He was kneeling on the ground of Iax. The Sword of the Emperor was buried point down in the cracked earth. Its fires had turned everything around him to glass. Burnt-out suits of armour lay around him. Only he was untouched.

Mortarion was nowhere to be seen.

He stood. Whatever presence had inhabited him was gone. The air was clean. There was no sign of taint nearby, and he knew that the Emperor's Sword had burned the Godblight away. Natasé's psychic shield still limned the duelling ground, but through it he could see clearing skies, and clouds heat-shocked by lance fire. A ferocious orbital bombardment was laying waste to Mortarion's army, which retreated, leaderless and outmatched, under the cover of poisoned fogs.

The air crackled. All around him, golden giants appeared. Further out, other spikes of energy announced the arrival of more Custodians into the rear of the Death Guard's lines. There would be a great slaughter of the traitors before the day was done.

Maldovar Colquan stepped forward.

'It is done then?'

'It is done. Mortarion is gone. His network is broken,' Roboute Guilliman said. 'The Plague Wars are over.'

And he sheathed the Sword of the Emperor.

Teleportation was an instantaneous means of travel, but there was an infinite gap between moments where one could feel the warp. Sometimes it lasted an eternity, but it was always forgotten.

Pontus Varsillian the Many-Gloried experienced this moment again, as he had many times before. Only this time it was different.

It was written in the books of his order that in the ancient days, the Emperor touched the mind of every one of His Custodian Guard. That He saw through their eyes, and that they shared of His thoughts. For ten millennia, they had been bereft of this communion – alone, without awareness of their loneliness.

For that brief, eternal moment when Varsillian hung between

materium and immaterium, that gap was filled. He could have sworn something looked through him, that he had been alone all his life without realising, and now he was not.

The sensation passed.

Teleport flare opened his way to a scene of devastation. He and his force of eleven others arrived upon a field where a battle had been fought and lost. Wrecked tanks dotted muddy hillsides. The cadaver of an Ecclesiarchy war train loomed a few hundred yards away. There were scattered bodies, most green bones that appeared to have been there for decades. Patches of slime marked the places daemons had fallen. Whatever had happened there was over now. Smoke raced along the ground in the face of a strengthening wind. Mist escaped before it, fleeing over the horizon. It was night-time, but in the east over the marshes was the promise of dawn.

'Fan out,' Varsillian told his brethren. 'Locate the survivors. Gelistan, Hadrianus, with me.'

Varsillian set out to the medicae facility. They passed a couple of Adeptus Astartes grav-tanks on the way in. Both were resting on the ground, grav-fields out. There were a dozen Novamarines within and around them. Several were still alive, all unconscious.

'Mark their positions,' Varsillian said. 'Send for medicae evacuation transports.'

They went within. Derelict halls greeted them, ripe with centuries of decay although it was not so long since the facility had been overrun. There were dead stands of fleshy plants, and more noxious puddles where daemons had died. But they saw no sign of active Neverborn, either by sight or upon their sophisticated armour sensoriums.

They headed further in. A deathly stillness lay over everything. There was no sign of life other than the wind. Above, the cloud was clearing. Shreds of sky appeared.

'I mark five living Adeptus Astartes in the central chamber,' Hadrianus voxed. Location dots sprang up on Varsillian's helmplate.

'Let us start there, then,' said the Warden.

They picked their way through corridors blocked with falls of rubble. They came across the corpses of dead Novamarines. They marked their positions. Though they were too badly affected with plague or rapid mutation to allow their gene-seed to be harvested, honour would be done to them and their battlegear.

The five life signs pulsed weakly from battleplate running on emergency systems. The Custodians entered the central chamber, and found the Adeptus Astartes laid out around the origin point of a blast.

'The artefact site, no doubt,' said Gelistan. There was nothing left of it, only a black starburst on the floor. Varsillian walked over to it while his comrades checked the Adeptus Astartes, and found a sixth body, standard human, so small he took it at first for a pile of rags.

'This one is alive too,' said Varsillian. Hadrianus joined him.

'How is that possible?' he said. 'And these others have been flung aside by explosion. Why is he still here?'

'He is sick,' said Varsillian. Gently, he rolled the body over. A diseased, emaciated face looked up at him with blind eyes. 'The militant-apostolic,' he said.

Mathieu drew in a wheezing breath. His hands spasmed.

'Help me,' he said.

'Rest easy, help is already on the way,' said Varsillian.

'Not help,' Mathieu moaned. 'I must... I must go to him. I have one last message to deliver, at the Emperor's command.

'I must speak to the primarch.'

CHAPTER THIRTY-NINE

THE RAINFATHER'S GAMBIT

'*The thing about you psykers,*' said Rotigus, and it cast a torrent of stinking water at Tigurius, '*is that you overestimate yourselves.*'

A shield of blue spiritual power flared in front of Tigurius, and Rotigus' deluge splashed against it. The water slopped around the Librarian, diverted away by his power, sluicing down priceless tomes and turning them to piles of sodden rubbish that sprouted knots of brambles.

The Rainfather continued to hurl spells at the Librarian, driving him back. Tigurius sent bolts of corrupting power away from himself with sweeps of his staff, but they hit the caged books lining the corridor, rotting them, transforming them, or setting them ablaze. Smoke and noisome gases filled up the narrow way.

'*I hear much about you being some mighty warrior. How disappointed I am, when I finally face you, to find this... this... example.*'

Rotigus flicked its rod forward. Screaming loops of crimson

power raced towards Tigurius that he was hard-pressed to deflect. They burst among the cages, causing them to implode with screams of metal.

Tigurius said nothing, refusing to be drawn into debate with the Rainfather, but answered instead with his own display of might. He drew at the warp so hard Fabian felt reality flex. Lightning raced from the tip of his staff. Rotigus attempted to block it with a wall of boiling filth conjured from nothing, but the energy speared through it, hitting the Great Unclean One in the centre of the chest, leaving a spiderweb of burns in its decaying skin.

Rotigus coughed, and a geyser of maggots gushed from its principal mouth.

'*So you do bite,*' it said, wiping vermin from its lips. It flung out its left arm, and hurled a ball of flies from the mouth below its hand at the Librarian. They hit as hard as a catapult-cast stone, knocking Tigurius back, then burst on his armour, and began to gnaw at his ceramite. '*But I have more teeth than you,*' it said.

Tigurius wreathed himself with flame, burning the flies to dust.

'Try harder, daemon,' he said.

Fabian rolled onto his front and got onto all fours. Once there, he felt dizzy and had to steady himself, taking deep breaths of stale, recycled air. He hurt all over. Nausea threatened his stomach. Reality warped like melting glass under the punishment of the psychic duel.

The library is still here, he told himself. *I am still here.*

He checked through his suit systems one by one, as he had been taught, to distract himself from the madness unleashed by Rotigus. The air shook to unearthly laughter. Flopping worms as big as his fingers were pushing their way out through the walls and up from the floor. One brushed his hand, and he snatched it back in terror, but it thrashed about and did him no harm.

That gave him the energy to get up, though he nearly passed out, and had to lean against the wall.

Smoke was thickening in the side room. Rotigus and Tigurius were still fighting, but drawing away from him, back towards the higher stacks.

His eyes fastened on the book on the floor. All the rest in the room were unreadable mush. What terrible secret was hidden between the survivor's pages?

He could not move. He should leave. He should not pick it up, but, he reasoned, what harm could it do? He had seen his share of forbidden grimoires that held mind-destroying secrets. This did not appear to be one of those, for it had been kept in this side room, which though protected by a heavy door, did not possess the warding sigils or psychic circuitry usually employed to restrain such things as sorcerers' tomes. It was just a book. It lay face down on the floor, the title hidden.

The sounds of fighting echoed up the corridor. Tigurius was striking at Rotigus with his staff. Crystalline matrices within the shaft burned as walls of light, leaving crater wounds on the daemon's surface. Rotigus smashed its rod down, and Tigurius caught it on the horned head of his staff, and poled it away and aside. He slammed the butt on the ground, sending out a shockwave that rolled up Rotigus' flab in visible waves, making its jowls flap. The mouth in the daemon's belly snapped at the Librarian, and in reply Tigurius shattered its teeth with a concentrated blast of energy.

Fabian could not get out. Their melee blocked the corridor completely. He glanced again at the book. Should he take it?

Rotigus sprawled into the caged shelves, destroying them completely. Tigurius slammed the staff head into the mouth in its arm, breaking fangs. The tongue was severed and flopped on the floor. Rotigus shrieked, a surprisingly high and girlish noise, and grabbed at the wound.

'This is over, daemon,' said Tigurius, raising his staff to strike again.

A tolling rang through the library, faint but powerful. Three rings that made reality wobble further, and the library shake. Books fell in avalanches from the stacks, and hung on their chains like dead avians strung up by vengeful agricultors. Tigurius staggered.

Rotigus heaved itself back upright.

'That it is, human.' It brought its rod down hard on Tigurius. The psychic hood around the Chief Librarian's head exploded, stunning him. His massive suit of armour toppled to the floor, and the lights on his hood and around his staff went out.

'Not very impressive at all,' said Rotigus with a tut, then rubbed its wounded arm-mouth with a grimace.

Rotigus turned its attention back to Fabian.

'Ah, still there. Very good.' It came rolling up the corridor, stooped like an ape.

Fabian had nowhere to go. He was numb to all sensation, past fear. Rotigus was such a terrible sight, it was easy to believe the daemon was not real, and that Fabian was in a nightmare. But it was happening. He stood rooted to the spot as Rotigus approached.

'I mean you no harm, truth seeker. Look, look at me!'

It pushed a hand out at Fabian, and the historitor saw it disintegrate before his eyes. Skin slid off muscles green with decay. Veins shrivelled. Sinews dried and snapped. Its fingers fell off and melted on the floor.

'See? It is over,' said Rotigus, displaying its stump. *'Mortarion's plans have come to nothing, and therefore I must go. The network of decay he wasted so much establishing is undone, and the warp's grip loosens on Ultramar. I bid you farewell. Enjoy your book, little reader.'*

Rotigus collapsed into itself, its skin ripping like old silk, and a wash of dirty water rushed out. Its head was last to go, folding in on itself like a discarded mask before dissolving into black smoke.

After a moment's thought Fabian picked up the book, saving it from the puddle of filth oozing from Rotigus' remains, and limped up the corridor to the Chief Librarian's side. In the corridor, those books that were not rotted black were ablaze, and fire was spreading into the main body of the library. He heard data crystals shattering in the distance. If he had not been wearing the environment suit, he would have been dead of disease or smoke inhalation within moments.

He activated his vox, and found the channels clear.

'Chapter command, Fabian Guelphrain, historitor majoris, seeking aid. Lord Tigurius is down, and the Library of Ptolemy ablaze. Please, *please* come and get us.'

There was a short delay.

'Affirmative. Position logged. Incendor suppression teams and Apothecary on their way. Stay where you are.'

'I do not know if that will be possible,' Fabian murmured.

The vox-link went dead.

A stack of books collapsed with a roar at the end of the corridor, sending a storm of embers racing towards him. He felt a profound sadness that so much knowledge was to be lost, and gave a little prayer to the Emperor that some would be saved.

Prompted by that thought, he turned over the book he held. It was wholly ordinary. There was no author's mark, but there was a title. Fabian read it aloud.

'The Reign of the Emperor Sanguinius, a history.'

He frowned at the title. It meant nothing to him. Sanguinius had never been an emperor of anywhere, so far as he knew. Had he been given a fanciful work? Was this some kind of cosmic jest at his expense?

The thought that a god would wish to tease him filled him with terror.

Tigurius' hand twitched. Within the smoking remains of his psychic hood, his helmet rolled.

Fabian hurriedly stuffed the book into an ammo pouch on his thigh. It only just fit.

'The daemon,' said Tigurius.

'It is gone,' said Fabian.

The Librarian slowly got up. Fabian dismissed the idea of helping him. There was no way he could move that mass of metal and flesh. He'd only be a hindrance.

'There are people coming for us,' Fabian said. 'I suggest we wait in there, with the door shut.' He pointed back to the room. 'You will survive out here, probably, but I don't want to burn alive.'

Groggily, Tigurius agreed.

CHAPTER FORTY

SAINT MATHIEU

'He is still alive?' Guilliman asked.

Chiromancer-Captain Bazhiri of the isolation ship *Sanctuary* nodded solemnly. Guilliman doubted if the man had any other expression but solemn, for his duty was a weighty one. The vessel he commanded was a death ship that few who entered left alive. The diseases Bazhiri treated were maladies of the soul as much as of the body. He had seen the worst the warp could conjure. By necessity, he was a psyker himself, of a middling sort, a rare individual somewhere between surgeon and sorcerer.

What times are these, Guilliman thought, *that individuals such as this must serve the Emperor.*

'Yes, lord regent,' the chiromancer-captain said. 'He is alive.'

Guilliman let out a thoughtful breath that came out close to a sigh. He was weary, yet had so much still to do. He asked himself if meeting Mathieu was more indulgence than necessity. On the one hand, appointing the priest could be seen as one of his rare errors. On the other, he wondered if it had been his choice at all, and if it had not, how much of anything was his choice.

He thought back to the garden.

He looked through a triple layer of armaglass into the treatment room. Sacred symbols were engraved into each pane. Somewhere nearby, esoteric machinery worked to hold back the influence of the warp.

Mathieu occupied the single bed in the centre of the room. Medical equipment crowded the space around him. He was wrapped in a white shift that was stained by seepage from his many sores. He had no wounds; all the lesions that covered his skin were the result of disease. He more resembled a bundle of sticks than a man, crudely assembled into human form and draped with skin. One of the few things Mathieu had taken pride in was his hair, and that was falling out, covering his pillow. His cheeks were sunken beneath an oxygen mask. His eyes stared blankly at the ceiling, and wept tears of pus.

'How is it possible that he still lives?' Guilliman glanced at the doctor. 'From a purely physical, medical standpoint.'

'Medically?' said Bazhiri. 'I do not know how. It should be impossible. He went into the most contaminated part of Iax without protection. From what the Adeptus Astartes who brought him here told me, he faced down one of the great plague creatures of the enemy. He touched a tainted artefact. He would have been exposed to all manner of disease, and the malefactions of the warp, as you can see. But he lives.'

'I can see,' said Guilliman.

'Although the psychic element of his afflictions is no longer active, we have seen to that, the sheer number of morbidities afflicting him should have killed him hours ago. This man should not be alive.'

'As you have said,' said Guilliman softly. 'And what is your opinion from a non-medical point of view?'

'There is his desire to see you, my lord. In other cases, I would say that this was keeping him alive. I have seen soldiers who should have succumbed to their wounds cling on for hours in order to receive final benediction from regimental priests. I have seen others suffer injuries that would kill a Space Marine outright so that they might complete their given task before they will allow themselves to die.'

'But not in this case?'

'No. He should still be dead. There is something going on here I am not familiar with. He is being kept alive by an outside influence, I am almost certain. These keep out any kind of psychic energy.' He gestured at the sigils in the glass. 'We are warded technologically and to the best abilities of the fleet's psykers. But even so, something is reaching him from the outside.'

Guilliman was silent for another moment.

'Is it his faith?'

'What is faith, my lord?' said Bazhiri. 'It is only another expression of the warp. No mortal man could believe so strongly to keep themselves alive through this. It is impossible. The actions of gods are stymied by these wards.'

'The evident practical is that he is alive,' said Guilliman. 'What is your theoretical?'

Bazhiri had seen too much horror in his life to fear anything, not even the primarch, and the look he gave the giant son of the Emperor had a hint of admonishment.

'We are seeing the work of the Emperor before us. A miracle. That is my only feasible theory. Do you not think so, my lord?'

Guilliman chose not to answer.

'I will see him now. I wish to know what he has to say. Then perhaps he can die in peace.' He turned to face the chiromancer-captain. 'There will be no record made of this meeting. You will leave. You will deactivate all machinery tasked with the gathering of data, do you understand?'

'Yes, my lord.'

'Clear this area for two hundred yards on all sides.'

Another little glance, another dose of admonishment. 'I am not sure that is strictly nec–'

'This is your ship, chiromancer-captain, but this is my command as Lord Commander and Regent of the Imperium of Man. Do as I say.'

'Gladly, my lord.' Bazhiri gave a bow. 'But I must remain to open the chamber.'

'Afterwards, you will leave also,' said Guilliman.

'Yes, yes, as you command.'

Bazhiri went to a locker, where a soft plastek hazard suit awaited him. He was practised in its use, and put it on quickly. Guilliman went to stand by the door.

Bazhiri closed the fastenings on the suit. 'My lord, I would advise you to wear your helm. He harbours many sicknesses, and I do not know if you will be immune.'

'I will not need my helm,' Guilliman said, and faced the entrance. 'Open the door.'

Bazhiri attached the breathing tubes and inflated the suit. 'Very well,' he said.

The first thing that hit Guilliman was the smell. There was a sickening sweetness in the room, of failing organs and decaying flesh. It made Guilliman's eyes water. Sweat prickled his brow as his post-human biology marshalled itself to fight off infection, and the devices of the Armour of Fate shifted into a higher state of activity.

It was possible that Bazhiri was correct, and that there would be something in that room that could affect him, perhaps a last gambit of Mortarion. His incisive mind weighed all these possibilities, but he was not concerned. He could not know he would be safe, no theoretical could support that, but somehow he believed it.

He approached the bed, pushing his way through the plastek sheeting, unafraid of contamination.

The priest stared up at the ceiling, still in his repose but for the rising and falling of his chest, and even that was not his doing, for machines breathed for him. When he inhaled and exhaled he did so to the click-hiss of a pulmonary stimulator plugged into his chest.

'Militant-apostolic?'

Mathieu did not move.

'Mathieu,' Guilliman said softly. He examined his emotions. He had expected anger. He had anticipated grudging acceptance; the priest had done a great service, after all. He had experienced confusion recently, and that was an emotion he was not fond of. But seeing the priest like that, gripped by a dozen different diseases at once, what he felt most was pity.

The crusts at the corners of Mathieu's eyes lifted. His face moved. Very slightly, he turned his head towards the primarch. It took a moment for his expression to clear, and his eyes to focus.

'My lord, is that you?'

'It is I,' said Guilliman, not sure if Mathieu saw him.

'Yes, yes, the regent,' said Mathieu as if that confirmed it all. His eyes closed and opened, and he swallowed, all actions performed with a glacial slowness. 'You came.'

'I heard you wished to speak with me. I could not deny a dying man his last request.'

'You considered it though,' said Mathieu. He smiled. The skin on his lips cracked and bled.

'I was debating the mer-'

'You do not need to explain yourself, my lord. We are moved by the Emperor, you and I. We have little choice over our actions.'

'So you believe.'

'So I know!' A little energy came into him, and he moved a hand encased by tubes. 'And so do you. You have witnessed it, His power. You have seen the light.'

'I must disappoint you. I do not believe that my creator is a god,' said Guilliman. 'He is something...' He paused. 'He is something else, if He is anything at all. All this faith and desire for salvation is a blind hope. He will not help us. He cannot. We must save ourselves.'

'A shame. A shame,' Mathieu said. His voice was a vox-ghost on an unreliable channel, fading in and out of audibility. 'This would be so much easier if you believed. Perhaps you can't. I do not think it is your fault either way.' He sighed, and seemed to shrink into himself, as if every breath depleted him. 'You must listen to me, carefully. Your father supports me, but His strength is needed elsewhere.'

'Then speak, militant-apostolic, I am listening.'

'This is my final gospel, and it is the finest news of all. The Emperor is waking, my lord.' Mathieu smiled. 'He stirs from His slumber after long millennia. The armies of the faithful trail Him, they bear Him aloft, they empower Him.'

Guilliman had his own opinions on this, but now was not the time to voice them.

'How?'

'It is the warp, my lord,' croaked Mathieu. 'The enemy has made his greatest mistake by opening the Rift. It may damn the Imperium, but it also may save it. The Rift has empowered the Emperor. The energy of the empyrean saturates the universe, raising up mankind, filling the lowliest psyker with power.'

'The rise in psychic incidence across the Imperium. This is what you speak of.'

Mathieu managed a tiny nod. The movement broke pustules on his neck that wept clear fluid. 'Yes. Your father is the greatest psyker of them all. How could He not be affected?'

'Then why does He not step down from His Throne? If He is capable of acting, why must I do His work for Him?'

'He is not ready, that is why,' said Mathieu. 'Not yet. You must help Him.'

'And how would I do that?' said Guilliman neutrally.

'I cannot answer that. It is your task.' Again a painful swallow. Mathieu took a moment before speaking again. His words were a precious currency, and he was fast running out of coin. 'He has spent millennia arranging the pieces so that you might return, my lord. You are His only hope. You are mankind's only hope.' A look of pain played over his face. 'We all have our part to play. Yours is to come. Mine is done.'

His eyes closed, and his next words were weaker still.

'Rejoice, Roboute Guilliman, and give your praise.' Mathieu's head sank further into the pillow, smearing the plastek covering with fluids. 'Praise be, the Emperor is awakening. You must guide His return. You came back. He can come back.'

'You have a fool's optimism.'

Mathieu smiled a final time. 'You deny the evidence of your own experiences. You know it to be true. You will find a way. Have faith in your father... and all... will be well.'

Mathieu's head rolled to the side.

Guilliman turned the man's face back to him. Though the smile remained, his spirit had gone, and the primarch thought he had never seen such a look of profound peace on any man.

He almost left, then bent low to whisper to the corpse.

'My father is no god. It is men who do His work for Him, as

419

I must now. He uses people. He always has.' Guilliman stood up, and with an armoured hand reached down to close the dead priest's eyes.

'Thank you, Mathieu, for your service to the Imperium. I am sure when I tell your successor what you did, they will make you a saint, and I will not dissuade them.'

CHAPTER FORTY-ONE

REMEMBRANCE

In the room there was an adjustable medical couch and a wide rank of inks in pots, and incense burned in every corner. It was paved with rough stones. Panels of the same rock covered the walls, all taken from the mountains of Honorum. Within, Chaplain Vul Direz awaited Justinian. Though a servitor stood inactive by the couch – a human torso on a delicate wheeled carriage – and elements of technology were visible throughout, it was as much a shaman's cave as a room aboard a voidship.

Justinian was escorted in by a pair of hooded serfs, clad like him in robes that were quartered midnight blue and bone white. They were silent, striving sincerely to create an air of mystery that Justinian could take only half seriously. He was born in less superstitious times, and the pseudo-Legions of the Primaris cohort he began his service in were free of the centuries of accreted rites that all the Chapters of the firstborn were prone to.

'Brother-Sergeant Parris,' said the Chaplain, his lugubrious voice invested with a certain power by occasion. 'You are ready to accept your first honour mark?'

'I am,' said Justinian.

'Do you submit yourself to the ritual of remembrancing?'

'I do.'

'Then recline,' said Direz.

Justinian got onto the couch. It rose up to human chest height so the servitor could more easily do its work.

'I have taken the liberty of suggesting a design, as you are still new to our ways.' Direz crooked a finger. One of the human serfs went to a stainless steel table and took up a piece of paper. It was folded in half to hide its contents, and the serf smoothed it out to display this to Justinian at Direz's command.

Upon it was a stylised image of Justinian, a serpent wrapped around him that Justinian had just beheaded. Three drops of blood spurted from its neck, and its head was pinned under one of his feet.

'Ordinarily we take the image of our defeated foe, or some other memorable element of the action to be commemorated,' explained Direz. 'A fortress, a weapon, but in these circumstances it is forbidden. To wear a depiction of the Great Enemy on our skin brings ill fortune. The same goes for the blighted land in which you fought, and the artefact you helped destroy. In this case, we must rely on allegory. Do you approve?'

Justinian looked at the artwork, then into the red lenses of the Chaplain's skull helm.

'I cannot.'

The Chaplain's helm tilted in question.

'I want this.' Justinian took out a printout on a semi-translucent flimsy. It was a pict-capture taken from his helm vid-feed, and showed the face of the girl they had encountered upon the island near the town of Hiastamus. Vul Direz took the print and looked at it.

'I want this child on my neck,' Justinian said.

'She is no foe,' said Direz.

'And yet I slew her,' said Justinian.

A hard exhalation growled out of Direz's respirator mask, amplified by his voxmitter.

'I heard what occurred on the planet,' the Chaplain said. 'Be advised that those people would have died anyway, and that Third Company Lieutenant Edermo was right to order you to do what you did. Imagine what would have occurred if even one of them had lived, and through them the enemy had learned of the mission. It would have failed, the artefact would remain, the primarch might well be dead and Ultramar lost in the warp.'

'It was we who had to pull the triggers,' said Justinian. 'They saw us as saviours, and we killed them.'

'It was a dark deed done for the best of reasons,' said Direz. 'These are terrible times. The future of our species hangs in the balance. You have given up your life so that we might survive. In their own way, they had to give up theirs.'

'Nevertheless, I will take a tattoo of the image I have given to you. It is my wish.' He looked up at Vul Direz from the marking couch. 'I understand that to you of Honourum my request is strange. But I understand also that according to your custom the nature of each marking is the choice of the individual warrior. I do not wish to remember this action through the image you presented to me.'

'I see,' said Vul Direz quietly, and Justinian could tell the Chaplain was weighing the worth of his soul. 'I will ask you why, then, that you choose this dishonour for yourself?'

'You misunderstand, Brother-Chaplain,' said Justinian, settling back into the couch. 'I do not feel dishonour. I do not punish myself. It sorrowed me to do it, but it had to happen.'

'Then why take this image?'

'Honours may become chains that keep us from our purpose. The allure of glory corrupts. I take this image not in penance, but so that I do not forget our duty as warriors of the Emperor, and protectors of humanity. I take it because I would remember that sometimes we must kill what we seek to protect in order to protect it.'

Vul Direz gave a grunt of approval. Justinian had been judged and had passed whatever test the Chaplain had applied to him.

'Very well. The child it is.' He stood back with a purr of motors and beckoned to the servitor. With an ugly jerk it came to life, as if started from sleep by a noise in the night.

'This child, one inch by two, in the position of the first honour.' Direz showed it the image. Its bionic left eye clicked, sectioning the picture for processing and transformation into art.

'Compliance,' it wheezed, and pivoted on its wheels. It dipped needled fingers into pots of ink with a dexterity that belied its otherwise unsteady motions. Pistons clicked. Pipes wheezed. The small bottles screwed onto the bones of its hands filled with colours, and a small pump spun into life.

'The Emperor has chosen you well, brother,' said Direz.

'Do you think He moves among us?' said Justinian.

'Explain yourself, brother.'

'Did you truly mean that? Was I chosen? Does the Emperor move? The priest gabbled something to me through his pain when we returned to the fleet. What I saw there made me think.'

'Never trust the words of the Adeptus Ministorum,' said Direz. 'They make a man into a god.'

'Then what I witnessed was not He?'

Direz chose his next words carefully. 'One does not need to be a god to wield the influence of one. I do not need to believe that the Emperor is a god to be sure of His power. Undoubtedly, He reached out and touched Iax. These are terrible times, as I said, but they are glorious also.'

The servitor's wheels squeaked. The whole delicate-looking assembly shook over the gaps in the uneven paving. Little tremors ran through it as it came to rest by the couch.

'Present chosen site for marking.' Its original vocal cords were still in place, but weak from infrequency of use, and its voice was a chilling rasp.

With some trepidation, Justinian turned his head aside to expose his neck to the creaking cyborg, but though it bent uncertainly down a change came over it once in position, and its fingers moved with deftness, sure and quick, needles stabbing into his neck at uniform depth and speed.

He had been told that sometimes, a Novamarine might experience a trip to the Shadow Novum unbidden during the remembrancing – the strange meditative state they induced in themselves – but Justinian felt nothing but the pinch of the needle points. The only vision he'd experienced was a flash of burning as Guilliman unleashed voidship killers to cleanse Iax in order to save as much of it as he could. He'd watched along with many of his new brothers. It was rare to witness atomic cleansing so clinically applied.

His mind drifted further, though still not to Honourum. He remembered his years in the Unnumbered Sons, first with others of his kind, and towards the end mixed in with all the gene-lines. Felix, always so serious. Bjarni, heartbroken that he would not return to Fenris. Many others, brief fraternities, sundered by assignment to Ultima Chapters, as reinforcements to the firstborn, and far too many by death.

All in the past, all gone. A new life awaited. A brotherhood forever. Each stab of the needles overwrote old loyalties with new, but he swore he would never forget.

Then it was done. The biting at his neck ceased. A subsidiary arm unfolded from the servitor's chest and wiped at his skin with a wet rag, bringing the sting of counterseptic. He made to move, but the servitor said with surprising force, 'Remain still.'

One of the human serfs came forward and placed a dressing over his tattoo.

'There,' said Vul Direz. He returned to Parris' side. 'I welcome you to the Novamarines, Justinian Parris, though the welcome has always been here. I understand it has been hard to give up one brotherhood for another. You were torn, but no longer. You are now one of us completely and utterly.'

Vul Direz held out his hand upright for Justinian to grasp. He did so, and Vul Direz pulled him up off the couch, bringing him close in to his chest in a half-embrace.

'My thanks, brother. I swear to serve the Novamarines faithfully until the day of my death, and through their good offices, the Emperor of Man.'

'I am sure of it,' said Vul Direz. 'For Honourum and the memory of Lucretius Corvo.'

'For Honourum and the memory of Lucretius Corvo,' Justinian responded.

CHAPTER FORTY-TWO

OTHER FORMS

Rotigus hunted carefully for his rival, and it took him a very long time. The groves of gnarlwoods stretched into an infinity of rot. From their boughs depended slick birthing sacs, each one burgeoning with the promise of rebirth. Decay and renewal, life and death, the gnarlwoods epitomised Nurgle's cycle, and ordinarily Rotigus felt a thrilling sense of belonging there, a charging of the soul. To be part of such purpose, and to see the truths of his lord presented to him in metaphysical form as solid as himself, gave him a heightened sense of joy, and he wandered there whenever he could. But the occasion was far from ordinary, and that took much away from his victory. He felt as hollow as the trees, rotted out from inside with no new, wriggling life to replace what was lost. He and every other aspect of the Great Grandfather felt the same, for at the beginning and at the end, they were all a part of him.

Wound the garden, wound the god.

The neverground shook. There were whispers in the hierarchy

that perhaps the burns would never heal, and that Nurgle tossed uneasily in his sleep with the pain. The upheavals in the liquid earth would last for some aeons to come, at the very least, like loose bowels incapable of rest. Rotigus could taste it on the air, a clean burning in Nurgle's holy foetor. He could feel it in his soul as a hot scar. He shifted his gut around to settle the pain, and it did not work. The mouth in his belly and arm were sealed tight in discomfort.

It would not do to dwell on it.

'I am not Ku'Gath,' he said to himself, 'full of misery and woe.' He felt disquieted though, gassy, full of painful bubbles. He sighed and pressed his ear against another slimy trunk, and knocked. The things in the birthing sacs hanging from the branches jiggled, but the noise was unsatisfactory, and he moved on to the next tree.

'A setback is not a defeat, and a defeat does not mean the loss of a war. Chaos is eternal. Often, it is simply a matter of waiting, isn't it, my friends?' He addressed this to the daemons in their pods, but they responded only to the knocks upon their mother-plants. They were deaf to his words while they slept.

He sighed, and splashed broad-footed through the mires and the bogs, pushed his way through stands of pink-lipped flowers that gave out leper's moans when touched. Lazy yellow flies hummed about, lethargic to the point of death. As usual in the garden, it was hot, and sticky, and everything was either in a state of frenzied growth or extravagant decay. Another thing that would ordinarily gladden him, but not that day.

He stopped from time to time to knock on the sodden trunks of further promising trees, but after embracing and listening carefully to each, he would tut, shake his head, and shamble on to the next grove, the next brake, the next copse, until he had walked a million miles and an aeon had passed in the garden.

Outside, it remained the same day it had been when Rotigus entered. A day in the garden was a billion wet, hot Seventhdays compressed. It rotted the soul with its tedium.

This did not make him happy either.

Finally, he knocked upon a tree that pleased him. His eyebrows arched, and he dashed to the next, and the next, knocking and listening, listening and knocking, until he reached a majestic gnarlwood, so huge and fulsome with decay it teetered on the brink of collapse. Most of its branches were bare of leaves, and from them dangled flaccid birth sacs black and hard with age, within them the half-formed bones of daemons who had returned to the garden but never won back Grandfather's approval, and so had truly died. Only one living sac hung from the sole living branch, and this held out with the promise of a dunking over a small mere.

Rotigus did not need to knock upon the tree. He had found his rival.

'Ku'Gath!' he said. The bloated birthing sac reacted to his call, and twitched and rolled, shaking the gnarlwood tree. Rotigus leant his staff against the trunk and went to the sac, placing his fat, wet hands on the slick tissues, stroking until the movement inside calmed. *'Shh, shh, my old enemy. Be calm. Now is not your time to emerge again into the world. We all must wait on Grandfather when we are foolish enough to get ourselves killed, is that not so?'*

The outline of an antlered head, prenatal and unformed, pushed out into the rubbery surface, and revolved out of sight.

'There there,' Rotigus said, and sat down by the mere. *'I thought I'd just come to tell you that you may not be getting out for a little while. In fact,'* Rotigus gave a small, embarrassed chortle, *'Grandfather is a little upset with you.'* He pulled a thoughtful face, and his pursed lips let out a spill of maggots. *'Actually,*

he's a lot upset. You see, not only did you ignore his command to withdraw from the Anathema's realm to fight the Changer, you failed to achieve your own goals.' He laughed, and maggots fell in a torrent from his maw. *'I mean that would be bad enough, if that selfsame error had not allowed the son of the Anathema to wave His blade about in the garden, and scorch it, and so Grandfather, and so me, and so you. You are, to put it somewhat mildly, in a degree of serious trouble, my friend.'*

The sac jerked with Ku'Gath's misery.

Rotigus allowed himself a satisfied sigh. Now this *was* fun.

'You may be thinking, how did I avoid censure? Why am I still strolling about, jolly as you like? Well, I'll tell you, it's why I'm here, in fact. So are you ready?' Rotigus looked at the sac. It did not move, but he went on anyway. *'It's simple, my friend. My plans are better. My plans,'* he whispered theatrically from behind a raised hand, *'are bigger. You sought to snatch Ultramar into the garden. Too modest! I have my eyes on a much, much more majestic prize. Imagine, if your limited intellect can encompass it, not just this disgustingly well-ordered corner of reality brought within the Grandfather's fold, but the whole of the Imperium, in all its rotting glory! This reality is falling apart. The powers fight over the carcass. Now is not the time to be meek, but bold, for the most daring scavenger shall have the greater share.'* He leaned forward, so his great head was reflected in the water. *'Let me show you how this is going to happen.'*

He waved a hand over the mere. The water shimmered, and an image took shape there, overlaid on Rotigus' diseased features. It showed a man in a dark room reading a small book. It was obvious from his body language that he was not enjoying what he learned.

Rotigus dabbled his fingers in the water. Pale things fled into the peaty murk. The image of the man wavered.

'This is Fabian Guelphrain. He is one of the primarch's most senior ferreters of facts. He is a poker-about-in-the-dust. A hoarder of forgotten dates. He is supposed to construct true histories. Remember that detail. In the book, which I led him to, is the only account of an empire deliberately unremembered. I thought it time to remind everyone about it, and the true scale of the oh-so-perfect Roboute Guilliman's ambitions. What this Fabian reads in there will infect him like a disease, he will not be able to divest himself of the knowledge. From this point on, he will never be free of doubt – it will fester, and that doubt will shake an empire.'

He chuckled, and stroked the tentacles of his left arm with his right.

'The rot is setting in, like a crack that lets in moisture or bad air, and with it comes the burgeoning of new life. An idea is as dangerous as the most potent virus.' Rotigus reached up and patted the sac. 'I came to tell you this, so you can think about my superiority while you wait to be reborn. Now I have done so, I shall leave. I have work to do. Unlike you.' He giggled.

Rotigus got up, the labour of lifting his flab causing him to grunt.

'Oh, and one other thing,' he said, as if he had forgotten, which of course he had not. 'When we next meet, you may address me as first in Nurgle's favour. That honour is no longer yours.' He dusted flakes of bark from his legs, smearing lichen into his slimes, and picked up his rod from the side of the tree. 'If I may be so bold as to offer you one piece of advice, Ku'Gath, it is that you are too limited in your thinking. You are obsessed with plague when the universe offers so many more paths to entropy.'

He whispered loudly, right against the sac.

'You forget that there is more than one form of corruption.'

Rotigus gave a cheery wave and departed, leaving Ku'Gath's

lonely cocoon dangling from its tree. The mists closed around it, and within, the half-formed Plaguefather began his wait for Nurgle's forgiveness.

He was going to be waiting a very long time.

CHAPTER FORTY-THREE

MATTERS FOR THE MAGOS

Shortly before Felix was due to depart, the primarch sent the Tetrarch of Vespator a command to attend him. Felix dropped everything, as one must when called upon by the most powerful man in the galaxy. He answered Guilliman's summons on an out-of-the-way observation deck in his palace. The place was empty of the bustle of diplomats and Imperial officials that had greeted him when he'd arrived, several weeks ago now. Felix liked it that way. He had a feeling Guilliman did too.

He found the primarch unarmoured, dressed in a simple uniform, looking down on Iax. The toxic clouds that had swathed the planet were receding. It was not natural that they had dispersed so quickly, but their provenance was not of this reality, and once the touch of the warp had loosened, Iax's natural cycles reasserted themselves. Felix did not allow himself to feel hope because of this, because Iax was ruined. The continents were all sludgy browns hardly distinguishable from the seas. There were a few places where the usual hues of the planet clung on, in the deepest oceans, in the most hidden valleys and points furthest from the cauldron's site. A few others leapt out from the devastation, and Felix wondered what had sheltered them, for only some variant of warp magic would have kept them pure. These spots were small, and dispersed. There were larger areas of lesser contamination, but lesser in this case was purely relative. There was a blackened patch around where First Landing had been. There was a matching field of devastation at Hythia, out of sight on the far side of Iax, where the cauldron had polluted space and time. But both these wounds had been inflicted by the Imperial fleet.

'You came quickly, Decimus,' said Guilliman. 'I thank you. I have so much to do, and so little time to do it in. Every second saved is a gift to me.'

'You order, I obey, my lord Guilliman.'

'I think it's about time you call me Roboute, don't you?' said Guilliman. He did not take his eyes off the planet, but stood bathed in its sickly shine. 'You have served me well. You are a man of rare qualities. No one can stand alone. We need comrades.' Guilliman looked at him sidelong. 'We need friends.'

'I am honoured that you bestow this privilege upon me, my lord–'

Guilliman raised an eyebrow.

'Roboute,' Felix said. Using the name felt like a transgression, and for some reason he had a flash of his childhood, and disobeying his tutors.

'It is no privilege to be counted among the friends of a primarch, trust me, Decimus,' said Guilliman. 'But is it not the case that we do not choose our friends, but that they choose us?'

'I do not know. I have no friends, only brothers,' said Felix.

'Then consider this an act of friendship,' said Guilliman. He looked down upon Iax with a sorrowful face. 'I called you here to bid you farewell. I will be departing Ultramar before the year is out, and you and I shall not see each other before I do. It may be that we never meet again.'

'Then you will still make the crossing, despite what is happening at the Pariah Nexus and at the Cadian Gate?'

'I have to,' Guilliman said. 'The forces of Abaddon are held at bay, at great cost in blood. The necron threat is temporarily contained. They gain no ground, but lose none either. Imperium Sanctus is in peril, but it is no longer on the brink. Now Imperium Nihilus must be saved. We face two great foes. I can beat neither of them with only half an empire.'

Felix considered carefully whether to voice his next thought before he did. 'If you can find any consolation in my words, I see the burden you bear, and it saddens me you must bear it. If there is anything I can do to help, then I shall.'

'You already help, Decimus,' said Guilliman. 'You and countless others like you. You are heroes in an age of horror. Without you, I could do nothing. I have felt and still feel alone.' He clasped his hands behind his back. 'I wish my brothers would return. The other primarchs are not all accounted for, but I cannot afford such hope. It strays into fantasy. The Logos Historica Verita has looked into many legends, and I can only conclude that my brothers' disappearances are heroic myths. They are doubtless all dead. The prime theoretical suggests that I am the last of the Emperor's sons and will remain so. But I realise that I am not alone as long as I have the likes of you.

'Calgar is bound for Vigilus again. The campaign there will drag on for some time, but the Nachmund Gauntlet must still be in Imperial hands when I complete my traversal of Nihilus. My fleet lords will continue the crusade on this side of the Cicatrix Maledictum. In the meantime, I leave Ultramar to the trust of you and the other tetrarchs. At your command are the fleets and armies of this realm, and ten Chapters of Space Marines who may heed your calls for aid. Be ready, Decimus, because what will be required of you is not only consolidation. After I return to Macragge, I will announce a decree to the houses of the rogue traders to seek out new worlds for Ultramar, places where the good governance we perform here and the noble culture it supports might be transplanted. It is too dangerous now to have the best of humanity located in one place. Mortarion's hate makes that all too apparent.

'There are a hundred billion stars in this galaxy, untold numbers of worlds that are suitable for human life, even more than can be made so, and we cling to this thin spread of a million planets. No wonder we are doomed. Our ambition has perished. We lost what made us human. When this crusade is over, there will need to be a time of rebuilding, then a period of conquest. Only through expansion can the Imperium survive.'

'If I may be forthright, my lord... Roboute, I look at Iax now and fear we may not succeed. What use is victory if the price is ruination?'

Guilliman nodded. 'We have won a campaign. We have won this war, but what will be left? Iax will take centuries to recover, and then I doubt it will ever regain the beauty for which it was known. We cannot sustain this endless struggle against Chaos. It cannot be fought. It must be contained, or destroyed.'

'How can it be contained, my lord?' said Felix, forgetting his permission for intimacy.

'This is a puzzle of cosmic scale and nigh intractable complexity, yet all the pieces exist, I am sure. The necrons and the aeldari know things we do not, about the nature of the warp, and the Emperor. Somewhere, amid the excesses of them all, a solution can be found.' Guilliman's eyes were losing their focus on the moment. He looked off into the void, gaze fixed on horizons only his primarch's mind could perceive.

'Cawl,' said Felix. 'You are talking about Cawl. Is that what he has been doing, trying to find a solution?'

'I chose you well. Yes, Cawl. He believes the work of the necrons holds the key. I have received a message from him, the first in some time. I go to speak with his proxy when we are done here. Is there anything you wish to say to him? I understand he is peculiarly fond of you.'

'Nothing,' said Felix, who found the idea of Cawl's affection repellent.

Guilliman nodded again, distant once more. He could be like that sometimes, merely accepting what was given him without recognition, his mind too busy with eternal affairs to engage too closely with human niceties, even the withered social conventions upheld by the Adeptus Astartes. The contrast with his earlier warmth was striking.

'What are you going to discuss with him?' Felix asked.

'Many things. But foremost I shall tell him that he has been gone too long. I will tell him I wish to see him before we depart for Imperium Nihilus. That will not be a request, it will be an order. If by any chance you see him first, please pass that on.'

'I will try.' Felix paused again. 'Can you order Cawl to do anything, Roboute?'

Guilliman made a noise of weary amusement. 'We shall have to see, shan't we?'

He turned to Felix and reached out. Felix took his massive hand.

'Farewell, tetrarch,' said Guilliman. 'Fight well, rule better. I leave a great number of my people in your hands. Try to save them. And, if you can, remember this – although the aeldari seer helped plot the course to our victory, our plan would have failed had I not had a little faith. Perhaps we all should have.'

Felix nodded, and the disquiet he had felt on Iax at Guilliman's beliefs resurfaced. He struggled to hide it. 'For the Emperor. I wish you good fortune on the far side of the Rift.'

'It will be needed, and I thank you for it. We march for Macragge,' said Guilliman.

'No, my lord,' said Felix. 'I march not for Macragge, but for you.'

Guilliman took the secure lifter down from his palace into the bowels of the ship where the Cawl Inferior lurked. He underwent the multiple security protocols automatically. He was deep in thought. The needs of war in material space seemed increasingly insignificant, and although he understood this, he felt poorly equipped to formulate a strategy against the powers of the warp. They were deep into the realms of the abstruse, the domain of psykers, sorcerers and hypertechnologists, and he was none of those things.

Guilliman arrived to find the armoured doors to the Cawl Inferior already open, where Guidus Losenti met him for once on the threshold of the machine. The astropath looked older and frailer every time Guilliman saw him. His files stated that he was a little over forty standard Terran years, but he appeared twice that age. The sureness with which he used to move was failing, and he trembled a little as he greeted Guilliman.

'Master-Astropath Losenti,' Guilliman said.

'Lord commander,' said Losenti. 'I felt a great weight lifted from the empyrean. I assume you have been successful?'

'Mortarion has been driven from Ultramar. His necrotic network is dispersed,' Guilliman said. 'But for enemy hold-outs, the Plague War is over.'

'That is good, that is good,' said Losenti. His lips were slack, and a string of drool trickled from the corner of his mouth.

The astropath wiped at it hurriedly with his sleeve. 'I am sorry, my lord.'

'Your duty weighs on you?'

'These months in Ultramar have been difficult,' Losenti admitted.

'They are done,' said Guilliman. 'Are you well, master astropath?'

'I persist,' said Losenti, forcing himself a little more upright and putting strength into his voice. 'My lord, I shall activate the machine for you. It will not be the last time. Not yet.' He smiled. The orbs of jet he had in place of eyes glinted in his sockets. 'You offered me mercy not so long ago. I see your concern. I am still not ready to accept it.'

Guilliman nodded. 'Very well,' he said.

A look of relief passed over Losenti's features. 'Thank you. If you please, my lord.' He stepped aside so Guilliman could enter the chamber.

They underwent the awakening of the Cawl Inferior. Although stripped of all the Adeptus Mechanicus' usual cant and ritual, the procedure still had the sense of an invocation. When Losenti called out the coded sequence he had received from Cawl, and the machine came online, it was as if some elder being rushed in to mundane reality from a place obscure to human knowledge.

Losenti retreated more quickly than was usual. The look of strain on his face was greater. Guilliman regretted his suffering. Another individual life used up for the sake of humanity. He could not bear to calculate how many more sacrifices there must be.

The machine concluded its activation. The severed heads in their containment tanks did their gruesome dance. The alien circuits flared into life. Psychic pressure built, and died, and the racket of the machines beneath the floor followed.

Finally, the Cawl Inferior was ready.

'Roboute,' it said. 'How very, very nice to see you.'

'Cawl Inferior, let it be known now that I have little time for your impudence.'

'A busy man, as always,' said the machine. It used one of Cawl's many voices, and today seemed to have settled on a sly, insinuating personality. 'Very well. My master, Archmagos Dominus Belisarius Cawl, sends this communique and hopes it finds you in good health. If this message has been activated, then you have been successful and have saved Ultramar from the designs of your brother. He therefore extends his congratulations to you.'

'And when will he extend his presence?'

The Cawl Inferior actually laughed.

'Such impatience! Were you always this grumpy, or was it death that robbed you of humour?'

'I see. We have to endure the impudence. Very well. When might I expect a visit from Cawl?'

'Not for a while. Not before you cross the Rift.'

'Then I must insist he follow me across.'

'You know, lord regent, your mistrust of Archmagos Belisarius Cawl saddens him. He does not need to be at your side to conclude the mission you have set him.'

'That he has set himself,' corrected Guilliman.

'Semantics. You would have set it for him, had he not undertaken to do so unilaterally.'

'He is arrogant to presume to predict my mood or my intentions.'

'Well, yes, but the point is, he has, so maybe we should allow him his superior manner and simply let him get on with things?'

'Just report,' said Guilliman.

'Testy, I would have thought victory would have pleased you. All right then. Archmagos Belisarius Cawl cannot return to Ultramar yet. But he will. There is an artefact upon the Eastern Fringes that interests him greatly. He will soon be heading there.'

'Which one?' said Guilliman.

'That which resides upon Sotha.'

'The Pharos,' said Guilliman.

'Give the man an honour,' said the Cawl Inferior archly. 'The Pharos. Archmagos Belisarius Cawl is now certain that this device is of necron origin, and that it will reveal much knowledge beneficial to his understanding of noctilith. All he requires is a key to access it. He is in the process of acquiring that key right now.'

'For what purpose does he wish to visit the Pharos?'

'For many purposes,' responded the Cawl Inferior. 'Do not think to stop him. He is aware you put a ban on the place long ago.'

'I was not going to stop him,' said Guilliman. 'If he wishes to plumb the depths of that device, I have full confidence he will do so without causing any harm. You will convey this sentiment to him. Is that clear?'

'It is committed to the return message code,' said the Cawl Inferior, after a pause.

'Tell him Tetrarch Felix now rules that part of Ultramar.'

'My master will contact him. He will be pleased to see him again.'

'How go Cawl's efforts to unlock the secrets of the blackstone pylons?'

'His work proceeds well,' said the Cawl Inferior. 'Access to the Pharos will enable him to accelerate the process. He will be successful. He is Archmagos Belisarius Cawl and he can do anything. Before long, he will have the knowledge he needs.'

'So he claims,' said Guilliman.

'It is more than a claim. That we are having this conversation is proof of it. There are many potential dialogues in my memory cores. He accounted for all possibilities, but he assumed a certain track of events, and so far, his calculations have shown a deviation of less than one per cent from his predictions. His great work will come to fruition, you can rely on him.'

'What is the content of these other dialogues?'

'Disasters. Deaths. Doom,' said the Cawl Inferior. 'I can be no more specific. I have delivered my encoded message. I have nothing more to relay. Please offer your response for encoding and transmission to my counterpart.'

Guilliman's face set. The machine waited expectantly.

'Matters are becoming complicated for me,' he said.

'Ah! A rare confidence,' said the Cawl Inferior. 'Pray tell, how?'

'Prayer is the crux of it,' said Guilliman. 'A grievous blow was struck against the Plague God.'

'Then you should rejoice.'

'What if I were not the one who struck it?' Guilliman replied.

'Explain.'

'I fear the Emperor may be moving. I fear that He worked through me. I refused to believe it at first, but the evidence that I have been presented with offers only one viable practical.'

'That is?'

'The Emperor is active again. He is at work through the tarot, through visions, so-called saints and acts of faith. I know I spoke with Him, but I am still not sure what I saw or heard in the throne room. My first solid indication that something real was occurring was the nature of the warning of the Pariah Nexus. I resisted the idea at the time, though the possibility was put to me early on. But evidence accrues. Now, I can no longer dismiss this theoretical out of hand.'

'Why fear?'

'What?'

'You used the word fear, not think, believe, consider, calculate, guess, hypothesise or any other appertaining to deductive psychological processes. Why fear?'

'Do you believe the Emperor is a god?' said Guilliman.

'Ah, I see why fear. Do I, the Cawl Inferior, believe that, or does Archmagos Belisarius Cawl?'

'Either. Both,' said Guilliman.

'The dogma of the majority of the sects within the Cult Mechanicus regards the Emperor as the living avatar of the Omnissiah, the third of the Machine-God that bestrides the galaxy clad in mortal form.'

'I know that,' said Guilliman patiently. 'A creed that the Emperor pointed out as false on numerous occasions, by the way. What I wish to know is what you and Cawl think, not believe, but *think*.'

The machine fell quiet. Mechanisms clattered loudly.

'I have no response.'

'Do you believe He can come back?' asked Guilliman. 'Can He be returned to full life, like I was?'

'Who?'

'The Emperor. Cease toying with me.'

'The question is meaningless. I have no beliefs.'

'I said do not play games with me. Respond. I command you.'

More silence. More clicks. The heads in the tanks twitched.

Guilliman was about to speak again when the machine's voice filled the room.

'If I were the Archmagos Dominus Belisarius Cawl, which I am not, I would have one cautionary advisement to give regarding this line of thought.'

'Then advise me, machine.'

'If it is possible to restore the Emperor, and if He could regain true life, then what went into the throne room of the Imperial Palace may not be what emerges. There is great peril considering this, even as a hypothesis, because thoughts lead to actions, whether we intend them to or not. Before you know it, we reach disaster, all from good intentions.' There was a pause.

'They used to say that. About roads to bad places. Paved with good intentions.'

'Why would it be perilous? Expand.'

'Because all gods are blights on existence, Roboute Guilliman, whether they call themselves gods or not,' the Cawl Inferior said. 'I think you know that better than anyone. Do not forget it.'

There was silence.

'Now, if there is nothing else?' asked the Cawl Inferior.

'No.'

'Then present the remainder of your message for encoding.'

Guilliman did, then returned to his wars.

Imperium Nihilus awaited.

ABOUT THE AUTHOR

Guy Haley is the author of the Siege of Terra novel *The Lost and the Damned*, as well as the Horus Heresy novels *Titandeath*, *Wolfsbane* and *Pharos*, and the Primarchs novels *Konrad Curze: The Night Haunter*, *Corax: Lord of Shadows* and *Perturabo: The Hammer of Olympia*. He has also written many Warhammer 40,000 novels, including the first book in the Dawn of Fire series, *Avenging Son*, as well as *Belisarius Cawl: The Great Work*, *Dark Imperium*, *Dark Imperium: Plague War*, *Dark Imperium: Godblight*, *The Devastation of Baal*, *Dante*, *Darkness in the Blood* and *Astorath: Angel of Mercy*. He has also written stories set in the Age of Sigmar, included in *War Storm*, *Ghal Maraz* and *Call of Archaon*. He lives in Yorkshire with his wife and son.

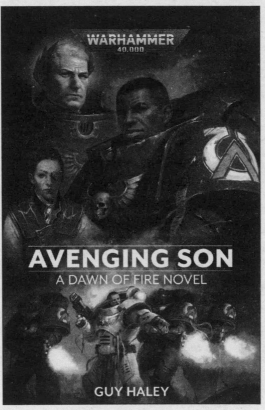

YOUR
NEXT READ

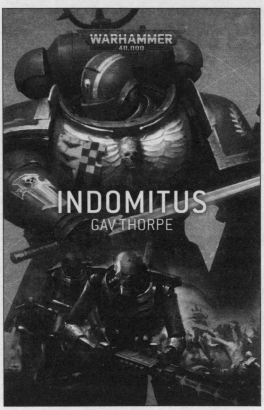

INDOMITUS
by Gav Thorpe

When their crusade fleet is drawn to a stricken world, the Ultramarines of the warship *Ithraca's Vengeance* encounter the dread necrons and face a terrible choice – to destroy the xenos stronghold, or bring word of their malign plan to the Lord Primarch Guilliman.